"Ava Gray's style is edgy, unapologetic, and take-no-prisoners bold. Ava Gray is a must-read!"
—*USA Today* bestselling author Larissa Ione

Her reaction betrayed her utterly.

Instead of taking one hand off the wheel to slap him away, her fingers tightened at ten and two. Her thigh went rigid, and then, ever so slightly, her knees splayed outward, as if willing him to go further. Wanting him to slide his hand higher.

Was that what got her off? Risk? Danger? He didn't move. Heat spilled from his skin to hers. Then he began drawing delicate patterns along her nerves, etching with his blunt nails.

"You didn't answer me," he said then.

"About what?" She didn't look at him. Didn't ask him to stop. A shiver coursed through her, and he didn't think it was from the wind blowing between their cracked windows.

"Your name." He slid his hand a little higher.

Her top clung to her breasts, damped by perspiration. No more than a scrap of lace and a thin layer of cotton covered them. In the tunnels of light cast by passing cars, he saw her nipples perk. Reyes thumbed her inner thigh, caressing as if he touched bare skin.

"Mmm. Kyra. I'm Kyra."

"Pretty." Inwardly he exulted that she hadn't lied. "I should know it if I'm going to keep doing this. Am I, Kyra? But understand—if I take my hand away, I won't put it back. So be sure of what you want before you give your answer."

AVA GRAY

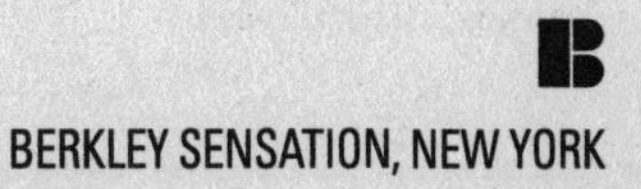

THE BERKLEY PUBLISHING GROUP
Published by the Penguin Group
Penguin Group (USA) Inc.
375 Hudson Street, New York, New York 10014, USA
Penguin Group (Canada), 90 Eglinton Avenue East, Suite 700, Toronto, Ontario M4P 2Y3, Canada
(a division of Pearson Penguin Canada Inc.)
Penguin Books Ltd., 80 Strand, London WC2R 0RL, England
Penguin Group Ireland, 25 St. Stephen's Green, Dublin 2, Ireland (a division of Penguin Books Ltd.)
Penguin Group (Australia), 250 Camberwell Road, Camberwell, Victoria 3124, Australia
(a division of Pearson Australia Group Pty. Ltd.)
Penguin Books India Pvt. Ltd., 11 Community Centre, Panchsheel Park, New Delhi—110 017, India
Penguin Group (NZ), 67 Apollo Drive, Rosedale, North Shore 0632, New Zealand
(a division of Pearson New Zealand Ltd.)
Penguin Books (South Africa) (Pty.) Ltd., 24 Sturdee Avenue, Rosebank, Johannesburg 2196,
South Africa

Penguin Books Ltd., Registered Offices: 80 Strand, London WC2R 0RL, England

SKIN GAME

A Berkley Sensation Book / published by arrangement with the author

PRINTING HISTORY
Berkley Sensation mass-market edition / November 2009

Cover art by Danny O'Leary.
Cover design by Lesley Worrell.
Interior text design by Kristin del Rosario.

For information, address: The Berkley Publishing Group,
a division of Penguin Group (USA) Inc.,
375 Hudson Street, New York, New York 10014.

ISBN: 978-0-425-23153-1

BERKLEY® SENSATION
Berkley Sensation Books are published by The Berkley Publishing Group,
a division of Penguin Group (USA) Inc.,
375 Hudson Street, New York, New York 10014.
BERKLEY® SENSATION and the "B" design are trademarks of Penguin Group (USA) Inc.

PRINTED IN THE UNITED STATES OF AMERICA

10 9 8 7 6 5 4 3 2 1

To Lauren, Laura, and Larissa:
three ladies who put the "l" in lucky.
As in, damn, I'm lucky to call you my friends.
Thanks for everything.

ACKNOWLEDGMENTS

Skin Game started as a glimmer, a "what-if" brainstorming session with my assistant, Ivette, wherein I speculated whether I could write paranormal romantic suspense, based in science rather than magic. Her enthusiasm fueled my own. If Ivette hadn't believed in this idea from the jump, I doubt I would've pursued it. Thanks for that.

Lauren Dane provided support along the way and helped me think my way out of a couple of boxes. Her superior brain really comes in handy!

I also need to send a big bouquet of flowers to Larissa Ione for reading this book, giving me a great blurb, and becoming its biggest fan. When a writer that talented likes your work, it means a great deal.

Thanks to Judi and Maria Szabo for checking my Hungarian. Much appreciation to those in law enforcement who answered my questions via e-mail. Any mistakes are my own.

Finally, Cindy Hwang is an amazing editor, and I will be forever grateful she took a chance on these characters. Kyra and Reyes aren't typical protagonists, but she let me push the envelope. It's a pleasure to work with her in bringing you dark, edgy romances. I like grit in my love stories, and I hope you will too.

CHAPTER 1

Kyra held the guy's balls in the palm of her hand. Literally.

Just for a second as she brushed by him, but it was enough. His eyes widened, and she knew he took the touch as a sign he'd get lucky after he won her last hundred bucks. The crumpled bill lay underneath his, weighted by a cube of pool chalk.

Poor, stupid mark.

She slid him a slow smile as she racked for their fourth and final contest. His friends stood with beers in their hands, half-smiling in anticipation of a sure thing. In a seedy place like this, they had only an old table with worn felt near the right corner, making it necessary to compensate. That wouldn't slow her up this game, though.

Her opponent had years of practice on this particular table. A scruffy, hard-drinking son of a bitch like him had no better skill, nothing else going for him. No, calling himself reigning champ at Suds Beer Factory defined him. She counted on that.

Spinning her cue stick between her palms, she paused before taking the first shot. "You want to make this interesting?"

Her voice had often been called throaty. Kyra sounded like she smoked unfiltered Camels and drank too many whiskey sours. In fact, she did neither. That was just one of nature's cons, more flash for the package to distract people from what lay underneath.

"Darlin'," drawled one of the barflies, "it already is."

Now somebody would comment on the sweet curve of her ass or the way she filled out her jeans. Kyra managed not to roll her eyes, but it was a near thing. If she ever sunk so low that she needed a boost by picking up a man in a place like this, she hoped somebody would shoot her and put her out of her misery.

The man she'd been reeling in for the past hour couldn't resist asking, as she'd known he couldn't. People were so damn predictable. "What'd you have in mind?"

"Double or nothing."

"You don't have the cash," he scoffed.

Her smile didn't falter. "No, but I have a fully restored 1971 Mercury Marquis parked outside. It's nice, fresh powder blue paint. You'd get a good chunk for it."

"That's yours? Big ride for a little thing like you," her opponent said. Chet, she thought his name was.

For that comment alone she wanted to smash his nose through his forehead, but he'd feel the hit worse in his wallet. It wasn't like he used his brain much, after all. Kyra faked a smile as she put her keys on top of the two bills.

A stocky guy near the bar shook his head, a crop of coarse, brown curls bristling from beneath his baseball cap. "Don't take the lady's ride. She probably has a gambling problem—don't know when to quit even when she can't win."

"I never walk away from a bet." She hadn't affirmed what he'd said, but these yokels would never notice the difference. "What about you? Scared?" she mocked gently.

Oh, that would never stand. As a chorus of "ooohs" arose from his friends, Chet shook his head. "It's your funeral, lady. You're on."

Finally. She never knew how long a boost would last, so she needed to get this game in the bag, or she really *would* lose her ride. Since the car was the only thing she owned, that'd be catastrophic.

Kyra broke then, a perfect scatter. The red three slipped into a pocket, deciding whether she'd shoot solids or stripes. Four more shots lined up for her, and she called them in a neutral tone.

A con could go south pretty fast if she didn't play it right. Chet might suspect he'd been hustled when she was done, but men seldom started a fight with "a little thing like her." If they did, they found themselves unpleasantly surprised—after she tapped the toughest among them.

Bank, carom, and suddenly she'd sunk half the balls on the table. Suds got really quiet and someone muttered, "I call lemonade."

"Yep," another guy said. "She's torching him."

If she hadn't been worried about the clock running out, she might have stalled a shot and put a ball in jail just to let Chet use his cue, but she needed to wrap things up. Kyra rounded the table and sank the next shot easily, as she knew everything about this game and this particular table. She didn't bother with showy play; the point was to win, not to impress.

The bar was dead quiet when she pointed to the far left pocket, called it, and banked the eight ball toward it. She narrowed her eyes as its roll slowed. She hadn't noticed the faint wear near that pocket as well, but it didn't matter. Chet had learned to compensate over long years of practice; thus, so had she.

The black ball sank with a quiet plunk.

"I believe that's a dime in all," she said with a smile. "Cash only."

A dime was a thousand bucks. Kyra knew pool-hall slang because she'd worked this particular con a lot. Now it just remained to be seen whether he'd pay up politely.

"You played me," Chet growled.

She pretended to misunderstand, opening her eyes wide. "So I did. I won, too."

This was the moment of truth. Most guys wouldn't take a swing at her, no matter how mad they were. She'd run across some real sons of bitches in her travels, though. So Kyra braced herself.

"Pay the lady," came a low, rough voice from the back of the bar. "Unless you want people to call you a welsher."

With a muttered curse, Chet handed back all the money he'd won, plus a few hundred more. Kyra smiled, claimed her keys, and the last two bills beneath the chalk cube. She thumbed the white rabbit's foot on her keychain, as she did after every successful con. Superstition had its place.

"Table's all yours, boys. Thanks for the fun!"

Before the mood could turn from puzzled to hostile, she grabbed her denim bag and headed out. It was best to hop into the Marquis and hustle down the road. Nobody prevented her from pushing past the front door and into the humid kiss of Louisiana twilight. Jasmine growing wild on a broken-down fence scented the air.

Kyra cast a look back at the timber roadhouse. Places like this made up her bread and butter. *So many suckers, so little time.* She loved the euphoria of getting away clean.

Then she heard the crunch of footsteps on the gravel behind her.

Shit, she thought. *I knew it was too good to be true.*

She picked up the pace to no avail. A hand on her arm spun her around, and she found herself craning her head back to see who had a hold of her. At five foot four, she was neither petite, nor average, and he topped her by a foot. More interesting, he hadn't been involved in the game.

"What did you do in there?" She recognized his voice—a cross between black velvet and a buzz saw—he'd demanded Chet pay up. The guy had been drinking alone near the back, but she hadn't gotten a good look at him.

She'd remember a face like this, hard angles softened by a spill of midnight hair, and eyes so dark they seemed to drink the light—black pools with azure lightning in their depths. He had skin like old mahogany, weathered but lovely. But his fine, unusual looks didn't give him an excuse to touch her.

Thanks to this ass, she'd be lucky if she didn't wind up in the fetal position, groaning through a migraine. With a prowess she must've snagged from him, Kyra neatly broke his grip on her forearm. Surprise flickered in his gaze, as if he recognized the maneuver but didn't understand how she'd done it. Well, hell, she didn't know how, either, and sometimes it got damn confusing, but it was a living.

"I won a pool game. And now I'm leaving." Her tone dared

him to try something, especially when she sensed the deadly readiness in her muscles. She knew without a doubt she could snap somebody's neck. *Comforting*. It'd be better if she wasn't nearby when the skill she'd stolen reverted to him.

"You think so?" He fell into step, alarmingly casual as they came up to her car.

"Who's going to stop me?"

"This is a nice ride," he observed. Suddenly he had a knife in his hand, but instead of threatening her with it, which she could've handled, he traced it down the front whitewall. "And I guess *I* could stop you." Understatement.

"Yeah." She wouldn't even breathe without his permission. Those Diamond Back tires had set her back a pretty penny in South Carolina, but nothing was too good for the Marquis. It was all she had left of her daddy, after all. "Just what do you want from me?"

Ten minutes with you *up against a wall.*

For a second, Reyes thought he'd spoken out loud, but she wouldn't be regarding him with the same mix of wariness and puzzlement in her tawny eyes, if he had. Up close, he saw the smattering of freckles on her nose and cheeks, making her look young and vulnerable. He'd bet she played that for all she was worth.

Not tall, but she gave the impression of being leggy, lean along with it. She wore strawberry blond hair in a wavy nimbus to her shoulders. Her jeans were old, torn at the knees, but her boots looked expensive.

And he absolutely couldn't explain his vicious urge to grab her with both hands, mark her with his teeth, and ride her until she begged for mercy. Maybe it was because he couldn't picture her crying uncle; spirit in a woman made his heart kick like a half-broke horse, and she'd shown such a roguish blend of guile and confidence inside the bar.

The first three games, she hadn't been able to play worth shit. He'd watched his share of hustlers over the years, and he always knew when a player stalled. They had a tell in the way they handled the cues, but this woman, he'd have sworn she barely knew how to hold the stick. Until that last game.

Until she turned into a tournament player before his eyes—like magic.

Reyes didn't believe in magic.

She'd done something when he touched her. He felt different. Energy coursed through him with no outlet, as if a customary corollary had suddenly been blocked. He felt slower, too, as if his muscles had forgotten how to move.

Just as well he hadn't intended to do anything here at Suds. He never acted without all the facts, and he needed to know more about this woman. It worked on him like a compulsion. He wanted to know her better than his own name.

Like most impulses, he'd resist it, taking satisfaction instead in leashing his appetites. Reyes almost enjoyed letting the longing build to fever pitch, only to turn his back on it. He never let hunger overwhelm him anymore. But for the first time in years, temptation tugged. She smelled like coconut oil and sunny days. He wondered what she'd do if he leaned down to breathe the scent of her. Would she fight? Scream?

"We'll take a ride," he said easily. "You probably should get away from here. Once those rednecks figure things out, they'll come running."

"You're *not* getting in my car."

Smart woman. But that wouldn't do her any good, not when he already knew her weakness. Attachments, whether to people, places, or things, only led to trouble.

He applied a little pressure on the tire. "Both of us go. Or neither. They're going to think I was your silent partner since I made them pay up, and I'm not taking a beating for you. But if you want to get away, I'd hurry. Sounds like they're getting riled inside."

No lie. Reyes heard shouting. Soon the men she'd swindled would come pouring out, looking to take the money back and maybe a pound of flesh. Chet had probably worked himself up to thinking she owed him sex to make up for the heaping helping of emasculation she'd served him with a smile. This couldn't have fallen out better if he'd planned it.

She swore. What a mouth she had, but everything sounded better when spoken in a husky undertone. "Come on. I'm only taking you as far as Lake Charles, and if you spill a drop of anything on Myrna's upholstery, I'll kill you with my bare hands."

"Myrna?"

The woman shot him a look that said it wasn't the time to talk about the name of her car. By the time she got the keys in the ignition, he'd settled into the passenger seat. She handled the big car with careless expertise, backing out in a spit of gravel.

Just in time, too.

The bar door flew open, and six men poured out. One chucked a beer bottle at them, and it smashed against the fender. To his amusement, the hellcat spat another curse and reversed hard into the lot, like she'd happily run *all* the rednecks down. They apparently thought so, too, because they scattered, fell on their asses. She shifted gears and then stuck her hand out the window, flashing the finger as they fishtailed out onto Rural Route 9.

"Myrna Loy," she said, as if they'd never been interrupted. "I'm nuts about her."

It took him a minute to place the name, and then connect it to her car. He tended to connect the dots, not make tangential leaps; logic, not Rorschach blots.

"You like her movies then?" This wasn't going at all as he'd planned. She still hadn't even answered his original question. He prided himself on being adaptable, however; it made him the best at what he did. So he'd circle back to it soon enough.

Before answering, she adjusted the radio and tuned it to KBON, filling the car with zydeco music and rushing wind. "Love them. Have you ever seen *The Thin Man*?"

"I'm afraid not. Good?"

Her smile flashed, a dimple in her right cheek. "Fantastic. She and William Powell were *the* couple back then—so suave and charming. When I was a kid, I wanted to be Nora Charles."

Nick and Nora Charles—the two names popped into his head as a matched set. Where had he heard them before? It would come; he had a nearly eidetic memory.

"Dashiell Hammett." He finally remembered. "I read the book a long time ago. I prefer Mickey Spillane."

She glared at him out of her peripheral vision, eyes practically throwing sparks. "Heresy. I should put you out of the car."

Reyes tried to picture that. Nobody ever made him do anything he didn't want to. Odd, she didn't seem in the least intimidated. Nothing in her manner indicated she was worried about acquiring a passenger his size, armed with a knife. She ought to be tense, sweating, and when things didn't add up, it troubled him. It was like she knew something he didn't. And he hated that feeling.

He slid the blade back in his boot. Threatening her ran counterproductive to his aims at this point, so he improvised. "So what did you do back at the bar? Or maybe I should ask *how* did you do it?"

That would give her a reason to be wary of him, thinking he'd noticed something askew. Which he had, of course, but it wasn't the big picture. Honesty often provided the best smokescreen for his other endeavors.

She lifted a shoulder. "Maybe you should."

"So how did you do it?"

"Do what?"

He had the feeling she could continue this line of circular conversation all night. Well, it didn't matter. In time, he'd wear her down. She didn't realize it, but she'd gained his company for a while.

That was something of a specialty of his—breaking down barriers, building trust. Reyes bet she'd yield what he needed to know before too much longer. A softness about her mouth said she liked what she saw when she looked at him. He was used to that, but this woman made him *want* to use sex, a tactic he seldom employed these days—too many complications, too many variables.

"What's your name anyway?" He played the rootless hitchhiker with a familiarity born of experience. That impression would be reinforced by his appearance and his lack of personal belongings. "And thanks for the lift."

"You didn't exactly give me a choice." Her husky voice sent a pleasurable spike along his nervous system straight down to his groin. Reyes shifted, unwilling to let the erection gain full-flag status.

"No, I didn't. You love your whitewalls too much to gamble with them."

"I love this car," she corrected, stroking a hand along the blue dashboard.

Reyes watched her fingers with a clawing hunger that astounded him. He wanted them on his chest, his abdomen . . . lower. He wanted two weeks with her in a hotel room, nothing but bare skin and cool, white sheets. Despite iron discipline, his penis swelled all the way up, straining his zipper.

"I can see that." His voice rumbled low, even for him.

"Isn't she a beaut?"

"Sure is."

So are you. But he didn't say that out loud. It was too soon. Like a wild thing, she would be skittish, slow to gentle. She *still* hadn't told him her name. Such a way she had about her—appearing to give away everything, when in fact, it granted nothing—could've come only through years of practice.

All in all, Kyra Marie Beckwith was a lot more intriguing than her dossier let on. Too bad he had to kill her.

CHAPTER 2

The sun rayed from the sky, giving it the look of frayed blue velvet. Night would fall soon, and Lord knew she hated to travel backcountry roads after dark. Lightning bugs might be the brightest light she saw for miles.

They hadn't been driving quite an hour, but Kyra was ready to get rid of her uninvited guest. He set off alarm bells, and she'd learned to respect her intuition, as it'd saved her ass more than once. So she'd stop for gas and ditch him.

He kept asking the same questions, no matter how many times she dodged, and that made him trouble with a capital *T*. Too bad, because otherwise she might have enjoyed killing a week in bed with him. The man had the hard, rugged look she found irresistible, but in her line of work, she couldn't afford to hang around people who showed too much interest in what she did or how she did it.

Thankfully, the flickering white fluorescent of a filling station caught her eyes up ahead. She still felt tough, strong, and didn't doubt she could deal with him, if he forced the issue. Leaving bodies behind would only get the authorities riled up, however, so she hoped it didn't come to that.

"You ready to stretch your legs?" She hadn't spoken in

miles. "I could go for a convenience store sausage or maybe some burritos and a slushie. What'd you say?"

For a minute, she thought he was asleep, and then he asked, "You buying?"

She could do that, Kyra decided. Flush from her win at the roadhouse outside Eunice, she could afford to feed the man before she cut him loose. They weren't far from Lake Charles, so he'd do fine with a meal in his belly.

"Yeah."

Making the turn without flipping on a blinker, Kyra pulled into the parking lot. Two other cars sat alongside the building, but she didn't see anybody. It was second nature for her to scan her surroundings, take stock before she made up her mind what to do. Being vigilant always paid off, one way or another.

She hopped out and tried to put some gas in the Marquis, but the lazy son of a bitch inside wouldn't authorize the pumps. The machine said she could use a card to pay, but she didn't have a bank account.

"I've got to go inside," she called. "They probably require prepay after dark. Do you need to use the restroom?"

He *had* to get out of the car. How was she supposed to get rid of him if he stayed right there? The gas in the tank would take her to the next town, so she'd drive off as soon as he disappeared around the side of the building. It was a shitty thing to do, given they were in the middle of nowhere, but her conscience wouldn't bother her overmuch. A man like him could take care of himself.

"Probably should," came his laconic response. The guy unfolded from the passenger seat with easy grace. "No onions on my dog, please. Bean and cheese if you go for microwave burritos."

Kyra stared at him, bemused. She'd intended to give him five bucks to buy his own dinner, but the way he sauntered off said he assumed she'd fetch it for him. He must be used to women waiting on him; that always made a man cocky.

Well, his loss. She wouldn't be here when he got back and he'd denied himself a few dollars with his big ego. To make it look good, she started across the parking lot, watching him every step of the way, but he slowed as she did, evidently wanting to make sure she went into the shop. Just her luck—she'd picked up a suspicious-minded, knife-wielding stranger.

Dammit.

Well, she'd duck in and out quicker than he could take a leak. A bell jingled as Kyra opened the glass door, squinting at the shift from shadow to light. Instinct slowed her step when she saw nobody behind the counter. The clerk could be crouched down taking inventory, she supposed, so she angled her head to check the security mirror in the far corner of the store. Several cartons of cigarettes lay scattered back there, some smashed or split open.

Two cars, no attendant. Shit. This wasn't good.

A muffled thump from the back room reinforced that impression. Robbery in progress—the idiot would be trying to get the cashier to open some hidden safe when most people knew convenience stores had drops in the floor that couldn't be opened except at shift change. If she had a lick of sense, she'd get out and call 911 on her cell.

Since she found herself stealing toward the back of the store, taking cover behind half rows of shelving stocked with Vienna sausages and condoms, she obviously needed her head examined. Her intervention might save a man's life, though. And while she loved taking money from suckers, she wouldn't have it said she was a coward.

Her muscles vibrated with readiness. Every stolen instinct screamed for her to kick the office door open and solve the problem with brute force, but that might get the clerk killed. She didn't want blood on her hands.

Never again.

So she had to marry caution to her martial prowess; they didn't have to like each other, just coexist long enough for her to save the day. Kyra shook her head over that. Talk about your unlikely heroines.

Her heart thundered in her chest. She'd nearly reached the door when she heard a cry of pain, quickly throttled. *What to do, what to do—*

Well, going in seemed out of the question so she knocked a can of chili onto the floor and then spun to one side, watching it roll toward the manager's office. The robber thought he was slick as he poked his head out, gun in hand, to check the situation.

Gotcha! She slammed both fists against his temples and then tangled her fingers in his greasy hair, yanking his head down as her knee came up. His gun went off as he fell, but the bullet only hit a two-liter bottle of grape soda on a distant shelf.

Kyra gave the would-be stickup artist a little one-two kick in the side, so easy it felt like dancing. No, this son of a bitch wasn't getting up anytime soon. A shiver ran through her when she realized just how tough her passenger was. With his expertise, she could kill, not just easily, but casually.

Damn, she hoped this *Natural Born Killer* thing wore off soon. The throb had already started in her temples, too much feedback when she stole more than one skill in a single day. That was why, among other reasons, she didn't like being touched by strangers. But it wasn't like tall, dark, and scary had given her any choice, threatening her whitewalls like that. She *hated* not having a choice.

"You can come out now," she called to the kid cowering in the office. "Might want to open a roll of that duct tape and get this son of a bitch wrapped up."

The clerk came out slow, as if he thought it was some kind of wicked prank. His eyes rounded when he took in the man sprawled at her feet. "What did you . . . how . . .?"

People sure have been asking me that a lot today, Kyra thought with a sigh. This was why she preferred not to get involved, why it was better to keep moving and take only what she could carry.

"Karate lessons," she said with a straight face. "You gonna get that tape or should I?"

"I—no . . . I will." Finally the kid seemed to shake it off and he hurried over to the aisle next to the freezers, where he tore open a roll of electrical tape.

"You'll want to call the sheriff," Kyra prompted gently. "And if it's not too much trouble, could you authorize pump four? I'll take twenty in unleaded fuel, two hot dogs, and two slushies."

"Are you shitting me?" The cashier, who was tall and

thin, spattered with acne, raised a brow. "This is reality TV, right? People don't do stuff like this."

She shrugged. "I do. I'd appreciate it if you didn't mention me when the cops get here. You can play hero. Put the fear in all armed robbers within a hundred miles."

"Huh," said the kid. "Okay, deal. I can't comp the gas, but the dogs and slushies are on me." He shook his head. "Damned if this hasn't been the weirdest night."

"You're telling me." Kyra stepped over the fallen robber, collected the food and drinks, and dropped a twenty on the counter for the gas.

When she stepped out into the humidity, she found mystery man waiting for her.

Reyes brooded.

The hot dog was not the worst thing he'd ever eaten, but he couldn't imagine why anyone chose to drink a blue raspberry slushie. Still, it seemed impolite to complain, and out of character besides. A man down on his luck would be grateful for whatever he got.

He'd watched her from the front of the store. Saw how she'd waded in without regard for personal safety, and that was fine—her business if she had a death wish. But she didn't get to die, not until he found out what he needed to know.

He'd been prepared to bail her out. He hadn't been prepared to see her unleash *his* moves. Head to knee, double kick? Remembering made him feel strange and queasy, prickly from the inside out.

"We're almost to Lake Charles." Her voice interrupted his increasingly tangled thoughts. "Where should I drop you off?"

She thought they'd be parting ways once they hit the city. He shrugged. "Anywhere is fine. Thanks for dinner and the lift."

More than an hour past, he'd pretended to lose interest in her. There was no surer way to disarm someone than to pretend you didn't give a shit. Reyes realized he wished it were true, but damned if she didn't fascinate him.

White lights sparkled ahead, dazzling proof of city and civilization, and he studied them instead of looking at her profile. Because he wanted to, he couldn't allow himself to take pleasure in her features. Business, not pleasure, had drawn him here. Kyra had led him on a merry chase, but now he had her, and he couldn't let himself become distracted.

"No problem." She paused, and then went on reluctantly, "But I can't just dump you off on the side of the road."

"Why not?" Reyes thought it was a reasonable question. "You didn't want me along in the first place, and if you hadn't gotten mixed up in trouble at the service station, you would've left me there."

Aha, flash of guilt in the quick glance she cut his way. He'd use it.

"So . . ." He drew the word out and shrugged. "What does it matter? I had dinner and I got out of Eunice. I don't feel like scuffling over the rest."

That was a big, bold lie. Despite the hour, he felt energized. Reyes wanted to run his hand along the seat between them and curl it around her thigh, just to see how she'd react. He loved her mouth and her voice. It felt like he'd been listening to her for days instead of hours.

His muscles twitched like he'd been working out. It ran directly counter to his impression before that he wouldn't know how to fight if he had to. Whatever she'd done to him—however little sense that made—had worn off. Christ, this woman would drive him crazy before he got the job done.

"I'm sorry about that," she said finally. "I didn't realize I was so transparent."

"Only to somebody who's used to being left behind." Reyes wished the words didn't contain so much raw honesty, candor used to cloak deception.

"Oh." She exhaled in a little sorrowful sound that made his hands curl up into fists on his knees. "Look, I'll get you a room tonight," she added. "I can afford it."

He wore this persona like a second skin, but he'd never before permitted glimpses of himself to show through. Reyes refused to let her disconcert him further. He had a job to do.

So he forced a smile. "I don't want one, unless you're sharing it with me."

"That's not going to happen." She tried to sound firm, but he caught the faintly breathless way she pronounced the *h*.

"No?"

That was when he decided to indulge himself. He wouldn't cut loose, but he could play with her a little. Reyes finally slid his hand along the seat as he'd envisioned over the past hours.

His palm settled near her knee, just above the ripped fabric of her jeans. It wasn't a threatening touch, more of a promise. And that same chain reaction shuddered through him, like an orgasm, only smaller, quieter. He felt drained again, but this time he was ready for the feeling, and he tried to capture its nuances for later study.

Her reaction betrayed her utterly. Instead of taking one hand off the wheel to slap him away, her fingers tightened at ten and two. Her thigh went rigid and then, ever so slightly, her knees splayed outward, as if willing him to go further. Wanting him to slide his hand higher.

Was that what got her off? Risk? Danger? He didn't move. Heat spilled from his skin to hers. Then he began to draw delicate patterns along her nerves, etching with his blunt nails.

"You didn't answer me," he said then.

"About what?" She didn't look at him. Didn't ask him to stop. A shiver coursed through her, and he didn't think it was from the wind blowing between their cracked windows.

"Your name." He slid his hand a little higher.

Her top clung to her breasts, damped by perspiration. No more than a scrap of lace and thin layer of cotton covered them. In the tunnels of light cast by passing cars, he saw her nipples perk. Reyes stroked her inner thigh, caressing as if he touched bare skin.

"Mmm. Kyra. I'm Kyra."

"Pretty." Inwardly he exulted that she hadn't lied. "I should know it if I'm going to keep doing this. Am I, Kyra? But understand—if I take my hand away, I won't put it back. So be sure of what you want before you give your answer."

Her reply came hushed and husky. "Don't stop."

Why did that make him hard as a spike? There was a certain adolescent lust mixed into what he was doing, feeling her up as she drove. They were on the highway now, cars speeding by on either side. She couldn't respond, only sit with the big engine vibrating the seat beneath her ass while his fingers slowly worked up her thigh.

"What's your name?" It was the first hint of curiosity she'd evinced toward him. Considering what he was thinking about doing to her, Reyes considered it a good sign. And then she slanted him a heavy-lidded look, belying the freckled simplicity of her face. Her eyes shone in the moonlight with maddening allure, as she quoted his words back at him. "I should know it, if you're going to keep doing this."

Despite himself, despite layers of calculation, he smiled. He heard himself say, "Rey—" before he managed to cut it off.

The woman was *charming*. Her dossier hadn't included that.

Christ. His fingers curled between her thighs. So many aliases and he'd almost told her his name. Maybe he should retire after this job, settle down on some small island. He was either losing his edge, or Kyra Marie Beckwith was dangerous in a way nobody had warned him about.

"Rey," she repeated. "Doesn't that mean king?"

"King of the road." He ran his fingers along her inseam, making her thighs tense.

"Cute." She sounded really breathless, squirming against the seat.

Her foot increased the pressure on the gas as he went further. Reyes smoothed in slow circles, tantalizing her with the question of when he'd move on. The worn denim felt soft and smooth beneath his fingertips, but it would be nothing compared to the satin of her sun-kissed skin.

She would be wondering how long before he took the metal tab and unfastened her jeans, how long before his fingers delved into the open V of her fly. If he did, he would find her panties damp. He wanted to make her come, just like that, a furtive touch creating a complete loss of control on her part.

Desire gnawed with near painful ferocity, but he wouldn't act on it. No, this was a calculated tease, an appetizer. Judging by her expression, she wanted more. It would be dangerous to go further with her behind the wheel of a car. He decided that was part of what appealed to her—that element of risk.

Good to know.

With a faint smile, he grazed the placket of her jeans, stroked the joined teeth of her zipper. She moaned softly, lifting her hips. Then trailed his fingers away. Eventually, she turned with a heated, foggy gaze, as if just figuring out he didn't intend to go further.

"So . . ." he said. "One room then?"

In answer, Kyra pulled into a motel parking lot as if her precious whitewalls were on fire.

CHAPTER 3

By the time Kyra registered them and paid cash for the room, she should've cooled down. The pounding in her head had receded, leaving other impulses in its place. She should start thinking better of this decision. Instead she could only remember how long it had been since she'd been touched.

Raw and hungry sex with strangers was the only kind she'd ever known. She'd need to stick around in order for it to turn into something more, and she never did. This guy wouldn't be an exception to that rule, but he might well turn out to be her best lay yet, if the way he looked was any indication.

She'd take what she wanted from him, and then ditch him. It might seem like a risky prospect to someone else, but maybe that was part of what she craved—the thrill of danger. He shut the door behind them while she took stock of their lodgings. Simple prefab furniture, paintings bolted to the wall, television affixed to the storage cabinet. The place had been decorated back in the 1970s, if the garish shades of burnt sienna and avocado were any indication. The chair by the window had a ripped vinyl seat.

"Nice," she said with a mocking smile. "Romantic. You

gonna run out for some protection while I slip into something more comfortable?"

The guy—Rey, he'd said his name was—cocked a brow at her. Surely he didn't think she rolled with a purse full of condoms in case she got lucky. Or maybe it was her tone that startled him; he probably didn't realize a woman could be horny as hell without losing her mind.

"Promise me you won't go anywhere," he said, spearing her with a midnight gaze.

"I won't leave before you get back." Which wasn't quite what he'd asked her to pledge, but he didn't seem to notice the difference.

"I'll be back in ten minutes. Get naked," he ordered as he went out the door.

Ordinarily the demand in his tone would put her back up and make her disinclined to sleep with him, but he'd been on her radar since before he ran a knife against her new tire. Kyra would bet he offered exactly what she wanted in bed: rough, demanding, no-holds-barred sex. She squirmed just thinking about it.

Because she wanted to, not because he'd demanded it, she stripped off her clothes and laid them on the chair. Most likely she should have closed the curtains first, but she didn't hurry as she sauntered over to do so. If anyone got a glimpse of her body, well, it was a good one. She'd used it often as a distraction.

Kyra rarely permitted anyone close enough to touch. That was work related, and she only reached out when she intended to steal. Sometimes she missed physical closeness with an ache that threatened to tear out her heart, but she lived with it, knowing she really didn't have a choice.

She took a quick shower and turned down the bed. Waiting for him, she couldn't help but picture how good his hands had felt on her thighs. Kyra felt herself grow slick, aching to be touched. It seemed a shame to waste it.

By the time Rey returned, she'd teased herself to quivering readiness. Just as he'd asked, she lay on the cool white sheets, naked. When he pushed open the door, she lifted her fingers to her lips.

"Goddammit, you started without me."

She lifted a shoulder. "You turned me on."

To her amusement he tossed a shiny silver box on the nightstand. "There."

Her mouth quirked. "A twelve-pack? You're ambitious."

"Never hurts to be prepared."

"You got that right," she murmured. "If you can keep up, you'll need three or four of those tonight."

Rey paused. "Is that a challenge?"

"It's a fact. Are you going to take your clothes off, or do I need to do it for you?"

A shudder worked through him. He closed his eyes and curled his hands into fists. It was a moment before he moved, and then it was to pull his shirt over his head. He didn't bother draping like she did, just flung his things in his haste to join her on the bed.

Ah, gorgeous. Kyra hadn't misjudged him. He actually improved when he got naked: broad shoulders, taut abdomen, and such delicious bronze skin. All told, she didn't think she could've picked a better partner for a night's pleasure. He had a lovely cock, made for exactly what she wanted.

In a move she hadn't anticipated, he went straight for her mouth, licking and nuzzling her lips with raw hunger. Though she usually preferred to get right to the fucking, she kissed him back, bit down on his lower lip until he whimpered. She ran her hands through his inky hair, surprised to find it was silkier than she'd expected. Heat kindled as he tasted her, so she threw a leg over his hip and rocked against him.

Surely he'd take the hint. Slap a condom on his cock and shove inside her. She'd never been with a man who made her wait after she made it clear she wanted to fuck. Kyra had already taken care of the foreplay, after all. Before his arrival, she'd caressed her own breasts and tugged on her nipples, stroked her own labia and teased her clit. She only needed him for the final act.

Rey didn't seem to have received the memo. He kissed her until she couldn't get her breath. She ran her nails down his back, wanting to punish him for being so slow.

He nibbled from her lips to her jaw and then down her throat. Kyra tipped her head back and made a low growling sound in her throat. He bit her. She felt herself lubricate even more, so slick and ready for him.

"Don't make love," she managed to say. "Just fuck."

In answer, he licked a slow circle around her nipple. "You're *not* in charge, Kyra. Try to tell me what to do again, and I'll stop. If you want to be completely in control, you should do it yourself."

"Bastard. Maybe I will." She reached between them, curled her fingers around his cock, and squeezed. "Who's in charge *now*?"

His hips bucked. "You make me come like this, and you don't get a hard cock inside you tonight. Let go."

She levered up on an elbow, working her fingers along his length in an irresistible rhythm. "Make me."

His eyes kindled like stars blazing into the dark velvet of a night sky. "You don't know what you're asking for."

"Are you as stupid as you are pretty?" She enunciated clearly in case he was. "Of course I do."

That seemed to be the last straw. He caught his breath and broke her hold on him in a move she'd used on him earlier in the day. Before she hardly knew what had happened, Kyra found herself facedown on the bed with Rey applying pressure on her upper back to keep her that way.

Ah, a kinky fuck. She liked that.

The condom packet crinkled as he presumably tore it open. Then she felt his hands on her hips, but he didn't need to guide her. She knew this position, so she raised her pelvis, and he slammed into her. His fingers knotted in her hair, smarting a little, but she liked it rough—always had.

He took her hard and fast, all the way in and then he drew almost all the way out, so she felt each push as if it was the first time. Kyra lifted her hips to meet him, grinding back on each inward thrust. Then it was like he read her mind—what she always wanted and seldom got.

His hands roved under her body, cupping her breasts. He pulled on her nipples and she felt an answering contraction in her pussy. Rey ran his hands over her like he owned her, slipping between her thighs to rub her clit. Kyra bucked as if she'd fight him off, but it was quite the opposite. She wanted to be tamed, but nobody ever rode her exactly like she wanted.

Until now.

She felt him cover her entirely, weighting her. Claiming her. He bit down on the back of her neck, hard enough to hurt. She'd wear his mark for days, and that idea pushed her over the edge. Sobbing for breath, she tensed and came. Clawed at the pillow.

Rey pushed her through that orgasm and two more before he let go. His thrusts became quick and shallow, his breath gusting in her ears. Kyra lay beneath him, quiet and quiescent, reveling in the afterglow. The raw groan sounded torn out of him when he shuddered atop her, his chest plastered to her back in sweet slick sweat.

How fucking brilliant. She might've met the man capable of wearing *her* out. It would definitely be a night to remember.

Reyes woke with a hard dick, the taste of her on his lips, and a bad feeling. In that order. After the night he'd had, the first thing indicated there was something seriously wrong with him. He should be set for sex. Instead the wild night seemed to have only given his penis unreasonable expectations.

Christ, they'd done it three times, not counting all the extracurricular exploration, vying for dominance all the while. Fighting her for control had worn him the fuck out—he'd never been with anyone like her—and now he wanted her all over again.

They had nine more condoms, and time for a quickie before checkout. He reached for Kyra and found only the slightly pilled cotton of cheap, well-washed sheets.

No shower running, no ambient noise in the room at all. Not. Good.

With immeasurable regret, he opened his eyes. The slant of the sunlight across old, green shag carpeting reinforced his impression something wasn't right. A quick scan of the room resulted in a resounding, "Fuck!"

Before he bounded out of bed stark naked, and headed for the window, he already knew what he'd find—a potholed parking lot that didn't contain a powder blue '71 Marquis. Chagrin and humiliation burned in his empty stomach, creating a bitter cocktail. She'd given him the slip.

Only sheer self-control, which had failed him last night, prevented him from slamming his fist into a wall. That would only injure him without adding anything of benefit. Reyes tried breathing exercises, needing to restore equilibrium so he could examine the situation logically.

Nothing helped.

The woman had fucked his brains out and then left him asleep in bed. He couldn't remember when, if ever, anyone had so bested him. Of course, given the teeth marks he'd left all over her neck and shoulders, it could be argued he'd taken his share from her as well, at least on a personal level.

But this was business, not personal.

She'd written him a note on motel stationary, short and to the point. *Best I ever had—thanks for an amazing night. Good luck!* Signed with a big swirling *K*.

Well, at least I was her best. Somehow, that knowledge didn't quell his wrath. Adding insult to injury, she'd also left him a crumpled twenty, as if he were a cut-rate man-whore she'd hired for the night.

Reyes swore.

A glance at the red digital numbers on the old clock radio told him it was almost eleven. Goddamn, he *never* slept this late. Clearly he'd underestimated Kyra Marie Beckwith all the way around.

Fury alone wouldn't get the job done, but if he tamped it, if he remembered how he felt at this moment, it might come in handy later. He took a five-minute shower and dressed in the same clothes he had on yesterday. Housekeeping would be at the door in a few minutes and he intended to be gone before then.

After giving the room a final, cursory scan, he snatched up the bill she'd left him. When he found the woman, he'd make her eat it. Or maybe not, maybe he'd put her mouth to better use. But first things first.

As he came out of the rundown motel, humidity hit him like a wet glove. Reyes retrieved his cell phone from a zipper pocket cunningly concealed in the lining of his jacket. Later, he'd need to take it off or sweat himself sick. He let the customer-service agent do her I'm-so-friendly spiel and then said, "You'll find my rental car parked at Suds just outside Eunice. Send someone to collect it, please."

The rep sputtered as he'd expected. He gave her thirty seconds to articulate her objections, and then he spoke over the top of her. "I don't care what it costs. Put it on the platinum card." He paused and pretended to listen. "No, thank *you*."

Spinning in place, he assessed his situation in a single glance—within a few miles of Lake Charles and a stone's throw from the highway. No wonder the bed vibrated all night, quite apart from their pelvic wrestling. An eatery called Motel Restaurant sat close to the access road, apart from the L-shaped building that intersected at the office. Since it offered his only option for breakfast, he headed that way.

Like the room they'd rented, this place had seen better days. Worn green linoleum had cracked and curled up near the counter. The tabletops were made of ancient white and gray Formica. It wasn't a large place, only one person inside, a scruffy, bearded guy who looked as if he'd be hard-pressed to pay for his coffee.

Nobody came to seat him, so he chose a booth near the back where he could watch the door. Old habits died hard.

The menu consisted of a single laminated sheet. It looked like he could have grits, eggs, hotcakes, bacon, or any combination thereof. This wasn't the sort of place where a guy could find fruit or granola. Reyes sighed; the food he ate while tracking Kyra Beckwith might succeed in killing him where everything else had failed.

Next order of business would be getting another car delivered. Enterprise claimed to do just that, so he dialed information for their local office. Five minutes later, he had the promise of a ride. He had to drive with the rep back to the branch to fill out paperwork, of course. It would be well into the afternoon before he finished all this crap.

If he wasn't the best at what he did, he might be worried about the delay. It had taken him months to track her down the first time because Kyra lived quietly, didn't flaunt her money, or take too much in a single score. Well, not usually anyway, not since Vegas. So people didn't remember when she passed through.

This time, however, he had a plan B. Reyes hadn't expected the woman to get away from him, but he'd taken steps, just in case. In his field, he was known for preparing for all eventualities. He drew out his phone and clicked a few keys, wanting to make sure the tracking device he'd planted gave a good signal.

Perfect. Someone else might've planted the transmitter on her clothing, but she'd change them, probably sooner than he could catch up to her. There was no telling how fast or hard she'd drive, how many miles she'd cover in one day.

But Kyra would never leave that car behind. He'd sussed out her love for it back in the bar, after glimpsing her quickly veiled reluctance to drop the keys into the pot. She'd wagered it, but only when she knew she'd win.

Reyes still wasn't sure how she'd done that, or what she'd done to him that left her able to kick the guy's ass in the convenience store. But he *was* positive of one thing.

Once he found the Marquis, all he had to do was stake it out. Reyes smiled, imagining her reaction. This would be fun. Anticipation spiked into his veins.

The waitress—a pink-haired, middle-aged woman with a beehive, who'd clearly watched too many *Alice* reruns on TV Land—came to take his order. His expression must have alarmed her because she took a step back. She fiddled with her pad and pencil. "Uh, if you're not sure, I can—"

With some effort, he dialed the menace down. "No, I'm set. Thank you."

He went for coffee, juice, and the special: scrambled eggs, bacon, and toast. Since there was nobody else, his breakfast arrived fast, and he was pleasantly surprised. By the time he finished the last triangle, liberally smeared with good strawberry jam, he felt almost agreeable.

"Don't clear my table," he told the waitress as he stood, throwing down the crumpled twenty Kyra had left him. Reyes offered a warm smile to make up for the fact he'd scared her earlier. He knew he could be intimidating, but he didn't generally try, not unless he was on the clock. "I'm going to get a paper, and then I'll be back to drink your fine coffee and wait for my ride."

She actually blushed, patting her hair with a plump hand. "Oh, we certainly have the space this morning. It'll be my pleasure to keep your cup warm, sir."

His lips twitched as he headed out. A machine in front of the motor lodge offered him a day-old *American Press* for fifty cents. Well, he'd take it. Scanning the headlines as he walked, he read about recalled meat, fragile college budgets, and mudbug madness.

Until Enterprise delivered his car, he had nothing but time.

Then the game was on.

That's right, Kyra Marie. Keep an eye on your rearview mirror, because I'm coming for you.

CHAPTER 4

Gerard Serrano gazed out over the skyline. From his penthouse, he had an excellent view of the Vegas lights. He should have felt some degree of satisfaction over what he'd achieved. Thirty years ago, he'd been a kid with nothing, coming to the Strip looking to make his mark. From there he'd clawed his way up to the top, stepping over a few bodies along the way.

"Like they say," he muttered, "you don't make the omelet without breaking some eggs."

Until a few months ago, he'd been feared and respected. That had all changed the night Rachel Justice humiliated him in his own casino. Serrano clenched his jaw against the remembered burn of it. That wasn't even her real name, of course. She wasn't a kindergarten teacher. She wasn't Presbyterian.

Kyra Marie Beckwith had played him for a fool like nobody had managed in twenty years. It didn't help that his chief of security, Foster, had suggested he run a background check on her, months ago. If he hadn't been so stupidly infatuated, he would have listened. If Foster had his way, everyone would be fingerprinted before they were allowed to talk to him, Serrano thought with amusement.

That faded slowly as he recalled his problem. If he'd listened to Foster, he'd have known who "Rachel" was before things escalated and he could have taken care of things quietly. Now that was no longer an option. He had to make an example of her.

She'd used her position as his fiancée to disgrace him completely. If he hadn't been out of town on business, she never would've been able to convince the cage cashier to pay out her money in large bills. She'd even gotten them to do it especially for her, not needing his approval because he'd told them to treat her word as his own. He'd intended to make her queen of his kingdom, the mother of his children.

He turned from the window as his security chief let himself into the office. Serrano recognized the cat-soft footfalls; nobody else who worked for him moved quite like Foster. He half suspected the man had a background in stalking and killing, but to Serrano's mind, that made Foster more suited for his job, not less. He was a tall, slim man of indeterminate ethnic background. Sometimes Serrano thought he was Nordic, other times, German, but Foster had no discernible accent.

"Any word?" Serrano asked.

Foster functioned as the go-between in communication with the pro they'd hired to make the problem go away. Serrano didn't dirty his hands with such things, and it wouldn't be smart to leave a trail. The money that paid for the hit came from various hidden accounts, and not even from the same one.

The security chief inclined his head. "He caught up with her in Louisiana. When he has information regarding the whereabouts of your money, he'll finish the job."

"That's good news." Serrano smiled. "I want to get this wrapped up. I'm heading to St. Moritz in a few days."

"I thought you hated to ski."

"I do, but the women there are fantastic."

His top man had the restraint not to say that his penchant for women had gotten them into this mess in the first place. Sometimes it was good for people to think they knew all about you. In some ways, this debacle could be turned to his advantage. It might be interesting to see who came snapping at the injured wolf's throat. When the time came, he'd handle all challenges in the same way he always had—without mercy.

Foster didn't know everything; he just thought he did. And the real reason Serrano was heading to Europe was a lot more interesting than he'd let on, even to his security chief. He didn't think it was smart to trust anyone with the big picture.

"How long will you be gone?"

"A couple of weeks, I'd say. Can you handle things here?"

"You can rely on me."

Something about Foster's cool, neutral tone set off alarm bells. Serrano had never been able to pinpoint it, but he always had the feeling his security chief didn't like him, not that it stopped the man from doing his job or cashing his paycheck. Maybe he was paranoid, but he hadn't survived so many years in a dirty business by being a trusting SOB. One of his competitors might see his humiliation as a golden prospect to take him down, and any employee could be bought.

That was why he'd started thinking about a family, a son to inherit what he'd built. It would take the right kind of woman to give him what he wanted. He'd thought Rachel Justice was that woman, but she was just a con artist's creation. That stung more than he liked, the fact that he'd been so cleanly taken. But Serrano didn't let his temper get away from him. It wouldn't do to show weakness, not even in front of Foster—maybe *especially* in front of Foster.

"Keep me posted, will you?"

"Absolutely, sir." Foster turned to leave.

"How long have you worked for me?" He knew the answer; he just wanted to measure the man's precision.

"One year, ten months, and twenty-seven days."

"When was the last time you had a raise?"

"Not quite a year ago."

"Was it a good one?"

He damn well knew it had been. Serrano rewarded efficiency. Foster was a solid, reliable employee who never asked inconvenient questions and always offered the best solution to any problem. In his experience, that meant something would break soon. Men like Foster weren't content nibbling at the edges of somebody else's pie. They wanted the whole damn bakery for themselves.

At least, that had been his experience in the past. Serrano was starting to think maybe he'd never met anyone quite like Foster before.

"Twenty percent increase," Foster answered, expressionless.

"Excellent. I'll see what I can do for you this year, too." With that, he turned, dismissing his chief of security with his back. Though he heard no movement, he knew the moment the man left by the nearly silent snick of the door.

He'd entrusted a great deal to a man nobody knew much about. Serrano had stolen him from a rival casino because he came so highly recommended and because Foster was dispassionate as a shark. The security chief didn't invite confidences any more than he shared them. He did his job and he went home, which as far as Serrano knew was a simple one-bedroom out in Green Valley, even though Serrano paid him enough to afford something ten times as nice. Foster could live in a penthouse if wanted, but his security chief wasn't motivated by money. Serrano wouldn't feel entirely at ease about the man until he knew just what did motivate him. In nearly two years, he *still* hadn't figured it out.

Still, he had no concrete basis for his suspicions. They were reflexive more than anything else. He hadn't kept his position by letting people put things over on him. If he really thought the guy was up to something, he wouldn't have put him in charge of cleaning up the Justice debacle.

Serrano shrugged into his suit jacket. He'd be damned if he was going to change his routine. Tonight his cronies would be showing off at an exclusive club, where the drinks were overpriced, the women wore very little, and the men came in one shape: powerful. Ordinarily, he'd be the first one there. Since his humiliation, he hadn't shown his face, but he couldn't hide forever.

On the way down, he called for his driver, Tonio, who

met him at the front doors of the Silver Lady. The casino was a blowsy whore, but he loved every inch of her from the red carpet to the silver neon that ran the length of the electric bombshell that had made the place famous. There was a healthy crowd in there, he thought, as he climbed into the limo. Lots of blue-collar Joes like he'd once been, begging Lady Luck for a break. He could've told them all to go home and invest their money in a good IRA, but that would be bad for his own bottom line.

Serrano poured himself a drink. He didn't have to tell Tonio where he was going. Most of the time, his life ran like a Swiss watch. The driver dropped him off outside the club, seventeen thousand feet of pure luxurious debauchery. At the door, the bouncer waved him in and he took the VIP elevator up to the private suite. He didn't like mixing with all the drunks on the main level.

When he arrived, he found two guys waiting, Lou Pasternak and Joe Ricci. They had drinks in hand, watching the greater floor show. It wasn't just the dancers, but the way the men reacted to them. From up here, you could get the big picture, which was one of his favorite things about stopping by the security room at the Silver Lady. Sometimes he liked keeping a finger on the pulse of the place.

"So you finally crawled out of your hole," Joe said, raising his glass. "I think I'd just kill myself, if I was you. Nobody's ever gonna forget this."

Pasternak showed his teeth. "You know one of your guys put that thing on YouTube? When she held up the sign, I thought I'd piss myself laughing. Have you seen it?" The big man threw his head back and laughed.

Serrano froze. *Son of a bitch.* He'd known rumors would get out, repeated by those who were there that night. There was no avoiding that. He couldn't have imagined this would end up on the Internet. Somebody at the Silver Lady, somebody who worked in security, had copied the footage, sneaked it out, and put it up to disgrace him further.

He'd find out who was working that night, identify the culprit, and make an example of him. He hadn't dumped a body in years, but he still knew how to go about it. They had to see he wasn't soft.

A sick feeling overwhelmed him. Killing her might not be enough. He needed to do something big to make people in this town remember why they'd feared him.

Something big . . .

Addison Foster returned to the security room precisely ten minutes after he left his boss. The guards came to attention when he slid inside. They always became more conscientious by virtue of his presence. If he hadn't been distracted by other things, he would have found their nervousness amusing, not that it would have found any outlet in his expression. Foster prided himself on his inscrutable mien.

Where Gerard Serrano was concerned, it had saved his ass more than once.

"What's the situation on the floor?" he asked.

Rodriguez gave the report. "Making money almost everywhere, but table eight is losing steadily to a guy in a porkpie hat. I haven't been able to ID him yet."

Amateurs.

"Did you figure out his system at least?"

"Not yet."

He'd have to do it himself before their losses got big enough to piss Serrano off. "Show me the footage on the backup screen." Obligingly, Rodriguez sent the images over where he could examine them frame by frame. Foster sat down, and within forty-five seconds, he said, "Bring me the blond at the slots behind the table . . . and the guy in the hat. She's signaling him."

"Right away," the other guard said.

With a sigh, Foster let himself into the interview room. He could do without these idiots who were so sure they had a foolproof way to beat the house. There was no such thing as money for nothing. The guy in the porkpie hat didn't come quietly. It took four security guards to get him up there, and his blond accomplice wouldn't stop crying.

After conducting the required disclosure and confiscating their ill-gained goods, he turned the would-be Bonnie and Clyde over to the cops. It amused him how much play Serrano got out of the local authorities when he was probably the biggest criminal on or off the Strip. The only difference was, nobody ever caught *him*.

The rest of his shift passed quietly enough, but it was 4:00 A.M. by the time he clocked out and headed for his gold Nissan Altima. It was two years old and in excellent condition. Foster had learned to take care of his possessions as a child, and it didn't matter their actual value. He safeguarded what belonged to him.

So very little did.

It was a fair drive to his apartment so late at night, but he wouldn't live near the casinos. That brought back too many memories. Once he reached his apartment building, he checked the lot out of long-ingrained habit. Though it had been years since anyone had tracked him down, he never knew when the past would come calling again unexpectedly.

No shadows, no telltale signs of pursuit. Not even a car passing to another residence. That was good. At this hour, everything should be quiet—and it was—another reason he liked working this shift. It made it easier to spot things out of order.

Foster got out of his vehicle, hit the lock button on his remote, and kept an eye on the landscaping. It was impossible for him to walk to his building without constantly scanning side to side. As it always did, his heart pounded a little harder in going up the stairs to the third floor. If anyone had chosen tonight to try and kill him, this would be their best chance.

But as it had been for the last six hundred nights, he made it to his apartment unimpeded. Sometimes he almost felt disappointed in the ones hunting him. In that regard, he had some sympathy for the woman against whom they'd dispatched a professional. But if they'd only tried a little harder, they might succeed in making his life interesting. Instead he'd slipped into the skin of this nonentity, Addison Foster. Doubtless this man had grown up in New Hampshire and summered in the Poconos. He'd attended all the right schools.

Most days, he hated the son of a bitch, even as he was forced to live his life.

But not entirely.

The woman was waiting for him, as she was paid to, three nights a week. He did not speak to her as he hung his jacket in the closet. As instructed, she was already wearing the blindfold. She'd chained one of her wrists to his bedpost, and he took care of the other one himself. Then he left her that way, anticipation flooding his veins. He took a slow, leisurely shower, washing off the smoke and stench of a night at the Silver Lady.

The prostitute knew better than to make small talk. She was slim and lithe, younger than he wanted to think about, most likely, but not *too* young. His tastes didn't run in that direction. At his request, she had no body hair, just the dark mane on her head. It was dyed, of course. She'd been a mousy blond the first time she came to him, but in Vegas, you could have anything, if the price was right.

Just looking at her cuffed to his bed made him hard. She didn't move when he opened the table beside the bed and produced a condom. He rolled it on with the ease of practice, and she lay sweetly still and passive as he came down on her. The good girl had already lubricated herself, so he slid in easily.

Foster found it easier to do this with whores, who didn't question his preferences. Regular women always wanted to know *why* when he said, *don't look at me, don't talk to me, and for God's sake, don't touch me.* He'd given up on that type of exchange years ago. In many ways, this was cleaner and more honest.

Holding himself away from her on his arms, he began to thrust. They touched nowhere except this point of penetration. He could tell by her breathing when she started to like it. That was the thing that surprised him most about their arrangement. He found it strange that a working girl could take pleasure in his very particular tastes, but this one did, no question. She came almost as silently as he did—with a soft exhalation and a nearly imperceptible tightening of muscles.

It was exercise, nothing more.

As soon as he finished, he rolled away from her and unfastened one of her arms. He went to the bathroom and shut the door. She knew her cue. While he washed and disposed of the condom, she would dress and disappear. She'd never once seen his face.

That was the way it had to be. If she ever found out who he was—or more important—who he had been, things would change for her—and not in a good way.

By the time he came back into the bedroom, she was gone. Doubtless she envisioned he had some kind of hideous deformity, something he didn't want her to see or touch. Maybe she even got off on the thought that she was fucking a circus freak. There was no accounting for kink.

The truth was, his difference lay beneath the skin, nothing that could be measured or quantified. He merely accommodated it as best he could. Foster shrugged into a silken robe. The maroon dressing gown would surprise Serrano, he thought. He reckoned Foster a complete ascetic or possibly a homosexual. That too was part of the plan.

Then came the next part of his nightly ritual. Foster checked all the traps in the apartment, tiny cues that would tell him if something had been moved or touched. If the girl had shown signs of letting herself in and prowling in his things, well, they would not have continued their association. But she only did what she was paid to do, the consummate professional. He respected that in a woman.

He had a downright soft spot for the one who'd humiliated his boss on closed-circuit TV. Giving one of the guards the idea about YouTube had been priceless. Foster didn't think Serrano had seen that yet. The fireworks would be spectacular.

When he was content the apartment was still clean, he drew a titanium case out from its hiding spot. Inside, there was a laptop. He powered it up and input eight different passwords, taking him through various layers of encryption. He waited for a connection, then two words popped up on the black screen:

KNOCK KNOCK.

Despite his general distaste for the drama, he typed: WHO'S THERE?

MOCKINGBIRD.

Ah, he'd gotten lucky then. Foster smiled as he input, SHRIKE HERE. I KNOW HOW WE CAN TAKE HIM DOWN.

CHAPTER 5

Kyra had crossed the state line into Texas awhile back.

Now she just needed to decide where she was going to stop and how long she'd stay. She'd been running ever since she left Vegas, having the uneasy feeling if she lingered in one place too long, they'd catch up with her. She had to assume Serrano had people looking for her. God, if only she could've seen the look on his face.

Laughter overwhelmed her, almost drowning out the sound of the wind rushing through the car. If she had any sense, she'd be making arrangements to get out of the country, but she had no idea how to smuggle a large sum of money past customs. Unfortunately, the kind of people who might help her seemed equally likely to kill her and take the cash.

Plus, she didn't want to go anywhere she couldn't drive. She just wasn't leaving the Marquis, so that limited her choices. Canada might be an option, if she could get across the border with the money, but they'd tightened security lately, and she didn't want to wind up in jail. The same went for Mexico, and she'd have a language barrier to overcome there. No, Canada looked like the best option. She just needed to wait for Mia to get back—and stay free until she did.

She tapped her fingers against the steering wheel, gazing out over the plains. No help for it. Her shoulders were burning, and her ass was sore. She needed to rest, maybe take a couple days off and have a little fun. In every town, there were always idiots who could use some separation from their money. Sure, people would say she had no reason to work anymore, but that would be like telling a composer to stop writing music, just because he'd earned enough doing it. Some things you did for love.

Making a split-second decision, she yanked the car to the right, taking the exit. She followed the sign pointing toward Mount Silver. It looked to be no more than a tiny dot, several miles off the highway, but they'd have a cheap motel at the very least. Places like this always did. In the morning, she'd take a look around and consider her options.

Sure enough, she found a place on the outskirts of town called the Sleep E-Z. It was a concrete block U-shaped building that looked as if it had been last updated in 1957, and a series of motion-detecting lights flickered to life as she parked beside the office, illuminating an unholy collection of lawn gnomes. After climbing out of her car, Kyra stretched to pop the kinks out of her shoulders and back.

There was no restaurant attached to the property, but she had some ramen noodles in the trunk. With any luck, there would be a coffeemaker in the room. When she got to the office door, she found it locked, but there was a bell for after-hours service. It took almost five minutes, but eventually a man wearing low-slung tan pants and a dingy wife-beater came shuffling out through a curtained area in the back. He surveyed her suspiciously through the door and Kyra raised both hands to show she wasn't armed.

"I need a room," she said through the safety glass. "Do you have any vacancies?"

That was a ridiculous question. There were only two other cars in the lot, and one of them probably belonged to him. Still, it didn't hurt to be polite, not when he looked so grumpy about being woken up.

"Yeah," he grunted. "Just a sec."

She heard the sound of about ten locks being disengaged. What the hell did he expect to happen out here in the middle of nowhere? But maybe this was a high-crime route, based on factors she didn't know about.

With a smile, she stepped into the office, which smelled of burned coffee and stale sweat. The manager or owner—whatever he was—didn't speak as he set out the guest registry. The nicer hotels would demand a credit card and a picture ID, which is why she generally wound up in places like this. She wrote Cassie Marvel, one of her favorite aliases in the line below the last guest, whose scrawl was illegible.

"Forty-five bucks. Cash," the guy told her, as if he suspected she might try to pay in food stamps or bingo tickets.

Kyra laid out the money in small, crumpled bills. That seemed to relieve his mind somewhat and he plunked an old-fashioned metal key down on the counter. "You're in 117. No parties, no unregistered guests. Basic cable is free. Check-out is at noon. You're not out of there at 12:01, you pay for another night."

"Got it." She nodded and snagged the key. "Thanks."

She left the building and hopped back in the Marquis, pulling it around the building to the corner of the U nearest her room. The exterior lights seemed too few and far between. The dark was more profound out here, broken only by the stream of her headlights. Once she turned them off, she couldn't see, and that made her uneasy.

For a moment, she sat listening to the engine tick over. Then she told herself she was being stupid. Nobody knew where she was. Hell, she couldn't even pinpoint the town without half an hour and a map.

Before getting out, she locked the other doors, and then clicked the lock button on the driver's side. Then she grabbed the keys and her bag from the backseat. Try as she might, Kyra couldn't dispel the foreboding as she slid out of the car. Her fevered imagination conjured footsteps crunching across the parking lot, even though she didn't see anyone. Her heart was pounding like a jackhammer by the time she got in the door.

For a long moment, she leaned up against it, eyes closed. It was a thin barrier between her and imagined danger, but it helped a little. She turned and engaged both the bolt and the chain. It was a wholly irrational response to the dark, but she'd been afraid of it ever since she was a kid.

Normal people grew out of it, but normal people didn't deal with a dad who'd left her on her own more nights than she could tally. He meant well, and most times, he did come home with breakfast money from whatever game he'd gotten into. Kyra understood what kind of man he was, not the sort who could work a day job, and she'd loved him fiercely. But she'd always gone to sleep with the lights on. The worst time she could remember was a bad storm in Pensacola, when the power went off. She'd been nine.

Thunder rumbled in the distance. Ah. That probably explained her nerves. Lightning in the air always made her nervous.

"Looks like I got off the road just in time," she said aloud.

A tired driver coupled with a fierce Texas thunderstorm didn't make a good match. She took stock of what forty-five dollars had bought her. The room was shabby but fairly clean, if you didn't look too long at anything. She was thankful to find a coffeemaker in the tiny bathroom, so she could heat water for soup. First Kyra checked it for telltale signs it had been used for cooking meth, but it was dusty, not rusty looking. Next she filled the pot and poured it in the top, checked and then rinsed the filter area, and flicked the machine on. It immediately began to hiss.

As she laid out some clothes for the next morning, rain began to spatter on the roof. Kyra couldn't help but repress a shiver. In her life, rain never signified anything good. It rarely rained in Vegas, but it had been pouring on the August night when she found him discarded in an alley off the Strip like yesterday's garbage.

Her hands shook as she opened the carton of noodles. She didn't want to remember that night. It would only give her nightmares. There was nothing more she could do. She'd avenged him the only way she could, and it hadn't given her any peace. His wet, battered face still rose up to the surface of her dreams like a corpse floating free of its weights in a night-dark river.

"Who did this?" she'd whispered.

"Serrano," he'd gasped. "But listen to me, baby. Stay away from him. Promise me—" But he wasn't able to force a promise out of her.

He died.

She remembered with crystalline clarity how she felt, kneeling in the rain, which contrasted to the heat of the night. All around her, neon had flashed with maddening regularity. If she closed her eyes she could visualize everything about the moment.

With effort, she forced the memories away. She needed to eat something or she'd get sick. Since her weird ability sparked to life, she'd had a crazily high metabolism, as if what she did cost a certain amount in terms of energy. That made sense, actually, not that Kyra had asked any doctors about it. She hadn't seen one in years.

She got the coffeepot and poured the water into her ramen noodles. What a glamorous life she led. Everything would look better in the morning. It always did.

It was almost 3:00 A.M. when Reyes pulled into the motel parking lot. He found the Marquis right away, verifying that he was still on target. He wouldn't have been surprised, actually, to learn she'd found the thing and planted it on another car.

That would have complicated matters significantly, as it would mean she'd made him, and he wouldn't be able to coax the information he needed out of her. He'd have to gear up to pain and coercion immediately.

The tracking device simplified his job; now he had to work out why she'd add him to her routine of her own volition. He'd forced his way in once, and she'd ditched him, even after the smoking-hot sex. He thought that was probably the norm for her. In fact, Reyes doubted she'd given him a second thought since driving away.

Another man might've been flattened by that. For him, it just presented a challenge, a problem he needed to think his way around. She'd proven more capable than he expected, not just a pretty little gold digger. Foster had warned him she had hidden depths and was dangerous as the day was long. She'd apparently killed her own father to cut him out of the score; Reyes had visited the grave himself.

Maybe he should have thought twice about sleeping with

the evil little bitch, but he'd thought that was a way to reach her. Women who couldn't be manipulated emotionally could sometimes be bound with sex. The way she walked away proved she wasn't one of them. It was quite the fucking problem, considering he needed information before he finished the job.

At the moment, however, he needed a room for the night. It was a break she didn't know the car he was driving. There would be nothing to tip her off when she woke up in the morning.

The failed gambit would make things more difficult. If he'd known how slippery she would prove to be, he would have planned his first approach a little more carefully. But there was no changing the facts now. He'd have to find a way that didn't set off all her alarm bells. That might prove tricky.

First, he needed sleep.

Reyes rented a room from the surly proprietor and headed to it, intending to crash for the night. It amused him to let himself into the room right next door to hers. When the manager turned his back, he'd checked the record behind the counter: Cassie Marvel. He added it to her list of known aliases, along with Rachel Justice and Lisa Baker. He admired that she didn't stick with one set of initials. People often made that mistake unconsciously, their egos imprinting their true selves on whatever persona they adopted.

As he passed her room, he noticed through the filmy curtain that her light was still on. Reyes was surprised to find himself curious as to why she'd be up so late. She must be exhausted.

It had been a long day of driving, even for him. He knew it was unwise to linger where she might catch a glimpse of him, but with the light reflecting off the inside of the glass, he wouldn't be more than a dark figure to her. So he permitted himself a glimpse through the gap in the curtains, and was startled to see her curled on her side, fully dressed, facing the door. A pang spiked through him; Kyra Beckwith slept like a child afraid of the dark.

He walked on. His shoes made no sound as he slipped into his room, forcing away the oddly vulnerable impression she'd left. There was probably a weapon hidden beneath her pillow. He'd been briefed about how dangerous she could be, but he still hadn't sorted out why her hand-to-hand combat style so closely mimicked his own. Reyes also couldn't explain the bizarre drain when she touched him.

Things seemed to be back to normal now. He tested that theory with a few advanced katas. They came to him naturally, so whatever she'd done to him, he had gotten over it.

Before he slept, Reyes rearranged the room a little. He slid the end table beneath the window, so anyone coming in that way would knock over the lamp. He hated motel rooms on the ground floor—getting into them was like shooting fish in a barrel—but he had to stay close to his quarry. Then he pushed the desk a little too close to the door, so if anyone tried to kick it open, it would rebound back, giving him time to ready himself for the fight. It was a primitive alarm system, but it would do. You didn't get to be his age in this particular field without perfecting precaution to a fine art.

Reyes fell asleep with his gun next to him.

In the morning, the pavement was still wet from the storm he'd driven through to find her. He took a shower and then ate a protein bar, considering his options. When she left, he didn't follow her immediately, merely kept an eye on her signal. No further than it went, he'd guess she was looking for breakfast in this two-bit town.

If she ran true to form, she'd be looking for a place to run her next con. That made little sense, based on the amount she'd gotten from Serrano, but she didn't seem to be touching her principal. From what Reyes could tell, she was living off what she made along the way, not the cash from the casino. That told him she must have stashed it somewhere for the time being. But where? And why?

He collected his things and stopped by the office to check out. There was a young woman, maybe the guy's daughter, working the desk today. She couldn't have been more than nineteen, bottle blond and corn-fed. The boys probably loved her.

She blushed as she took the key from him, letting her fingers brush his. "Too bad you can't stay another night."

He smiled faintly. "Well, you never know. I might be back."

Depending on what his quarry decided to do.

The clerk took that as a compliment and giggled slightly, gazing up at him through heavily mascaraed lashes. Every inch of her face had been covered with some kind of cosmetic, trying to cover up a slight complexion problem. In the morning light, he saw the bumps on her chin raying outward toward her jaw like a Braille map of awkward teenage hormones.

"I'll leave the light on for you," she joked.

He got the reference, vaguely remembering some motel chain that used that as a slogan. *Well, why not make use of her? The kid's in the mood to talk, unlike her old man, and you might get some useful info.* Reyes leaned on the counter, offering a slow smile that told her he thought she was the finest thing in all of Texas. Like most of his smiles, that one was a lying bastard, but it served the purpose. She softened visibly, leaning in. He almost regretted how easy it was.

"Are there any decent bars in this town?" he asked.

"The Blue Rock," she answered at once. But she sagged with disappointment. "But I can't . . . uh, my dad doesn't like me hanging around in there," she finished, chewing the color off her bottom lip.

As if I didn't know you aren't old enough to drink. She assumed the question came as a precursor to an offer of a date, and he left her that illusion.

"Well, I wouldn't want to cause trouble for you," he said gently. "Do they have a pool table there? Darts? Maybe a poker game in back?"

She shrugged, likely sensing she wouldn't be getting a free dinner or felt up in his car. "Yeah, to the first two, not sure on the last thing. Take care, mister."

Reyes pushed away from the counter. Being polite entertained him because in the back of his mind, he carried the knowledge that for the right reasons, he would have put a bullet through her brain. In his opinion, some scumbags needed killing, and he could earn a good living doing exactly that.

He strolled over to his rental car, thoughtful. Ten would get him twenty that Kyra Beckwith would check out the Blue Rock before she left town. She went about it like a compulsion, as if she didn't know any other way to live. It would have been harder to track her if people didn't remember her little swindles here and there, but she wouldn't think of foregoing them.

If he was wrong about her, he could try again in the next town . . . and again . . . until their paths crossed naturally. He wasn't sure how he would parlay an opening into a permanent opportunity at her side, but he thought well on his feet, always had. Reyes rubbed his hands together, full of anticipation that came in the form of a low, almost sexual hunger deep in his belly. He wanted another chance against her.

With some effort, he drove away the images of her clawing him like a cat. He still bore her marks on his skin. There was no way he could continue to think about that and stay professional, so he pushed the images aside with consummate control.

It's almost time for round two, and this time, you won't come out on top.

CHAPTER 6

Kyra had miscalculated.

There probably wasn't a score here. The guys at the Blue Rock weren't typical yokels, and they almost seemed to expect her to try something. They'd been watching her with avid suspicion ever since she sauntered in the door. Something wasn't right. There was something fishy in this little town, echoed by the paranoia of that motel owner.

She just couldn't figure out how they'd made her. At this point, she hadn't done anything but order; she'd only been in here for two minutes. Maybe they simply had something else to hide, and she was paranoid, thinking their secret had to do with *her*. A place like this might front any number of unsavory enterprises. Kyra took a pull of her beer and locked eyes with the bartender, a big bald guy who watched her like a hawk.

Instinct told her to finish her beer, eat a few stale pretzels for the look of the thing, and then hit the road. There would be another town, another round of suckers. Instead, she tried a smile.

"Gonna be a hot one," she said, conversational.

A ceiling fan stirred sluggishly overhead, not doing much

more than moving the warm air around. Two guys played pool behind her, but she took care not to watch them overtly. Too much interest would seem out of place in a casual barfly.

"Yep," he agreed with a nod. "What brings you to Mount Silver?"

The question surprised her, the modern equivalent of "what're you doing in these parts, stranger." She wondered, smothering a smile, whether it would be followed up with "we don't like your kind around here." The bartender propped his elbow on the counter, waiting for her reply. Generally, a lean like that meant the guy wanted a closer connection. In this case, it meant he wanted her near enough he could grab her.

So she shrugged. "Just passing through."

Before the guy could reply, someone strolled out of the bathrooms in the back. Her nerves were on edge, so she wanted to categorize everyone in the place. Through smoky sunlight, she recognized him immediately as the guy she'd left exhausted in her bed at a motel somewhere outside Lake Charles. What the hell was he doing here? Her bad feeling exploded into a flash fire.

But he drew up short at seeing her. "Are you following me? Look, lady, I appreciate the ride and everything, but whatever it is you think I did, it wasn't me. I didn't touch your stuff." Rey tried a placating smile. "If you're mad I wasn't there when you got back, then . . . uh . . . I promise our night was special, the best I ever had, but I'm not really the settling-down type." His dark, rough face gained an expression of manifest horror. "You're not pregnant, are you? It's not mine." He glanced at the other guys in the bar as if for moral support. "I wore a jimmy hat, every time. I swear."

Furious color burned in her cheeks. Now everyone in the bar thought she was a slut. If it hadn't been so embarrassing and inconvenient, it would have been funny. Much funnier if it happened to someone else. *Coincidence?* It seemed unlikely, but he seemed as shocked to see her as she was him. Sometimes life threw unexpected curves, and you just had to catch them.

"I'm not pregnant," she muttered. "I just seemed destined to run across you."

Rey grinned. "Some people are just born lucky, I guess. So . . . just to be clear, you *weren't* looking for me?"

The room felt hot and thick. Somebody snickered. "Of course not."

She couldn't tell if the heat came from remembering how he'd woken her twice before morning, imprinting himself on every inch of her body, or embarrassment from his fear she might be hunting him down for seconds. Her bedroom show came to town one night only, no encores. So she'd never slept with the same man twice.

"You two know each other?" the bartender asked into the silence.

That roused an uneasy reaction from the guys playing pool. One of them whispered, "They gotta be cops, trying to play us."

"Yep," the taller one agreed. "It's the only reason we'd have two strangers who 'happen' to be acquainted in on the same day."

The big guy stepped forward, pool cue in hand, but it looked more like a bo staff, the way he held it, than an instrument of recreational fun. Kyra took a step back and came up against the bar. Rey took a position at her side that was oddly reassuring.

"If you think we're cops," she offered, "then it would be stupid to try anything. Just let us walk out of here and nobody gets hurt."

She'd been right about them having something to hide. At this point, she had no idea what it could be. When she'd inquired about bars in the area at checkout, the girl at the motel had said her dad didn't let her hang out here, but Kyra had thought that was because the man didn't want his underage kid drinking. Maybe there was something worse going on.

The big guy grinned. "I got a better idea. We could just end you quietly, and bury the bodies out back. How many nosy cops we got out there anyway, Ed? Four? Five?"

Before answering, the bartender, presumably named Ed, did some math, counting on his fingers. "Five right now. Seven if we do these two."

Rey shifted, leaning most of his weight against the

counter, as if they weren't outnumbered and receiving death threats. "Go on. Take your best shot."

If she hadn't stolen and used his capacity for mayhem, she'd think he was being cocky. She knew better. Kyra took care not to touch him. Crippling her only ally wouldn't do them any good. It would serve her best if she borrowed from one of these guys; she just had to hope her target didn't hide a secret gift for macramé.

Enraged, the ox lunged with the pool stick, but Rey stepped aside neatly and came into a fighting stance with an ease that said he was on a whole different level. He beckoned, curling his fingers up twice, and three guys ran at him.

Kyra didn't take time to watch their tussle, as she had the smaller guy to worry about. He wouldn't think he needed to use his best stuff on her. That assumption would cost him. She slapped him on the forearm as he came at her. Her sissy move stopped him dead in his tracks as laughter overwhelmed him.

"Is that the best you can do?" he demanded. "My ex-wife hit harder than you."

She had no idea. Maybe he was really good at watercolors or refinishing old furniture, and just took a casual interest in fighting. But no . . . his technique flowed over her within a few seconds. *Tae Kwon Do, huh?* Okay, she could work with that.

"No," she said, smiling. And spun into a jump kick that connected with his head. "This is."

She fought him easily, using his own style against him, while he fumbled as if he'd taken no classes at all. There was almost nothing better than taking a belligerent man's best ability and turning it against him, except maybe relieving some mean, greedy bastard of his money. The best moment of her life had come when she won at 21, playing with Serrano's money.

Her opponent reacted with disbelief, rocking with every hit. His kneecap popped out of socket and he went down hard. Kyra kicked him in the head for good measure. The sound of the bartender cocking a shotgun put her on the floor. No matter whose skill she stole, she wasn't bulletproof.

That didn't seem to stop Rey. She heard him dive over the bar as the gun went off, and then there was the sound of breaking bottles. Something gave a wet pop and she thought it was probably a body part. Then there was a thump from the body falling.

She stood up, carefully. There were four guys on the floor, including the one she'd dropped, plus the bartender. Rey had taken on three men at once, and only suffered a scratch on his cheek from the flying glass. He vaulted lightly over the counter.

"So," he said, "come here often?"

Kyra couldn't help it; she laughed. "No. You ass. Did you kill any of them?"

"I don't think so. That guy won't be walking around for a while, though." He tilted his head toward the bartender.

She sighed. "I just wanted a drink." *And a score,* she added silently. "What the hell was this about anyway?"

"I dunno. But I'm thinking I'd like to find out."

His target followed him toward the back room, where he found nothing but stored beer and booze. "It has to be downstairs then."

"What does?" She watched while he broke the lock.

"Whatever they were trying to hide from the cops."

He flicked the light on before they went down the stairs. If there had been anybody else on the premises, they surely would've come up if they heard the brawl, so he wasn't expecting trouble. They came on an old unfinished basement with concrete block walls and a stained floor. The strong sulfur and ammonia smell gave away the secret before he spotted the paraphernalia, containers with tubes and funnels, coolers, boxes of supplies.

"Meth lab," Kyra said from behind him.

Reyes wasn't surprised she could ID one on sight. That was probably the least of the trouble she'd been involved with during her colorful career. He didn't like ending women, but he'd done a little research before accepting Serrano's job offer, and she had quite a record.

He pulled his drifter persona close and tight before turning to face her. "Don't touch anything."

"I know. It's volatile." Her eyes narrowed. "I'd like to

burn this place down. Scumbags like that make their money dealing to high school kids. I have no problem with adults who choose to rot their brains like this; it's sort of like natural selection—"

"They win the Darwin Awards," he put in, smiling.

She looked at him in surprise. "Yeah. Exactly like that. But when kids get sucked in, not knowing what they're in for, it totally pisses me off."

"So do you want to?" He met her gaze levelly.

"Want to what?"

"Burn the place down."

Her eyes widened. "Are you crazy? That'll have the real cops and firemen out here before we get far enough away. I don't want to attract attention."

She'd said "we," he noticed. His smile widened into something sharp and feral. It demonstrated progress for her to incorporate him into her plan, and he intended to capitalize on this opportunity.

"Okay," he said easily. "I'm gonna disconnect some stuff. You go on up."

Too trusting, he decided, as she took the suggestion at face value. He could be stealing meth for all she knew. Instead he rerouted some things and lit a cigarette, leaving it burning in a fashion that would wind up working like a fuse. This place was going up, one way or another. He didn't like drug dealers any better than Kyra did, so he'd work this like a freebie. Nobody was paying him for this job, but sometimes it was just good karma to offer your services gratis to the universe.

Before they left, he made sure the men were still unconscious. If one of them woke before the blast, well, he was welcome to try to find Reyes for some payback. That kind of thing made life interesting.

In the gravel parking lot, he had the odd feeling they'd played this scene once before, but he wouldn't threaten her tires a second time. His rental car was still at the motel; he'd hitched a ride over, as that was more in keeping with his role.

"Fate brought us together again for some reason," he said, lying through his teeth. "You walk on the wild side, you're gonna hustle the wrong person someday, and then what? You need some muscle at your back, and I need wheels. Let's see where it takes us. We don't have to hook up again."

His body protested immediately. Since he'd first seen her ponied up to the bar, he'd had an insane urge to shove her down and take her, any way she'd let him. The scratches she'd left on his shoulders stung a little—in the best possible way.

Damn, they didn't have time to stand here talking about this. But she didn't know that. He had to reel her in slowly, or she'd fight the capture.

"Get in," she said finally. "We shouldn't hang around here. And maybe you're right. I never thought about taking on a partner before, but you might fit the bill."

Her eyes slid over his shoulder, as if seeing someone who wasn't there—a former cohort? Hell, maybe she'd killed him. Reyes rather liked the idea of living dangerously. He also liked that she didn't bother to deny what he'd noticed her doing at the last bar.

"You know anything about the biz?" She went around the vehicle.

"Not really." He slid into the Marquis on the passenger side. "But I learn fast. I can watch your back while you work and just jump in if something goes wrong."

She started the car, backed it out faster than anyone he'd ever seen, and slammed the wheel so that they spun onto the road. He loved the way she drove, all attitude and swagger, underscored with complete control. Reyes would bet she knew this car better than most women knew their own anatomy. It made sense; she practically lived in it.

She thought for a while. Neither of them turned on the radio. They had come about a mile when a big orange glow and a distant boom rose up behind them. Kyra noticed it in the rearview and said, "What the hell did you do? I thought I said not to burn the place down!"

Reyes grinned. "I didn't. I blew it up."

Would she get all girly on him and cry? *Oh, hell. Please, no.* To his delight, she burst out laughing. "Ah, shit. So much for low profile, but they had it coming."

Something tightened in his gut. After a moment, he identified the feeling as pure lust. Most females couldn't stomach the things he did; most flinched away from his eyes, seeming to sense the kind of life he'd led. She was brash and brave and full of wickedness.

Damn, he wanted her.

He made himself speak casually. "There was enough chemical in that place that they won't find any sign of us, even if you're in the system."

"Are *you*?" she asked without looking away from the road.

She had to know the answer to that, if she had any skill at observation. But she didn't seem to judge him for being an ex-con. Most people would.

"Yeah."

"You've had military training," she told him. "Probably not Special Forces. But I don't think you enjoy taking orders. Is that why you opted out?"

"More or less." It astonished him how much she'd picked up.

"And I think you must've gone East to study martial arts, the way you fight."

"The East isn't the only place you can learn."

She picked up on the fact that he didn't deny studying abroad. "Then where?"

"The Philippines," he answered honestly. He didn't let himself think about why he was answering her questions as Reyes. Maybe something told him she'd sense a lie. Professional liars often had a built-in bullshit detector, so whatever he said to her, he had to mean it. "Brazil. Indonesia."

That was the key, he realized. She'd catch on to any elaborate ruse. To get to her, he had to be himself. In some ways, this would be the hardest job ever. He'd been pretending to be other people for so long, he didn't even know who lived inside his own skin anymore.

"I thought I recognized some of your moves. Capoeira, combined with tarung derajat? Maybe some Jendo? You've blended the styles in a way I've never seen. But . . . it's beautiful. You're beautiful when you move."

She didn't seem to realize she'd just called him beautiful. In his experience, women didn't think so. He scared the hell out of most of them. Reyes didn't know how to respond to that, so he addressed the first part of what she'd said. "Yes, you caught all three. How'd you know? They're not common."

"I'm a fan." Her dimples flashed as she smiled, cutting him an appreciative look. "UFC, mostly. I watch martial arts on ESPN whenever I get a chance."

Mmm. He put himself in the picture beside her, a beer in one hand and her in the other. It was deliciously seductive. She'd clearly studied some herself, so maybe she'd even make a decent sparring partner. He could picture them on the mat, breathing hard as he took her down, fighting their way into the hardest, hottest sex ever. Her skin would shine with heat and exertion, sweaty-slick beneath him. She had a strong body, deceptively leggy. He wanted them wrapped around him.

Ah, damn. His cock went hard as a spike. He should *not* be thinking along those lines. Reyes shifted to cover the fact that he wanted to wrench the wheel, shove her into the backseat, and take her. By some miracle, he kept his breathing steady, though his hands curled into fists.

"I'm the brains," she told him. "I've been doing this longer than you can possibly imagine, so I pick the targets. I plan the score. You just do as you're told and maybe we can work something out. I'll give you twenty percent to start."

What just happened? She'd decided to hire him while he was thinking about sex? There was something to be said for keeping his mouth shut.

"Twenty-five percent," he countered, knowing she'd expect it, which was why she'd lowballed him. "And we'll renegotiate once I learn the ropes. This sounds like it'll be dangerous."

"Deal," she said promptly, making him think he could've gone to thirty.

And I'm in.

It was a ballsy question, but he had to ask. "What about sex?"

"What about it?"

"Are we going to have any?"

She looked thoughtful, almost abashed. "I don't know.

I've never done it twice with the same person." At his elevated brows, she amended, "Well—on a different night. So *if* we do, it'll be a major event, and I'm thinking you'll have to work for it."

And a lance of pure lust ran him through.

CHAPTER 7

Kyra hadn't spent so much time with one person since before her dad died.

It was disconcerting to ride with Rey all day and then hang with him in the bar at night while he watched her work. It was even weirder to wake up and meet for breakfast somewhere. She had to admit; it was helpful having someone at her back. He'd extricated her from a couple of shaky situations with only a dark look, not a single blow exchanged, and that made for a nice change.

Since they were accomplices, jointly responsible for what went down at the bar, she figured she should be able to rely on him to some degree. He couldn't turn on her without implicating himself. A down-on-his-luck ex-con like him needed the income she provided, too, if he didn't want to wind up back in prison or homeless. That was too bad because he might've made something of himself on the fighting circuit, based on his other training, but they didn't take convicted felons, and on the underground fight arenas, he would wind up dead or brain-damaged. Safety wasn't exactly a concern for the handlers there.

Everything was easier with him around, but she didn't

trust easy, never had. Maybe she'd just traveled with her dad too long; his paranoia had seeped in through her skin, making her unable to trust anyone completely. No matter how providential their partnership seemed, she'd still sleep with one eye open, so to speak.

To his credit, he hadn't tried to push their relationship. After asking about sex, he made no moves on her, and he seemed genuinely interested in learning the tricks of her trade. That wasn't so hard to understand. If a body had any brains at all, it was possible to get by doing this instead of real work.

They'd come north through Texas over the course of the week, earning enough money to cover food, gas, and shelter along the way. His cut was slim, but he didn't complain. Today, if everything went according to plan, they'd be rolling into Pecos in early afternoon.

Kyra yawned, stretched, and hit the shower. The hot water beat down on her skin, waking her up better than coffee. She made it quick, knowing Rey would be waiting downstairs by the car. She'd almost had enough traveling for a while. After Vegas, she'd thought she would want to be on the move constantly—six months was a hell of a long con—but she found she missed waking up in the same place.

Maybe she'd never be ready to go straight, but she wouldn't mind settling in a big city somewhere that had a lot of ready marks. The danger about small towns was that people tended to remember her, but they also made it easier to find gullible targets. At this point, she had it perfected. Find the local bar, identify the mouthy big shot, and then relieve him of some loot and ego at the same time. It was practically a public service.

Once she got dressed, Kyra did a quick check of the motel room. Nothing left behind. That was good. She could pack in five minutes these days; she'd perfected the art of living out of a backpack. As she left the room, her damp hair clung to her cheek, irritating her. So she tugged it over her shoulders in two messy sections and braided it up. A quick rummage through her pack unearthed two bands, so she was set.

Like most days, she wore her favorite ratty jeans, matching jacket, and a plaid button-up shirt. Kyra knew she didn't look sophisticated enough to be up to something, particularly with the braids, and that was sort of the point. Rey reinforced that conviction as he slid off the hood of her car. Ordinarily she'd tear him a new one for that liberty, but she was in too good a mood—and too hungry—to waste time snarling this morning.

"You look about fourteen years old," he said in the gravelly voice that plucked at her nerve endings.

She grinned as she slid in behind the wheel. "Good thing for you I'm not."

"No joke," he muttered. "So we're for Pecos today. What's the plan there?"

Kyra shrugged. "I won't know until I take the lay of the land."

To her surprise, he left it there, turning away from her to stare out the window. Most people would be questioning her, trying to get her to spill her secrets so he could take off on his own sooner. Her new partner didn't say much, which should have been peaceful. Instead she found herself wondering what lay behind his silences.

She found a diner a few miles down the road, where they stopped for breakfast. Actually it was more of a truck stop, but from the number of semis out front, the food and coffee must be good. Kyra guided the Marquis in between two shiny big rigs and hopped out of the car. After snagging her backpack, she glanced at Rey over the roof of the vehicle.

"Hungry?"

"You have no idea," he muttered.

Her lips curved in pure feminine appreciation. That was the first indication he'd given of being aware of the smoldering sexual tension. With every passing day, she wanted him a little more, but she'd meant it when she said he would have to work for an encore. If she broke her rule about entanglements for him, Kyra wanted to be sure he was worth the risk. So far he appeared to think abstinence would do that job for him without any real effort on his part. Well, he obviously didn't know her very well.

Inside, the restaurant was full of potbellied men in plaid, their jaws bristling with whiskers and their hair covered in baseball caps. The crowd made her anticipate breakfast in a big way. It wasn't the sort of place where you waited to be seated, so they snagged a booth with rusty tangerine seats and a scarred Formica tabletop.

She plucked a menu from the silver metal stand by the window. Over the years, she'd eaten in countless places like this one, and they all ran together after a while. After a thirty-second perusal, she decided on the Country Scramble: eggs, bacon, and sausage all fried up together and topped with yummy white gravy, biscuits on the side, of course. Her mouth watered just thinking about it.

A perky blond waitress bounced over. "What can I get you folks?"

"Fruit and yogurt," Rey said. "Topped with granola if you have it. Plain whole wheat toast, no butter."

Kyra raised a brow. "On a health kick?"

He shrugged. "Just tired of fried eggs, I guess."

"You're gonna be sorry when you see my biscuits."

"I've already seen 'em," he murmured. "But I wouldn't mind another look."

Was he flirting with her? Her smile widened. "So tell me a little about yourself. How does a guy get to be your age, totally unencumbered?"

He met her look levelly. "I could ask you the same thing."

"You could, but you didn't."

"Fair enough."

The waitress arrived with their drinks: coffee for her, herbal tea for him. Kyra was starting to notice he avoided caffeine and sugar whenever possible. It was an interesting quirk in someone down on his luck. Generally people without financial recourse would order the cheapest items, not the healthiest. Rey added a squirt of lemon, no sweetener, and took an experimental sip. If Kyra didn't know better, she'd think he was stalling.

"Well?" she demanded.

"It's not bad." The amusement in his dark eyes said he knew she was losing patience, and that he found it entertaining.

"Not the tea. What's your story?"

"So you want my life story at Stuckey's? Not very atmospheric."

"It's Gayle's Gas-N-Go, actually," she corrected. "And if you don't want to tell me, just say so."

He thought about that for a moment, long dark fingers tracing a pattern against the scarred tabletop. "Okay," he said at last.

"So you don't want to?" Her good mood evaporated.

"Is that so surprising? Would you spill all your secrets to *me* over pancakes?"

"Probably not," she admitted.

"Well, there you go. Trust takes time. I won't be telling you everything until I'm sure you won't use the information against me." His mouth curved into an ironic half smile. "I'm sure you've heard the saying—familiarity breeds contempt—and all that."

"I don't think it would," she found herself saying. "The more I get to know you, the more I like."

Something sparked in his eyes. Kyra couldn't decipher the expression, but for a moment, she thought he might reach across the table for her. She scooted back, knowing that would be disastrous for the day's take. Rey narrowed his eyes, scowling at the implied insult, but before he could ask, the waitress delivered their food and they ate in silence. She felt sad and sick, but she couldn't explain why she'd recoiled.

Half an hour later, Kyra took the ramp back to the interstate, a charcoal gray ribbon bounded in white lines that cut through the center of some bad country. *This part of Texas sure is ugly.* The scrubby land was uniformly dry and brown, broken only by occasional desert flora. As the day wore on, it got hotter, so she rolled down the windows, letting the wind roar through the Marquis like a contained cyclone. She threw back her head and laughed, mashing down on the accelerator.

Live fast, die young. It worked for James Dean.

With her peripheral vision, she caught Rey looking at her with dark and hungry eyes. The strength of her response astonished her. The things he could do to her with just a look should be illegal—and probably were—in the state of Texas. When he realized she knew he was watching her, he turned away. He could have lied back at the diner. He could have made up a background, or a sob story, and she would have never known the difference. Instead, he'd let her know he wasn't ready to open up. She respected that.

As she pulled off the highway, taking the road that led into Pecos, she smiled. He wasn't so different from other men; he just restrained himself better. Oddly enough, that reassured her. If he could control his behavior in this area, he'd make a reliable partner. She needed someone she could count on to respond the same way, every time they played the game, no deviations. That was what made a con successful—even the smallest tell could cost them everything.

You're a crazy woman, looking for an honest liar.

But maybe, just maybe, she'd found him.

This was the fourth town they'd hit, but it was the first time she'd let him in on the game. By prior arrangement, Reyes arrived first at the bar they'd targeted: Lefty's Tavern. It was a redneck dive, full of wildcatters and refinery workers. He ordered a beer and sat down to wait, as instructed.

Kyra arrived half an hour later, and she drew the eye of every man in the place. He'd never seen those particular jeans on her before, but they were a work of art, strategically ripped down the backs of her thighs, and then laced together with black satin ribbon. The design showed cunning glimpses of skin.

Her movement gave everyone in the room a peek down her black tank top. It would've been plain if not for the deep V and the slim line of sequins that drew attention to her cleavage even when she was standing up. When she leaned down to snag the keys that had "slipped" from her fingers, his temperature spiked. Along with ten other guys, Rey saw she was wearing a red scalloped bra with black polka dots and a cute little bow in between her breasts.

The other guys had to be thinking about the matching underwear. Even though he knew it was a calculated display, meant to distract, he could no more prevent himself from picturing her in polka-dotted lingerie than he could stop his heart. And he was no Tibetan monk. Unfortunately, he had actual experience to draw upon, making his imaginings painfully accurate. He even knew the way she sounded when she came.

Physical satiation should have made it easier to focus. Instead, he could only think about having her again. And again. Reyes knew he was making progress with her by biding his time, increasing her levels of trust. He wanted to believe it was sheer perversity that made him want her so, knowing she was dangerous, the closest thing to a black widow he was ever likely to meet.

He couldn't wholly credit that, either.

Reyes made sure not to stare too long, no longer than anyone else, before he went back to his beer. Sometimes she went for the Lolita look in braids and plain cotton. Tonight, she was someone else entirely. Since he'd been doing the same thing for more years than he could count, he admired her ability to slip from one skin to another. Like him, Kyra was pure chameleon; she could be whoever you wanted her to be.

Her walk was smoke and honey; she could stop a train with those hips. Predictably one of the local Romeos headed for Kyra before she made it to the bar. He was tall, brown-haired, mostly fit, but Reyes noted he'd gone soft around the middle.

"Buy you a drink?" the guy offered.

Her mouth curved up. Only her eyes gave her away. Despite her smile, she wasn't sweet; she was a tigress with tawny eyes to match.

"You asking me or telling me?"

"I thought I'd start by asking." Her would-be one-night stand reached out a hand, like he meant to touch her, but she danced away, firefly light.

Interesting. So it's not just me. She doesn't like being touched. Reyes filed that away under potentially useful tidbits about his target.

"That works for me." She flashed a smile, pure carnal sweetness.

"Cal, get the lady whatever she wants." The guy tossed a crumpled bill onto the counter. Reyes couldn't make out the denomination from where he stood.

"Can I get some Anakin?" Kyra asked.

The 'tender frowned. "Like . . . Skywalker? I don't do fancy mixed drinks."

She bit her lip, adorably confused. Her body language practically shouted: *I'm cute, but not very bright. Take advantage of me.* Oh yeah, she was good, all right.

"You mean Heineken?" her "date" offered.

"Yes!" She beamed up at him. "Thank you."

"I'm Rick. And you are . . .?"

"Sasha," she told him without a single tell. "I just moved here from Reno."

While Reyes watched, Kyra sipped her beer and worked her new friend for a good half an hour, milking him for information about the other patrons. She did it without apparent guile or intent, encouraging him to ply his wit. Within an hour, she knew who had money, who wished he had money, and who deserved to lose some.

"I feel like a game of pool," she said eventually.

That was his cue.

"I'll play." Reyes pushed away from the bar, sauntering toward her. "But why not make it interesting? Five bucks says you can't beat me."

Rick sized him up and immediately protested. "Leave her alone. She's with me."

That set up a slow burn down low in his gut. He had to force himself not to curl his hands into fists. "So you don't want to play?" he asked Kyra.

She gave a sweet, confused smile. "No, I do. This won't take long."

He beat her by a landslide, which was the point. With a tremulous lower lip, Kyra turned over a crinkled five-dollar bill. "I thought I was getting better," she said with a sad little sigh.

"You're so pretty, you don't need to be good at a dumb game like that." Rick had it bad already.

In response, Kyra let him buy her another beer, adorably despondent. "I wish that was true. Maybe my daddy would have more time for me if I could play the games he likes. I can't throw a football, either."

That's genius, Reyes decided. Now she'd tugged on

Rick's heartstrings. The man would be filling in all kinds of scenarios, wanting to play white knight.

"Do you have brothers or sisters?" the guy asked.

She shook her head. "Nope. I'm an only child. I think he'd have been happier if I was a boy."

"That would've been a crying shame, sweetheart."

Reyes ground his teeth. Something dark and primitive swept over him at hearing this asshole practice his sloppy endearments on her. It was all Reyes could do not to punch the son of a bitch in the face, which told him he had a problem. No wonder she'd played Serrano—and so well. Kyra was a pro, all right, well schooled in manipulating a man's emotions. And that made him twice the fool—because even knowing what she did, he found himself susceptible.

The con went down as planned. After she'd established herself as cute and harmless by losing a few games of pool, she challenged the champion thug to a game of darts. Reyes watched as she brushed her hands over his forearm, eyes imploring. As predicted, the man couldn't say no. Rick watched with a half frown, not seeming to understand why the woman he'd wanted was playing with someone else.

"Let's do a pool," Reyes suggested, as the two competitors lined up. "I'll put my money on the lady."

Kyra flashed him a smile. "That's so sweet, but I wouldn't. My daddy says I can't hit the broad side of a barn."

"He's an asshole," Rick said, supportive.

A few of the guys took the bet, kicking in money. The rest bet on the local dart champ, who according to Rick, also did some drug running on the side. The pot swelled to five hundred bucks, wagered on a single toss.

Kyra let the champ go first, and he barely hit the board. Everyone booed, and then somebody said, "Maybe he's too drunk."

"Shit. I wish I'd known. I'd have bet on her."

She fretted her lower lip, supposedly sighting and aiming. Then she gave a girlie toss, but the dart soared true, striking the center of the target. Scattered whoops went up, and then Reyes counted out the winnings to the two guys who'd bet on her. Rick was one of them.

He liked this particular con because it spread the money

around. This was the first time they'd tried it, but she'd explained the premise in detail. Nobody could cry "hustle" if a few locals made a little cash, too. He pocketed the rest, knowing Kyra had to trust him to turn up at their rendezvous point on his own, carrying her cut. It would be the first time she'd done so.

If only he knew how she'd been so certain she'd win. Instinctively, he knew it had something to do with the way she'd touched the guy. She never did that; she went out of her way to avoid physical contact.

Still brooding over that, Reyes headed out. He knew it would be driving her crazy—the fact that she couldn't just follow him and make sure he didn't split with her money. She had to be patient. She had to trust him.

Two hours later, when she came knocking at his door, he smiled.

CHAPTER 8

***An awe-inspiring** view,* Serrano thought.

He gazed out over white mountaintops up into the impossibly blue sky. St. Moritz was such an intriguing dichotomy of cosmopolitan and quaint ski village. From up here, the view was positively panoramic. He was staying at Badrutt's Palace Hotel, ostensibly enjoying a long-overdue vacation. His detractors said he'd fled town, not wanting to deal with the fallout from being bested by the woman he'd asked to marry him.

To some degree both were true, but neither comprised his chief aim. Among other things, he was in Switzerland because he anticipated needing an ironclad alibi. And what better place than a famous hotel? The hotel swarmed with staff as well as old-world charm. He'd make sure to order room service and let himself be seen now and again, quietly nursing his wounds. It was all rather poetic, actually.

He'd taken the penthouse suite of course. Though he had no need for three bedrooms or a one-hundred-fifty-meter wraparound terrace, he'd gotten into the habit of living ostentatiously. His lip curled as he took in the heavy stone and dark woodwork. The carpet was old and expensive; everything was a bit too European for him, but that was to be expected, here. He preferred the clean lines of his Vegas condo.

At least the bedchamber he'd taken as his own wasn't too formal. It had heavy cream and blue patterned tapestries pulled back from the windows, a soft floral rug, an enormous bed, and a dusty blue armchair. Serrano regretted that he'd be sleeping alone, but companionship wasn't part of the plan.

If he was to put on a convincing show of grieving for his lost relationship, he couldn't bring any women up here. No, he meant to be the picture of a spurned lover, saddened but not angry, lonely but not vengeful. Image was everything, after all.

It still stung, remembering how much he'd wanted her. How much he'd ached for her. That damned woman's smile made his heart twist. At one point, he'd have done anything for her, anything at all. Which was how he'd wound up on one knee, offering her a four-carat diamond.

He didn't like to admit his judgment could be faulty but in this case, it had gone completely off the rails. It galled him that he missed her. Rachel—*Kyra*—had been a good listener, and he'd thought she would make a fine mother. God, she'd sunk her teeth into him but good.

But business was business.

A young man came out of the second bedroom, tying his tie. His name was Wayne Sweet, and until twenty-four hours ago, he'd worked security at the Silver Lady. "I'm almost ready. It was so cool of you to bring me with you."

Serrano allowed himself a tight smile. "Think nothing of it. I needed a bodyguard; you wanted the credential for your résumé. It all works out very neatly, doesn't it?"

"Yeah. It sure does, sir."

"Shall we go?"

They made their way to the funicular. At this hour, people were heading for the pubs and discos downtown, but he had other plans. They took the train first to the Chantarella station, and then continued upward again to Corviglia. There were a number of mountain restaurants open, if that had been his aim.

"Before dinner, I want to show you the highest point," Serrano said, smiling.

He led his employee along a little-used hiking path, not toward the viewing area. It was cold up here. Dark. When the trail ended in a steep drop that could only be navigated by angels and mountain goats, Sweet said, "I think we came the wrong way."

"No, this is it. Turn around. Take a look."

Like a lamb to the slaughter, obedient, Sweet spun around, gazing out. Serrano drew a pistol, a cheap .22 fitted with a silencer, and plugged his former employee in the back of the head. Sound carried a long way in the mountains, and he preferred not to take chances. He liked a .22 for executions; it wasn't a high enough caliber for an exit wound, so there was no blood spatter, no messy cleanup. In the same motion, he gave Sweet a nudge forward, enough to topple him off the cliff.

He glanced down. *Hell of a drop.* Casually, he tossed the weapon. It would be spring before they found him, if something didn't drag him off and eat him first. And let that be a lesson to all the men who worked for him. They'd know the score when he came back from Switzerland alone; some things didn't need to be spelled out. Sweet had been dead wrong for thinking he could get away with posting that video on the Internet. He hadn't done a guy himself in years, but this would prove to everyone he hadn't gone soft.

Nobody would miss the guy.

Though it was cold at this altitude, Serrano stripped off his leather gloves. He'd incinerate them later. Calmly, he retraced his steps to the funicular station, and then chose a path at random. He would have a nice dinner up here, where everyone could see him. Then he'd head for home.

Later, he'd order room service for Sweet, enjoying a free week on the boss in St. Moritz. When the authorities checked things out, they would discover that Sweet had gone missing long after Serrano had returned to the States. It would be impossible for anyone to tie him to this, no matter what they suspected.

"Looks like a nice place," he said aloud, and strolled into the lodge to dine.

Several hours later, replete with truffles, venison in polenta, and caviar, he returned to his suite and powered up his laptop. It would be the middle of the night in Vegas, but Foster should be at work for another hour or two yet. The Silver Lady needed constant attention, and his chief of security would be extra careful in Serrano's absence.

Foster took his sweet time answering the request for a video conference. By his watch, which never ran fast, it took fifteen full minutes. He tapped his fingers, gently impatient, until the call sprang to live feed.

"Took you long enough."

From his side of the camera, the chief of security regarded him with cool blue eyes. "I have twice the workload with you on vacation, but the Silver Lady is doing well. How can I help you, sir?"

"Has your guy checked in this week?" He knew he didn't need to elaborate. In fact, he wouldn't. Never say anything on the phone that could be used against you.

"Not yet." Foster frowned, just a flicker of twin lines between his well-groomed brows, and then the look vanished, but not before Serrano saw it.

"What does that mean?" he demanded. "Is there a problem? I need this finished."

"He's a pro. At this point, he's trying to unearth the answer to your first pressing question, sir." Such as where she'd hid his money. Serrano appreciated Foster's discretion. "If you want to disregard that inquiry, we can step up the timetable."

And put an end to the irritation named Kyra Marie Beckwith.

That was tempting. He'd like to forget this ever happened, but conceding the loss would send a lesser message to his competitors. At this point, he couldn't afford weakness. He'd have to be patient a little longer.

"No," he said finally. "Give him a little more rope. What do we know about this guy anyway?"

Foster had handled the hire. Serrano didn't want certain details. As long as he didn't, he could pass a polygraph if he had to. Being able to say, "I really don't know" sometimes offered immeasurable value.

After a minute's hesitation, Foster said, "I'll send you the personnel data. You should have it in the morning. I think you'll find his résumé fascinating."

Foster would use a private, bonded Swiss courier. Documents like this should never be trusted to FedEx. He was breaking his policy of noninvolvement, guaranteeing him plausible deniability, but he needed to know what kind of contractor was handling his business. If the man was employing finesse, that was fine, but if he thought he could stretch this task, and add billable hours, Serrano would show him the error of his ways.

"That'll do. I'll let you know if I have further questions about our new hire. See you in a few days."

It irked him that Foster rang off without another word, but like the best Germanic stock, the man was nothing if not efficient. With everything handled to his satisfaction, he straightened his tie, ran a hand through his dark hair, and headed for the bar downstairs. He needed to make sure people remembered seeing him tonight.

It wouldn't be hard. Serrano hid a smile. If these people knew where he'd been born, they'd choke on their caviar. He nursed a drink, held on to his receipt. Within the hour, he had a glamorous redhead trying to convince him she could heal his broken heart.

Foster was proud of the file he'd sent Serrano just before leaving work the night before. There was nothing so useful as lying with the truth. It was chock-full of impressive—and true—information regarding the man they'd hired.

Reyes was an interesting man, a bundle of contradictions. Like most of his ilk, he worked under a pseudonym, but Foster wouldn't have hired him if he hadn't been able to dig up the truth, including his real name. They'd exchanged e-mail addresses initially, free anonymous accounts from which Reyes doubtless bounced his messages to other locations, maybe several of them, depending on his paranoia. By now, Serrano would be reading the information and congratulating himself on hiring top personnel to deal with his problems.

It was not quite 2:00 P.M., which meant he was operating on less than five hours sleep. Since it was Thursday, there was no help for that. He'd make it up tomorrow. Foster parked his car and leaned over, pulling a bottle of cologne from the glove box. After dabbing on a little, he got out, his long legs eating up the sidewalk.

Shortly, he came to a set of mirrored doors, set in a white, ultramodern building. Inside it was cool and quiet, tinted glass protecting the residents of this place from exposure to the desert sun. The nurse on duty raised her head as if to challenge him, and then she relaxed, offering him a warm smile. She was in her mid-thirties, and slightly interested in him, if he offered any encouragement.

Foster wouldn't.

"I'll sign you in," she said. "Your mother's waiting for you."

He nodded and continued down the pale hallway. Here, the tile was not bile green or scarred by hundreds of feet. This was a costly private nursing facility, where people received the best care money could buy. Too bad it couldn't buy hope or comfort as well.

Foster stood for a moment, gazing into the room. The old woman sat by the window, dressed in her best housecoat in honor of his visit. Her snowy hair had been styled, and someone had painted her thin mouth with bright red lipstick. The jar beside her bed that held her teeth was empty, which meant she'd put them in today.

Beulah Mae Finney was eighty-seven years old, and she wasn't his mother. She *thought* she was, but her son had been incarcerated for the last five years, and hadn't come to see her for four years before that. He'd initiated the visits to test his ability to mimic voices. If he could fool someone's mother, he reasoned, his gift would stand up to any scrutiny. Since she suffered from cataracts, she was perfect for his purposes.

He'd slipped into the state-run hellhole where her natural son had dumped her, signed the register, and gone to see if he could imitate the street-rough cadences favored by James L. Finney, prison-bird esquire. He knew Jimmy Lee wouldn't be back to interfere; he was doing hard time in Mississippi for messing with an underage girl.

They visited for months, and he took quite a liking to Beulah Mae. Once he'd established his ability to fool her, he didn't have the heart to leave her languishing in a rundown nursing home that smelled of urine, decay, and morbidity, and it had been astonishingly easy to commandeer someone else's mother. He supposed people were not crawling out of the woodwork, eager to foot the bill for aged and infirm seniors who didn't belong to them, so there was no protocol in place.

Foster took a step then, knowing to the inch when he would get close enough for her to smell the cheap cologne Jimmy Lee had always worn. Her lined face brightened into a smile, showing a smear of lipstick on her porcelain teeth. He'd just bought her a new set of those, too.

"Jimmy Lee!" she exclaimed. "Right on time. I can set my clock by you these days. Have I told you lately how proud I am that you turned yourself around?"

His voice came out low, harsher than his usual tones. "Ever' time I see you, Ma."

She laughed. "Well, then. Come on over here and give me a kiss."

Foster did as he was bid, brushing the old lady's cheek in a gentle peck. Then he sat down opposite to hear who was cheating at cards, who was sneaking into whose room at night, and who probably wouldn't last the month. It had to be depressing to get old, he thought, not for the first time. *Good thing I am not likely to live to a ripe old age.*

He spent the requisite hour with her and wrapped up the visit to the second. She wanted a second kiss, but he dodged away from a hug. Close physical contact would reveal that he was taller and slimmer than her incarcerated offspring, and he'd miss Beulah Mae if his deception were exposed.

With a muttered, "See ya next week, Ma," he stepped out into the hallway.

Time for part two of his weekly pilgrimage. Foster made his way to the other part of the facility, where they kept long-term, no-hope patients. Oh, the administration wouldn't call them that, but the people in this section would never wake up from their comas. They'd never pull out their wires and IVs and go dancing down the hall. These people were locked into whatever worlds their minds could conjure because their bodies were done.

The nurse here recognized him, too, but not by the name he'd received at birth. Unlike Beulah Mae Finney, he *was*, however, related by blood to the girl who lay pale as snow against her linen sheets. It had seemed to make sense to bring Beulah here, where they took such good care of his little lost one. She had his blond hair and pale eyes. Such fair coloring looked fragile as glass in her unnatural repose.

Infirmity had stolen away most of her puppy fat. She was small for her age. Though she should be a young woman by now, time had passed her by. Now she lay there stick thin, nourished by needles in her veins. Nurses trimmed her nails and cut her hair. They washed her and dressed her like the living dead while the heart monitor tracked every little blip. If he were so inclined, he could chart her permanent sleep.

Foster closed the door, and stood for a moment with his forehead resting against the cool wood. Each time, it hurt a little more, and yet he returned, week after week. Apparently, he represented some brave new world of masochists who liked their wounds so deep nobody else could see them bleed. It took almost more strength than he possessed to straighten and square his shoulders, if it mattered that she shouldn't see his weakness.

She hadn't seen *anything* in six years.

He'd decorated the room with her drawings and her favorite things: pictures of unkempt kids skateboarding, a teddy bear she'd painted in art class. He paid enough money that the staff didn't complain. Deliberately, he lowered himself into the chair beside her bed.

"Hey, Lexie." He waited a count of fifteen as he always did, offering her the opportunity to respond. It was a ridiculous ritual, one he could no more discontinue than he could fly.

She lay pale and quiet, but no number of kisses could rouse her. He'd tried that at first and then desperate arms around her, and then finally, his tears. Like the Ice Queen, she could not be moved. She could only sleep and dream.

So into the bleak silence he spoke of Gerard Serrano, his own plans and schemes. The medical equipment that kept her alive offered a steady accompaniment to his voice. Sometimes, in this closed room, Foster felt more alone than anyone else in the world. There was no one left who knew who he had been, the people he'd loved.

Loss motivated him. At last, as the light waned, he stood. Bent to brush a kiss across her cool brow.

"I'll see you next week, *min skat*."

In the old days, she would have hugged him around the neck. She would have wrestled with him, spilled grape juice on his freshly ironed shirt, and laughed like a hyena over it. When he got home from work, she would've demanded a pint of ice cream. So many things had changed—so much he loved, lost, and all for the sake of greedy men.

Most likely, he should sign the papers and let her go. In the six days between his weekly visits, he considered the problem from all angles. Logically speaking, it was the wisest course. He knew it; he just couldn't make himself go to the director and request the forms. On some level, he hadn't stopped wishing for a miracle, even though he didn't believe in such things. Not for him. But maybe God, if such a being existed, could spare some grace for Lexie.

On another level, she kept him from deviating from his self-appointed task. When she wound up in the hospital—and he'd discovered who was to blame—he had promised himself he would not rest, would not allow himself a moment's peace, until the guilty paid with everyone and everything that they loved.

So he'd worked quietly. Cleanly. Sliding from one disaster to the next like an albatross in human form. Gerard Serrano was the last one on the list.

And no matter the cost, he wouldn't stop.

CHAPTER 9

Kyra peered past Rey's shoulder, stunned speechless by what she saw.

Through the gap between cheap curtains, she'd been able to tell the lights were out—and she'd thought that meant he was gone. But she'd knocked anyway, digging up a tiny bit of faith. *Maybe he's asleep,* she'd told herself. But he wasn't. She'd heard him stirring inside; in a motel like this one, the walls were tissue thin.

First, relief surged through her. Then he swung the door wide, and she glimpsed a sea of flickering candles. *Ah, crap.* Maybe he'd picked up a woman somewhere between Lefty's Tavern and Motel 5, which sadly wasn't up to the rigorous standards set by the Motel 6 up the road. But at least he'd come back.

If it had been anyone else, she would have just assumed he'd split and gone to bed herself. Kyra wouldn't even have bothered knocking. In fact, she'd never taken such a leap of faith before. If it had been her father, she wouldn't have hesitated to run that particular con, but without him, it hadn't been possible in years.

As she'd driven back from the bar, she'd wondered

whether he had skipped out with their night's take. She could afford the loss, which was why she'd taken the risk, but joy ricocheted right through her at finding him waiting for her, just like he'd promised. Maybe she'd really found a new partner.

"I'm sorry to interrupt," she muttered. "I didn't realize—"

"That I was making dinner?" Rey cut in smoothly.

He stepped back to reveal the rest of his room. Nothing could disguise the cheap furniture, but the candlelight helped. From somewhere he'd found a red-and-white-checkered tablecloth, which he'd spread over the cheap café table beside the window. He'd laid the table with Chinette, plastic silverware, and wineglasses. The man even had a wicker basket for the food.

"I don't understand." Kyra took a step back, puzzled.

In answer, Rey reached out and snagged her hand, tugging her into the room. "Come in already."

There was a little sizzle, but nothing like the usual reaction. Though it meant she might get sick later, she didn't jerk away. She felt completely ambushed—in a good way. Kyra let him seat her, and then he laid out her choices, mostly sandwich makings and fresh veggies. He sat down opposite her, smiling. His teeth gleamed white in the dark. Mechanically, she started assembling an enormous sandwich with turkey, Swiss cheese, sliced tomatoes, lettuce, some Colby, and roast beef. The thing was six inches thick by the time she finished.

"What are you doing?" She gestured at her sandwich.

"Feeding you."

Her new partner was particular about what he put on his sandwich, she noted. Rey took his time selecting the bread, and he went with whole grain. He chose lean turkey, and the trimmings, lettuce and pickle. It reinforced what she'd already noticed about him—he was careful and he took his time with things, great attention to detail.

"Yeah, I figured that out. But why?"

"You're starving by the time we finish for the night. I wanted you to have something more than ramen noodles or vending-machine junk. You have a high metabolism."

So he'd noticed. That rocked her a little. Nobody had paid

that much attention to her in years. Even her dad hadn't. Since she was sixteen and she'd told him they needed to keep moving on, he had trusted her to make her own decisions.

"I do," she acknowledged. Kyra took an enormous bite to cover her confusion. She chewed while contemplating his acuity. "How'd you transport all this stuff?"

"Carried it." He dismissed her concern with a loft of one broad shoulder. "It's only a mile and a half to the market from here. Don't worry," he added, "I took the food out of my part of the cut. Here's yours." He handed her a wad of bills across the table.

Kyra stuffed those in her bag, now on the floor at her feet. She didn't bother to count the cash. If he'd wanted to cheat her, he would have done it by disappearing, not skimming five bucks off the top.

Her sandwich went down quickly, as he'd doubtless known it would. She felt less enthusiasm about the raw vegetables he lined up on her plate, but when he poured the wine, she decided it was a worthwhile compromise. Kyra nibbled on a stalk of celery, none too enthusiastic about its healthful benefits.

He'll have me taking multivitamins before long.

"So after you left Lefty's, you were just overcome with the desire to feed me?" Somehow she just couldn't wrap her head around it.

"Altruism doesn't ring your bell, huh?"

She quirked her mouth up in a half smile. "Not so much."

"Brutal honesty it is, then. Remember how you said if we ever had sex again, I'd have to work for it?" Rey grinned and swept his hand toward the candles. "Consider this my first day on the job."

Now there was a motive she could understand. He wanted something from her, and he'd hit on this as a possible way to get it. Kyra smiled back.

"It's beautiful," she said softly. "Who'd have thought a few votive candles could be put to such good use?" She felt compelled to warn him, though. "But you should know . . . I don't really do romance. I mean, I'm not susceptible to it."

For a long moment, Rey studied her in the flickering

light. She felt as if his onyx eyes stripped away layers of skin, flesh, and bone to see into the parts of her she didn't even examine too long. When he finally spoke, she shivered a little, freed from a spell that stole her secrets.

"How would you know?" he asked.

Another shudder worked through her. It was as if he could see down the years, and he *knew* she'd never lived anywhere long enough to have someone come to the door with flowers, not when it was real. Serrano didn't count. Rey knew she'd never been taken to a fine restaurant by a man she esteemed and respected. And she'd never regretted her life, never regretted her choices.

But here in the vanilla-scented dark, she wondered for the first time what might have been. She didn't like him for making her speculate. Her stomach cramped tight around the sandwich she'd inhaled.

"I just do." She dismissed the strange, otherworldly moment when she'd felt like he knew her to her bones. "But you get points for trying. I'm weirdly flattered you'd go to the trouble since you've had me once already."

"Three times," he corrected in a soft, savage voice. "And it wasn't enough."

Her nerves fired to life, remembering that night. She'd never been with anyone who could be as rough as she wanted without actually hurting her, but Rey had carnal brutality down to a fine art, knowing where to press, how to hold, when to restrain. He used fingers and teeth with expert precision. Kyra squirmed in her seat, squeezing her thighs together.

She tried for a dismissive tone, not wanting him to see how badly he'd shaken her. "Sex is sex."

"No." He shook his head. "We had something else entirely, and you know it, too."

"Something more than sex?" Kyra went caustic in self-defense. "With a guy I picked up—unwillingly, I might add—outside a cheap beer hut filled with yokels. I don't think so."

Leaning in, he asked, "Then how did I know to bite your inner thigh? How did I know you like to be subdued and taken from behind?"

Those memories sparked awareness between them. If she were honest, their night together had fueled her solitary fantasies more than once. But she wasn't going to let herself be suckered into a two-person fantasy that ended in him getting what he wanted from her so easily. She'd said he would have to work for her, and she'd meant it.

Kyra shrugged. "Sometimes people share the same kinks. It's pure serendipity when they meet."

"I can see you're going to be a challenge."

"That makes it more fun, doesn't it? You wouldn't want me to just strip naked and lay down for you."

His dark gaze slid to the bed as if imagining her there, spread out for him, and he gave a little groan that turned her on. "Wouldn't I?"

"I think you're a man who enjoys the chase."

"More often than not," he admitted. "I intended to seduce you in traditional ways, candlelight and flowers. I had a feeling you hadn't seen much of that, but now I'm not sure what'll get me what I want."

"I'm certainly not going to tell you. That would take all the fun out of letting you figure it out yourself."

"Will you give me a hint?" Rey smiled.

Kyra found herself staring at his mouth. The rest of his face was sharp, reflecting some lovely, arcane union of Hispanic and Native American features, but he had a lush, gorgeous mouth. In response, near smiling, she wanted to kiss him so badly that she had to curl her fingers around the armrest of the chair.

"I'd better not. You know too much about me already." That was, without a doubt, the truest thing either of them had said since she got back. "I'm going to bed. Thanks for dinner. And . . . see you in the morning."

Reyes reached for her before she could scamper to her room like a frightened rabbit. His grip wouldn't hurt her, but neither would he permit her to escape. Not yet. He ran his thumb against the delicate skin on the inside of her wrist. She trembled.

There was a little surge, like that electricity from the first time, but it was faint and thready, almost nonexistent. He didn't feel drained, just a little dizzy. That could almost come from her softness. Reyes hadn't known until this moment how much he loved the scent of coconut.

His hard cock surged against his zipper. Painful, but tolerable. When she'd teased him with the mental image of her naked on the bed, he'd turned to stone from the waist down, just as she intended. Well, he didn't intend to suffer alone.

"I think a good night kiss is in order, don't you? It seems to fit the mood . . . and it's in keeping with dinner."

Her eyes looked huge in the candlelight. "Just one?"

"Absolutely." He etched a cross over his heart, which would've been laughable if she knew anything about him.

Kyra tilted her face up, and her trust struck him in the solar plexus. Something was screwy. She didn't act like the hard-edged, treacherous bitch depicted in Foster's file. Maybe he should do a little more checking.

For now, though, he would take the lips she'd offered him. Reyes curled his fingers around the nape of her neck and leaned in with his whole body, bringing her up against the door. Kyra wound her arms around his neck, startling him with the sense of rightness that accompanied the motion. Reyes kissed like he fucked, all possession. In her case, it was more furious than usual; he didn't want to leave her a spare brain cell for anything else.

Her mouth opened on a gasp, and he took more, nuzzling deep with each sweep of his tongue. She tasted faintly of celery and spicy mustard, clean flavors that made him want to lick away everything that didn't come from Kyra. He slid his hands down her body, relearning her curves, and then cupped her ass in his hands, lifting her up against him. He tasted her from lips to jaw and then downward, biting tenderly at the sweet column of her throat. Then he nibbled his way back to her luscious mouth.

Her nails dug into his shoulders, tiny little bursts of pain that insisted they should be naked. Kyra's tongue lashed against his, slick and hot. He swore he could feel her heartbeat in the heat of her lips, an echo to his own thundering in his ears. Then he lost his mind as she tried to climb him. His hands came up to drag her hips against his and he couldn't help but thrust. She pushed back, undulating her hips. Her breath came in sharp little pants; he recognized the sound of her escalating arousal. If he touched her inside her panties, she'd come in a fury of clenched teeth and fierce cries.

God, she felt good. Reyes remembered that she'd fit him like a glove. With her long legs curled around his hips, he should be canonized for not unzipping them both and sinking into her. For a long moment, it was touch and go.

Then he opened his hands and stepped back, letting her drop. Kyra swayed for a moment, eyes opening. She pressed two fingers to her bee-stung mouth, seeming to try to figure out what had happened—or what hadn't.

"That was more than one kiss," she accused, breathless.

Reyes made himself smile. "My bad."

He was pleased to see her knees weren't altogether steady when she tried to open the door. Kyra supported herself on the door frame for a few seconds, still looking dazed. "Well then." Her gaze slid to his bed. Lingered there, as if awaiting an invitation. "Good night, I guess."

You made the rules, sweetheart. No changing them now. Keeping her off-balance would work better than any tactic he'd yet devised.

"G'night, Kyra."

He shut the door in her sweet, sun-kissed face. Reyes stood listening for the click of her door, making sure she'd gotten in safely. Only then did he push away from the wall and allow a muffled groan. As he went, he stripped off his clothes.

Straight into the shower. Another man might take the high road, but he wasn't big on self-denial. More importantly, it would undermine his purpose if he couldn't control himself around her, and there was only one way to make sure of his discipline. He had to be practical about such things, so he stepped into the shower and turned it on.

The hot water felt tepid against the heat of his flesh, as if it could evaporate to steam just from touching him. Reyes wanted to be businesslike as he wrapped his fingers around his dick, but he couldn't force Kyra out of his mind's eye. As he began to stroke, water pouring down on him, he saw her sinking to her knees in the tub, face upturned as it had been for his kiss. To his disgust, he lost it in less than two minutes, as soon as he imagined her lips touching his cock. A shuddering orgasm ripped a cry from his throat, and he slumped against the tile wall, heart still racing. A woman hadn't gotten to him like this since he was a kid.

A few minutes later, he staggered out of the bathroom, steam slipping through behind him to coil in the air. After pulling back the covers to reveal thin off-white sheets, Reyes sank onto the bed, slightly dizzy. The worst part—he wasn't anything like satisfied. He still had a need for her twined like barbwire in his belly. Nothing would do but for him to have her again.

And he was starting to get chills when he pictured ending her. He didn't want to be close to her when he did it; that was beyond even his considerable professional acumen. And that ruled out knives and strangulation.

He told himself to focus. *Keep your mind on the job, asshole. And don't worry about the details. Just get the information. By the time you have it, she'll show her true colors. They always do.*

Still, he couldn't help but want to double-check what he'd been told. Maybe he needed to dig deeper. His attention to detail was what made him one of the best—and most principled—assassins in the country. Sometimes people were desperate enough to have the job done right that they tried to put one over on him.

Reyes prided himself on taking on jobs where the target needed killing anyway. The fact that someone's just deserts and his skill intersected? Serendipity, as Kyra claimed regarding their sexual compatibility. Privately, he considered himself a vigilante for hire, though not for such an altruistic reason as righting a wrong. Nobody he knew wore a white hat, too hard to keep it clean.

Without further deliberation, he plucked his cell phone from the hidden zipper inside his jacket. He also had a pocket-sized quick charger since his cover didn't permit for plugging in the phone in his room. Speed dial number four connected him to someone he did business with frequently.

Favors begat favors in his line of work. He didn't like owing people, but he'd done a good turn for this guy recently.

"Monroe," he said, when the call completed.

A rough, disgruntled male voice asked, "Do you know what fucking time it is here?"

Since he had the man's cell number, he had no idea where Monroe might be. It was better that way. "No. And I don't care, either. Can you check someone out for me?"

A stream of colorful invective followed—seasoned by curses in Chinese, Turkish, and Russian. Reyes waited, listening to the rustling of papers. Finally Monroe said, "Shoot. I'm ready."

"Get me everything you can find on Kyra Marie Beckwith. I have three socials here for her, but I'm not sure which is the real one." He listed the numbers.

"Ah," said Monroe. "One of those."

"Yep. How soon can you get it?"

"That depends."

A prickle of irritation pierced his calm. "On what?"

"On whether she's lived on or off the grid."

"Okay," he acknowledged. "Just do the best you can and get it to me fast. You do this for me, and we'll call it square over Prague."

"Appreciate it," Monroe said, and Reyes heard the smile in his voice. "I'll be in touch, *patron*."

They had history, Monroe and him. He never asked anyone else for help.

Shortly thereafter, he disconnected and lay back in the dark, staring at the ceiling. Outside, he could hear the hum of the fluorescent light in the hallway. Reyes wondered what Kyra was doing on the other side of the wall. Was she a cold-shower sort of woman?

And then he didn't have to wonder; he knew.

Listening to her muffled thumps and moans, he discovered she was a self-sufficient type. It sounded like she was tearing up the bed without him. With her, his plans never seemed to work as anticipated.

Ah, Jesus.

He recognized the throaty cry she made as she came, but

her movements didn't show any signs of slowing. Reyes would give a kidney to kick a hole in the wall and have her, and say to hell with his job, to hell with his reputation. He burned with wanting her.

It was going to be a long night.

CHAPTER 10

"We've had a good run," Kyra said.

She counted the money a second time and then pushed Rey's cut across the bed toward him. Ordinarily, she wouldn't share mattress space with him, even under the most innocuous of circumstances, but this room didn't even offer the usual café table and rickety chairs. They had to split the take somewhere.

He'd been the perfect partner ever since they shared that scorching kiss. She had no idea what to make of his withdrawal, but maybe he'd decided not to tempt the chemistry that crackled between them. That was no doubt the prudent course.

They'd passed from Texas into New Mexico. Back in Louisiana, she'd realized she wanted to escape the heat, so they were wending their way north slowly. Kyra had heard Colorado was nice, and she couldn't remember ever wintering anywhere cold. That would be the last place anyone looked for her, the next best thing to Canada.

As an added bonus, Kyra had a friend who would be taking a job soon in North Dakota, and she hoped Mia would be able to tell her what to do with her stash. She couldn't get out of the country on her own, but she trusted Mia Sauter more than anyone else in the world. When she first fled Vegas, she'd known she needed to kill some time, as Mia was working a contract overseas. She'd tossed her cell phone a few days back, not wanting to take the chance Serrano could track her somehow, even though it was a cheap, prepaid device.

Just stay one step ahead, that's all. Just a little longer.

Frankly, she'd thought Serrano would have had her killed before she got out of town, but she'd had to take the risk. The bastard couldn't be allowed to kill her father and pay nothing for it. Men like him, men with money and power, thought they could do whatever the hell they wanted without consequence. It had been a stroke of luck that he hadn't seen the tape for twenty-four hours, giving her a priceless head start.

She'd been running ever since.

"If I'd known there was such good money in this, I'd have looked for an apprenticeship years ago," Rey said lazily.

A small quirk of conscience pricked her. She really should warn him that it wouldn't go this smoothly—and the money wouldn't flow as well—if he didn't have her help. But that would open the door to things she had no intention of sharing. Worse, it might sound like she was trying to convince him to stay with her indefinitely.

"It beats honest work," she agreed.

"Can we take a night off?"

Kyra glanced at him in surprise. She could certainly afford to, but she didn't want to tap into her stash until they got to North Dakota, and she had some idea what to do with the money. Flashing large amounts of cash would get her noticed—and Serrano would have goons on her in no time. It was definitely best that she live and work as she always had. And there was the fun factor as well. Fact was, Kyra *liked* what she did.

"Sure," she said, trying to hide her disappointment. It was natural he'd want a break. "Knock yourself out."

She took in the dingy motel room, which was like a thousand others she'd stayed in: tiny, cramped, a polyester, floral bedspread in garish hues, lackluster prints affixed to the wall, and furniture so cheap that it made pasteboard look luxurious. Rooms like this always seemed to hold a faint musty odor, as well, and she'd learned not to peer behind the headboards or beneath end tables for fear of what she might find. This place didn't even have a coffeemaker, so no ramen for dinner.

Before she spent those six months with Gerard Serrano, letting him lavish her with expensive things and posh surroundings, she never would've thought twice about a place like this. *The bastard's spoiled this for me, too,* she thought with a scowl. Though she still enjoyed life on the road, she missed fine jewelry and a Jacuzzi tub to soak away her sorrows. Money might not be able to buy happiness, but it made misery more bearable.

Kyra remembered how Rey had walked more than a mile, carrying heavy groceries, just to feed her. Nobody had ever done anything like that for her. Until he did it, she hadn't even known she'd like it. And now, damn him, she found herself searching for hidden meanings in his small kindnesses. He didn't look like the considerate sort; he looked more like he cut women's throats and left them for dead. But she'd learned people weren't always what they seemed. Her father had called himself a professional student of human nature—and she'd taken her lessons from him for many years before he died.

"What's wrong?" If the question caught her off-guard, the gesture certainly did. Rey reached over, ignoring the pile of bills between them, his fingers cupping her chin.

She started to recoil, but there was only a faint, thready echo. It felt oddly as if her ability had short-circuited somehow.

"Nothing," she said quickly. How humiliating. If he realized she had a minor thing—okay, a major sexual obsession—for him, she'd wither up and die. Kyra made herself smile. "See? Totally cool."

"You think I want to go out in search of snatch." Statement, not a question.

She tried to make a joke of it. "Wasn't that a Larry Flynt show?"

He sighed then. "I obviously phrased the question wrong, if that's what you extrapolated from it. I asked if *we* could take the night off. Together. You and me."

His words hit her like a closed fist in the temple, and she felt dizzy, breathless. "I don't understand. I have no idea what you want from me."

"You know exactly what I want."

"You already *had* it," she protested. "Damn, Rey. I'm not Chinese food . . . men don't come back in two hours, hungry for more."

His actions made no sense and didn't follow the rules by which she'd lived. In her experience, one warm body was much like another, interchangeable. Sometimes the skill levels varied, but with enough imagination almost anyone could serve the purpose. Hell, given her lifestyle, she often worked in that capacity alone.

He shook his head, darkly intent. "You're out of your mind if you think anybody else will do. I could fuck a hundred women, and still go to sleep with this ache in my gut. It has to be you."

In that moment, she wanted more than anything to crawl across the bed toward him and give him everything. Feelings she'd never dreamed or imagined surged through her, but sex with him wasn't simple anymore. Though it galled her to admit it, Rey scared her because he possessed the potential to matter.

"So what is it you're offering?"

And the man surprised her again. "A drive into the mountains. We spend so much time with the dregs that sometimes I start to want something clean and pure."

Kyra only considered for a moment. "That sounds great."

She snagged her share of the money, aligned the bills, and then she slid them into her wallet. After shouldering her bag, she glanced at him, oddly uncertain. If there were rules for this kind of thing, she didn't understand them. She'd never been out on a true date. In some respects she was as inexperienced as an Amish girl.

They locked the door behind them as they left using the analog metal key, and she took a cursory look across the parking lot. No signs of pursuit, but there was always a chance. Kyra found the Marquis right away.

In contrast to the darkening sky, it gleamed pale blue like the sky at the highest altitudes, all delicacy. It cost a mint to fill the thing up these days, but she'd never considered selling it. Everything she loved had somehow become bound up in the metal.

"I grew up here," he said, gazing out over the shared balcony that ran the length of the motel.

He'd requested a second-floor room because he didn't trust people. At least here on the corner, they would hear someone coming up the stairs; there would be some warning before disaster struck. Rey had tried to insist that they should share a room—that he didn't like the feel of this place, but Kyra had stayed in enough fleabags to know this one was much like any other, no better, no worse.

"Here, as in Taos? Or here, as in New Mexico?"

"New Mexico," he answered. "Not far from here, actually."

"Did you stay in one place?"

A flicker of something passed across his dark, sharp face. "More or less."

"That must have been . . ." She trailed off, not knowing what to call an experience that differed so vastly from her own.

Part of her wanted to say boring; another part thought comforting might apply.

As a kid, she'd thought her life was one big adventure. Most days, she still thought so. Dismissing profundity, Kyra stepped away from the flimsy, rusted railing and headed for the stairs. His tread followed immediately, giving her the ridiculous impression that he had her back—that she could rely on him.

"It was what it was," he said, as they reached the car. The look she'd noticed upstairs had winnowed down to something fierce and quiet and sad, like a titanium needle lodged deep.

Before she could rethink the impulse, she went to the passenger side and tossed him the keys. She told herself the offer didn't serve to cheer him up or ameliorate emotional baggage she wasn't equipped to deal with. Rey caught the jingle of metal, blessed with her genuine lucky rabbit's foot, looking astonished.

She muttered, "It just makes sense. You know where we're going and all."

"You're letting me drive?" As if he needed to hear it.

"Your Marquis?"

"Yeah," she said softly. "Be gentle with her."

"As much as I know how to be." Rey laid his long fingers atop the roof, and she felt it on her skin. "Let's go."

Reyes knew he'd lost all perspective. For a man who had been accused, more than once, of lacking a heart, it was disastrous. The woman had given him the keys to her car, for God's sake, not the crown jewels. But as he drove, he couldn't help feel . . . something.

He didn't know what it was, exactly, because he'd never known anything quite like it before. Whatever it was, it made him keep stealing glances at her from his peripheral vision, just watching the way the wind blew her hair.

It wasn't too much farther now. The Marquis, being a sturdy car, would make it to the lookout point if he took care with it. And he intended to. Reyes felt strange and unsteady, as if masquerading as himself had weakened him in unanticipated ways. He hadn't known how dangerous it would be, how thin the line between candor and truth.

The silence lasted until he parked the car. There was nothing but open space and mountains for miles around, topped by a black canopy littered with stars glimmering like crushed ice. You couldn't find a sky like this over any city in the world.

"It's so peaceful," she said.

In the old days, if he'd ever brought a girl up here, if he'd ever had a car, he would've first lain with her on the hood and pointed out the constellations. At one point he'd wanted to be an astronomer. If that gambit went well, he'd have attempted to talk her into his backseat. He'd dreamed of that scenario more than once, wishing on stars he climbed to see. But neither cars, nor girls comprised a significant portion of his past, at least not until he was well out of his teens.

"You think Myrna would support us?" He tilted his head toward the hood.

Kyra smiled. "Are you kidding? This is a car built for love. Of course she will."

To his surprise, she dug into his pocket for the keys, and

then went to the trunk. When she returned, she had an old quilt, the sort of thing that people packed in their emergency kits, along with bottled water, kitty litter for traction, and granola bars. Someone, probably the father she'd allegedly killed for his cut of the money, had cared enough to teach her to be prepared.

He no longer wanted to believe she'd done it, even though it complicated his life immeasurably. If he balked at this job, he would forfeit a pristine reputation. And Monroe wasn't making matters any easier. The last public record he could find for Kyra Marie Beckwith came from a free-clinic vaccination. She couldn't have been more than eight years old, either.

Oddly enough, it was run by the same corporation that administered the free medical program in the Wyoming town where he'd grown up. Reyes remembered that because he'd spent hours sitting with one of his father's women, waiting his turn amid crying children. He'd learned early on that crying didn't do any good.

The woman didn't have bank records, didn't have credit cards, so there was nothing to track. All he had to go on came from Serrano, who wanted the woman dead. But Kyra didn't seem like the kind who would turn on her flesh and blood. The few things she'd said about her father seemed to indicate fondness, and he had a pretty good built-in lie detector.

Could he stake everything he'd built on a feeling? Reyes had no ready answer for that. For now he could only steel himself and stay with her.

She spread the quilt over the hood and climbed up carefully, her back propped against the windshield. Kyra brought her knees up as if to ward off a chill, but he could read her body language. For some reason, she felt uncertain and exposed.

Not waiting for an invitation, he slid up beside her, leaving enough space between them that she shouldn't feel crowded. But he'd read her wrong. Instead of inching away, she eased closer, as if she wanted to be in his arms. Or maybe he was projecting because he wanted her there. The movement carried her scent to him, more coconut. Reyes couldn't tell if it was body lotion or shampoo, but it made him think of slick, bare skin, every time he breathed her in.

"I used to hike up here when I was a kid," he told her quietly.

Self-preservation said he shouldn't share any more of himself with her—it was fucking dangerous—but his infallible instincts told him that the only way he'd win her trust was by giving of himself. He could get the job done this way, no doubt, but Reyes wondered what the cost would be.

"You must've lived in the middle of nowhere then." Her gaze swept the landscape, for what he didn't know, and was afraid to ask, for fear of what she might see. More clearly than he wanted, he could picture the way her eyes gleamed during the day, shining like sunlight through honey.

"Not as much as you might think. It was a ten-mile trek. I'd usually stay overnight if the weather was good."

"How old were you?" she demanded, visibly outraged. "Didn't anyone worry about you?"

God, he didn't want to answer. It gave her too much. But with her, it had to be a give-and-take, and she was too canny to be fooled by creative fiction.

"Thirteen. And not really. Not so much."

She reached for him then, compassion outweighing the caution he saw in the lines of her body. Her fingers touched his. "My dad left me alone at night sometimes. When he was looking for a game. I'd lock the door, put on the chain, and try to sleep."

Reyes remembered how, when he'd first caught up with her, she'd been sleeping in a pool of yellow light, a small isle against the dark. That was why she still slept with the lamp on. He knew it as surely as if she'd said it, and he knew a quiet burst of rage for the man who'd used her as an accomplice, not cared for her as a father was supposed to. If she'd killed him like Serrano claimed, then maybe he had it coming.

She saw something in his face, something that alarmed her. He couldn't even guess at what. And she hastened to add, "We had a secret knock for when he came home. A password. I was never in any real danger."

Unless there was a fire. Or someone came in through the window. He didn't say that aloud. Every little girl wanted to believe her daddy loved her, no matter how untrue, or how much of a son of a bitch the man might've been. He found himself glad that that old bastard Beckwith lay six feet down.

Instead of replying to that, he threaded his fingers through hers. Her flesh felt hot, and she had soft skin. It was a silly little intimacy that shouldn't have moved him, and yet it meant everything that she'd sit with him, hand in hand, beneath the sky of his boyhood.

"That's Lyra," he said, changing the subject. Reyes lifted their joined hands and traced the outline of the harp. "Do you see it?"

She narrowed her eyes. "I think so."

"And there's Sagittarius, the Archer." He continued to sky paint, finding each star in the constellation for her.

"Did you learn this in school?" she asked, eventually.

"Some. Most of it I got from books on my own."

Kyra kept her eyes fixed on the heavens. "I never went."

That startled the hell out of him. "To school?"

"Nope. I watched a lot of *Sesame Street* early on. And my dad taught me some. I can read." At his look, she became defensive. "I learned a lot traveling. More than most kids do just sitting around some Podunk town for eighteen years."

"I didn't say anything."

She glared. "You were thinking it. This is why I don't tell people shit. They always think they know something about me from how I was raised."

Reyes reached for her then, not calculating the probable outcome of his actions. He pulled her into his lap and sifted his hand into her tangled curls. She surprised him by yielding, not fighting him like a wildcat, and her body felt like seven kinds of heaven in his arms.

"I think you turned out fine," he said quietly, knowing she needed to hear it as much as it was true. "You're smart and funny, skilled and resourceful. And if you were any more appealing, I'd lose my mind."

"You mean that." Her voice came out soft and wondering, as she turned her face against his throat.

"I do." At this point, she'd cast some kind of wicked spell on him, and he couldn't do anything but tell the truth. Reyes genuinely feared what might come next.

Jesus, he thought, shaken. Then he realized—whatever had happened the first time he'd touched her, it didn't seem to be happening now. That new development had to mean something, but what?

And her mouth took his in a kiss that threatened to burn the leather off his shoes.

CHAPTER 11

Clearly she'd lost her mind.

But Kyra didn't stop. His kisses were like potato chips; she couldn't stop at one. She nuzzled, tasted. Her tongue teased his lower lip until he took control, devouring her until she felt her blood might turn to steam. If she focused on his mouth, she wouldn't have to think about the way Rey made her feel. This wasn't about sex anymore; it was something else entirely.

She had no experience with it.

His hands roved her back, urging her closer. Rey made her want to huddle closer, as if he were a roaring fire. She ran her hands up his hard chest to his shoulders, and nipped his bottom lip. A strangled moan slid out, and he turned her on his lap, so that she straddled him. She'd never felt anything so good in her life. Experimentally, she circled her hips. Even through their clothing, need seared her.

Eventually, he pulled away and leaned his head back on the windshield, breath coming in sharp rasps. "I didn't bring you up here to have sex on the hood of a car."

"I have a backseat."

"I'm not sixteen." He waited a beat, then added through his teeth, "No condoms."

"Some Boy Scout you make. You're not prepared at all."

"I never said I was. You have to get off me, Kyra. If you have any mercy, lift yourself straight up and sit there." Rey pointed. "*Way* over there."

For about half a second, she considered torturing him with a slow slide and wiggle, but if he lost his mind without a condom, she wasn't sure she'd have the common sense to tell him no. She didn't need the complication of an unwanted pregnancy, let alone some social disease. So she did as he'd asked, pushing up with her knees and moving away from him neatly, no unnecessary contact.

"I never knew it could be so hot," she said, musing as she settled on the quilt.

"What?" Rey sounded half strangled.

"Teasing the same man. I always thought it would get old . . . boring, you know? Like once you've done it, there's nothing more to see. But it's not like that."

He shifted, angling his body toward her. "You've really never been with the same guy twice? Never had a relationship?"

Great. Now he's going to focus on how strange I am. But it was better he notice her lack of social skills instead of her weird ability. She could handle the first better.

"When you move around a lot, you don't make many friends. And if you don't go to school, you don't get the usual milestones." She ticked them off. "Kissed at twelve, felt up at fourteen. Give it up in a backseat after prom night." At his surprised look, she added, "I've seen the movies. I know how it goes. And I didn't miss much. I never had anybody making fun of my clothes or telling me I'm too weird to be homecoming queen, either. Only a wuss fixates on how crappy he had it."

He studied her for a long moment. "You never wanted to change anything? Never got tired of constantly moving on?"

She sneered. "And do what? Get a job I hate, taking orders from somebody else? Everyone I ever met who works in an office is constantly scheming a way to get out. Well, guess what? I'm *out*. Why would I want to get in?"

"You make a good point," he said, seeming thoughtful.

"Just because it's different doesn't make it worse."

Kyra remembered her dad saying those words almost verbatim, the rare times she'd complained about packing up and leaving a town where she'd made a few friends. Usually they were drifters' kids like her, but it had been nice to have somebody to play with. But after a while, she hadn't even seen the point of imaginary friends. It was better to live in the real world and accept your situation fully.

Mia was the only one who stayed in touch. At first it was hard because Kyra was always moving and her dad didn't encourage her to maintain ties, but she learned to time her runs to the post office while he was asleep, mailing cards and letters to Mia, who always wrote back right away, as soon as Kyra had a new address. It had been the sweetest thing, a little secret that made all the difference.

They seldom stayed in one place more than a month, usually in some by-the-week motel, but Mia had always been amazingly loyal. After Kyra was old enough to be trusted with a portion of their cut, she spent a good portion of it on pay phones, so she could talk to Mia for a few minutes. She liked hearing about the regular stuff her friend did, childhood by proxy. And Mia seemed to enjoy hearing about her adventures.

"I'm not arguing with you, Kyra." He smiled, his gaze warm and . . . tender? "You don't see me punching a clock, do you? You're preaching to the choir."

Embarrassment surged. "I forgot you're more like me than everyone else."

"That's truer than you know."

She drew her knees up, gazing out at distant mountains gone purple in the dark. "You owe me a story. You know too much about me now, and I don't know nearly enough about you."

"What kind of story?"

Kyra cut him a look, smiling. "One about you, something nobody else knows."

In profile he looked pensive. His cheekbones and chin showed in strong relief, shadowing his eyes. She could watch him for days. That alarmed her.

"Couldn't we have sex on Myrna's hood instead?" he asked, at length.

"No." She leaned far enough to jab him in the chest with her finger. "That ship has sailed. We're going to talk instead."

"Oh, hell."

"Your fault," she said without pity. "If you'd thought about how beautiful it'd be up here under the stars, you'd have brought protection in case you got lucky."

Then it hit her. He'd handled her, touched her all over. They'd kissed, and she'd just poked him again for good measure. No spark. No shock. No surge indicating that she'd taken something from him. While he ostensibly considered what he wanted to share, she tested her realization by brushing her fingers against his biceps.

Still nothing.

Incredulity warred with excitement. There was a reason, other than nomadic lifestyle, that she'd never been with the same man twice. For Kyra, physical contact didn't offer comfort or closeness. It was business, or it was sex—and she only enjoyed the latter once the workday was done. Inevitably, she wound up with a piercing migraine from a deluge of too much energy, another reason she avoided big cities.

Vegas had been the worst for her, and she'd only survived it because she convinced Serrano she was terminally shy, afraid of loud noises and big crowds. He'd taken her to quiet, expensive little bistros, places where they wouldn't be bothered. Kyra had thought it was ironic that a bastard like Serrano craved soft, delicate women in need of his protection.

"Kyra." Rey's voice brought her back to the here and now, husky with strain. "If you don't stop stroking me, we're going to have a problem."

She pulled her fingers away as if he'd burned her. "Sorry."

He gave a rueful laugh. "I'm sure I deserve it. I disagree with Sartre, though. Hell is *not* other people. Hell is you, me, a romantic sky . . . and no condom."

"I blame you," she said firmly. "No more stalling, now."

"Can I hold your hand again?"

For a moment, she looked down at the hand he wanted. It was serviceable but nothing special, pale at night though it would show a faint tan come morning. She flexed her fingers and then offered them to him, feeling odd and adolescent.

"Sure." Kyra shook her head. "You're the weirdest hobo I ever met."

"Met many, have you?" He curled his fingers through hers.

"A few." Mostly her dad's acquaintances and cronies.

It seemed to Kyra they were going about this all backward. They'd graduated from mind-blowing sex to hand-holding, and the man seemed self-congratulatory about it. She shook her head, smiling, silently marveling that she *could* just hold hands with someone and have it be that, only that.

"I was born on the Crow reservation in Montana," he said quietly.

Kyra sensed that he was about to honor her request; he was going to tell her something nobody else knew. A little ache sprang up that he was willing to trust her. She stilled, focused with every fiber of her being. Though she didn't even nod to encourage him, she thought he knew she was riveted. His fingers tightened on hers.

"I don't remember anything about it. My mother left there when I was just a few months old, and she caught up with my dad in New Mexico. He was a musician from Guatemala. Always said he didn't know she was pregnant when he split." Rey shrugged. "One-night stand, traveling man. I have that much in common with him."

He seemed to expect her to say something at this point, but hell if she knew what. Since she'd invited his confidence, she had to try. "Did they get married?"

That surprised a sharp little laugh out of him. "No."

"Then what happened?"

"She left me with him, went out for bread, and never came back."

"So you were raised by your dad, too." She should have been surprised to find they shared a common cornerstone, but somehow it seemed almost inevitable.

Rey thought for a moment, face set in brooding lines. His fingers smoothed against hers reflexively, incessantly, as if she were worry beads that gave him comfort. Why should such a small thing make her feel this way—all hot and fluttery?

"If you want to call it that. He lived his life, and he did more for me than my mother. He didn't give me away, at least."

Revisiting the past wasn't as painful as he might have expected. After all these years, it felt as though he were talking about someone else. Reyes wished he could pull her back into his lap, but with need blazing like a lighthouse beacon inside him, that wouldn't be smart. This chat would serve a purpose, which was why he'd gone along with it. She'd feel all soft and tender toward him, listening to the world's smallest violin.

Eventually, he'd get her story out of her. She'd confide in him about the money. Then he could walk away. He'd been hired to do exactly that, and he'd never failed, once he took a job. He'd just have to get over this internal conflict.

"There's more," she said, soft. "You going to tell me?"

"I don't know. Should I?"

"If you want. I'd like to hear it."

"He didn't know what to do with a baby," Rey went on. "So I spent a lot of time with various female friends of his. Nobody thought to call social services because excessive use of babysitters isn't against the law." It just made a kid wary of strangers because the minute you got to liking somebody you were sent elsewhere. "I was five when I started seeing more of my dad. He put me in school. Played a gig in the evenings, hung out with me in the afternoons."

Not like a father, though. That had been beyond Cesar Reyes. He'd enjoyed smoking a bowl and playing Bob Marley while his son did whatever the hell he wanted. Cesar wasn't big on rules.

"That doesn't sound so bad," she said then.

To her, it wouldn't. From what he could tell, they'd been raised by the same sort of man, one who put his personal pleasures first. Kyra would never admit that, however, because her father had loved her in his way, at least in the beginning. He didn't know what had gone wrong between them. From the jump, Cesar just hadn't cared enough to kick him out. In a different way, indifference could be almost as powerful as abuse.

He shrugged. "No. I don't have any hidden scars. No beatings. No cigarette burns. I did pretty much whatever I wanted."

"Like hike ten miles and camp on a mountain by yourself."

Reyes glanced her way, seeing the belated disapproval. Ah, she got it now. When all the other kids had somebody telling them to be home at a certain hour, making sure their homework was done, he'd had a musician offering him 'ludes and malt liquor. It was a wonder he hadn't wound up dead with a needle in his arm.

"Yeah," he said quietly. "Just like that."

"So you grew up big and mean and joined the army. Because you wanted somebody telling you what to do for a change."

A little flare of alarm sparked through him. She knew him a little *too* well. But he didn't let his uneasiness show.

"Yeah, pretty much. But it was the Marines."

She grinned at him. "And then you realized that you don't much like it since you'd spent your whole life doing what you wanted. So you didn't re-up the next tour."

"Again, true. Who's telling this story anyway?"

"You are. I'm just an interactive listener." Her gleeful self-satisfaction did something crazy to his insides.

Unable to help himself, he tugged her closer then and brushed a compulsive kiss against her temple. *Coconut.* She shouldn't even be here. Kyra belonged on a white beach somewhere, surrounded by palapas and the crystal blue ocean.

"Well, that's about all."

"No, it's not. I'm willing to bet you joined up at eighteen. That leaves years of your life unaccounted for. What've you been doing all this time?"

He didn't want to ruin the rapport but neither did he intend to tell the truth. The road he'd walked to his current life didn't bear close scrutiny, particularly with a target. "You asked for something nobody else knew, not my life story."

"I've been cheated. I bet a lot of people know that," she

said, frowning. "How your father raised you, I mean, especially the ones you knew growing up."

Actually they all thought he was dead. But he wouldn't tell her that, either. Reyes rubbed her shoulder lightly, luxuriating in the feel of her.

"Yeah . . . but I told you something nobody else knows in all that."

"Which is?"

"That I minded it."

He'd never let on he wished for something different, not once. Never gave anyone a hint he wasn't thrilled with complete freedom. It smacked of weakness, wishing for what you didn't and could never have. Cesar played a mean guitar; that was all he needed.

"Are they still alive?" she asked. "Your parents?"

"I don't know."

"Have you ever looked for them? Since you got out of the service."

"I think the better question would be did they ever look for me?"

He knew the answer, too. They hadn't needed to. The government had sent his old man a polite, regretful letter saying they appreciated his sacrifice. Reyes liked to think Cesar might've smoked a bowl in his honor. They sat in silence for a little while.

Then Kyra said, "Since my dad died, I don't have any family, either. My mom died when I was four."

Finally, something he hadn't known.

"I'm sorry."

"No big. I don't remember much about her."

"But you were close to your dad?" He had her in a receptive mood; it was the perfect time to mine for info.

"Very. It broke my heart when he died." Her chin firmed and she bit down hard on her lower lip, making him think she was fighting back tears.

Shit, that wasn't how a woman looked if she'd killed a man. Kyra had no reason to pretend with him, unless she'd figured out his game, and she was enjoying a colossal mindfuck at his expense. But no, all his instincts said she was being straight with him.

"What happened?"

Lost in memories, she didn't realize how important her answer was. She closed her eyes and turned her face against his shoulder. Her voice came out muffled. "He made some rough enemies. My dad was a hustler, strictly small-time. Then he got it in his head he could work the system, put us on easy street. He failed in a big way."

"So . . . ?" he prompted gently, every muscle clenched.

"This . . . guy had him beaten as an object lesson. They'd pounded him like meat. When I found him, he was dying." Kyra squeezed her eyes shut, but a tear still slipped out from beneath her closed lids.

Object lesson. Yeah. Knowing what he did about Serrano, that rang true. Reyes could fill in the pieces. Her dad had tried a cheat at the Silver Lady, maybe won a bit. But when Serrano found out, he sent his thugs after old Beckwith. Kyra wouldn't have taken the loss quietly. No, she'd done something to Serrano besides steal his money—and she hadn't murdered her old man, as Serrano claimed.

Goddammit, he should've looked longer at this job, but the money had been unbelievably good, twice his going rate. He should've done more background, but the problem with people like Kyra and her dad—they left very little record of their passing, an oddity in the modern world. But still, he should've known not to trust the neat package Serrano's lapdog Foster presented. When something seemed too clean and clear-cut, it usually was.

What now, genius? If he walked, Serrano would just hire someone else, someone without any care for the niceties. Where Reyes liked to be sure he was doing the world a karmic service with the jobs he accepted, some guys just wanted the money. Women, kids, nuns, politicians . . . it didn't matter as long as the wire came in on time. Reyes didn't work like that, but he knew plenty who did.

Belatedly he said, "Sounds like a real douche bag. Sorry about your dad."

"Me, too. I miss him." She hiccupped a little, laughter splitting the tears. "The car's all I have left of him, you know?"

"No wonder you take such good care of it."

"Exactly."

As they'd talked, the sky had clouded over, and now the first fat raindrop fell. He remembered the sudden mountain storms well. More than once, he'd nearly been washed off the mountain. The access road would be swimming in a few minutes, and nothing but a four-wheel drive could get them down.

"We'd better get in." He canted his head toward the back-seat.

"Are you trying to take advantage of me while my guard is down? Remember, the no-condom rule is still in play." Then she felt the rain pick up. "Ah. Yeah, I see the problem."

He snagged the quilt as he slid off the hood and made a break for the back door. She went around the opposite side and they slid in simultaneously, meeting in the middle. It was ridiculous, a ploy straight out of high school—and he was as sexually unprepared as any sixteen-year-old. Kyra showed some willingness to snuggle in and without overthinking, Reyes drew her to him, then wrapped them both up.

"I'm afraid we'll be stuck here all night. It should dry up by late morning."

"It's okay. It's not like you planned it."

And that was the most alarming thing. He, who planned everything down to the second, factoring in every possible variable, hadn't planned for her at all.

CHAPTER 12

"So do you do this a lot?" Kyra asked.

Beside her, Rey stirred. "Depends on what you mean by 'this'?"

"Lure women into their own backseats and then *don't* take advantage of them."

"No condoms," he reminded her in a long-suffering tone.

Man, she couldn't believe she had to do this, after the sex they'd had. But it seemed he needed a nudge. The man had taken her joking comment about working for it far too literally.

"There are other things we could do."

"Oh, really?" His lazy tone belied the sudden tension in his body.

"Mmm-hmm." She rather liked the switch, the pretense she was seducing him.

Rain drummed on the roof, shrinking their universe to two. Body heat had already started to steam the windows. Imagine what they could do if they put their minds to it.

"Did you have anything particular in mind?"

"You talk too much."

Kyra pulled his mouth to hers and wrapped her arms around his neck. His response sent tiny bursts of pleasure careening through her bloodstream, as his lips toyed with hers, every bit as darkly sensual as she remembered. But there was an added edge to his kiss; they both knew he couldn't go beyond a certain point, and it added a layer of thrilling risk. She shivered as he ran his mouth down her throat, teeth sinking lightly into the delicate skin. The light pain heightened her senses, making her more aware of his body heat, the hardness of him.

"Better," she breathed, tipping her head back.

In the sultry dark, she couldn't see him, but she felt his smile on her skin. "I know a fun game for us to play."

"Oh, yeah? What's that?"

"Teenagers," he whispered. "Neither one of us have ever been in a backseat, have we? You've never worried about letting a boy touch your breast under your shirt, but over your bra."

He wasn't touching her there, but at his words, she felt the heat of phantom fingertips. Her nipples furled, and her breath came a little faster. She could envision it so clearly: a desperately horny kid wanting to touch her, so primed he could come in his pants just from the idea.

His gravelly voice dropped even lower, rasping, "And you've certainly never felt the temptation to let him inside your jeans and stroke you over your panties, where in his clumsy eagerness he brushes your clit for the first time."

She sucked in a shuddering breath and had to clench her thighs against the resultant image, but she got into the spirit of things. "I don't think we should do more than kiss," she told him primly. "It's too easy to get carried away."

Rey brushed his fingers against her bare belly, revealed by the gap between shirt and jeans. "Okay," he whispered. "Just kissing."

"Good. That's good."

When he lowered his head, she expected a gentle mouth kiss in keeping with their game, but instead he touched his lips to the base of her throat, measuring her pulse. He could surely feel it skipping like mad against his mouth. His hands skated up to her sides as he nuzzled her collarbone. Her breath went in a dizzying rush.

She pressed her thighs together tighter, not in self-preservation, but to try to ease the need building there. Each point where he touched her, fingers along her ribcage, thumbs circling on her upper belly, felt impossibly warm. Those thumbs would feel so good on her nipples, big and rough. Kyra made a sound in her throat, as he nibbled his way up to her jaw and on to her ear. When he took the lobe between his teeth and bit down with exquisite gentleness, she arched her back, trembling.

"Are you sure I can't go under your shirt, Kyra? I'll stop the minute you say."

More than anything, she wanted to say to hell with it and take him inside her, but the no-condom problem was still in effect. She managed to keep the game alive by whispering, "Only on top of my bra. Don't take my clothes off."

God, how could she feel this tremulous excitement over role-play? But as heat trailed up her belly to the side of her breast, she felt as if she'd never been touched before. Rey caressed her in slow sweeps, like a kid getting bolder. His fingertips fanned while he circled his thumbs closer, centering her yearning on one tiny point. A little whimper escaped her when he finally brushed her tight nipple.

"You're so pretty," he murmured against her throat. "Am I turning you on? Are your panties damp, Kyra?"

Yes. God, yes.

Thinking a good girl wouldn't be able to say it aloud, she nodded, eyes downcast. He played with her for what felt like hours, smoothing through the thin silk of her bra. She didn't need much support so she went with decorative scraps, and she felt every touch, every stroke, every caress. Rey kept his touch heartbreakingly gentle and delicate when he knew she liked it rough. Kyra hadn't known she'd enjoy this, too.

"Can I touch you over your panties?"

She just moaned, needing an orgasm fiercely. Heart beating like a trip hammer, she broke character and went for his zipper. She had to struggle to get it down because of the straining erection. His breath caught when she curled her hand around his cock, but he didn't try to stop her. Rey's fingers were busy now, too, delving beneath the waistband of her panties.

Kyra arched as he found her clit. No more pretense now. They weren't innocent kids, however powerful the play might have been. He knew how to strum her body into quaking, and he did it like a virtuoso. She was less sure about the way she handled him, but by the way he bucked and shook, she must be doing all right. They came in each other's hands, shivering, shuddering, as rain crashed down overhead.

"Mmm." She stretched and licked her fingers.

He caught her to him and buried his face in her hair. "God, woman. What you do to me . . . why do you always smell like the beach?"

She was too dreamy to answer. Shortly, she slept, and in the morning, they moved on. A quick stop at the motel permitted them to wash up and collect their belongings. Reyes could probably tell she had a plan, but she wasn't sharing the details even now. It was driving him nuts.

New Mexico yielded to Colorado. This time of year, it was brown and dry, spiked with occasional greenery alongside the road. Kyra loved the west and how the sky seemed to stretch on forever. It made for easy if monotonous driving, and their route angled lazily northeast.

Kyra had known without him telling her that Rey would rather not go through Wyoming. It would be hard not to look for his mother there especially, and she wondered if he found himself searching the eyes of strangers for a hint of recognition. For the first time, she was glad her mom had died; at least she didn't have to live with knowing she was unwanted.

By tacit agreement, they decided to stop in Denver. It was a larger city than she usually selected, but they might make a little more money here. That wasn't her primary concern, of course. She had money, and if she could get to Mia in North Dakota, she'd be able to do something with it at last. She'd be sorry to ditch her new partner when the time came, but those were the breaks. He'd do fine with what he'd learned from her.

For a change, Rey had the wheel as they drove into the city. Since he'd proved he knew how to handle a delicate machine, Kyra let him spell her now and then. She lifted her arms over her head and gazed out the window at passing buildings.

"This all right?" He'd picked a cheap motel within a couple miles of downtown.

"Fine. We can work from here. I'm thinking we'll want to spend two or three days working different joints."

"Do you have somewhere in mind?" he asked as he parked.

Kyra shook her head. "I've never been to Denver before. It'll take me a little while to nose around and find a couple of likely spots. I'll ask the desk clerk first. They're usually a good source on local color."

"Good thinking."

She couldn't help but notice that he seemed distracted. He'd been a little strange and distant ever since they spent the night in the back of the Marquis, doing nothing but snuggling. "Everything okay?"

"That guy on the bike—no, don't look—use the rearview mirror."

A little shiver went through her as she did as he asked. Pretending to fluff her hair, she checked out the scruffy-looking dude on the red Kawasaki Ninja. His personal hygiene didn't match the gleam of his bike, which meant it was new. He'd recently come into money.

"What about him?"

"I'm pretty sure he's been with us since we crossed the state line."

"But that was hours ago!"

"Yeah." Rey nodded. "Maybe he just likes the look of your Marquis."

"Your gut says no."

Rey angled, regarding her seriously. "Is anyone hunting you?"

She hesitated. "There might be."

"If you don't trust me, we'll just have to be on our guard.

Pay no special attention to him as we get out. I'll be watching for him, though."

The man on the Kawasaki pretended not to see them. He was ostensibly fiddling with something on his bike, but Reyes could tell he was watching with his mirrors. Looking in that direction would tell him Reyes had made him, so he followed Kyra into the office.

This motel was nicer than the ones they had been staying in. Denver had an upscale vibe that had reached even the seedy portions. It was a small lounge done in lemon yellow with two scratchy new sofas, assuming somebody would want to hang around here. The linoleum had seen better days, but they'd covered it with a cheerful area rug in primary colors, geometric pattern.

The girl at the counter looked to have at least as much Hispanic blood as Reyes, and her name tag read "Maria." "Hi there, can I help you?"

"Two rooms," Kyra said, and disappointment slid through him. "Three nights. We don't have a reservation."

"Not a problem, unless there's a convention in town . . . and there isn't."

"Do you have any adjoining rooms?"

Well, that's better than nothing.

While Kyra took care of check-in, Reyes found the men's room. Immediately, he dug out his cell phone and dialed Foster. The man answered on the third ring every time without fail.

"I trust you have something to report," Foster said in lieu of greeting.

"I hope to shortly. Trust takes time, as I've told you before. I have a question. Did you hire anyone else to locate Ms. Beckwith?"

There was a weighty silence. "Do I *need* to?"

"No," Reyes said. "But it seems as though we've picked up a tail along the way. I wanted to find out if he's one of yours before I neutralized him."

"If my employer has done this, he did not discuss it with me," Foster said. "Therefore, anything that befalls the man would be a result of poor planning."

That would be tacit permission to off the guy. "Are you positive your employer lets you in on every move he makes?"

"I am sure of nothing, but I consider this ninety-nine percent. I must warn you, however . . . my employer lacks both subtlety and patience. You have a week at most to finish the job."

Shit. Serrano had reached the point where he wanted results ahead of method. It wouldn't matter to him if Reyes had to torture the woman extensively or beat her into ground chuck to get the information out of her. Fear spiked through him.

"I'll deliver," he said. "I always do."

Foster made a brief sound of amusement. "I know. That's why I hired you."

He hit "end" on the phone and leaned his head against the cool tile. Reyes had to face it. Somewhere along the way, he'd gotten emotionally attached. He didn't do that; he *never* did that. Though he didn't like killing women, he'd done four in his career. He'd walked away from more offers than he'd taken; he didn't want a payday that came from offing some guy's middle-aged wife so the asshole could marry the mistress without worrying about alimony.

"Fuck," he bit out.

Reyes fought the urge to punch something. He didn't want to forfeit his reputation, but he didn't want to kill her, either. Not anymore. Not since she'd come beneath his fingers, his name stretched into a sweet little cry. Maybe he was every bit as much of a sucker for her as Serrano had been, but he couldn't muster up any indignation. He just wanted to make love to her again.

Rock, meet hard place.

By the time he came out of the bathroom, he'd managed to compose himself, phone tucked away into its secret hiding spot. Paranoid to a fault, he kept it turned off when he wasn't using it. Kyra had finished, and she stood with the key cards in their little envelopes, chatting with the clerk.

"Just pool halls . . ." Maria was saying. "Umm. Rack 'Em in Aurora is good for pool. Or you could try Pete's on East Colfax."

Kyra nodded. "Great, thanks."

"You ready?" He didn't know whether she'd want to go out tonight after driving all day. It was sobering to realize how short a time he'd known her, relatively speaking.

"Yep." She headed back to the Marquis.

Reyes walked behind her, scanning the parking lot for trouble. The red Kawasaki was still there, but he didn't see the bearded guy. Maybe he was just visiting somebody here—or meeting someone. People often didn't want to have affairs on their home turf, so they'd meet up in a town where nobody knew either of them. The biker might've come from New Mexico to meet his piece on the side. They might be upstairs right now, doing the horizontal mambo, moaning over how much sharper and more exciting it was to do it when it felt like they were getting away with something.

She cut him a look as she demanded the car keys. "I'll pull around back. We're on the other side, upstairs."

"Thanks. I hate ground-floor rooms." Not that he'd stayed in such places for years. He had a gorgeous condo in Long Beach that he hadn't seen in weeks.

Ducking her head, she looked a little shy. "I know. I remembered."

"So you booked upstairs for me?" Damn. He couldn't remember the last time anyone had taken note of his personal preference and tried to accommodate. A weird sensation made his chest feel like it was too small.

"I guess. It's no big."

It was, but he didn't embarrass her by pursuing it. "What numbers?"

"Two-ten and two-eleven. We're in adjoining rooms. I hope that's okay."

Reyes raised a brow. "Planning to visit me?"

"I dunno." She shrugged. "Maybe."

That invited all kind of questions, but she seemed edgy this afternoon, so he didn't push her. Kyra inserted the key and popped the trunk, but before she could move, he took her things along with his. To his surprise, she didn't argue; she just shut it, locked all four doors, and headed up behind him.

External stairs, he noticed. No elevator. No security, not even an old bellhop. This place was a disaster waiting to happen. Reyes held the bags lightly. If need be, he could hurl them at an attacker, and disable him in less than five seconds. He was almost disappointed when they made it to their rooms unscathed. She handed him his envelope with the key card in it.

"I'll take two-ten, if that's all right." He'd be better placed to hear anyone coming for her, unless they circled the long way from the other side.

"Sure." She hesitated, fidgeting, quite unlike herself. "You want to order pizza later and watch a movie on pay-per-view?"

Astonishment swamped him; it was a wonder his mouth didn't drop open. Was she asking him on a *date*? He said the first thing that came to mind: "This place has pay-per-view?"

That answered his question about whether she wanted to get right to work. The answer was no. Apparently she wanted another night off . . . with him. Shit, he was in so much trouble . . . because he wanted it, too.

Kyra gave a little huff and smiled. "Yeah, they do. Not the newest releases, I'm sure, but I haven't been to the movies in years, so they'll all be new to me."

"Sounds good. Give me a few minutes to take a shower?" After the long, dusty ride, he needed one.

Her tawny gaze swept his body, making him feel downright naked. "I guess you're worth waiting for."

With her looking at him like that, he felt like dragging her into his room and doing her hard, regardless of what she said about it. The little taste in the car hadn't done anything to diminish his desire. In fact, he could still feel her hands on him whenever he thought about it, her smooth fingers working his cock convulsively, fueled by her own rising orgasm. Heat slammed through him.

"Shower first," he muttered, nearly undone by her husky laugh as she noticed her effect on him. He handed Kyra her bag. "Cold one. I'll be there later."

"I'll be here."

"You better be."

She took a step toward her room, and he focused on the sweet curve of her ass, nicely framed in faded denim. Reyes found himself unable to let her step away without putting his mark on her, claiming her as his. The instinct went deeper than anything he'd ever experienced. It made no sense at all. Not caring who might be watching, he came after her and took her mouth in a deep, fierce kiss.

The hell with this. He wasn't made for denial. No shower, at least not alone.

"Unlock the door on your side," he bit out. "Now."

CHAPTER 13

Gerard Serrano returned to the United States with a minimum of fuss.

It took a day for talk to start circulating, and he eavesdropped on his employees using the technology he'd installed in the break rooms and changing areas, expressly for that purpose. He hadn't gotten where he was without a deserved reputation for being prepared. If he didn't know everything about his domain—or at least have the potential to do so—then he deserved whatever happened to him.

Settling into his leather office chair, he powered up his desktop system and input a password. He didn't keep it written down anywhere. It wasn't a personal fact that someone could guess, and he changed it on a weekly basis. Serrano prided himself on being a careful, methodical man.

Smiling in anticipation, he brought up the streaming feed from the lounge. A couple of security guys whose names he didn't recall offhand sat at a table covered in the remnants of a fast-food lunch. At first they only talked about things that had happened so far on their shift. They mentioned an elderly couple trying to make off without paying for the breakfast buffet. Serrano shook his head; that was the least of his worries.

While they gossiped like little girls, he looked up their personnel files: Rick Calloway and Dave Brody, both in their late twenties, both a couple of slackers with little to no ambition. Calloway was a tall, thin drink of water, and Dave was just average in every respect. Just as he was about to get bored and attend to more pressing business, the conversation shifted.

Dave leaned in over his cheesy burger wrapper. "You heard yet?"

"Heard what?" Calloway picked at his fries, which looked cold and disgusting even through the grainy feed.

"About Wayne, man. He didn't come back with the boss."

Rick wasn't as dumb as he looked because he said, "Shit. He heard about—"

"Totally," Dave said.

The other man's hands clenched on the table. "You think he knows our part in it?"

Ah. Interesting. So it had been a team effort. Serrano tapped his fingers against his mahogany desk, thoughtful.

"Nah, man. If he did, he woulda invited us to Sweden and pushed us out of a plane over the ocean somewhere, too."

Calloway looked nervous. "I dunno. Maybe we should get out of town. I don't think we should work here anymore. You never know what might happen."

"C'mon. This is a great job. Where else could I sleep instead of doing real work? As long as nothing catches on fire, it's cool."

Serrano narrowed his eyes. So he was paying Brody to slack? He'd tell Foster to ride him like a cheap whore, if he didn't have the loser killed. He was still considering the angles.

"I'm telling you, Dave, if you're smart, you'll get the hell out. Serrano runs this place like he's Don Corleone. He thinks he can just disappear somebody and nobody will ask questions. Hell, man, think about it. He *did*."

Brody shrugged. "It's not like this is the Wild West. It's not even old-school Vegas these days. The Feds are everywhere . . . gangsters don't run the town anymore. I'm not dumb enough to get on a private plane with him, and I'll watch my back. I'll be fine."

"If you say so." Calloway didn't sound convinced. "I think it's time I went to visit my ma in Kissimmee."

Dave shook his head. "You're such a puss."

Shortly thereafter, they left the lounge without cleaning up their mess. That didn't concern Serrano directly, but it bothered him to know he had such idiots in his employ. They were in charge of supervising things when he was busy elsewhere at a higher level. If they didn't have Foster riding herd on them, they'd doubtless be happy to let tourists rob Serrano blind.

"That's the problem," he said aloud, as Foster came into his office.

"What is?"

The security chief had an unnerving way of knowing when he was needed. Today he wore an impeccably cut, gray pin-striped suit, one that put Serrano in mind of 1930s gangster film. All Foster needed was a fedora and a tommy gun to complete the picture. It galled Serrano that his own clothes didn't hang as well; he'd done too much manual labor in his youth, packed on too much bulk.

"No loyalty these days."

"Times have changed," Foster agreed.

"What do you know about it? You're little more than a kid yourself."

Foster didn't even blink; it was impossible to rile him. "As you say, sir."

"Great suit. Who's the designer?" He wondered if the right cut would result in him looking so polished. For once in his life, Serrano thought it might be nice to look like a prince instead of a thug.

"Domenico Vacca."

The name meant nothing to him. He'd heard of Boss, Lauren, and Armani. That was the limit of his knowledge regarding male couture. "He expensive?"

"Very," Foster said, as if he didn't want to talk about money. "I presume you'd like to discuss the future of Brody and Calloway here at the Silver Lady."

Serrano let it go. He studied the other man, who never sat

in his presence unless explicitly invited. Damn if he didn't like the feeling it gave him, sort of a feudal rush. "Did you know the other two were involved when you gave me Sweet?"

"I did not. I identified Sweet via his IP."

The particulars doubtless involved a lot of illegal technical nonsense that he didn't care about. He drew one important conclusion. "So he posted the video from home?"

"Correct."

"Maybe Brody and Calloway gave him the footage. Do they work those cameras?"

"They're part of the rotation," Foster answered without checking the schedule. The man could keep a hundred different balls in the air without breaking a sweat.

"Take a seat," he invited at last. "Let's talk about this."

Foster tugged his pants up as he sat, an old-fashioned gesture that protected the creases. Serrano hadn't seen anything like it since his grandfather's day, before wash-and-wear clothing, before permanent press. Serrano shook his head. *Foster's a weird one.*

Foster folded his hands in his lap and looked expectant. "What would you have me do, sir? Do you wish to terminate their employment?"

"I'm asking your advice, man-to-man. What would *you* do, Foster?"

"What is my goal in this situation? To instill fear or command respect?" As he spoke, the security chief's eyes looked ancient, somehow wrong in his youthful face. Serrano thought he saw dark things stirring beneath the veneer of silvered ice.

"Both, preferably."

"Then I would kill the one who is stupid enough to remain. Since he betrayed me, he cannot continue to live off my largesse. As for the one who is smart enough to run, I would allow him his life while making sure he learned of Brody's fate."

Serrano arched a brow, wondering if Foster was as canny as he seemed. "Why?"

"Sometimes a living man who fears you is more beneficial than ten dead ones."

"Because he'll tell other people," Serrano said. "And your legend spreads."

"Precisely."

He smiled. "You're a smart guy. That's exactly how I intend to handle this. Do we have someone local for the job?"

Foster nodded. "I'll take care of it, sir. Will that be all?"

So eager to do my dirty work. Serrano killed a smile before it could blossom. It wouldn't surprise him a bit if Foster strangled Brody himself.

"Not quite. I've been giving this some thought . . . and I'm not sure if doing the girl is going to be enough. We need something big, something to prove I'm still a power in this town. I'm targeting Pasternak and Ricci." Serrano named the partners who owned the Pair-A-Dice Casino, the shitheads who'd laughed at him a few weeks back. They wouldn't be laughing when this was over.

"Violence or personal misfortune?"

He considered. "I'm feeling subtle. People already know I'm willing to fit somebody with cement shoes. Now they need to realize I'm smart, too. Dig me up some dirt on them, will you? For instance, I wouldn't be sad if the IRS took a long, hard look at their books."

"I'll get right on it." Foster stood, evidently sensing his imminent dismissal.

As if he'd let him walk out without an update on that damned bitch. "What's the story with the guy you hired to retrieve my money?"

For the first time, Foster looked uncomfortable. "He's having some trouble with her, sir. She still hasn't confided in him. I gave him a week deadline to wrap it up."

"I'm not surprised," Serrano muttered. "She's a pro all the way . . . it won't be easy to get inside her head. If he can't get the money back, just give him the order to end her. I can afford the loss, and I want this finished, one way or another."

Foster inclined his head. "I'll let him know the next time I speak with him."

Serrano let him get nearly to the door before adding lazily, "Oh . . . and give my regards to that little old lady and the kid, the next time you see them."

He didn't turn. His expression would give away his horror. So Foster kept walking and ducked into the first men's room. This was the executive lounge, all stone tiles and marble countertops fitted with motion-activated gilt spigots. It always smelled of oranges in here, and there were four rock fountains on tiered shelves, intended to drown out the sound of pissing men.

Taking refuge in a stall, he sank down on the toilet and let the shakes come. Nausea boiled up but he wouldn't let it out. Serrano, that crazy, paranoid bastard, might have the bathrooms bugged, too. He'd have to get himself together in silence.

It's fine, he told himself. *Serrano doesn't know everything.* If he'd put the pieces together, he'd have done something about it. The man had all the finesse of a lawnmower; he lacked the patience for a long-term scheme.

But still, it shook him that the man knew that much. He'd been so sure nobody was watching him. He'd never noticed a tail. As long as he paid the bills, Lexie and Beulah Mae would be fine, but he hated the thought of abandoning them. More importantly, Serrano would take a break in his routine to mean there was something significant in his discovery. He'd remember the two females as Foster's weakness.

And they were. He battled an overwhelming urge to run for the garage, get his car, and drive like a bat out of hell over to Desert Winds to make sure Serrano hadn't done anything with his new knowledge. Maybe he'd made a mistake in keeping Lexie close. Grief plucked at his heartstrings, old and familiar as a well-worn pair of shoes. It wasn't like she knew the difference.

The most alarming aspect was that Serrano might not trust him fully. Serrano might have somebody digging into his background. While Foster didn't think highly of the man's acuity, he'd built an empire on brute instinct, and he had the resources to hire good people.

So close. This couldn't be happening now. Not when all the threads were starting to unravel. He just needed to stay in place long enough to give a few more good tugs.

Foster allowed himself five minutes to panic quietly, indulge in worst-case scenarios, and then he mastered himself through breathing. By the time he came out of the stall, he was entirely composed. He washed his hands and blotted with a paper towel. In the mirror that ran the length of the counter, he looked much younger than he felt, just another cog in the corporate machine.

Because he could do nothing else without arousing suspicion, he completed the workday. Foster handled all the minor annoyances that Serrano couldn't be bothered with, squatting like a spider in his penthouse office. When he was sure his boss wasn't watching, he tended to be lenient, and today he let a couple of college girls go with a warning. *Damn stupid kids.* He wished genital warts on whoever had turned prostitution into a fairy tale by way of *Pretty Woman.*

Finally, it was quitting time. Since he'd constructed this whole persona around routine, deviation would mean the end of everything. To make matters worse, he wasn't due to visit for nearly another week. Perhaps he could call and check on them. Since he wasn't paying attention, and it was the middle of the night, he didn't expect to collide with a shapely brunette as he came out of the corridor that led from the business offices onto the casino floor.

Reflexively Foster steadied her with his hands on her upper arms. His blood heated as he inhaled her light scent: cinnamon and vanilla. Since he had sex regularly, three times a week like clockwork, the response perplexed him. She wasn't classically beautiful by any means; the woman had a spill of inky hair and darkly hooded eyes. Her skin bespoke Mediterranean origins, but she had almost a Middle Eastern hook to her nose. He could usually categorize people at a glance, but he didn't know a thing about her after that inspection, except he'd been holding on to her a fraction too long.

"I'm fine," she said pointedly. Then her gaze slide behind him to the door marked "Private." She brightened visibly. "Oh, do you work here?"

It was four in the morning, and Foster was in no mood to deal with a casino groupie. He ran across them more often than he cared to contemplate. They thought sleeping with a floor manager or a security guard would get them upgraded to a high-roller suite when all it entitled them to was a night of sex, generally of dubious quality.

"Talk to Cecilia with guest services," he said tiredly. "She'll give you a certificate for a free meal at the buffet."

"Do I look like a freeloader to you?"

Foster took in her expensive Italian shoes and matching handbag, her tailored black pantsuit livened up with a red silk blouse showing a hint of cleavage. The jacket had been nipped in at the waist to flaunt her curves. She wore diamonds at her throat, but subtly understated . . . a single teardrop on a platinum chain. He couldn't have dressed her better himself.

"No, you don't," he admitted. "I apologize. What can I do for you?"

"My name is Mia Sauter," the woman said quietly. "And I'm looking for my friend, Rachel. Last I heard, she was living here, dating the owner of the Silver Lady, but I haven't heard from her in weeks. I got worried and came looking, but according to the man who owns her apartment building, she doesn't live there anymore."

He kept his expression impassive. Maybe he could do something with this opportunity, but it would depend a great deal on "Rachel's" friend. "Yes, I think I can help you. Let's get something to eat." When she started for the all-night café, he shook his head. "Not here. We need to talk."

She hesitated. "It's late. I haven't slept in over twenty-four hours."

If that was true, she looked amazing. "Did you catch the red-eye?"

"Last night," she confirmed. "Two nights ago technically I suppose, but it's all a blur at this point."

"Where did you come from?"

"Vancouver," Mia answered promptly.

Another lie. She probably didn't realize it, but she had a tell. Most people, unless they were sociopaths, did. Just as when she'd said she was looking for her friend Rachel, when she said she'd come from Vancouver, her eyes slid up to the left, accessing the center for constructed images instead of the one that controlled memories. Mia wasn't a bad liar—not on the level of Kyra Beckwith, but better than average. That didn't recommend her to him, despite her superior fashion sense.

This would be the perfect time for him to get the truth out

of her, but he couldn't seem to push. "If you'd rather get some sleep, I understand. But I'll give you some words of warning—don't talk to anyone else here about this. And don't stay at the Silver Lady." He pulled a silver business-card holder from the inside pocket of his jacket and wrote his private cell number down. "Call me when you want to know something about Rachel."

Mia took the card and read it over. "Addison Foster, chief of security. I guess that means I've lucked into someone in the know. Let's just go somewhere and talk now. I'll have some coffee. I've been up this long, I can manage another hour."

A faint smile curved his mouth. "Do you want to accompany me in my car or do you have a rental?"

"I caught a cab."

"Then you can taxi to the diner if you prefer. They make great pancakes. . . . I'll give you the address."

She shook her head, lustrous black curls brushing her cheeks. "I may as well save the cab fare, and you know where we're going."

Foster found her trust alarming, but since it suited his purposes he didn't tell her she was being foolhardy. He took her to Pancake House, keeping to well-traveled roads so she wouldn't get worried. The light was just starting to tease along the horizon as he parked his Altima. Everything about him guaranteed respectability from his suit to his conservative car.

"I haven't been to one of these places in years," she said in delight. "You were right about the pancakes."

They made an amusing picture, overdressed for the occasion, but there was no shortage of tables. It was too early for breakfast, and the heavy drinkers hadn't come up for air yet. Apart from the bored crew, they had the place to themselves.

He chose a table near the bathrooms, set into a niche away from the front door. Though Foster hadn't noticed a tail, he hadn't seen one when he went to Desert Winds, either. He needed to amp up the caution. Polite conversation sufficed until the waitress took their order, delivered coffee, and headed back to her station to chat.

"So," Mia said, taking a sip after she'd doctored her drink with cream and sugar. "You know something about Rachel. Spill it."

"I know everything about her," he replied quietly. "And I think you mean *Kyra*, don't you? More regrettably, my boss knows as well."

The woman dropped her spoon and leaned her head on her hands. "Then I'm too late. She already went through with it."

Oh, yes, Foster thought. He could get a great deal of use from Mia Sauter.

CHAPTER 14

Kyra darted into her room and then said through the adjoining door, "Take your shower first. Cold one, remember?"

"You have to be kidding."

She stifled a laugh, sensing he wouldn't appreciate her amusement. "I do not kid about cold showers."

When she'd offered pizza and a movie, she'd meant only that, regardless of his intentions. He stomped off and if she pressed her ear to the door, she could hear the water running. Good enough. Kyra could use a quick one as well after driving all day. She didn't intend to have sex with him tonight, but it wouldn't hurt to tease him a little by smelling good.

He seemed to have a thing for layered scents. Somewhere along the way, she'd picked up a bath set steeply discounted, and it had matching gel, lotion, and shampoo, all basic coconut. Nobody had ever reacted to it like Rey, though.

A quick shower seemed to be in order, not a cold one, though. She made sure to apply the lotion everywhere and let it sink into her skin. Then she dressed in clean jeans and a fresh tank top. No bra. That was a delicious cruelty. Kyra pulled her wet hair back into a ponytail.

In fifteen minutes, he tapped on the adjoining door, scrupulously polite. "Can I come over now?"

"Sure." She unlocked the door and he stepped through, black hair still damp. His black T-shirt clung to his chest, revealing muscles that made Kyra want to dig her fingers into them. His skin still carried that bronze glow, which she knew to be natural, now. He was unfairly delicious, a real test to her self-discipline.

He offered a lazy smile, a frisson of awareness sparking between them. "Do I pass inspection, sergeant?"

There was no point in being anything but honest. "You know you curl my toes. What do you want on your pizza?"

"I don't usually eat it."

That astonished her. "Really? How come?"

"When I was growing up, I rarely had a home-cooked meal," he told her. "But I ate a lot of pizza. So whenever I can, I do my own cooking."

Kyra pondered that, nonplussed. "What kind of stuff do you make?"

His obsidian gaze went to the tiny kitchenette at the far side of the room. She hadn't particularly wanted to pay ten bucks extra for a kitchen, but the clerk claimed only the mini-suites came with connecting doors. And maybe that was true. This kind of room was probably good for families on vacation.

"I make a great chicken picatta. I also do salmon with red pepper sauce. Angus and bleu cheese salad—"

"Holy shit, that's real food." Her mouth watered. "If we went to the grocery store instead of ordering out, would you mind cooking? I can help," she added, thinking he might take it wrong. "I'm sure I can chop stuff." She'd never tried, mind. In her experience, food came two ways, delivery or takeout.

Before answering, Rey went to check out the kitchen, counting pots and pans or something. The kitchenette consisted of a tiny two-burner stove, sink, microwave, and half-size oven. She wasn't sure she'd ever seen a fridge so small that wasn't also half again as short like a dorm unit.

"I can work in here," he said finally. "Chicken piccata would be easiest. The recipe doesn't require a lot of sophisticated equipment."

Kyra grinned, anticipating her first home-cooked meal in . . . well, she couldn't remember, actually. Her dad didn't cook. She'd never learned. It seemed pointless when she never stayed in the same place, certainly never had a kitchen for very long. In Vegas, she'd rented a place for the long con, but she never actually bought food or anything. From the moment she started the game, Serrano was always taking her out somewhere.

"Let's go shopping."

He smiled back. "Men all over the world just shuddered without knowing why."

"Funny. C'mon." She grabbed her bag and room key, then reached for his hand, towing him toward the door.

God, how weird it was to touch without an agenda. She'd grabbed his arm without even thinking about it. Rey might be the only person in the world with whom she could do it. With him, she could wrestle, tickle, snuggle, anything she wanted, and it didn't have to be factored into her day's work. Touching him didn't create a gridlock in her brain that resulted in painful feedback. Once her ability kicked in, she'd stopped receiving even casual hugs from her dad; she hadn't realized until this moment how much she missed it.

Rey went easily enough. He thought she didn't notice him watching the lot from the balcony like a hawk, but she remembered his wariness about the biker. She hadn't forgotten the guy, either. It was possible Serrano had sent someone after her. Kyra wasn't sure how Mr. Kawasaki had tracked her down, but she'd bet on herself in a fight. All she needed was one point of contact, and then she'd turn whatever skill the guy had against him. She'd done it more times than she could count.

"Let me ask Maria about where we can find a market nearby," Rey said as they climbed down the stairs.

He ducked into the office and Kyra watched them through the glass. The clerk leaned on the counter while talking to him, saying with her body language that she'd be open to any invitation Rey might offer. A jolt of pure rage startled her. She wanted to stomp into the building and drag him out of there, snarling all the while.

She shook her head to clear it. "Well, that was weird."

"What was?" Rey asked, stepping outside.

"Nothing."

"When a woman says nothing, she means everything."

"I get grumpy when I'm hungry." Kyra would be boiled in oil before she'd admit to a spurt of possessiveness. That feeling ran counter to everything she stood for.

"Then let's get you fed."

Everything that followed seemed very surreal. Rey drove them to an upscale little supermarket called Whole Foods, where he picked his ingredients with the utmost care. Sometimes it felt as if she didn't know him at all, particularly when he spent five minutes examining the asparagus, which she'd never seen uncooked in bunches before. They looked like tiny spears.

"Organic, naturally produced," she read aloud. "So you're into healthy stuff."

"When I can be. Whenever it makes sense."

Well, that was a weird quality in a drifter. Maybe he was more like those hippie types who didn't work and wanted to grow all their own food. That had always seemed like a contradiction to Kyra. If you didn't work, how could you afford to buy the land to grow stuff on? But she'd met a few people in her travels who just planted gardens in vacant lots, regardless of who owned the property. She wouldn't put Rey in that category, however. He wasn't the idealistic type.

Finally, they had a cart full of exotic ingredients, like capers and heirloom tomatoes. She couldn't believe he needed so much stuff to make *one* meal. The clerk at the register looked at the ingredients and said, "Somebody's making chicken piccata."

Damn, could everyone cook but her? She pondered that on the drive back. Kyra carried her half of the bags, eager to see how this worked. There wasn't space for both of them so he dismissed her offer to help.

She watched in awe as he pounded the chicken thin and dipped it in flour. He made some sauce to pour over it and then he served it with grilled asparagus. She'd never eaten so well in her life, not even at any of the fancy restaurants Serrano took her.

Doing the dishes seemed like the least she could do, so she washed up in the tiny kitchenette. Afterward, Kyra moaned a little, rubbing her stomach. She unfastened the button on her jeans, which had to be the least sexy thing in the world.

"That was . . . amazing. Thank you."

He watched her lounge against the headboard with hooded eyes. "I should be thanking you. I haven't cooked for anyone that appreciated me in a long time."

"You could get a job doing that. Seriously."

"We already discussed how I don't like working for someone else."

She agreed, "So we did. Let's see what's on."

It was much later than she'd realized, and the food made her sleepy. Rey found something to watch, not on pay-per-view, and settled down on the bed beside her. Cars chased each other and then exploded; gunshots rang out. Men cussed. By the time it ended, she was dozing.

"Kyra," he whispered.

"Mmm?"

"I'm going to bed now, sweetheart. I . . . can't stay here."

Why couldn't he? She could think of worse things than to snuggle up to him and sleep. It was a decent-sized bed.

She opened her eyes, bleary and confused. "You're leaving?"

"Just going to my own room. You're too much temptation. If I spend the night, you'll be under me by morning." His fingers felt exquisitely gentle as they brushed the hair from her face.

She gave a sleepy siren's smile. "We can't have that. G'night then."

Kyra roused enough to shuck her jeans and slipped into bed in her tank top, leaving the lights burning as she always did. She heard the click of the door as he left, but he didn't lock it. That felt reassuring rather than risky. If he'd intended to press her, he would've had his hands all over her while she catnapped. Rey must respect her. It was the only explanation that made sense, however little experience she had with such things.

She went to sleep smiling and woke with a heavy weight squeezing all the air out of her chest. An unfamiliar male voice growled, "Don't scream."

A strange sound popped Reyes from a sound sleep. He rolled out of bed, unconscious to battle-ready in three seconds. Listening, he couldn't identify what had woken him. He didn't hear anything now.

But something had definitely roused him. He hesitated, unwilling to wake Kyra over nothing. Then a lamp crashed to the floor and he spun into motion. Reyes came through the adjoining door like a hurricane, surprising the guy who had an arm around Kyra's neck. It was definitely the bearded biker from this afternoon. Reyes didn't know if the bastard meant to kill her or choke her out for easy transport.

Either way, it wasn't happening.

"Put her down," he said softly. "Or I will pull your head off with my bare hands."

"Who the fuck do you think you are?"

For half a second, he thought about saying, *your worst nightmare*. Instead he canted his head at Kyra. "She's mine. This is your final warning."

The guy still didn't move, his loss. Reyes snagged the lamp from his side of the bed and whipped it at the guy's head. It smashed against his skull; the asshole cried out, dropping Kyra, and Reyes bounced over the bed, cord in hand—too easy.

He whipped it around the target's neck and choked him out. Red bled at the corners of his eyes. He wanted little more than to end the son of a bitch who'd dared lay hands on his woman. Reyes forced him to his knees, feeling his flesh yield.

"Please," the guy begged.

Reason prevailed—he needed information—but it was a near thing. "Who sent you? Who do you work for?"

The cord cut into the man's throat, so he eased it off to let him speak, but the sound still came out strangled. "Dwight.

He's had all the road warriors looking for you two since you blew up his place. He greenlit you two, and the Marquis is memorable. It's a land-boat. I figured I'd take the girl and you'd come for her. Two-fer."

So at least one of the meth dealers had survived the explosion. He didn't know if he was glad or disappointed that Serrano wasn't behind this attack. That way, his choice would be made for him. He wouldn't have to decide to toss his reputation down the toilet over a woman, one he still wasn't entirely sure he trusted, however much he wanted to.

He'd spotted the guy earlier on his shiny new bike, but then he'd disappeared. Reyes had thought perhaps his caution had crossed the line to paranoia. Now he wished he hadn't left Kyra alone. This son of a bitch was going to suffer.

"What's your name, asshole?" He tightened the electrical cord just a touch.

"Steve."

"Get this, Steve. I know a thousand ways to kill you, and I'm only letting you live because I need a messenger, and you're here. You ride on back to Dwight. Tell him to write the bar off and move on. All I wanted that day was a beer. He called the play by accusing me of being a cop." Reyes let that sink in. "Do I *look* like a cop to you?"

"No, sir," Steve gabbled.

"If he sends anyone else after me and mine, I go scorched earth on this. Not just Dwight, I'm talking his friends, his family, anybody who ever looked at him kindly." Reyes bent, letting the other man look into his eyes for a full minute. "Are we clear?"

Whatever he'd seen, it made him shudder. "Crystal."

"Get out."

Steve scrambled out the door on hands and knees. The tool he'd used to pop the door lay forgotten on the floor, right beside Kyra. Goddammit, he hadn't put the chain on for her when he went back to his room. Reyes did that first and then knelt beside her. She'd curled into the fetal position on her side, so tightly coiled that he was afraid she'd hurt herself. A soft little whine came from her throat, like that of a wounded animal.

Looking at her, he didn't think she'd been injured enough

to warrant this reaction. Something weird was going on, something really weird. He touched her shoulder lightly.

"Kyra, it's over. He's gone."

Nothing. But she tucked her face farther, brought her knees up higher. Shudders ran through her in deep waves, almost like a convulsion. That scared the shit out of him.

"Did he drug you?"

With the lamps broken, he wouldn't be able to see a tiny pinprick. Jesus, what if she was going into anaphylactic shock? Helplessness swamped him. He had no experience with rescuing people or helping in their time of need. The trick with the cord was more his forte.

"Come on, Kyra. Talk to me, baby. What's wrong? What do you need?"

"Bathroom," he thought she whispered, but it was hard to tell through her chattering teeth.

Okay, that he could do. Reyes scooped her up, ran to the tiny lavatory, and flicked on the light. He started to put her in the tub, but she shook her head, eyes wide and wild. He'd never seen anything like her expression right now, blanched almost to bone and sick as death. Bewildered, he set her down and she fell to her knees beside the toilet. The dinner he'd cooked came up in a liquid rush.

"Do you need to go to the emergency room?" he asked.

"Get out!" she demanded, wiping her mouth. "Go!"

Then the next wave hit her. As she vomited, she sobbed. Since she'd gone to sleep in a ponytail she didn't even need him to hold her hair back, and she clearly wanted him gone. So he grabbed the ice bucket and stepped outside. The balcony was clear. If he'd moved on the asshole when he'd noticed him earlier, this wouldn't have happened, but he couldn't go around killing people for potential offenses. He didn't want to leave her even for a minute, but she might want cold water or ice chips when she finally recovered. If she did.

When he returned, he found her huddled beside the toilet, wracked with dry heaves. Her eyes were red with weeping, her nose running, and she smelled disgusting. Quietly, he wet a washcloth, added a touch of her coconut bath gel, and then began to wash her face. It warmed him when she didn't pull away.

"Jesus, Mary, and Joseph," she said, gazing up at him

with dull, wrecked eyes. "Why didn't you kill him? I wish to God you had."

That was the last thing he expected to hear, and it sent a shock of unease through him. Reyes was no stranger to taking human life; he did it for a living after all, but it was a job to him, not something that gave him pleasure. He'd started on the path inside, after he went down for raping a white girl, one with money, who liked it rough and then when she realized the enormity of what they'd done—and what it said about her particular tastes—recanted her consent.

They'd come at him hard, but after he killed the third inmate in as many months, a child-molester that time, they'd accorded him some respect. And it felt *good,* taking out some scumbag. At that point, he started wondering whether he could turn that rush into an entrepreneurial venture.

"Why?"

She didn't seem to hear him, just mumbling into space. "It's a funny thing, touch. Sometimes I get something good, other times, not so much. You know what he was best at? Rape. But when he touched me, he lost his wood. That's why he was so pissed at me . . . he couldn't do it to me like he planned when I had his mojo. But now . . . now, it's what *I'm* good at." And she began to cry, long lusty sobs that broke his heart, even though he had no idea in hell what she was talking about.

"Kyra . . . , sweetheart, you're not making sense."

But he couldn't get anything else out of her; she just cried quietly, tears slipping down her face. Even though he didn't like to risk staying the night here—let alone three nights like they'd planned— because Steve might have called in their location, he couldn't just bundle her into the Marquis and take off. He didn't know where they were going for one thing. Reyes was sure she had some destination in mind, however meandering their route had been thus far.

Morning light would have to be soon enough. He'd stay awake in case of trouble. Kyra let him brush her teeth and comb her hair. It wasn't a shower, but he didn't think she needed to be handled further in her condition. He'd never seen anything like it, except in women who survived the harshest battlefield conditions, and possibly . . . those who'd been raped.

But the bastard hadn't done that. Reyes was sure he'd gotten there in time. Puzzled, he lifted her into his arms and took her back to the bedroom. This bed had been violated, though, so he carried her on through to the connecting room. He went back for her stuff and locked the door from his side. They wouldn't be going back in there.

Kyra had a thing about being touched, he reasoned. Maybe having a strange man break into her bedroom and grab her had all the traumatic weight of a rape. Reyes settled against the headboard and pulled her into his arms. She didn't fight him, just settled her head on his chest. His heart gave a queer squeeze.

"I don't understand what's wrong," he finally whispered. "And I can't help if I don't understand. I feel like I'm missing something here. Can you explain?"

"You'd never believe me."

"Maybe I'll surprise you."

"You always surprise me," she admitted. She finally sounded close to coherent. "I'm sorry about your dinner. Sometimes I can't help it. Touching the wrong people makes me sick."

Reyes couldn't believe she'd just apologized for puking. He waved that away, feeling like he was on the verge of figuring her out. She'd said, *Now it's what I'm best at,* after the guy had touched her. Reyes had forgotten something key, but he couldn't put his finger on it, and it would be better if she confided in him.

"Tell me why."

CHAPTER 15

Kyra closed her eyes. Maybe that would make it easier. After everything she'd put him through tonight, she owed him an explanation.

"It doesn't work with you anymore," she began. "But the first time I touched you, I stole your ability to fight. You may even have noticed the theft, felt sick or slightly dazed. Sometimes people do, depending on their sensitivity. The loss isn't permanent . . . I never know how long I'll have a talent, so I generally work fast after I've tapped a mark."

She felt him stiffen against her and waited for the derision. When she was a kid, she'd confided in a couple of people, despite her dad's insistence it was a bad idea and would cost them their edge in the game, but it never worked out. They always thought she was a liar, and over the years, she'd stopped trying.

"So . . . I *didn't* imagine it," he said slowly.

She lifted her head, surprised. "You noticed."

"I did, the first few times. But it started to slack off, and then eventually, nothing happened at all, so I thought I'd hallucinated the whole thing."

Kyra looked puzzled. "That's new. I've never had it stop working before."

"Which means you can't touch without stealing something."

"Yeah." He couldn't know how depressing that thought became. "And if I make contact with too many marks, take in too much, it feels like my head's going to explode."

"That's why you're so careful about touching people."

"I can't believe you haven't said I'm crazy yet." She shook her head.

"Well..." He smiled. "You are, but not because of this. I'll be honest . . . if I hadn't noticed some of this stuff on my own, I wouldn't believe you. But you've given me proof that's hard to deny. You kicked that guy's ass in the convenience store using *my* moves. There's no way you could've learned those independently. You hardly knew me."

"You saw that." She sat up. "How come you didn't help me?"

"It seemed like you had the situation under control." Rey sank his hands into her hair, smoothing it gently with his fingers. "So this . . . ability . . . how does it work? Is it random? Do you have any idea why you can do this?"

"Based on what I've figured out by trial and error, I get whatever the other person's best at. In your case, that's combat." She leveled a long look on him. "Since this is out in the open now, we're going to talk about *why* that is, at some point. The duration might be random for all I know. I tried timing it at first to see if that made a difference, but the results came back so varied, I didn't learn much. Now I just work fast and hope for the best."

"There's some adrenaline in that," he noted.

"Yeah," she admitted. "There is. I like the risk and the rush. Will I get the job done before I lose it?"

"That's how you manage the pool and darts hustle," he realized aloud. "You seem so unskilled in the first few matches because you really are. Genius."

Kyra nodded, wondering if he would put the rest together. "As long as I don't repeat the game in the same place, it works like a charm. Keeps me from honest work."

"But it also makes it impossible for you to settle down."

She gave him a look. "Do I look like I *want* to?"

"Point taken." Rey's dark brows drew together, and she could almost see him tracking through everything that had happened. "The biker who broke in . . . you said—"

Kyra nodded.

"I let a rapist go, didn't I?" He swore, low and virulent in some mixture of Spanish and Portuguese. "If I'd known, I never would have. . . ." Rey broke off, as apparently something else occurred to him. "You felt what he's best at. Is it still with you? Christ, no *wonder* you were sick."

"No." She shook her head. "It's been gone for a little while now, just residual nausea left. Staying power isn't his forte."

"I'll track him down if you want. I don't care how long it takes."

Tempting. She hated to think of the son of a bitch hurting other women. But she couldn't afford to backtrack to Texas, and she didn't want to send Rey away at this point. In a few more days, they'd be in North Dakota, where she'd find Mia, and then . . . well, she'd see. But she had a gnawing impulse to ask Rey to go away with her, someplace warm and sunny that didn't put U.S. extradition high on their priority list.

She thought about what he'd said to Steve. "What do you think Dwight's going to do when he gets your message?"

Rey started to smile. "If he's as dumb as I think he is, he'll shoot the messenger and ignore everything he said."

"I live in hope."

This would be the perfect time to tell him everything, but she wasn't ready. Trust didn't come easy to her, and she wasn't about to put all her eggs in one basket, in case he turned out to be different than she thought. Money talked a good game, and while Rey might sneer at a small-time punk, Serrano was in a different league. He could lay down serious currency.

"This means we need to watch our backs," he was saying. "We might have more assholes coming, and he was right about your car. It's memorable. If they have people looking, they'll spot us pretty fast. I don't suppose you'd consider trading it in?"

"I'd rather die."

"Hope it doesn't come to that," he muttered. "If you're

feeling up to it, we should pack and get on the road. We may have people heading for us as we speak."

In answer, she slid out of bed and started gathering up her stuff. The room next door was trashed, so she left some cash on the night table to cover the damage. She didn't intend to discuss the issue with the night manager. Within five minutes, they were ready to roll out.

Rey jingled her car keys. "Me or you, sweetheart?"

Until meeting him, she'd always hated endearments because they were either meaningless or representative of emotional entanglements she couldn't experience. For the first time, she felt like she might matter to somebody else. And she liked it.

"You can," she said. "I'm still a little shaky. I better not be driving if I have to hurl again."

"Is that likely?" He looked a little worried.

"Hope not. But I wouldn't know. Never run across anybody like him before."

Kyra hoped she never did again. Words couldn't describe the horror of someone who gloried in his ability to use his body to inflict pain. The bastard liked it and knew he was good at it, a real virtuoso in fact. He'd been thinking about doing it to her right up until he laid hands on her. A hard breath shuddered through her, and she fought the feeling that he'd contaminated her somehow, deep in places where she could never scrub it out.

"You're okay," Rey said quietly. "Now come on, let's get out of here."

It wasn't even dawn as they crept out of his room, bags shouldered. She'd collected all the supplies—like the spices—that would travel well. Maybe he could cook for her again. There was something homey about a meal somebody made for you, even if he cooked it in a cheap motel kitchenette. If anyone had asked her if she craved home cooking, Kyra would've said no—but now that she'd tasted it, she wouldn't mind seconds, preferably under circumstances where she got to digest the food. She'd liked watching him work, knowing he was doing it to impress her.

Nobody else was stirring as they slid into the Marquis. Kyra watched the lot every bit as carefully as Rey at this point. After tossing their things in back, he hopped in, stuck the key in the ignition, and they were off toward the lightening horizon.

"Where are we headed?"

She could tell him that much. "Do you know how to get to I-76 from here?"

"Yeah."

"Head for it. We didn't get much sleep, so we won't drive far today. I'm thinking we'll stop in Alliance, Nebraska, and try to get some rest. From there, it's Sioux Falls, and then Fargo."

"So that's our final destination."

"Yep." She wasn't telling him why. "I don't think we should take two rooms anymore. We can get two beds if you prefer, but it would be safer if we stayed close."

"That's true," he agreed. "But let me ask you this . . . are you out of your mind?" His tone was level, almost pleasant, belying the sharp words.

She glanced at him in surprise. "Huh?"

"You've been teasing me longer than any woman has a right to. *Now* you ask if I prefer two beds? No. I want you under me. I want to wake up smelling you on my skin. Is that clear enough?"

"I don't think it's normal for you to feel like that. You just saw me puke." *Jesus.* She couldn't believe she'd just said that. *Why bring it up? Let him forget, for fuck's sake.*

"We're not exactly poster children for normal, are we? Get some sleep."

Kyra balled one of his sweatshirts to make a pillow, and it took her all of three minutes to fall asleep. Reyes could follow the signs to Nebraska, no problem. But could he still kill her? This was the first time since he'd gone into the business that he'd run into trouble completing a contracted assignment, but he was sure Foster had lied about her. There wasn't a vicious bone in her body. Sure, she could be wicked, but cruelty was a different instinct.

She hadn't stolen the money, either; Reyes was positive

of that now. Kyra was a con artist, not a thief, and she used her unique ability to power her games. Given what he knew of her, he'd bet she had won the money, maybe not fairly, but it was hers. He didn't know why Serrano was so determined to see her dead for it. Given his personal wealth, he could afford to shrug off a couple mil. He'd make it back in less than a week.

So it had to be something more. It rankled him that she hadn't confided in him when he'd tried so damn hard to be receptive. His first instinct had been to call bullshit, but he'd restrained it, telling himself to hear her out. By the time she was done, he had to admit her story made a crazy kind of sense and dovetailed with what he knew of her. Trouble was, he didn't know enough.

For one thing, he had no idea why they were stopping in Alliance, Nebraska. He'd never heard of the place, and couldn't imagine it would be big enough to support a con. They hadn't made any money in Denver, either. On the surface, Kyra had shared a lot with him. When you took a closer look, she'd told him just enough to shut him up.

Frustrating.

Reyes drove in silence. Every now and then, his gaze slid to the woman slumped in the passenger seat. In sleep, she seemed smaller somehow, stripped of the attitude that gave her presence. He realized how much weight she carried alone . . . and her shoulders looked downright fragile. Even the smattering of freckles on her cheeks made her look younger, more vulnerable.

She'd hate him thinking along those lines so he kept his eyes on the road. Things greened up as the day wore on. The closer they got to Nebraska, the more farmland surrounded the road. As they crossed the state line, Reyes read the sign "Welcome to Nebraska, the good life," with an ironic quirk of his mouth. He couldn't ever recall visiting this particular state, surely for good reason.

In late morning, Kyra stirred.

"Are we almost there?" she asked sleepily.

He'd been seeing signs for a while now, driving well over four hours without a break. His legs were screaming, as were his shoulders, and Reyes wouldn't mind a pit stop, but they were within reasonable distance now. He didn't like getting off the highway unless he had no choice.

"I think so. Thirty more miles according to the last sign. Are you good for it?"

Kyra considered. "I could use a bathroom, but I can wait. We'll be looking for the Sunset Motel, by the way."

Yet another seedy fleabag, he guessed. What he wouldn't give to take her to a five-star resort somewhere. Lately, he'd been enjoying a fantasy about them sunning on a white, sand beach together somewhere with a waiter bringing frozen drinks on demand.

"I'll keep an eye out."

She shifted in her seat, crooking her knee toward him. Reyes felt her studying his profile in an odd prickle of awareness. Out of the corner of his eye, he could see the tear in her jeans, revealing a shapely knee.

"I never said thanks," she said softly.

"For what?"

She tugged at raveling strands of worn denim. "Taking care of me. It's rarely been that bad. Usually I can deal with it, no big."

Instinctively he knew he needed to answer right, not too much weight, not too much levity. "I won't say it was nothing. You freaked me out. But I suspect being good to you will have its rewards."

Her lips curled into a feline smile. "You know, you're right about that. I'm thinking what I put you through last night counts as working for what you want, probably harder than a man should have to. Don't worry, Rey. I'll make it worth your while."

"I have no doubt." A billboard caught his eye. "I think we're coming up on our exit in a few miles. What's so special about this place? Do you have business here?"

She shook her head. "No, this is vacation. Business starts up again in Sioux Falls. Ever heard of Carhenge?"

Reyes lofted a brow. "Ah, no."

"Basically, this family made a replica of Stonehenge out of wrecked cars. It's a memorial for the guy's dad. They did it on their farm, and at first the town council tried to shut them down. But now it's a tourist attraction, and there's a society dedicated to preserving the place. They used a 1962 Caddy as the heel car," she added with visible enthusiasm.

He understood the appeal of it for her now: rebel spirit, memorial to one's father, and cars. "Sounds interesting."

"I've always wanted to see it . . . and I figured since it was kind of on the way . . ." Kyra bit her lip, adorable in her uncertainty, although she wouldn't like to hear that. "Well, I kind of wanted to share it with you. I mean, you probably think it's dumb—"

"No," he cut in, oddly touched. "I think I'd like to see it, especially if it's important to you."

"I wish I could do something like this for my dad," she went on. "But this place is special because the guy's dad used to live here. We don't have anything like it . . . we never stayed in one place long."

Yeah, he'd gathered as much. "Maybe there will be something you can do on-site, something to commemorate him."

Her smile radiated so much frank gratitude it almost tore out his heart. "Let's get a room first. From the motel, it's less than three miles. They're open daily during sunlight hours."

It wasn't difficult to find the Sunset Motel, which aimed for quaint more than sleazy. He supposed that made sense, given its proximity to an Americana attraction. They got a room without trouble and stashed their things. If he didn't quite like it, he was getting used to constant travel, but he wouldn't mind visiting a Laundromat. That concern would be out of character, however. A vagabond like he purported to be would just hose things off in the shower and hope for the best.

When he let them into their room, his gaze focused on the bed, one queen, more than adequate to accommodate them in any position she wanted. Reyes stifled a groan. Instead of wrecked cars, he'd rather see her naked. He tossed down their bags and visited the bathroom. As he washed up, he hardly knew the man in the mirror.

Reyes hadn't worn jeans and T-shirts of his own free will since he could afford better. Dressing like this reminded him of wearing cast-off clothing because Cesar didn't see anything wrong with telling anyone who would listen that his kid was growing so quick he couldn't keep him in pants. He'd never known—or maybe cared—how much it stung to know nothing he'd touched had ever been bought just for him.

Fuck it. Clothes didn't make the man. He needed to call Foster to placate him, but his phone was in the other room. If he went out to get it and then went back into the bathroom, it would look suspicious. He'd come too far in her esteem to jeopardize it now. It was only a matter of time until she confided in him completely. And then he could figure out the best way out of this mess, maybe some compromise that would satisfy Serrano, safeguard his own reputation for getting the job done, and leave Kyra her life.

At least that was what he told himself as he blotted his face dry. He could use a shave, but that could wait, too, preferably until just before he made love to her. If she could take a vacation, so could he.

Kyra took her turn, and when she came out, he saw she'd brushed her hair and put on some lipstick. The paint on her mouth made her eyes look that much more innocent in comparison, and he didn't understand it at all. How could someone who lived like she did have such an unsullied soul?

Reyes held out a hand. "You ready to check this place out?"

CHAPTER 16

Carhenge was everything Kyra expected.

It had a campy Americana charm, but she found herself reluctantly impressed by the precision of the replication. She'd never been to Stonehenge, but she'd seen pictures. Rey seemed a little bemused by the idea of a monument like this erected in a random field, but he was patient with her desire to wander around.

A man at a souvenir shop down the road told them they held pagan celebrations, music festivals, poetry readings, and of course, the occasional car show here. Kyra bought a T-shirt and tried to forget what'd happened earlier. Unfortunately, when her gift went wrong, it went *way* wrong.

The site had picnic tables, so they bought lunch and came back. As the day wore on, other tourists showed up to check things out, but nobody tried to make conversation. Kyra stifled a smile over that, but Rey didn't look particularly approachable, even in direct sunlight while eating corn on the cob. Right then, she could almost forget all the complications in her life.

She'd never felt this kind of warmth directed at one man. When he turned his head, the sun gleaming on blue highlights in his dark hair, heat coiled in her stomach. His sharp features no longer looked fearsome, only sweetly familiar. Her heart felt strange, a little too large for her chest, when he smiled at her.

They spent almost the whole day, doing nothing in particular. She knew he was trying to give her a good day to make up for what she'd gone through this morning, and she appreciated it. He had to be bored, but she felt weirdly close to her dad as she walked around the attraction.

While she considered that, he cleaned up the remnants of their picnic and then jogged over to a trash can. He paused on the way back to talk with an older man who wore a Carhenge hat. Kyra watched them, knees drawn up to her chest.

Rey came back in a few minutes later. "If you apply for a Friends of Carhenge membership, you can sponsor one of the Aubrey holes and name it after your dad."

"Really?" For reasons she couldn't explain, this would mean a lot more than a simple engraved stone.

"Yeah. If you want to come over here and spend fifteen minutes with this guy, we can take care of it right now."

Her smile of thanks felt strange and tremulous. "Thanks for checking on it."

Half an hour later, they climbed into the Marquis with a receipt and a promise that the job would be done. She felt at peace for the first time in longer than she could recall, and Kyra knew she could thank the man beside her for that. As she drove back to the motel, she smiled. He was tough, no question, but he had a tender side, too.

"What?"

"Just thinking about how lucky you're getting tonight."

He grinned. "I still have two-thirds of the condoms I bought in Louisiana."

As she pulled into the parking lot, she slid him a serious look. "I'm glad fate brought us together again. I can't remember when I've been this happy."

A shadow flickered in his dark eyes. "Me, either. Let's go upstairs."

The stark, sensual lines of his mouth told her there wouldn't be any teasing this time. He wanted her as much as she wanted him, and Kyra found that reassuring. Rey took her hand and led her to their room. They'd just tossed their bags inside the door, and he swept them aside with a foot as he tugged her through the door.

He bent, rummaging for the aforementioned condoms and tossed the box on the bedside table. She had enough presence of mind to pull the curtains and put the chain on the door, but then his hands slid over her hips, drawing her to him for a long, drugging kiss. As soon as his lips touched hers, pure lightning crashed through her. Kyra ran her hands over his hot, hard chest, up and over his shoulders. Her nails dug in as he nipped her lower lip, demanding a deeper taste of her.

By the time he broke away long minutes later, they were both trembling. She gloried in the fact that his hands weren't steady as he pulled her shirt over her head. Kyra wriggled out of her jeans on her own, leaving her clad in peach panties and a matching camisole. His gaze found the dusky points of her nipples through the satin, and she felt the look between her thighs.

Kyra pulled the cami over her head and tossed it toward a chair. His touch skimmed upward over her ribs, hesitating only a few seconds before closing on her breasts. It wasn't a fierce touch, more reverently possessive, as if he were acknowledging something beautiful that belonged to him. She knew she should be worried or offended, but she couldn't resist the seduction of his hands. Rey rubbed his thumbs back and forth across her nipples, abrading them, but he knew not to pinch. Instead he tugged with tender fingertips, mimicking suction.

Her breath went in a shuddering rush. She needed his mouth there. As if in answer, he bent his head, laving her nipple in a tight circle, then he bit, lightly. *Yes, like that.* Kyra swayed, breathless with the delicious contrast between demand and delicacy.

"We're going to slow things down now," he murmured in a black velvet voice. "Lay back."

Instinctively, she wanted to protest. She didn't need foreplay, but by the look in Rey's eyes, there would be no arguing with him today. Kyra sank onto the bed, conscious of every angle and curve. His dark gaze seemed to skim her skin, touching the lees and hollows of her body.

"Want me?" she whispered.

He didn't waste words. Instead the heat of his mouth brushed the inner curve of her ankle, a delicate kiss that curled her toes. Kyra spread her legs, stifling a moan. She knew where he was heading, but nobody had ever done it before. Men didn't tend to waste such niceties on a woman they picked up for the night.

His teeth followed his lips, grazing a path up the curve of her calf. When he licked the soft skin behind her knee, Kyra lifted her hips. It was impossible not to imagine his mouth at work elsewhere, devouring her with the complete intensity and focus he dedicated to every task. Levering up on her elbows, she reached out to touch his head, smoothing the raven strands.

"Close your eyes," he whispered. "I don't want you watching me. I want you *feeling*."

"Oh, I am." A shiver swept over her, but she did as he asked.

Everything intensified when her lashes swept down. Flashes of sensation punctuated the darkness, and her world centered on the gifted mouth now nuzzling her inner thighs. Rey fastened his teeth gently on the skin and tugged, then swirled his tongue in lazy circles. Heat and dampness contrasted with the rasp of his jaw.

A little moan escaped her as he licked along the edge of her panties. Hoping he'd take the hint, she lifted her hips again. This time, he slid them down her thighs and off to join her clothes on the floor. Dimly she realized she was naked, and he was fully clothed. There was a certain titillation in that awareness.

When his fingers grazed her labia, she stiffened a little. She'd thought he would use his mouth, but what he was doing felt good, so she stayed quiet. Rey pressed and caressed her outwardly until she felt a steady stream of moisture within. The longer he delayed touching her more intimately, the more sensitized she felt. With what felt like thumb and forefinger, he massaged her lips until she found her pelvis rising and falling, trying to force a little contact with her aching clitoris.

Kyra moaned as he shifted and a phantom flare of heat

traced along her folds. By the time his mouth graduated from teasing to greedy, she'd come unhinged. Her hips bucked and she tangled her hands in his hair. He worked his tongue against her, licking up and down everywhere but the spot she wanted it most. She tried to raise his head up, but he seemed determined to drive her out of her mind.

"Come on," she begged. "Finish me."

Silky hair brushed her thighs when he slid upward. Strong hands cupped her ass, lifting her to his mouth like a pagan sacrifice. Kyra's thighs spilled open, and she had no hope of hiding anything from him. His lips closed on her clit, firm, soft, heated. Each pull made her writhe against him, utterly open, taken by his lips and tongue to a place where she could only thrash and groan, beyond speech.

Orgasm broke upon her hard, leaving her shivering in his arms. The waves went on and on, subtly enhanced by the magic of his mouth. He whispered to her in languages she didn't know. When she opened her eyes long minutes later, his hands were on her back, stroking her as if she were a wild thing he had to tame.

Kyra felt like she should say something poetic, but that wasn't her style. Instead, she offered, "Those pants have to be strangling you by now. Wanna take 'em off?"

Hell, yeah. **She** lay there like a contented kitten while he stripped out of his jeans. Her tawny eyes following his every move reinforced the feline image. He'd loved watching her unguarded emotions while he touched her. That was why he'd demanded she close her eyes, so that barrier would drop. It had been even better than he'd imagined, and over the last few weeks, he'd imagined a lot.

Need ricocheted through him—and that was exactly why he couldn't take her right now. Reyes left his boxers on out of self-defense. She might take his decision for tenderness or consideration, but it was more basic than that. His response to her pleasure had rocked him too much. For an agonizing moment, he'd feared he would come, too. That gave her an unacceptable level of influence over him, compromising his ability to make good decisions. Therefore, he had to prove to himself he was still in charge, both of his emotions and this operation. Things had gotten murky; time to clear them up.

So Reyes wrapped his arms around her and tucked her close. Kyra gazed up at him with sleepy eyes. "Not tonight, you have a headache?"

"No," he said quietly. "I'm going to let you recharge for a little while. There's no rush. We have all night, right?"

Her lips curved into a heartbreakingly sweet smile. "Right."

Kyra spooned up against him, back to his chest, and tucked her sweet little ass against his dick. At first he thought she was wiggling to try to drive him nuts, but eventually he realized she'd been trying to get closer to him. She nestled her head beneath his chin and sighed softly.

Reyes sensed the moment she drifted off, languid and warm. Next to her, he felt like a live wire, every nerve jumping, but he wouldn't be ruled by his emotions or his urges. When he took her, it would be controlled and methodical. It would serve his purposes, not simple biology. Through force of will, he relaxed his body by muscle groups and then he too closed his eyes and slept.

When he woke, he realized with crystalline clarity that he'd never have detachment where she was concerned. His dick still felt diamond-hard, nestled up against her ass. If he had to wait another minute to get inside her, he'd die. His hands shook as he reached behind him for a condom. He pulled his penis through the slit in his boxers. The packet crinkled as he tore it open and rolled the latex on.

She murmured a little in her sleep at his movements; the idea of waking her with an orgasm had him nearly ready to come, added to the previous stimulation. Damn, she'd tasted sweet, and she felt even better. He brushed his fingertips between her labia and found that she was still wet, still warm. *Good.* She must be enjoying her dreams.

With a gentle hand, he tilted her hips, lifted one of her legs gently, and pushed into her from behind, inch by tantalizing inch. She gave a little whine, almost in protest, but he thought that came from the excruciatingly slow speed of his penetration.

He'd never made love to a woman soft with sleep before. Reyes always woke them up before pouncing like a tiger, giving them the opportunity to say no; he liked it hard and rough with plenty of teeth. Given his general preferences and his history, it was safer to acquire consent beforehand—and just because a woman said yes once that night, it didn't guarantee her cooperation again. They'd done it that way the first night, but nothing had gone as planned with her since.

Tonight, however, he trusted that she wanted him. Alarm and excitement warred for supremacy as he began to move, gentle strokes into her that made him feel as though *she* did the taking, sinking hooks deep into his heart. Reyes ran his hands over her body, caressing her breasts and belly until she arched beneath his hands like a cat.

He knew the instant she roused to full wakefulness, swiftly confirmed by her murmured, "Mmm. So it's *not* a dream."

"No," he managed huskily.

"That's good. Can we . . .?" In answer, he angled her hips slightly, pushing her forward for stronger thrusts. "Yeah, that. Exactly."

His breath came faster as he took her with fierce tenderness. He had to be closer than she was so he found her clit with his fingers, jacking her intensity to match his own. They came together, shuddering, with only the quiet rasp of their breathing to mark the moment. It surprised him how much he wanted to hear his name on her lips . . . and she didn't even know, at least not in its entirety. He'd almost forgotten his name wasn't Rey.

Reyes rolled away to dispose of the condom, and then he reached for her again, so needy that it frightened him. She curled into him, arm across his waist. It wasn't that he wanted to screw her again—although he did—it was that he simply craved her closeness. He wanted to lie with her in the half-light and listen to her breathe, inhaling her scent.

It was totally fucked up. Now he could only see one way to end her, assuming he wanted to complete the job. He'd cup her head in his hands, bestow one final kiss, and then twist. Clean. Fast. She wouldn't feel much pain. Contrary to what he'd thought before, it *had* to be up close and personal, however great his distaste.

He didn't want to, but he'd taken money for this job. He couldn't throw away years of work, establishing himself as *the* go-to man who always got the job done. He couldn't walk away from this job with his reputation intact; Foster would see to that.

Maybe there was some middle ground, some acceptable compromise.

But he doubted it.

No, if he let Kyra live, he had to commit to her cause. It would be all or nothing. Could he do that for a con woman with even less a sense of responsibility than *he* had? Did he want to?

"That was amazing," she said dreamily, rubbing her cheek against his chest.

Reyes gazed down at her face, studying the fans her lashes made against freckled cheeks. "I hope you didn't mind . . . I couldn't wait for you to wake up."

She smiled. "I think that's the nicest thing anybody ever said to me."

His heart clenched. "That's pretty sad."

Her expression clouded. "It is, isn't it?" Kyra dipped her chin, hiding her face from him then. Her words came out soft and abashed, muffled by his skin. "I think I'm falling in love with you. I'm probably not supposed to say it first because you'll get all panicky thinking about mortgages or something, but . . . it's true. And I get fed up with telling people what they want to hear. I won't do that with you."

Each word struck him like a fist in the chest, and he couldn't get his breath, not because he was freaked out by the idea of a mortgage—he owned his condo free and clear—but she'd given of herself so freely when he knew how closely she guarded her emotions. Hell, she wasn't even used to being touched.

And he was going to use that against her.

"Are you saying you trust me?" he asked quietly.

Kyra considered that and then nodded. "Yeah. You've been straight with me, told me things nobody else knows about you. You saved my life, and you listened when everyone else thinks I'm full of shit."

"Then don't you think it's time you leveled with me?" It was a calculated risk, but there would never come a more opportune moment.

"What makes you think I haven't?" She immediately went on the defensive, a tactic most liars utilized.

"Your eyes slide ever so slightly over my left shoulder instead of making direct contact when you lie." He'd noticed she didn't do it with other people, which told him she didn't enjoy deceiving him. "If you don't want to tell me, that's fine. I'm just somebody you picked up along the road, but realize I know you haven't been honest with me." Now she'd think he hadn't confessed like feelings due to her lack of faith in him. Reyes understood how women thought, and he held the silence and then added, "You know what? Never mind. It doesn't matter."

"Yes, it does," she said. "You're right. I have my reasons for keeping quiet, nothing to do with you. But know this . . . you're *not* a throwaway fuck to me."

He gathered her close. "You aren't to me, either."

It wasn't a declaration of love, but it was the closest she'd ever get from him. Now the seeds had been planted; he just needed to wait for them to bear fruit.

CHAPTER 17

Serrano never put all his eggs in one basket.

He would've given a lot to see Foster's face when the man realized he knew about his secret visits to the nursing home; then he'd know exactly how valuable the information was. Regardless, it never hurt to have leverage over somebody. He couldn't have Foster thinking he ran things. Trouble started that way.

Foster's efficiency couldn't be questioned, however. Serrano already had a dossier on his desk, detailing Ricci and Pasternak's financial peccadilloes. He skimmed, underlining the more interesting transactions. Then he tapped his pen, thoughtful. There was something almost erotic about controlling someone else's fate. He didn't let himself think past that because he'd had some ridiculous, romantic idea about marrying a woman who was a virgin on their wedding night. Ruthlessly, he refocused his attention, refusing to acknowledge the bitter humiliation that lay beneath the surface.

Based on the patterns, it looked to him like the idiots at the Pair-A-Dice were laundering for somebody. Just as well, they lacked the brains to succeed at anything requiring more initiative. If he could figure out who they worked for, it might be more fun—and more devastating—to wreck that relationship. The IRS would mean possible jail time and loss of revenue, but criminals . . . well, they could be real animals.

Serrano smiled as an idea came to him. He rang through to his assistant and told her, "Hold my calls and cancel my ten-thirty. I don't want to see anyone today."

"Even Mr. Foster? He'll be up in the evening to check in with you before he takes over for the night."

"Yeah, even Foster. As far as the world's concerned, I'm in Barbados."

"Very good, sir."

He made a few calls and worked through lunch. The faxes started coming through around noon, sources that owed him money and knew they'd better keep him happy. Serrano had Sandy bring him a sandwich and kept digging. A good brain had separated him from the rest of the punks in Philly, which was why they were dead and he was rich.

By half past five, he had a good idea who Pasternak and Ricci worked for. He gathered up all the financial documents—illegal, of course—and stashed them in a briefcase, intending to have someone reputable validate his conclusions. At this hour, he knew where to find Bobby.

Next, Serrano grabbed his coat and shrugged into it on the way out the door. Sandy had gone home at five, after poking a nervous head in the door to say good-bye to him. Generally, he would wait around until Foster arrived in the evening, exchange info, and then he'd head for home himself. Tonight he had another destination in mind.

His driver came out of the bar as Serrano strode toward the doors. He shook his head at Tonio. "I won't need you. You can take the night off."

"Really? Sweet." The other man returned the way he'd come, presumably to finish a conversation he'd abandoned when he heard Serrano was on the way down.

In the garage, the limo was parked next to his silver Lexus SC430. He had a whole section devoted to his cars, as he occupied the top floor of the casino. Tonight flash would be important, however. Sliding behind the wheel of an expensive sports car always made him appreciate every dime.

Traffic was heavy since he'd come out near rush hour.

With the light spiking crimson over the palms, he made his way to a club at the outskirts of town. No tourist would ever find this place. From the outside, it looked like an office building—no neon, no flashing dice, no showgirls in silhouette, just a low-rise white building with mirrored windows. You had to flash a membership card to get into the lot, and if you got close to the building, it simply read "Farraday's" in elegant copperplate on the brass plaque.

Serrano flashed his card again at the door, where a uniformed servant became obsequious at seeing the VIP symbol beside his name. "The dining room just opened, sir. For dinner tonight we have lamb with rosemary-mint sauce."

That sounded good, but he hadn't come for dinner. Whether he stayed depended on how his errand went. "Is Bobby here?"

"At his usual table, sir."

He smiled his thanks and stepped past into an open space that borrowed heavily from exclusive gentleman's clubs so popular in Victorian times. From the subtly patterned rug to the maroon leather chairs and heavy paneling, you expected to be surrounded with men in bowlers, bristling with mutton chops. Instead the patrons all shared a certain sharkish slickness.

Serrano let his eyes adjust to the contrast between sunset brightness and oblique light thrown from strategically placed sconces. He found Bobby Rabinowitz without difficulty. The man was short and round with a balding fringe so neat it could've been a tonsure. In different times he would surely be wearing a rough brown robe and skimming from the parish take.

Black framed spectacles sat on a short, broad nose, and rosacea spattered his round cheeks. He was also one of the few people who looked genuinely delighted anytime Gerard Serrano entered a room. He should since he'd been doing his books for the last ten years—and had made a pretty penny off them.

"Ger," Rabinowitz said, half-standing from the padded leather chair. "This is an unexpected pleasure. Please, sit. Do we have business?"

Serrano patted his briefcase as he complied. "We do. But it can wait until you finish your dinner."

"Have you eaten? The lamb is to die for."

"I could eat," he admitted.

His accountant signaled for another plate. This wasn't the kind of place where they offered a menu. If a person wanted buffet choices, he could go elsewhere. For the best cuts of meat and exquisite side dishes, a man came to Farraday's, if he could afford the annual membership.

A waiter spread a snowy white napkin in his lap, something that always made Serrano slightly uneasy. The wrong sort of guy could take advantage of that proximity, and not just in a gay way. It would be fast and easy to slip up to somebody, stoop to serve, and stick a knife in his neck. He didn't relax until the man moved off by a good ten feet, leaving him with Bobby.

Rabinowitz waited until they'd brought him a plate of lamb with artichoke and new potatoes on the side and then resumed his own meal. They made small talk while they ate, as he'd learned the hard way that gentlemen never put business before good food. There was a time and place for such things; money matters went perfectly with cigars and cognac, for instance.

After they cleared the table, Serrano lit up a Black Dragon cigar and leaned back in his chair, exhaling in a perfect circle. Bobby enjoyed that little trick. The bean counter didn't smoke, but he liked the smell.

"So what did you bring me?" Rabinowitz asked, practically rubbing his hands together. "Fodder for a tax shelter? Shell corporation? Dummy import/export business? I could use something juicy. Work's been dull lately."

"I think," he said, pushing the briefcase across the table, "this might be better."

Bobby snatched it up, nearly pegging a waiter who'd brought a silver tray full of coffee fixings and flavored liqueurs. Serrano accepted a shot of espresso and waved the rest away. He sat, patient, while the other man read.

At last Rabinowitz looked up. "Where did you get all this?"

He raised his brows. "You really want to know?"

"Better if I don't, actually, so I'll ask a different question. To whom do these records pertain?"

"Ricci and Pasternak."

"So you figured out that they're working for the Armenians now?"

"I wasn't sure. I wanted you to double-check the paper trail. I might make a mistake in following the patterns, but you never do."

The other man looked positively cherubic. "Everybody has a gift. That's mine. But damn . . . the Armenians—"

"Split from Odessa in 2006," he supplied. "Odessa has San Fran locked up. The Armenians took L.A., and they're rolling east."

The other man whistled. "Shit. This is a landmine, Ger. If we found this info, anybody else could. It could start a real bloody turf war, if the wrong people found out. What do you want to do about it?"

The old Vegas was gone, no question. Mobsters no longer ran the casinos, at least on paper. Everything was corporate-held, but corporations had officers; there was a hierarchy, in fact, and Bobby Rabinowitz was his CFO on paper. A guy could order his business according to the old ways if he wanted to, give thugs titles such as, Vice President of Marketing for breaking heads, and pay everybody a fat executive salary.

"An excellent question," he said, smiling. "But I have some ideas."

As Rabinowitz ate a slice of pie, he outlined them.

Mia Sauter looked as lovely as she had the day before, but this time she sported a lemon pantsuit paired with a retro silk blouse. On anyone else, the pattern would be too bold, but with her dark coloring, she pulled it off. She wore her lustrous dark hair pulled into a complex and daring chignon, no doubt intending to convey the message that she intended to be all business with him, but she was showing a little too much cleavage for the hairstyle to be compellingly persuasive.

"I don't remember agreeing to date you," Mia snapped, as Foster strode up.

He didn't smile. "This isn't a date. We broke off our discussion yesterday so you could sleep, and I worked last night. Today we should be able to complete our business."

For the last five minutes, he'd watched her waiting with ill-concealed impatience outside the Venetian. She was agitated; he could tell that. Despite what he'd said the day before, he hadn't terminated their discussion due to her exhaustion. Foster had wanted to give her another day to stew, worrying about what might be happening to her friend. It was a trouble-free way to soften her up. He always liked to begin negotiations from a position of strength.

He signaled the valet, who hadn't even bothered to park his car. Foster tipped him well and set off without waiting to see whether Mia would follow. The answer was obvious, and when she slammed into the car beside him, he smiled. Since he kept it well maintained, the Altima purred to life.

"I'm starting to actively dislike you," she muttered.

"And here I've gone to such trouble to make myself pleasant," he returned with a delicately ironic inflection. "I hate wasted effort."

She subsided into silence that might have seemed sullen if he hadn't caught her twisting her purse straps in a subtle manifestation of her anxiety. Good. That meant Mia took the situation seriously. She *should*. They left the Strip behind, taking Las Vegas Boulevard to Flamingo and then he headed for I-15.

"Where are we going?"

Given how much trouble her friend was in, she'd trusted him too readily. Lucky for her, damage to Mia Sauter didn't fit into his agenda. No, she was a means to an end.

"My apartment," he said briefly.

"No. Oh no. I want to do this somewhere public. For all I know, Kyra went off with you and nobody's seen her since."

Foster smiled. "You should have thought of that before you got into my car."

He accelerated as they merged onto the interstate. Beside him, she stiffened, dark eyes wide and livid with fear. "Stop. Pull over and let me out."

"You know I can't do that." Foster pointed at a "no stopping, standing, or parking" sign as they blew past. "Not here. Shortly I'll be taking 215 toward McCarran. From there I'll exit at Stephanie Street, which is about a mile from my apartment. If you still want to leave, I'll drop you off at a gas station. I'm not going to make you talk to me."

"You promise?"

What value she thought his promises had, Foster couldn't imagine, but he nodded nonetheless. Her panic seemed to scale back. He drove in silence, tracking her body language in his peripheral vision.

"We're almost there," he said eventually. "Are we doing this or not?"

Mia parried with: "Why does it have to be your apartment?"

"Honestly? It's the one place I'm sure we won't be overheard. And I can't risk being seen with you." It was an intentional swipe at her feminine vanity, but she didn't respond to that portion of what he'd said.

"You think somebody might be spying on you?"

"I have reliable evidence," he muttered, thinking of his monitored visits.

"Then it has to be your place," she decided. "I can't put Kyra at risk."

Nice. Loyal.

In response, he navigated the last mile to his apartment, checked the parking lot, and then led the way up the stairs. On the surface, everything appeared quiet. Nothing seemed to have been touched, but looks could be deceiving.

"Don't move," he whispered to her. "I mean it, stay *right* here."

While she watched in bewilderment, he went through the rooms, checking all the little traps and landmines that he left for anybody who might be dumb enough to break in. In the bedroom he found the thread he always tied across the threshold snapped. It was so thin, nobody would feel it break, but somebody had been here.

Foster tore the place apart then. He did it quietly but methodically, and each time Mia tried to ask him something, he held up a hand. They couldn't say a word until he found what he was looking for. And then he did. In the wall vent in his bedroom he found a small listening device no bigger than a dime.

This was a hell of a mess. One of two things had happened. Either Serrano had decided he didn't trust him, or more dangerous people had tracked him down. Terrible timing, too, any way he spun it. His options were limited.

If he removed it, the person would know he'd been detected. And if Serrano had sponsored the tap hoping to get some dirt on his second in command, it would strike him strange that Foster had already found it. Disposing of the thing would raise red flags. If it wasn't Serrano, he could think of a number of unpleasant alternatives.

After debating with himself for thirty seconds, he left the bug in place. Foster walked back to the door, where he'd left Mia waiting. Without saying a word, he took her purse. She had the sense not to protest and he rummaged, looking for a notepad. Thankfully she was as organized as she looked. He scrawled:

Plan B. This location is no longer secure.

"Just let me change my shirt," he said loudly. "And then we'll get dinner."

Play along, he mouthed.

By the way she narrowed her dark eyes, he could tell she'd nearly reached her limit with him. "Sounds great."

Foster banged around just long enough to lend credence to his statement and then he led her back out the way they'd come. Every muscle tensed as he came down the stairs. By rights he should have a weapon in hand, but if he had to, he could take someone bare-handed. He'd been playing a suit for years, but his reflexes were sharp enough.

There was an old woman walking her dog, and a woman taking her toddler to the swing sets on property. Everything looked peaceful. Normal. Things had never been that way for him, at least not since the Foundation got their hooks into him.

Mia amazed him by cooperating fully as he searched his car from top to bottom, but it appeared to be clean. By the time they climbed back in, he felt the adrenaline. He wanted to fight, wanted whomever it was to come straight at him, but he'd learned that trouble often came sideways or snuck up from behind.

"I'd think you were jerking me around," she said shakily, "with all this spy-games shit, but I saw your face. You don't have much of a sense of humor, do you?"

No, he thought. *Lexie had been laughter.* He didn't laugh anymore.

"'We at the FBI do not have a sense of humor that we are aware of,'" he quoted, remembering the last movie they'd seen together before things went south.

"*Men in Black,*" Mia said. "Are you saying you work for the government?"

"I could, but it wouldn't be true."

"Then what is? Who's spying on you?"

"There are a number of answers. I doubt you care about any of them, except as relates to your friend."

"True enough," she admitted. "I'd rather not have your trouble rub off on me. No offense."

"None taken. In a nutshell, this is the situation." Foster summed things up for her, including how Kyra had duped Serrano and eventually humiliated him at the tables, gambling her engagement ring on a high-stakes game of 21. "And then—this is the real pièce de résistance—she held up a sign for the cameras that read, 'I was only in it for the money. I'd rather die than marry you.' Quite dramatic. The security footage wound up on YouTube." He didn't mention his own part in that, however satisfying it had been.

"That's . . . more or less what she told me she planned. The sign is new, though. Interesting twist. God, I never thought she'd *do* it." Mia closed her eyes. "I can guess that he didn't take it well."

"Serrano? No. She's gone to ground, and he's hired someone to . . . dispatch her."

"A hit man," she said, looking numb. "He's contracted someone to kill her."

Foster nodded. "Unless we find her first. That's why I need your help."

CHAPTER 18

They rolled into Sioux Falls in late afternoon.

The city was prettier than she'd expected, lush, green, and clean. Kyra drove through to downtown to scope out their options. It had been several days since they'd earned any money, and Rey would get suspicious if she didn't get back to it soon. Not to mention the fact that she simply missed working.

There was a dive called the Cue Club two blocks south of downtown, which showed promise. She always canvassed a town personally, getting the lay of the land before she looked at the phone book. Kyra had a good memory for locations, and afterward, she'd be able to tell whether a place was upscale, based on the address. Sometimes the assholes that frequented yuppie clubs should be relieved of their money, but they were more likely to contact the police if they thought they'd been cheated. That was why she practiced her art on people who made their money outside the law and hung around in seedy bars.

In truth, she missed the rush of pulling off a more intricate con, but she shouldn't hang around the same town for more than a few days. As the asshole had said, the Marquis was memorable. If somebody caught up with her, either Serrano or Dwight's people—man, it was nice to know they cared—it wouldn't take long to run her to ground.

Next she found a motel with Kelly green neon lining along the roof. The rates were cheap enough and the rooms were clean. Kyra concluded their business without grilling the desk clerk about local attractions. He didn't look like the helpful sort.

Rey had been quiet today, making her uneasy. She knew he wanted her to confide in him, but it went against all her personal experience. If she told him about the money, what was stopping him from killing her and taking it? Her ability didn't work on him anymore—and she'd really like to know why—that left her vulnerable where he was concerned. She'd seen him fight. She knew what he could do with his bare hands.

Right now, she trusted him to do the right thing by her, but how *far* could she trust him? Would his reliability stretch to millions of dollars? No, it was better to keep him in the dark until they reached Fargo. Mia should be there by now. If Kyra had done the math right, Mia would've finished her job in Amsterdam, and the last time they'd talked, several weeks ago now, the other woman had said she intended to take a short-term contract in Fargo.

"You're quiet," he said, as they stepped through into another motel that was pretty much like the long series of its predecessors.

"Funny. I was thinking the same thing about you."

Rey paused, his features shadowed by the light from the open door at his back. He pushed it closed and leaned on it, gazing down at her. "Look, I understand. People say things they don't mean after great sex. All the happy endorphins make them stupid."

Is that what he thinks? That I'm trying to figure out a way to recant? For no reason she could name, it made her sad that he would assume nobody could mean it, if they said they loved him. Except for her dad, *she* might feel more or less the same.

"At least you admit the sex was great," she said dryly, dropping her bag.

She took a step and wrapped her arms around his waist. It wasn't a natural move for her; over the years, she'd learned to restrain her urges for physical contact. Even now, she half expected the shock, half expected the surge that signaled she'd taken something from him, but she felt nothing but warmth. His arms came around her slowly.

"So you haven't been trying to think of a way to disavow me?" Though the tone was teasing, his eyes were serious.

"Just the opposite, in fact."

His brows rose. "You're trying to think of a way to keep me?"

"Pretty much."

"Am I going somewhere?" he asked.

"You tell me."

"I have no plans, but you never know what the future holds."

Kyra sighed and stepped back. "You can be very irritating, do you know that? Let's go."

"What's the plan for tonight?" He fell in behind her.

"I won't know until we get there." She flashed a smile.

"That's reassuring. Thank God one of us is a pro."

They went to the Cue Club. It was a homey place done in dark wood and the occasional neon beer sign. The men wore Wranglers and flannel. The women wore Levis and cowboy boots. Everyone seemed at ease in his own skin, happy, friendly. They were familiar with each other, but not closed to outsiders.

She took a table near the door, and Rey sat on the other side. Nobody there struck a vibe with her. She listened to guys talking about bids on a drywall job versus overdue mortgage payments. One man mentioned how the wife was hosting a makeup party, and he'd been booted out. Another rambled on about peewee football and fantasy baseball. Kyra watched the flow of the place for half an hour before deciding they wouldn't find any targets here. Oh, she could probably amaze the locals with her talent somehow, but she didn't want to. Cheating honest people left a bad taste in her mouth.

"I can't believe it. Everybody in there seems to work for his money. No dirt, no gossip. I wonder where all the dealers, thieves, and bag boys are."

"It seems like a pretty wholesome town," he agreed.

She slammed her hand against the table, drawing a few eyes. "Well, shit."

"Problem?"

"I'm down to my last hundred bucks. I don't know if it'll get us to Fargo."

Well, unless she dug into the stash. Kyra didn't want to do that until she made contact with Mia, who would help her get the money out of the country. She didn't know if the bills could be tracked somehow. It might be standard in case they were stolen. In her case, they hadn't been, but she didn't want to risk leaving a trail.

"What's in Fargo?"

"A friend. Somebody who will help us out."

"Why would she help *me*?"

"Because you're with me," she answered.

He appeared to accept that. "So you prefer not to target honest folks?"

"I like going after people who deserve to lose their money."

Rey nodded. "So what now?"

"Hell if I know," she muttered. "It's usually as simple as picking a dive and identifying the key players. Any ideas?"

Over the years, she'd developed a real instinct for it. Tonight, however, her instincts had gone to hell. She'd led them straight to a family bar, full of married men. Kyra shook her head in disgust.

"None of my ideas relate to making money," he said.

"Then, what—oh. Don't you ever think about anything else?"

"I used to. I had hobbies, watched movies occasionally. And then I met you."

She laughed reluctantly. "You're good for my ego, I'll give you that."

Coming up from behind in soft-soled shoes, the waitress touched her shoulder. She was a motherly type with laugh lines around her eyes. Kyra jerked, but it was too late. A soft little sizzle went through her, signaling whatever she'd taken. This ability was nice, warming, and it rolled through her like honey. It was also rare, but this woman seemed to be equally good at two things, which meant Kyra got dual gifts for the price of one.

As it turned out, she knew how to make a little money. They weren't screwed for the evening after all. Flashing a smile at Rey, she stood.

"Would anybody mind if I played?" Kyra canted her head toward the piano. It had a tip jar on top, no dust, which told her somebody used it—probably on weekends.

"Help yourself." The waitress—Molly—smiled at her. "I bang on it a bit myself sometimes on breaks. There's no entertainment tonight, so it's all yours."

She felt Rey watching her as she sat down. Any other time, she would have no idea what to do with the keys, but her fingers settled in place on the ivories and soon the place filled with the soft, seductive notes of "Georgia on My Mind." The waitress sang, too, every bit as good as she played piano. Maybe at one point she'd dreamed of making a career of it, singing to people instead of bringing them beer.

Kyra sang, low and husky, of moonlight through the pines and places left behind. It was her voice and yet it wasn't, just her sound powered by Molly's talent. At first nobody paid much attention, but then Rey came over and clicked on the mic atop the piano. Conversation slowed.

The other woman had apparently worked up a set of songs that had states in the name because those were the ones Kyra found she knew by heart. If there had been any sheet music on the piano, she could've played it, but these tunes she played from memory: "Mississippi Queen," "Kentucky Rain," "Sweet Home Alabama," "Tennessee Waltz," "California Dreamin'," "and "Yellow Rose of Texas." She lost herself in the sweet and yearning music.

Reyes watched her. Just when he thought he had a handle on her, she shifted the ground beneath his feet. There was no money guaranteed in this, but right now, she was a performer. She played for the love of it. It might not be her love, but she was giving that waitress a priceless gift, letting her experience her own talent in a way most singers never would. By the time she finished the set, her throat had to be parched, and she'd gathered quite a crowd.

A few people had moved the tables and started to dance.

It had to be amazing, doing this. How would it feel, knowing you didn't have to be the same person, day after day? Kyra Marie Beckwith could be anyone she wanted, at least for a little while. But maybe it eventually got hard to remember who you *really* were, living like that.

He stood back from everyone else, just observing her. At this moment, she was radiant, energy sparking from her strawberry blond curls, reflected in the shine of her tawny eyes. If she'd asked the people to empty out their pockets, he had no doubt they would. Magnetism like hers could be downright dangerous.

She'd gotten so carried away with the music that he didn't think she'd even noticed people had started dropping money in the tip jar. There were a substantial number of crumpled bills, but he couldn't guess at denominations. Most likely it would fill up the gas tank, though, leaving her hundred for incidentals. They'd get to Fargo on it.

Kyra refused all requests for encores at that point, gathered up the bills and waved to her dispersing audience. She almost glowed from the attention, as if she soaked it in like a solar panel. The waitress brought them both a beer.

"On the house," Molly said, eyes shiny and moist. "You know, it's the strangest thing . . . you played every song I know, all my favorites."

She smiled. "I hope I did them justice. They're classics, aren't they?"

"More than. You two come back anytime."

Reyes set his hand in the small of her back as they walked out. He couldn't help the small, possessive gesture, wanting the other men to know she belonged to him. It had been impossible not to glimpse the desire in their eyes, even the ones who had been speaking moments before of their families. Kyra had a particular incandescence that made a man want to touch her, glory in her warmth.

"That's what I call a clean con," she said quietly. "It's impossible to plan those."

"Because you never know what you'll get from someone unless you've been watching them," he guessed.

"Pretty much." She climbed into the Marquis and pushed her bag toward him. "Count the take?"

He delved into her denim sack-style purse and came up with a handful of crumpled bills. It took him all of a minute and a half to straighten them out, sort by denomination, and tally them up. "Looks like seventy-seven bucks."

"Not bad," she decided aloud. "That's a tank of gas anyway."

"Back to the room then. You can't do that again tonight."

"Right," she said in an approving tone. "You catch on fast. I must admit, you're taking this a lot better than I ever imagined anyone would."

"It's a lot to take in," he admitted. "But it's amazing. *You're* amazing."

"You're biased."

"Maybe."

Christ, maybe he was.

Reyes fell quiet as she drove. He hadn't heard from Foster since he'd given the deadline. In anyone else, he might suppose other matters had distracted the man, but Foster had all the focus of a pit bull. He didn't let go once his jaws clamped down. Worst-case scenario, he'd hired someone else to complete the job Reyes had been contracted for. If that happened, then the decision had been made for him.

"You look worried," Kyra said, as she pulled into the motel lot.

This late, the neon green gave the place a strange, surreal air. Reflexively Reyes checked for men loitering, motorcycles, or anything out of place. He made sure to hop out of the car first, ready to fight. In fact he kind of wanted to; it would make a nice change from indecision. Belatedly he realized she wanted a response. He wasn't used to anyone thinking for more than fifteen seconds about his emotional state.

"I guess I am, a little."

To his surprise, she didn't ask why. Maybe she had some idea, and didn't want to get into it. In silence they walked along the cement path to the stairs and he went up first. Everything was clear until they hit the room. The place looked like a tornado had hit it, clothing strewn, mattress slashed, holes in the walls. The attackers had pissed all over Kyra's stuff, leaving a clear message.

She hunched her shoulders. "Dwight's guys?"

Unless Serrano had hired some seriously insane SOBs, then yeah. It had to be.

"Do you have any other enemies I should know about? This guy you pissed off . . . is he likely to send people after you?" It was more than slightly ironic for him to be asking her that.

Kyra didn't even give the question ten seconds' thought. "Yeah. If his guys find me, I'm dead."

They have to go through me first. The primitive thought astonished him. He'd kill for her. Not such a big step, given that he killed for money, but he'd never had anybody matter to him enough that he'd be willing to unleash his skills on her behalf, at least not without being paid first. And the twenty bucks that comprised his portion of tonight's take wouldn't even buy a minute of his time.

"We can't stay here," he said decisively. "They have to be tracking you through sightings of the Marquis. The only question is, do we drive on to Fargo and hope for the best or do we pick another place here?"

"Goddammit," she bit out. "This sucks so hard it's not even funny."

Reyes paused, astonished at her vehemence. "Explain?"

"This is everything I own," she added. "This stuff may not seem like much to you, but it's all I have, and I'm going to have to leave it behind. To make matters worse, the last two rooms I've rented have been damaged—" Reyes remembered the broken lamps at the last place. "—and that means the motels are going to call the cops. I had to leave my tag number here, too."

"Shit." The last thing he needed was interference from the local authorities. He could handle drug-dealing thugs; he could handle other hired guns, but he wasn't a cop killer. "Then we need to get out of South Dakota before they run your plates. Do you have warrants in any other states?"

"Yeah," she admitted. "I do." She didn't tell him what the warrants were for, though a shadow flickered in her gaze. "But I'm too wrung out to drive for long. I need food and sleep."

In the sickly neon glow, he could see the shadows beneath her eyes. He'd never noticed before how fragile she seemed after using her talent. It seemed to require an insane amount of energy to fuel it. Instinct made him want to stand and fight. They'd flown from trouble once too often for his tastes; he didn't like running when he didn't even know what he was running to. It required too much faith from a man who had nothing of the kind.

"I have reserves," he heard himself say. "I can go all night if I have to."

Kyra offered him a wan smile, looking weaker by the minute. "I bet you've been waiting your whole life to deploy that line."

"Pretty much. Let's ride, sweetheart. I'll stop for hot dogs and a slushie from a convenience store up the road." Reyes finally understood her predilection for junk food. It offered the fastest boost in quick sugars, preventing her from crashing after a job. The beer had been a bad idea, depressive when she needed energy.

"Can I talk you into buying me some chocolate, too?" She turned her back on everything she'd lost and went with him back toward the Marquis.

Chocolate, roses, a Shelby Mustang, or a condo in Aspen . . . shit, he'd buy her any damn thing she wanted. He was so lost. "Yep."

"Rey, I do believe you're the sweetest-talking man I ever met."

"Dammit," Dwight said, stepping out from the shadow of the car. "And I was so hopin' that would be me."

CHAPTER 19

Kyra sighed, trying to hide her nerves. "You just don't learn, do you?"

The sound of a gun being cocked drove home the seriousness of the situation. If she didn't play this just right, she'd wind up with a scarlet hole in her forehead. With her life in Dwight's hands, she might wind up worse than dead. She'd always thought people who wound up on life support long term suffered worse than those who went out clean.

"Toss me your keys. Now. Or I kill you two here, foregoing the fun of beating the shit out of you first."

She weighed her options. The barrel pointed at her forehead made resistance unwise, and she didn't know enough about this bastard to risk touching him. He might be like his henchman . . . or she might wind up with something worse than useless, like a gift for making great meth. It was too damn bad she couldn't take Rey's skill anymore. This would be over in a heartbeat.

But her lover would handle this. In a one-on-one fight, she couldn't imagine the guy who could beat him. Dwight was beyond stupid for coming after them personally.

"What'd you do with Steve?" she asked, buying time.

"Shot him in the head," the asshole answered promptly. "And tossed his worthless ass in the river. Which is exactly what I'm gonna do to you, if you don't make this a mite more entertaining for me. I said keys. *Now*."

"I'm not going to give you another chance to walk away from this," Rey said conversationally. "You do understand that, right?"

Dwight shifted his focus to Rey and signaled with his left hand. Motorcycles roared all around them, headlights splitting the dark like crossed laser swords. "Your warnings mean shit to me. I brought enough guys this time to put some serious hurt on you. You do understand *that*, right?"

Kyra chose that moment to hurl her keys at Dwight's face. As she'd suspected, he was a righty, and his gun hand came up to try to catch them. As soon as the pistol stopped targeting her, she hit the ground and scrambled toward the Marquis. The car was a grand old dame and would offer a hell of a lot of cover, if she could just get there. A gunshot rang out, and she felt a bite in her calf. Fire slammed up her leg; her knee buckled, dumping her face-first on the asphalt.

Fuck. The son of a bitch shot me.

Hot blood bubbled from the wound, but there was nothing she could do about it at the moment. Kyra heard a crash, and she wriggled around so that she could peer out from beneath the Marquis. From the wreckage, she guessed that Rey had toppled the line of bikes, as they were crashing together like dominoes. A number of bikers had allowed themselves to be distracted by the damage to their rides. Others looked more interested in taking it out of Rey's hide.

He vaulted over one of the fallen motorcycles and wheeled into a group of five like a wrecking ball. Kyra heard Dwight cursing, but he couldn't open fire without risking injury to his own guys, and the bikers wouldn't forgive him if he shot one of them. She hadn't gotten a clear look at how many men there were, but from what she could tell from her low vantage point, Rey was kicking the shit out of them.

He was a terrifying combination of brute force and elegant violence. Like a born killer he wheeled into a move that left four men groaning on the ground. His left leg lashed out, a sweep swiftly followed by a one-two kick. She remembered using that move herself. As he fought, Rey radiated beautiful kinetic energy, always in motion. That flow came from both tarung derajat and Jendo.

She didn't doubt he could take them all on. All she needed to do was wait and stay out of trouble, not offer herself as a bargaining chip. Her calf throbbed, but she tried to ignore the pain. Dwight swore as he scrambled around the car, trying to get the drop on Rey. Then, in the distance, she heard sirens. The motel manager must've called the cops.

"You have to make a choice, Kyra." Rey spoke near the left rear tire. "How bad is it going to be if the cops take us in?"

The police would just haul in everyone who didn't run. They used a butterfly net approach to sorting out situations like this. She squeezed her eyes shut. Little as she liked to admit it, given the circumstances, Dwight would be the lesser of two evils. It should prove to be a lot easier to escape his custody.

She exhaled unsteadily. Using elbows more than knees, she pulled herself out from under the car. "Surrender. Let him take us."

"Glad to know you're not complete punks," Dwight said. "It's better to finish this without local law enforcement. You've gone and pissed the boys off. Now get your asses in the trunk." He popped it and slammed his hand on the side for emphasis.

Given the way Rey had just decimated his muscle, she marveled that the guy still wanted to take them somewhere private, but maybe Dwight had sampled his own product. He didn't seem too quick with logical deductions. Dumb as a stump, her dad would've said.

Now she could see lights on the horizon. If they didn't get the hell out of here, they were done for. With a record like hers, it would take months to sort through the red tape. Rey boosted her into the trunk and then slid in behind her. The top slammed shut, leaving them precious little room. Somebody—presumably Dwight—took off in the Marquis, tires squealing. A squad car squawked its siren as they tore onto the highway. Kyra heard the sounds of pursuit as a sudden turn slammed her face into Rey's shoulder.

"That's gonna leave a mark," she muttered.

"See if you can roll away from me. It will be better if we spoon."

"Okay." Kyra struggled, trying to get some weight on her knee. She heard an *oof* as she hit him with an elbow. She managed it, but a spike of fire lanced through her leg. Biting down on her lip, she tried to strangle the whimper, but he heard it.

"What's wrong?" Rey took a deep breath then. How he could smell anything besides rusty metal and exhaust, she had no idea. "Shit. You're bleeding."

"I've got a slug in my calf," she said, trying to sound casual. "No big. It didn't hit anything vital."

"Shit," he bit out. "If I'd known, I would never have gone this route. You need medical attention. The authorities could have provided it."

"That and two years in prison," she muttered. "No, this is better. We can outwit this asshole. He thinks he's some kind of redneck Harvey Keitel. Don't worry, my leg will be fine. Just get me a bottle of Thunderbird and I'll dig it out myself."

"Is that supposed to be funny?"

She didn't answer. But if he felt with careful fingertips, he'd find a small scar in the fleshy part of her upper arm. This wasn't the first time she'd been shot. Her dad had been nearly hysterical with remorse. After things went bad in Reno, he'd wanted to quit the life. He'd promised to get a real job, rent a house somewhere. By then sixteen, Kyra hadn't been able to imagine what the hell that would be like.

How could she go to school when she couldn't even touch somebody casually? There would be no dances for her, no senior prom. No, the way they lived was better, and she'd convinced her dad of it, too. God, she missed him. After he died, she'd felt so alone, like nobody would care ever again whether she lived or died.

They careened wildly in the trunk and the sirens seemed to fade away. At least Dwight was good for that much. Kyra closed her eyes, half sick with memories, movement, and fumes. The reverberation of the car felt strange beneath her ear, and as if in response to an unspoken request, Rey's arms went around her, one beneath her head and the other across her waist.

When he spoke next, she felt the warmth of his breath against her ear. "You cut him, you know. When you flung the keys at his head."

Kyra smiled. "Good. The son of a bitch deserved it."

"And then some," he answered grimly. "He'll get his, have no doubt. We just didn't have time to deal with him and the bikers that were still standing before the five-oh rolled up."

"How many did you drop out here? I didn't have a great view."

"There were nine on the ground who couldn't run for their rides." Rey sounded matter of fact, like he hadn't broken a sweat over it.

"Who the hell *are* you? The bionic man?"

"Yep. Didn't you hear? They rebuilt me . . . they have the technology. But it cost twenty million this time." She felt him smile against her hair. "Inflation."

"Fine," she muttered. "Don't tell me."

"You want all my cards on the table? No problem. Someday I'll tell you all my secrets . . . right after you spill yours."

He had her there. Kyra hadn't exactly been straight with him. "Fair enough. You think this is the time and place?"

"You have something else on the agenda?"

Reyes waited. He'd never known anybody like her. At its core, the magnetism between them felt elemental. Everything he'd spent his life working toward seemed ephemeral when compared to Kyra's fire. He tried not to hold his breath, but the truth was, he wanted to get this shit in the open. She needed to stop being so damn stubborn and let him in. He wanted it with every fiber of his being, not because he wanted to finish the job, but because he wanted to help her.

But she would have to take the first step.

"No," she said eventually. "I don't have anything else planned, but I'll be damned if I'm going to be backed into a corner. I don't want your secrets that bad."

Damn her for being a stubborn pain in the ass. Maybe he'd have to do it. If he told her about his contract with Serrano, it would start a shit storm, and she was injured. Better for them to focus on getting out of this mess, and then he'd tell her. In that moment, Reyes realized he'd made his choice. He had no intention of doing this job any longer. He'd jumped feetfirst into her mess and overall, he wasn't unhappy with the decision.

"I trust you," he said then. "But I can see why you wouldn't think that I do. I mean, you don't even know my real name."

From her tone, that surprised her. "I don't?"

"Nope. Rey's just a nickname."

One nobody but Kyra used, he added silently. The men who hired him knew him as Mack, a tongue-in-cheek nod to Mack the Knife. He figured it was healthy to have a sense of humor about his work.

"Then what is it?"

A ghost of a smile flickered and disappeared. "Porfirio Ten-Bears Reyes."

She was silent for several long minutes. "Huh. Hope you don't mind if I keep calling you Rey."

"I'm used to it."

Whatever she might have said became moot. The car skidded to a stop and the trunk popped open. Since Kyra was closest, a pair of hands reached in and dragged her out first, tearing her away from him. The hauler took no care with her injuries, and she cried out when he banged her leg against the fender.

"Let go of me, shit for brains!"

"I don't think so," Dwight said. "I made the mistake of looking away from you once. I'm using you as collateral to make sure your boyfriend behaves himself. Otherwise we'll have some *collateral* damage." The dealer laughed as if he'd made a really hilarious joke.

Frankly, Reyes was a little surprised he knew the word. From the strangled sound, he guessed somebody had an arm around Kyra's neck. He remained still in the trunk, considering his options. His course of action depended on how many bikers had kept up with Dwight in outrunning the cops. He'd left a number of them too incapacitated to ride.

"Up and at 'em, cholo." That had to be Dwight. Doubtless he'd follow that witticism with wetback, greaser, and spic. "Hands where I can see them."

"Technically speaking, that's inaccurate usage." Reyes climbed out of the trunk slowly, assessing. They stood in a salvage yard, surrounded by miles of wreckage. Ten men, including Dwight, ringed them. A burly bastard held a knife to Kyra's throat, mandating good behavior. "No chinos, no wifebeater, no hairnet. I don't even have a low rider. Now in the Peruvian sense, it's accurate. I *am* a person of mixed mestizo descent."

"Shut up, bitch." Somebody slammed the butt of a gun into his nose, smashing the cartilage. Pain blazed like a red comet through his brain. "The way I figure it, you owe me an ass load of money . . . damage to property, lost revenue, and the like. Since I'm a businessman, I'm going to give you a chance to repay me."

"What makes you think we've got money?" Kyra wheezed out.

"Who said anything about cash?" Through the blood in his eyes, Reyes saw the man shake his head. "I figure I'll make a ton if I drop this crazy fucker into some bare-knuckle cage matches. And you . . ." Dwight ran a thick fingertip down Kyra's cheek. "With a mouth like you've got, you'll earn me a fortune."

"You're dumber than you look, if you think that'll work long term," she snarled. "The minute you turn your back, I'll put a knife in it."

"See, that's the thing," Dwight said, remarkably composed, "when people care about each other, they're reluctant to take risks. They'll put up with shit they'd never tolerate otherwise. Tell me, cholo, what would you do to keep me from ordering him to cut her throat here and now? Would you suck his dick?" He gestured to one of his sweaty henchmen, standing ready with a .45.

Across the distance between them, he met Kyra's gaze with his own. She was trying to tell him something with her fierce tigress eyes. They slid downward, lighting on the thug's arm around her neck. The man was enormous, his biceps the size of redwoods. *Of course.* He started to smile. Whatever ability the man brought to the combat table, she owned it now.

"Sure," Reyes said quietly. "But I can't deep throat. You broke my nose."

"See?" Dwight smirked at Kyra, ostensibly helpless in the big guy's grip, and then jerked his head at Reyes. "So prove it. On your knees."

Without an instant's hesitation, he walked over to the guy Dwight indicated and dropped to his knees. *Dumbass.* He reached toward his zipper as Kyra made her move. Instead of a small woman, the shithead found himself holding a juggernaut who tossed him like a Frisbee. He landed on two other guys, and she roared with rage.

Reyes went for the .45 in his target's hand. He broke the other man's arm in a smooth motion, and then rolled knee to knee, plugging anything that moved and wasn't Kyra. She fought like a berserker, no skill, just strength and rage. She picked up a hunk of metal and went to town. It wouldn't have surprised him at all to see her pull somebody's head off with her bare hands.

In the end, it was a little bit like skeet shooting. She'd knock 'em down and he put a bullet in them. A few bikers managed to make it to their cycles and spun the hell out of there, but Dwight went down with lead in his thigh. Reyes strode up to him, intending to end him, just as Kyra got there.

"He's mine," she said, forestalling him. "This fucker shot me and then took some lame idea about pimping me out."

He'd never had a partner before, never known anybody who would make good on his threats. Reyes hesitated; he'd promised Dwight he would go scorched earth, and every instinct told him to just put a bullet between his eyes, making sure the job got done right. That was the way he'd always operated. The dealer writhed on the ground, moaning in pain.

At last he stepped back. "Take him, if you're sure you have the stomach for it."

"He *hurt* you," she said in a voice as dark as night. "Hell, yeah, I do."

Kyra lifted a foot high in the air, balancing on her bad leg for a moment, and then brought her instep down on his throat as hard she could. With the strength she'd stolen, her weight carried the same force as if she were a three-hundred-pound biker. His throat collapsed, leaving him choking out a few last desperate breaths before he died.

She took no chances, checking Dwight's pulse, and then she reached out for the .45. Reyes passed it over in a kind of fog, stunned and bewildered. A final shot rang out, a bullet between Dwight's eyes, just as he'd intended. Kyra meant to leave nothing to chance; she understood the meaning of scorched earth.

A shudder went through him. She'd *killed* for him. Reyes found that both profoundly disturbing and . . . erotic. They needed to leave. He wanted something else. Despite his smashed nose, the dead body at their feet, and the bullet in her calf, he wanted to shove her up against the Marquis and take her like an animal. Something of his mood must've shown in his face because she put her mouth to his roughly, bit his lower lip.

"It's crazy," she whispered. "We need to get the hell out of Dodge, but I feel like every nerve just woke up at the same time."

CHAPTER 20

The look they exchanged should've set fire to flammable surface materials. Then he kissed her like he couldn't help himself, like he wanted to eat her up. Her arms went around his neck, mouth hot on his. Rey framed her ass in his hands, dragged her against him. Through their clothes, she felt him burning hot and hard. Kyra rolled her hips, seduced by the ferocity of him.

At last Rey wrenched away, his breath coming in hard rasps. With disbelieving eyes, Kyra took in the carnage around them. She'd forgotten everything else. He shook his head once as if to clear it and nudged her toward the car.

"We can't," he said thickly. "The cops won't be far behind and they're looking for this car now. That's going to make it tough."

He found the .45 and wiped it clean and then put it in Dwight's hand. Kyra understood why. They could do nothing else in terms of cleanup, but with luck nobody would find the mess until morning, giving them a long head start.

"We need a new set of plates," she pointed out, limping over to the passenger side. It was her right leg, so she wouldn't be driving until she got the bullet out. "And a fast paint job, no questions asked. The first is no problem."

"I can take care of that right now," Rey said.

Kyra watched as he scanned the junkyard, eventually settling on a trashed Datsun. Its plates hadn't expired, so he whipped out his knife and went to work. It took about five minutes for him to make the swap and then stash the old plates. He vaulted and slid over the hood to the driver side, so deliciously dangerous that she wanted to take a bite out of him. Her toes curled, sending a spike of pain through her right calf.

"You were amazing," she told him.

He shrugged. "I held up my end. There's no comparing it to what you did. Are you okay by the way?"

Kyra knew he didn't just mean the bullet in her leg, and she nodded. "I could eat, but afterward, I always need a boost."

"Headache?" he asked.

"Not yet. Adrenaline's keeping it at bay." When it hit, it would be murder.

"Any idea where we are?"

She shook her head. "I'm starting to think GPS isn't such a stupid idea."

"We'll just have to see where we wind up then."

His big hands held the steering wheel tightly, gleaming white-knuckled in the dark. Kyra watched him, bemused at the tension. Rey seemed so tightly wound he'd snap like an old guitar string if she so much as touched him.

"What's wrong?"

"I could lie," he said. "But there's no point. Instead of doing the smart thing after you shot Dwight, I wanted you on the trunk of the car. Right now it's all I can do not to pull over and push you into the backseat, regardless of who might be after us."

She shifted her gaze. "Damn. Does that hurt?"

He laughed, a slightly shaky sound. "A little. Give me a minute. It'll go down if you quit looking at it."

"I don't think so." The dark made her daring, the way they hurtled down the country road, seemingly alone in the world.

"It won't go down, or you won't quit looking?"

"Both," she said, smiling.

Kyra reached for him then, pleased to find him wearing button-fly jeans that gave way without putting him at risk of zipper teeth. She slid her fingers through the placket in his boxers; he inhaled sharply and his hips lifted before he caught himself. His thighs went hard as iron bars.

"What're you doing?"

"I'd think that would be obvious."

His cock was already stiff, throbbing beneath her fingertips. He jerked as she touched him, drawing him through the slit for better access. His breath rasped in the dark, hot and uneven, but he didn't try to stop her. Rey kept his eyes on the road, chest rising and falling with the apparent strain of controlling himself. "I'm starting to figure it out," he growled.

Since he was tall and he drove with the seat all the way back, it left her plenty of room between his lap and the steering wheel. Kyra silently blessed old cars with bench seats as she lowered her head. When she spoke, her breath fanned against the length of his hard cock.

"You liked what I did back there. You liked me fighting for you."

A tremor went through him. "God, yes."

"Would you like me to finish this?"

"If I had half a brain, I'd say no," he muttered. "I won't be paying attention to the road. I won't notice until somebody's right up on us."

She hovered, her lips a whisper away from the head of his cock. "And?"

"I want you to. Please." The raw need in his voice coiled deep in her stomach, making her ache in ways that surpassed sexual desire, deeper and more fundamental.

Kyra squeezed her thighs together as she took him in her mouth. Ordinarily she'd tease him a little, lick up and down, play with the head before going for it. Tonight she felt like she'd die if she didn't have him inside of her. He was the missing piece, and only he could make her whole.

Her saliva made him wet and she swirled her tongue along his length, learning his taste. It seemed strange that she'd never done this for him before, but she liked the feel of him, the shape and heat. He moved his hips, causing his foot to pump the accelerator. The car revved and slowed in response. To her surprise, he moved one hand from the wheel and sifted through her hair to curl his fingers around her nape. The gesture felt tender, not controlling. He applied no pressure, kneading her muscles as she sucked him.

It felt good, little spirals of pleasure shooting down her spine. In response she pulled harder, using her tongue faster against the sides of his cock. The new rhythm tore a groan from him, and Rey began to circle his pelvis, the most he could respond while still driving the car. The velocity acted as an aphrodisiac; Kyra could never have imagined how hot it would make her, speeding through the night with her head in a lover's lap.

Her pussy heated, dampening her panties. Kyra whimpered when she tasted him more strongly. He must be getting close. Her whole body felt flushed.

"Harder," he rasped. "God, yeah."

Then his whole body stiffened. A shudder tore through him, and he came in her mouth, long waves that had the Marquis wandering all over the road. Kyra swallowed and wiped her mouth. She still had no headache—first the adrenaline and now endorphins. Natural chemicals were the best. She'd almost forgotten about the pain in her leg, dulled to a low, steady ache.

"Good?" she asked, somewhat smugly.

"Fuck, yes. Open your pants for me, Kyra."

Oh, she liked where this was heading. Without another word, she popped the button and unzipped her jeans. "That what you had in mind?"

"Yeah," he breathed, fingers delving into her panties.

He found her already wet, swollen. Blindly, he explored, unable to take his eyes from the road. Kyra found that erotic as well. She lifted her hips. On the second sweep, he found her clit. Electricity sparked through her as he circled it with rough fingertips. Ordinarily she would need more buildup before he did that, but everything had blurred together in the shape of foreplay: his need, their explosive kiss outside the car, the helpless way he responded. She twisted and moaned, rubbed herself against his hand.

At this rate it wasn't going to take long.

"Like this." She repositioned his fingers, showed him the exact motion and pressure she wanted. "Circles now. Oh, fuck. Rey."

The vibrations from the Marquis added to her arousal. When she came, it felt as though every muscle in her body contracted. The orgasm went on and on, extended by his clever fingers. Kyra cried out and clawed at the seat. Signs flew by; lights flickered in the darkness. She was sobbing for breath when the world started making sense again.

"Damn." She slumped against the seat, eyes closed, while he petted her like a cat. "Do you always respond like this to a fight?"

"No. Do you?"

Kyra shook her head. "I never have before. It must be you."

"We're lucky we didn't get pulled over for drunk driving."

Eventually she rallied enough to straighten her clothing, and then she helped him with his. It felt like they drove half the night, and she began to wink in and out. Her head caught fire, nearly blinding her. If she didn't get something to eat soon, it wouldn't be pretty. At dawn, as the light edged pink and silver above the horizon, he pulled off onto a dirt road.

"Where are we?" she asked, muzzy.

"Safe house. Don't worry. I've got you."

When he lifted her into his arms, Kyra knew he did.

"This is going to hurt," Reyes said.

After feeding her, he'd allowed her to sleep as long as he dared, but that bullet had to come out. While she was out cold in the car, he'd made a quick call to Monroe, who'd come through with a hideout where he hadn't regarding info on Kyra and her dad. Now Reyes knew that was because there was nothing to learn.

The safe house wasn't much to look at, a plain two bedroom house set well off the road in a copse of trees. They had running water from an artesian well and a gas-generator powered the place. It offered only basic amenities, but more importantly, just a handful of people knew of its existence—and only Monroe knew they were here.

"I know." Kyra had peeled her pants off minutes before,

and now she sat in shirt and panties, waiting for him to get to work. "Just do it."

Reyes found himself squeamish. He didn't want to dig around in the wound; he didn't want to make her bleed. So he stalled.

"Do you have a first-aid kit? I need to be sure I have enough gauze and bandages." He glanced at the supplies he'd laid out and knew he was just delaying the inevitable.

"It's either in the backseat or the trunk," she said. "Make it quick, okay? I want to get this over with."

He nodded and headed out the back door. The Marquis sat behind the house, hidden from view if anyone came up from the road. Reyes checked the trunk and found nothing but other emergency supplies, like kitty litter and flares—no first-aid kit. Then he rummaged in the backseat, found it on the floor. As he pulled back, he noticed a ragged edge of the carpet, as if it had been peeled away and replaced.

Reyes stared at it for a long moment and then lifted. It came free, revealing a hidden compartment in the floorboard. Smugglers and drug runners used these all the time; they weren't complicated to install. He flipped it up and found a silver case. There was no need to open it; he knew what it contained.

That had to be Serrano's money.

She'd been carrying it all this time, living off what she made on the game. Since she never left the car behind, it made sense. He should have expected as much now that he knew her better. Kyra would never trust anyone enough to leave it with them, and she'd be afraid any hiding spot she chose could be compromised. In truth, he could have rolled the car long ago. Deep down, he just hadn't wanted to. He could now complete the job, salvage the reputation he'd spent years building.

Instead, he closed the hidden panel and fit the carpet back on top, being careful to leave it exactly as he'd found it. First-aid kit in hand, he made another call. It was past time for him to get in touch with Foster.

"You lied to me," he said, as soon as the other man answered. "Tell Serrano I don't work for him anymore."

Foster's voice was cool. "A pity. You came with the highest recommendations. It's always so disappointing when people's reputations outpace their abilities, but I'll let him know. You will, of course, return the retainer I wired into your account."

"Hell, no," Reyes said. "That'll cover the time you wasted. You're welcome to try your hand at collections, of course, but I don't think much of your chances."

"It's not my money," Foster returned, sounding amused. "Mr. Serrano will decide what he wants to do. If I were you, I'd expect company."

"I always do."

Just as he was about to disconnect, he heard one last thing. "Tell Kyra her friend says hello, won't you? Mia is such a charming woman."

Reyes slammed the door with more force than necessary and turned off his phone. For good measure, he popped the battery out. There had been rumors of technology that could track your location, even if the cell phone was powered down, and he intended to take no chances. Foster worried him. He was a thinker, unlike Serrano was reputed to be, and that made him a dark horse. It was impossible to predict how he'd move.

For the moment he put that aside. He didn't know who the hell Mia was, but Foster seemed to think Kyra would recognize the name. The other man also seemed to think he'd confessed all, broken his cover. He didn't look forward to that conversation. Reyes tipped his head back and stared up at the gray sky, hoping for answers.

Fuck it. Kyra was waiting for him to play doctor, and it wouldn't be fun. She was downright pissed by the time he got back, about to operate on herself, as she'd said in the salvage yard. Reyes waved the first-aid kit, trying to placate her.

"Got it, see?"

"I thought I was going to have to do this myself," she groused.

He rubbed a hand across his face. No more stalling. With an economy of movement, he washed up and then rubbed sterile alcohol pads over his hands. He blotted the outside of the wound for good measure. Her breath hissed through her teeth, but Kyra didn't say a word. Her hands went white from gripping the arms of her chair, though.

With a pair of sterilized tweezers and a penknife, he went to work. It seemed like ages where he dug around in her flesh, but Christ almighty, she was brave. The woman never made a single sound, from the moment he started, until he finally plucked the lead core from her leg.

He dropped it into a plastic dish and gave a shuddering sigh. The rest didn't take too long. He poured alcohol into the wound until she slapped at his hands.

"That's good," Kyra muttered. "I'll have a doc look at it soon, I swear. Just wrap it up, will you?"

She meant that literally, so he set the pads in place and wound the gauze around her leg. Finally he taped everything down, and she leaned her head against his chest. Her strawberry blond hair stuck to her forehead in sweaty strips, revealing how hard it had been to be stoic. Slow tremors ran through her, but she steadied as he held her.

"Okay?"

"You're no Trapper John," she told him. "But I'll live."

Damn right, she would. They'd sent him to kill her, but instead he'd protect her to his last breath. Kyra was his in a way that nobody ever had been—or ever would be again. He didn't know what the hell would happen between them, but he intended to make sure she survived it.

"I haven't had a lot of practice patching people up," he admitted.

Understatement. He put people in the ground; that never involved nurturing. Before Kyra, he could count the times he'd been touched tenderly on one hand. Before Kyra, everything had been different.

"No shit."

This was the time to tell her. He'd just quit working for Serrano; it was official. But as Reyes gazed down into her trusting face, he found himself reluctant to lose that. He told himself that a few days wouldn't matter. She needed peace to recover—it wasn't time for confessions or clearing his conscience. He stroked her hair.

There was one thing he could do, however.

"Who's Mia?"

She jerked back, eyes wide and scared. "Where did you hear that name?"

From the guy who paid me to kill you.

"You were mumbling in your sleep," he lied. "In the car. Who is she?"

Kyra relaxed slowly, and he felt like an utter bastard. "My best friend. You might even say, my *only* friend. I've known her a long time." She hesitated, and then went on: "We met when we were ten. Dad had rented a house in Pine Grove. He didn't do that often because people always came around, wanting to know why I wasn't in school. Mia lived next door. She was so excited to have a kid her age move in, she didn't pay any attention when I said I didn't like her, didn't want to play with her."

"She sounds great."

Her smile held definite warmth. "She is. Seventeen years later, and we've never lost touch. Sometimes we might go months without talking—Mia does contract work overseas, and I travel a lot—but whenever we get together again, it's like we've never been apart."

Well, fuck me sideways.

Foster had been telling him he had Kyra's best friend there with him in Vegas. That couldn't be a good thing. They'd use an innocent woman to get what they wanted, no question. Now he had to decide what to do about it.

CHAPTER 21

Serrano was in a fantastic mood right up until Foster entered his office.

Bobby Rabinowitz had come through, so he knew Ricci and Pasternak were laundering for one Armenian in particular, Krigor Akopyan. He'd been pondering the best way to use that information when Foster called. From the man's tone, he knew he didn't have good news. Serrano told him to come up. He respected the man for having the courage to tell him in person.

"So what's the story?" he said in lieu of greeting.

"I got a call from our guy." Foster squared his shoulders. "Apparently he's not working for us anymore."

He swore. "I thought he came highly recommended?"

The security chief gave no hint of how he felt, immaculate and well-groomed, but something of a cipher. "He does. He's the best the west coast has to offer, never failed to complete a contracted job."

"Until now," Serrano barked. "What happened?"

Foster shrugged. "If you want my best guess, the girl got to him. She convinced him she's the injured party."

Grinding his teeth, it was all he could do not to get up and hit something. "So we're out the retainer we paid him and the time he spent hunting her."

"And she now has a skilled professional on her side." Foster apparently didn't believe in pulling his punches.

"Were there any indications before now that he'd gone independent on us?"

"No. Do you want me to hire someone else?" Foster stood waiting for instructions with all the unconcern of a choir boy.

"You've done enough." He left that intentionally ambiguous. "I'll take care of it personally."

Foster didn't even blink. "As you wish, sir. Anything I should know going into the night shift?"

"It's been quiet today, just the AARP brigade scavenging the slots."

"I saw a new shill at table seven. Is he official?"

"Only in the sense that he works for me. I want you on the floor for a while tonight, understand?" That finally roused a reaction from the impassive son of a bitch, but Serrano couldn't read the flicker: puzzlement or confusion, possibly.

"Are you expecting trouble?"

Serrano smiled. "Let's just say I have a few irons in the fire and I want you to be extra vigilant. What's the status on Calloway?"

"He boarded a bus to Florida thirty-six hours ago. He didn't give notice. We can still get to him."

"No." Serrano shook his head. "And Brody?"

"He died in a two-car collision yesterday evening. There were no other fatalities. He lost control of his vehicle and crossed the median into oncoming traffic. Apparently he tried to steer out of the spin and got himself T-boned on the driver's side. Brody died on scene before the EMTs arrived."

That was subtler than he'd planned. People might mistake a car wreck for an Act of God when it was, in fact, an Act of Serrano. He frowned. "Any word on how the accident happened?"

To his surprise, Foster smiled. His bland face seemed to reflect a hint of smug self-satisfaction. "Bees, sir."

He blinked. "Bees?"

"Yes, sir. Brody was allergic to them. They were attracted

to the melted candy in his backseat. They slipped in through an open window, and when he took off, the wind agitated them. He was swatting at the bees because a sting could've killed him when he jumped the median, spun, and was taken out by Gladys Hossenfeffer of Poughkeepsie, New York, driving a 1962 Ford Fairlane."

"You're saying you put *bees* in his car?" Serrano didn't know if he was impressed or disgusted. Whatever happened to shooting a guy twice in the back of the head? That way, there could be no question of what happened or why.

"I didn't say that," Foster murmured. "But if I *was* going to kill someone, I'd make it look like an accident—no way for anybody to trace it back to me."

"There's merit in that," Serrano admitted.

Foster went on, "When a person known to be my enemy turns up dead in an unusual way, it—"

"Only adds to your legend." He thought about the hit a little more and decided he liked the weird creativity of it. "Talk about putting the fear in somebody. I mean, damn. You used an old lady as your trigger man."

The security chief lifted his shoulders. "She's a Sunday-school teacher. She won't take any heat. It was clearly Brody's fault, just one of those things, you know?"

Serrano smiled in appreciation. "Except to the people who know otherwise."

"Exactly. I mailed a copy of the story to Calloway, care of his mother. It'll be there by the time he arrives."

"He'll spend the next ten years looking over his shoulder and shitting his pants."

Maybe he'd been wrong to doubt Foster. The guy knew what he was doing. Still, he couldn't be sorry he'd checked him out. It reassured him to find the guy had an old lady to care for and a little girl in a coma. Those weaknesses made him human . . . in addition to giving Serrano leverage. He didn't trust anybody with no soft spots to hit; there was something innately wrong with that. Even *he* had his weaknesses—he'd just buried them deep years ago.

"Good work," he said sincerely. "That method was more oblique than I'd have chosen, but at least we don't have to worry about lead shoes and murder weapons."

"As I see it," Foster returned, "we need to be creative. Your enemies already know to be on guard against gun-toting men in suits. Now we've shown them there are other, less obvious ways to take them out. How are they supposed to function if they're constantly trying to figure out where you'll hit next?"

He got it. Loved it. "It'll make them lose sleep. Exhaustion steals a man's edge. He'll make mistakes."

"And it'll be even easier to move on him," Foster finished.

"You can go now. Remember, keep a sharp eye out tonight." If everything went as planned, things were going to get ugly for Ricci and Pasternak. The mess might splatter, and he needed a cleanup crew ready.

"Very well. Have a good evening."

He watched his chief of security stride from the office and then he switched to electronic surveillance. After hitting a button, a wall of cameras slid from his desk. He liked being able to monitor things from the privacy of his office; that way nobody knew for sure what he was watching. Just to satisfy his own paranoia, he observed Foster's trek from his penthouse office down to the floor. He went right to work as directed.

Excellent. Things were falling right into place. Serrano took out a prepaid cell phone and dug into his jacket for a number Rabinowitz had supplied. He took a deep breath and dialed.

A harsh male voice barked a Russian word.

"Is this Viktor Barayev?"

The man switched to heavily accented English. "Who is this? How did you get this number?"

"That's not important. I have information for you." Serrano paused, listening to the rapid-fire Russian. "Is this Viktor?"

"I don't pay for information," the man snapped. "I have a network for that. Don't call again or I'll find you."

It had to be him, or someone high up the food chain. He decided to drop his bomb without further prevarication.

He promised, "I won't call back, but I thought you should know that Krigor Akopyan is now doing business in your town."

The response was immediate and gratifying. Though he didn't speak a word of Russian he understood the virulence of cursing in any language. The sound of men arguing carried through the phone. "Give me names, so I can check it out. If your tip turns out to be true, I will make it worth your while."

Barayev and Akopyan had an old-school grudge, dating back to before the fall of the Soviet Union. He didn't want to take sides in the coming bloodbath. That kind of thing ratcheted up the cost of doing business. Huh, maybe he'd learned something from Foster after all.

"No need. This is just a genuine good deed. If you take a look at Ricci and Pasternak of Pair-A-Dice, you'll find everything you need to know about Akopyan. I suspected they hadn't cleared it with you first."

"This is my town," Barayev said darkly. "I will take care of it."

When Serrano hung up the phone, he was smiling. The Odessa Russians had divided up Vegas with the Jew mafia, and there was no room in the city for the Armenians; they should have stayed in San Fran.

Now he just had to wait.

After work, Foster made four unnecessary turns to lose anybody who might be tailing him. Consequently, he was fifteen minutes late when he met Mia for breakfast. She looked mildly irritated, but as ever, she was impeccably dressed. Today she wore a raw azure shantung silk suit, cut in severe lines.

Jewel tones suited her, he thought as he approached the table. He liked it when she wore her hair down; it softened her strong features. Inky tendrils spilled against her cheeks. She had a pot of coffee waiting, but she hadn't ordered anything to eat. Mia passed him the menu, though he already knew what he wanted.

"How do you work these hours?" she asked. "It isn't human."

"We do what we have to. Have you had a chance to think about where Kyra might've gone? Time isn't on our side."

He didn't care, of course. His objective was to detain Mia Sauter so she didn't realize she was being held, not help her in any fashion.

"I don't know," she said in frustration. "She doesn't have many friends."

"She wouldn't," Foster agreed.

"What's that supposed to mean?"

He met her hot dark gaze steadily. "She moves around a lot."

"Very true." Mia relaxed slightly.

The waitress came to take their order, and Foster got the special—pancakes, fried eggs, hash browns, bacon, and sausage. He knew he didn't look like he could pack it in like that, which was why he tried not to eat with other people. They commented too much on the disparity between his lean frame and his appetite. Mia got fruit and yogurt.

Putting the hooker on notice had been a bad idea. He found himself watching the way her lush mouth framed the spoon. It took everything he had not to respond to that, but Foster forced his body into quiescence. At the time, he'd thought himself a whisper from being caught. He'd already started making plans to move Lexie and Beulah, new state, new names. Now he wasn't sure what, if anything, Serrano knew. For a thug, the man owned a lot of sheer animal cunning. At this point he could only stay the course and will his nerve not to break.

"So you have no idea who she'd turn to."

"Since her dad died, she doesn't really have anyone." Mia wrapped slim hands around her coffee mug, the cream crockery contrasting in an oddly sensual fashion against her dark skin. "She's more alone than anyone I ever met."

Inexplicably he wanted to comfort her. "She has you."

She shook her head. "Not so it counts. I travel a lot, too. It's hard for us to stay in touch. I don't even have a home base these days."

"Why is that?"

Having deployed a question that would keep her busy for a while, he dug into his food. By the time he got off work, he felt like his muscles might be digesting themselves. Hunger didn't even begin to encompass it.

"I'm a consultant," she explained. "When I audit a company, I first see how the employees are spending their time in the network. Then I make recommendations that will positively impact productivity."

Foster smiled. "So you remove solitaire from all office computers and restrict net access?"

She offered an appreciative grin in answer. "Something like that. It's not always so simple."

"Nothing ever is."

They ate in silence—him with pure focus, her in distraction—until Mia said, "That's not all I do."

He didn't look up, didn't ask. "I guessed as much. Look, I'm not interested in your secrets. I just want to help you find Kyra."

"There's only one person she would turn to," Mia said then. "Me. But I was out of the country." She hesitated, as if something big had dawned on her. Her eyes looked too big for her face, skin going pale.

Finally, Foster thought. He'd suspected before she had. If Mia cared enough to come to Vegas, then Kyra cared enough to go looking for *her*, too. Doubly so, if she was the one in trouble. He just needed to hang on to this pretty little bit of bait long enough to finish what he'd started.

"Bad timing," he said, determinedly noncommittal. She would do all the running in this race.

"Are you trying to piss me off?"

Foster glanced up then. "No. Did you want me to write a dissertation?"

"Quit interrupting me."

Maybe he *was* trying to piss her off a little. He liked the way her eyes snapped sparks. "Yes, ma'am."

"I had told her I would be taking a job in Fargo next," she went on. "But that contract fell through. The company found the . . . problem on their own. They didn't need my services after all."

"Embezzler?" he guessed.

"Yes. Sometimes companies are reluctant to admit to executive error. It shakes up the stocks, scares the shareholders. They prefer to wrap things up quietly."

"Which is where you come in. You pose as a systems

consultant and find out who's swiping from the cookie jar."

Mia nodded. "Very good. The point is, I bet Kyra is headed for Fargo. If she's in trouble, she'll come to me."

"That's logical." Foster only marveled that it had taken her so long to work it out. He wanted to blame fatigue, not judge her a dizzy blond in brunette clothing. "Do you have a way to get in touch with her?"

"If I did," she snapped, "I would have done it already. I wouldn't even be here, would I?"

"She might've pitched her cell phone," he said reasonably. "I know I would, if I didn't want to be tracked."

She conceded the point with a tired nod. For a moment, she leaned her head into her hands, and then she looked up, a study in vulnerability. "I'm sorry. I know you're just trying to help."

If only you knew. Foster permitted a bland smile, completely in keeping with his cipher persona. Her anger couldn't strike off him; he was milquetoast, immune to strong emotions. It was time to take things up a notch.

"I'm afraid I have good news and bad news. Which do you want first?"

"I don't care. Just tell me."

"The guy Serrano sent after Kyra called in. He said he's off the job. He thinks my boss is a scumbag."

Mia's eyes shone with such relief, he felt like a bastard. "I agree with him. And that's fantastic!" Then her face fell. "Shit. What's the bad news?"

"When I told Serrano, he cut me out of the loop. I'm no longer privy to his plans, so I won't be able to give you a heads-up when he hires someone new."

"When," she repeated. "You're sure he won't cut his losses and let this go?"

Foster propped his elbows on the table. "I told you how it went down. What do *you* think?"

"Unlikely," she agreed. "He has to save face."

"You sound like you have experience with this kind of guy," he said.

Her slim fingers traced a name on the tabletop. Without seeming to, Foster watched the letters shape up one after another. Mentally he flipped them, assembling on his end into a word: *Sahir.* That must be a name, but it rang no bells with him.

"My grandfather was that kind of man," she said quietly. "His determination to keep my parents apart gives me a good understanding of what Kyra is going through right now. But you know Serrano better than I do . . . what can we expect next?"

He didn't even need to think about it. "He'll hire a pro, someone with all the skills of the guy he hired before, but with none of the scruples. Serrano will make sure this next guy is only in it for the money."

"And you're sure the man he hired first has walked?"

There was nothing so convenient as lying with the truth. "He said he was done—he knew Serrano had lied to him, and that he was keeping the money as payment for wasting his time."

"Pretty compelling," she said. "So we have a little time to locate her between the last guy quitting and the new guy finding her."

"Best-case scenario. I'll do everything I can to help you."

"Does that include quitting your job and going with me to Fargo to try and head her off? That's where she thinks I'll be."

"No," Foster said, still watching her graceful hands. This was a calculated gamble, revealing just enough of the truth to keep her docile and cooperative. "I took the call for Serrano, and when I found out what the guy wanted, I told him you were here. He's supposed to tell Kyra you're with me. So just sit tight. She'll come to us."

A brilliant smile lit her tired, worried features, and she spun out of the booth over to his side. Her hands felt hot as pokers as they framed his face. She leaned in, her lips soft, luscious, and red. Her face went vacant from the brief contact. No telling where her mind had gone.

Foster wrenched away, slamming his back against the wall. "Don't do that again. I mean it. Don't touch me."

Shock and confusion warred in her dark eyes, but she shook the disorientation faster than most. "I . . . I'm sorry. I was just—"

"I don't care what you were. Not again, you understand

me? Or I walk, and you can sort this mess out on your own. I've probably stuck my neck out too much as it is."

"I'm sorry," she said again. "Are you gay? I didn't realize."

"That would be a hell of a lot easier for me, wouldn't it?" he muttered. "No. I have to go." He waited while she slid out of his way, her movements choppy with humiliation. "Don't follow me. I'll be in touch."

CHAPTER 22

Kyra slept for a full day.

In sporadic bursts, she recognized that Rey was tending her, but she couldn't bring herself to object. She was too tired. When she woke for the last time into complete lucidity, she didn't recognize the room and panic echoed through her. The decor was plain and serviceable, but different than most motels: plain white walls and prefab furniture, no prints, no lamps.

A dirty window let daylight slip in through the faded blue curtains. From the angle, it had to be late afternoon. There were no clocks to confirm her guess, no ambient noise coming from beyond the bedroom. Had he left her? Alarm spiked through her. Shit, if he'd taken the car—with effort, Kyra put that fear down hard. If he'd wanted to take the Marquis and dump her in a ditch, he'd had ample opportunity while she faded in and out yesterday.

"Safe house, my ass," she muttered. "Who does it belong to?"

"I find it best not to dig too deep in certain matters," he said from the doorway.

"Nobody will find us here. There's no landline, no water lines, and enough gas in the generator to last us a week if we go easy on it and make use of candles. How are you feeling?"

"Better." She pushed out of bed and found herself weak, dangerously depleted. "At least I missed the migraine when I passed out."

"Always looking on the bright side. How's your leg?"

"Hurts. But I'll be fine. Is there anything to eat?" She took a step and her knee nearly buckled on her.

Rey moved so fast she almost missed it. He wrapped an arm around her shoulders, another beneath her knees, and lifted. Kyra had rarely been carried, but she found she rather liked it. "I'll get you settled in the living room. You need food."

"Do I ever," she agreed. "I could eat a raw ox."

"We're fresh out of ox, but I think I can fill you up."

Her mouth curved into a smile. "You know you can."

He caught the double entendre as he headed to the kitchen, after settling her in a worn, brown armchair. "Woman, please."

"I aim to." Was she actually flirting with him? Kyra enjoyed the mock-pained expression he wore as he rattled the pans.

"You do," he said quietly.

Inexplicable warmth surged through her. Despite the ridiculous number of obstacles they faced, she felt almost giddy. She'd never gone through teenage crushes, but surely she had the mother of them all now. Just looking at him made her chest feel tight, like the bluebird of happiness could peck its way through her sternum any minute, just because he smiled at her.

Jesus, you've got it bad.

While he cooked, she admired the blue-black sheen on his hair, spilling down to his shoulders. With his hard face, he looked savage, completely at odds with his domestic task. Kyra drank him in. It wasn't just the way he looked or the way he touched her. No, his magic went deeper still. Until she met him, she hadn't realized how much she missed having someone always on her side, no questions asked.

Ten minutes later, he brought her a plate. She glanced down at it in surprise because he'd arrayed a choice of grilled cheese, M&Ms, and potato chips—to be washed down with an ultra-sweet Coke. Better than anything else, the menu assured Kyra that he really understood. He'd made more healthful choices for himself, fruit instead of chips and candy.

"Good?" he asked, after she took a bite.

At some level, she understood he wasn't asking about the food. "It's perfect."

They ate in companionable silence. Kyra found herself uncharacteristically shy, unable to meet his gaze. Now it mattered too much what he thought of her. Instead she studied the living room, done in brown plaid. There were no pictures on the wall, nor any discolored paint to show there ever had been.

"Nobody lives here," she said then. "It's just a place people hide."

Rey didn't dispute it, merely continued with his meal. Since he didn't want to talk, she did the same, devouring every last M&M on her plate. As soon as she finished, she felt better almost at once. Kyra stretched and bent down to check her bandage.

"It should be clean," he told her. "I took care of it while you were sleeping."

He was right. Kyra didn't bother swapping the gauze, as it only had a little discoloration and the wound was draining nicely as it sealed up. "No red streaks, no swelling. Good work. I might think you treated gunshot wounds every day, doc."

"I've dealt with my share. We were lucky he hit you in an extremity. I wouldn't have risked a torso shot."

"And I'd be incarcerated right now," she said glumly.

Her dad had told her more than once what would happen if the authorities got their hands on her. First it would be tests, and then more tests. Then she'd disappear into some government-run facility, never having any say on where she went or what she did. Her gaze hardened. *They'll have to kill me first.*

To her surprise, he shook his head. "No. I'd have found a way to get you out of custody after you received proper treatment."

That sounded oddly like a promise, a commitment. Kyra

didn't know whether she was thrilled or terrified. "By jumping bail?" she guessed.

"It wouldn't have gotten to that point." Rey wouldn't elaborate on what he might've done, however.

"How long do you plan on staying?"

He smiled. "You'll see."

As it turned out, they lay low for three days. She'd never known anything like it. In fact, in most senses, Kyra would have to call their stay at the hideout a vacation. Rey insisted that they needed to give the cops time to get bored with the investigation and call off the dogs. He seemed sure that if leads didn't turn up within twenty-four hours, the police moved on, even if the case was still technically open. Since she'd done her best to minimize contact with authority figures, she couldn't argue with him.

More to the point, she didn't want to. He wouldn't even tell her what state they were in, insisting it was better she didn't know. Gradually, she had started to suspect his secrets might outstrip hers, given what she already knew of him. But for now, she refused to let the outside world intrude. Once she recovered somewhat and rebuilt her reserves, then she'd worry about finding Mia.

Mia, who specialized in retrieving funds from people who shouldn't have them. Mia, who investigated wrongdoing for a living. The irony of what she intended didn't escape Kyra, but if anyone could reverse engineer the process, it was her best friend. If she convinced her it was a matter of life or death, explained the situation fully, she was sure Mia would help. She wouldn't like it, and she would be risking a great deal—her entire reputation, in fact—but Kyra had no doubt Mia would come through.

They listened to music on an old radio until the batteries gave out. They napped, talked, and made love with a gentleness that often left her weeping. He was so careful of her leg that she almost felt breakable in his arms, not because of his vast strength, but because of her great vulnerability to him.

Each time he touched her now, she rocked with a quiet little earthquake of the soul. Because he *could*. Out of the billions of people on the planet, all of who were prospective marks to her, targets from whom she could steal, he could wrap his arms around her and bury his face in her hair. She would have felt impossibly exposed, if she hadn't sensed that he soaked in the contact as much as she.

On the fourth night, they lay curled together in the relatively narrow double bed, sweat still damp from lovemaking. His fingers stirred, stroking her back. Kyra put her head on his chest, listening to his heartbeat. That was something she'd never have done before Rey; she enjoyed the release good sex provided, but she never wanted any emotional entanglements afterward. And she'd always paid for her encounters with a splitting migraine because she took her lovers after the workday was done, after she'd already stolen what she needed to work.

Taking more via sexual contact often left her incapacitated the next day, moaning with an icepack on her head, but sometimes she needed to feel someone's hands on her enough to take the risk. Against all odds, she'd found someone she could be with . . . be normal with. In his arms, she was just a woman. It felt . . . phenomenal. And that meant despite a lifetime of self-defense, she had to let him in. He needed to know the whole truth of what he'd gotten into with her, if he was going to stay. Kyra's heart thundered in her ears.

"I need to tell you something," she said.

Then the front door creaked open.

Reyes shoved her away and rolled out of bed naked. Balancing on the balls of his feet, he crept toward the door, placing himself between Kyra and the man who'd taken up the contract in his stead. Nobody should've found them, period, let alone this fast. Something was wrong.

If they hadn't been awake, he might not have heard the lock pop and the faint groan of the hinges. In the other guy's shoes, he'd have used WD-40 on a structure this old, if he'd intended to make a quiet entry. That gave him hope. However good his opponent might be, Reyes was better.

He stilled. No time to search for a weapon. That would only make noise. If he listened, he could discern a good deal about his enemy before they engaged. Behind him, Kyra held herself quiet, not even seeming to breathe. No gasps or cries of panic, even though she had to be scared. *Good girl.* He willed her to stay that way and not offer herself up as a target.

Visualizing the layout of the house, he pictured the intruder's path. Just inside the front door sat the living room with couch and chair. Past that, the kitchen lay straight ahead. The invader would be able to tell they were in the bedrooms, which lay to the left. The first door on the right was the bathroom, and on the left, a smaller bedroom with two twin beds. They'd claimed the master bedroom at the end.

The tread told him a number of things about the guy he'd be facing. First, he was big, maybe as big as Reyes, and he'd been trained to move quietly. He was undoubtedly armed, but he thought he was going to catch them in bed. The guy was halfway down the hall now. Over his shoulder, he signaled Kyra to the other side of the bed. Reyes melted to the left of the door, back flush against the wall.

She slid out of sight as the guy ghosted into the room. Reyes lashed out, going for an open-hand hit to the throat, but his prey spun right. In the faint light, he could only tell that the man was nearly his height with buzz-cut dark hair, gun in his right hand.

Reyes spun, snapping a kick to his wrist and the pistol went flying. A curved knife slid into his left hand, and a bone-white smile flashed onto his face. *Fuck. He's ambidextrous. That'll make things tougher.*

They swayed with battle readiness, waiting for the other to make a move. This guy had some patience; he was scoping out Reyes's stance, hoping to learn something about the way he fought. But he wasn't giving anything away himself.

In a lightning-fast move, the killer slashed. He jumped back too late. Reyes felt the hot trickle down his chest, but he didn't look to see how bad it was. In retaliation he lashed out with a right uppercut, followed by a brutal left hook. The other man grunted, taking the hits like nobody Reyes had ever fought before, and he responded with an attempted stab to his kidney. If that strike had connected, it would've been a kill shot.

Reyes launched himself then. He had to take the knife away. They slammed into the wall. Leaning in, he used his weight to dominate, ignoring the shallow wounds all over his body. He slammed a knife hand into his enemy's throat, and his other hand took control of the man's left. He applied force to both locations, digging into the soft tissue. The asshole wheezed, but he didn't let go of the blade. Instead he slashed blindly at Reyes's forearms, and he felt each cut. His arms grew slippery with blood, making it hard to hold on.

The other guy got an arm between them, smashed an elbow into his chin, and he saw sparks. Reyes let himself yield, as if overbalanced by the hit, and then he flipped as they fell, bouncing against the bed onto the floor. In the drop, the knife clattered away.

There wasn't much room to maneuver between the bed and chest of drawers. For long, tense moments, they grappled, each trying to land a chokehold. This son of a bitch was strong, and he knew what he was doing. For the first time, he genuinely feared failure, not because it would mean the end of him, but because it meant the end of *her*.

Fear gave him strength. He wasn't just fighting for pay. He was fighting for home and family—well, the closest thing he'd ever known to it, anyway. Reyes slammed the bastard's head sideways against the metal legs on the bed frame. In the same motion, he jerked a drawer from the dresser and smashed it downward. Wood splintered everywhere, breaking the guy's face wide open. Blood spattered, but he still wasn't done.

He twisted, weakly, then the hit man's leg lashed out and caught Reyes square in the crotch. Pain and nausea surged through his entire body. Every instinct told him to roll onto his side and guard his balls from further harm, but he couldn't. Reining the urge to puke, he took a right cross to the stab wound. Knuckles ground down, making him feel every searing flash of agony.

Blood loss was making him slow and sloppy. Somehow Reyes found himself on his back, an elbow on his throat. He held the other man away from him with pure brute force. He had to escape this pin.

"Why won't you *die*?" the other man muttered in an unforgettable tenor, tinged with a Southern drawl.

"Van Zant?" he asked, disbelieving.

VZ was one of the good ones, relatively speaking. The

weight on his chest lifted a fraction; he used the distraction without shame or hesitation. In a smooth motion, he bucked and brought his knee up, slamming the other man's head down onto it. The next second he was kneeling on top of his chest, both hands around the other man's throat.

"Get off me, Reyes." The Alabama Ace tried to sound defiant.

Fuck, that wasn't good. He heard a soft inhalation from the other side of the bed. Kyra had noticed that recognition. There would be questions. Right now, though, he had something else to worry about.

"If you give me your word," Reyes said softly, "I'll let you walk out of here. But you have to swear you'll leave us be."

"Can't," he choked out. "I took the job, right? You know my work ethic."

Unfortunately, he did. If he let VZ go, he'd keep coming until one of them was dead. First, he needed to know something, however. Reyes tightened his hands around the other man's throat. By now he would be seeing stars, oxygen growing short. Still he struggled. "How'd you find us, V?"

"Monroe gave you up," Van Zant gasped, clearly enjoying the taunt. In their circles, everybody knew Monroe was the closest thing Reyes had to a friend. "Twenty large, and he sang."

That son of a bitch. Reyes closed his eyes, putting the blazing betrayal aside for the moment. He couldn't deal with it right now. With regret, he bore down, feeling the other man's neck give. His breathing choked out into a death rattle, and then ceased completely, leaving him dead meat on the floor.

Reyes found a lamp and flicked it on to survey the damage. In the physical sense, he had eight slashes that needed tending. In the emotional sense, Kyra was huddled in the corner, regarding him out of shattered eyes. From her look, he might have just raped and butchered her grandmother.

"He knew your name," she whispered. "*Why* did he know you?"

He felt wounded, weary, and sick, in no mood to go into this with her. Reyes hoped his expression didn't give away the sick fear eating at his insides. She shouldn't have found out like this. In self-defense, he brought the walls up, though she'd breached them weeks ago.

Even to himself, he sounded cold and remote. "We don't have time to talk right now. We need to clean this place up, bury the body, and get out of here."

"I'm not going anywhere with you until you answer me." Naked and wounded, she matched him for pure ice. Her shock and pain fused into a diamond-hard rage, making her dangerous.

There was something fierce and feral in her tumbled hair and gold-sparked eyes. The gun he'd knocked from Van Zant's grasp—a Beretta as it turned out—came up in Kyra's hands. Apparently she hadn't relied on him to win the fight, and she'd quietly located it during the scuffle. She could've shot them both at any time.

It was a little unnerving to realize that while he was fighting for her life, she was making contingency plans. He had no doubt she would have put a bullet between VZ's eyes if Reyes had lost, and she looked equally capable of doing it to him. No two ways about it—this sure as hell wasn't the situation in which he'd envisioned making a full confession to her. He hoped he survived it.

"I'm not kidding. Talk." Kyra cocked the gun to show she meant business.

CHAPTER 23

"Can I put something on first?" He stood before her naked and blood-smeared.

Kyra held the gun steady, refusing to reveal her nausea and heartache. "One article of clothing, and make it quick. I'm not feeling very patient."

In answer Rey found his jeans and slid them on, going commando. She wished he'd have a mishap with the zipper. No such luck. He sank down on the corner of the bed, keeping his hands where she could see them. He had a number of cuts that needed tending, but if she didn't like his answers, Kyra didn't care if he bled out.

"Serrano hired me," he said baldly, confirming her worst fears. "One of his guys contracted me to find you."

Anger blazed through her like a star going nova. Goddammit, she should have known better when he turned up for the second time, but he'd talked such a good game about fate bringing them together. At the time, it hadn't made sense that anybody tracking her would be able to get ahead of her, anticipate her movements. She'd thought it had to be coincidence.

By some miracle, she kept her voice level. Excess emotion would reveal how much he'd gotten to her, how much this *hurt*. "How'd you find me, asshole?"

"People remember your car. I stayed close on your trail until you hit Louisiana. You spent a few days in town, so I finally caught up with you. First thing, I put a GPS tracker on the bottom of your vehicle and then followed via updates to my phone. You got into town so late that I had a chance to scope out the bars. I picked the one I thought looked most likely and got lucky."

"How come you didn't just kill me outside the bar in Eunice? You had a knife."

"Serrano wanted the money back," he answered, toneless. "I wasn't supposed to proceed until I found out where you stashed it."

"But you decided to fuck around with me for a while first. I bet you play with your food before you eat it, too."

In the light cast by the small table light, his onyx eyes looked flat and dead. "I don't work for them anymore. If I was still on the job, why send someone else to finish it?" He hesitated and then added, "I found the money four days ago, and I didn't touch it. Go see for yourself."

A bluff, she thought. Not a bad one, but she already knew Rey was a fantastic liar. "Oh yeah? Where is it then?"

"Smuggler's compartment in the backseat, left side. It's in a silver case."

That shook her a little. He *did* know where to find the money. At any point during the last few days, he could've stolen the Marquis and left her stranded with nothing. Instinct told her to go check, make sure he hadn't stolen any, but she couldn't afford to turn her back on him.

"I'm supposed to believe that you decided you'd rather bone me than collect for killing me? You're one sick puppy, Porfirio."

Ah, that hit a nerve. Something like pain passed behind his empty eyes, a shadow sliding through an alley. Rey rested his hands on his knees, palms up. She knew his posture was intended to convey nonthreatening intent.

"At first you were just a job," he said quietly. "And then I got to know you. I realized Serrano's man had lied to me. I only commit to taking out people I'm sure deserve it. Unlike most, I'm particular about my contracts."

"Sure you are."

"If you'll let me, I'll show you the file they gave me."

She considered. It might be a ruse intended to distract her. Once she started reading, he'd take the gun, finish the job, and drive the Marquis to Vegas, along with the rest of her cash. Logically, it didn't make sense that he hadn't already done that. There had been no reason for him to hang around in the middle of nowhere for four days, if he already knew how to complete the job. Rey could have snapped her neck at any time.

"Get it." She gestured with the Beretta.

Moving slowly, he went to the living room and came back with his jacket. He retrieved a cell phone from a hidden interior pocket. Rey turned it on, pushed a few buttons, and then handed it to her. "Hit the bottom button to scroll down."

"Ruthless criminal," she read aloud, cherry-picking the juiciest bits. "Participated in her father's scheme to cheat the house, stole millions, and then killed him for his cut." Kyra looked up, eyes wide in disbelief. "*This* is what they told you? Why all the lies? Don't you assholes just take the money and do the job? Who cares about why?"

"I do. I wouldn't have taken the job if I'd known the truth."

"What difference does the truth make to such an accomplished liar?" Fury and anguish balled up in her stomach, tangling into knots: unshed tears and barbed wire. "I guess you figured out I didn't kill my dad."

"I know that. And I understand why you played Serrano. You really loved your old man. What are you going to do now?"

"I should kill you. But the sex was pretty good, so I think I'll just leave you here. If I see you again, I *will* shoot you."

"When this guy doesn't report in, they'll send someone else. If *he* doesn't get the job done, there will be another. They'll just keep coming. When are you going to sleep? You can't do this alone, Kyra. It's amazing you got as far as you did by yourself."

"Oh, *that's* a good idea. Call the woman with the gun incompetent." She raised the nose.

For the first time, he showed signs of agitation, scrubbing

a hand across his face. "Look, I didn't mean it like that. You need somebody watching your back."

"Like I'd trust you to do it," she snapped.

"Who else is there?"

That son of a bitch. He had to go and remind her how alone she was. If he thought emotional dependence would dictate her actions, he didn't know her at all. She hated that she'd mistaken sexual chemistry for something more. It made her feel stupid, gullible, another mark taken in by a strong chest and broad shoulders. Even looking at him now, she saw his bronze body on top of hers, his ebony head thrown back.

Her fingers trembled on the trigger; she was fiercely tempted to put a bullet in him. Now she liked the bruises around his eyes and his smashed nose. He deserved that and worse, the lying prick. If she could, she'd thank Dwight for roughing him up.

"Mia. I've been biding my time until she got back in the country. I just needed to keep moving. She'll be in Fargo by now . . . I just need to get there. And you stay the hell away from me."

She needed to get dressed, but she couldn't figure out how to manage it with a gun in one hand. Pulling a shirt over her head would give him more than the time he needed to take control of the situation. Kyra tried not to show any uncertainty while she considered the problem.

"She's not in Fargo."

Kyra froze. "How do you know that?"

"When I called my contact four days ago to tell him I quit, he asked me to pass a message. He said to tell you 'your friend says hello . . . Mia is such a charming woman.'"

She launched herself then, rage finally overcoming common sense. By some miracle, the hit connected, and the Beretta struck upside his head. "You asshole! They've had her for *four* days? When were you going to tell me? If anything happens to her, you're a dead man, you understand me?"

Kyra lifted her arm, and only then did she realize he wasn't trying to protect himself. He'd let her pistol whip him. She lowered the gun slowly, trying to understand what the hell he was doing. Nothing, it seemed. His hands were still on his knees, blood now trickling down his face from where she'd hit him.

"I should have told you sooner," he said. "So you get that one, free and clear. I deserved it, but don't raise your hand to me again."

"I don't think you're in any position to be making demands."

"Neither are you."

She lofted the gun. "How do you figure?"

"I could take that from you in less than ten seconds, now that you're within arm's reach." Then he did, disarming her with such lightning speed that she barely had time to dance back a few steps. "See? You may not like me, or want me around, but you need me. Mia's in the hands of your enemies. Just how do you propose to save her alone?"

She knows I'm *right.* Reyes watched conflicting emotions flicker over her expressive face. Kyra wanted nothing more to do with him; he realized that. Things as they had been were over, but he couldn't abandon her. He'd help her rescue her friend and finish things with Serrano. That meant returning to the scene of the crime, Sin City.

"I'll figure something out," she muttered.

"You have to take him out, you know. You started this; he has to finish it. He'll just keep sending people after you, no matter where you run, and there's no shortage of men looking to make a quick buck."

Kyra appeared to sift through his words, looking for mistruths or personal agenda. She wouldn't find any. If he had any sense, he'd walk away now, and try to forget what it had been like between them before she learned the truth. Even now he wanted to touch her, but she'd take his hand off at the wrist.

"All right," she said finally. "We make one last run together. Vegas. When Mia is safe and Serrano is out of the picture, we go our separate ways. I am *hiring* you," she added in a voice made of ice and knives. "This is business. You don't touch me again."

Regret, dusted with sorrow, settled at the back of his throat. It felt oddly like tears, and it made his voice raw.

"Understood. I'll do the job for a hundred grand."

"Let's be perfectly clear about what that entails."

"You give me the money. That makes Serrano a dead man walking."

Her smile said she liked the idea of hiring him away from the man who'd paid him to kill her. "How can I be sure you'll honor our agreement? You decided you didn't want to work for him, after taking the job."

Reyes fisted his hands, gritting his teeth against the urge to punch something. "Foster misrepresented the truth, knowing I wouldn't take the job any other way."

"And you're the best," she mocked him. "It had to be you. No other killer for hire would do."

"I don't know about that," he muttered. "I don't know why Foster wanted me bad enough to lie."

"Your good looks and charming personality?" Her scorn slid like razors against his skin.

He wanted to defend himself, but she was in no mood to hear about his ethics, such as they were. So he nudged the body with his toe. "I'm taking him out back. We can talk more later."

"Unlikely," she muttered.

Without answering, he shrugged into a shirt, found his jacket, and went outside. Reyes found tools in the garage that indicated bodies had been buried in the woods before. He took the shovel in his left hand and then went back for the body. He slung the corpse over his right shoulder. VZ hadn't been a light guy, and he was tired, injured, so he was puffing by the time he got deep into the trees. If the ground was frozen, he might have to settle for dumping it, though burial would be better.

He generally didn't dispose of bodies. When people wanted someone killed, they wanted it known, so they could remarry, teach somebody a lesson, or collect insurance, whatever the rationale was for the murder. This time, he wanted people wondering.

Reyes found a soft patch beneath a cluster of pine trees. Digging was mindless, and he almost enjoyed it because the repetitive motion took his mind off other matters. He wasn't surprised by how much she now hated him, just saddened by it. The loss of her hit him harder than he'd expected. Oh, he'd known it was inevitable; he just hadn't realized how much he'd mind.

Several hours later, he had a small grave. Without ceremony, he rolled the body into it, and filled in the earth. That took another hour. By the time he finished, he was filthy, hungry, cold, and tired. Reyes gave a satisfied smile as he went back to the house. Physical distress went a fair way to obliterating emotional pain.

Astonishment rippled through him when he saw the Marquis still sitting there. Despite their agreement, he'd half expected to find her gone. Good to know her anger hadn't overruled her common sense. She needed him and he'd deliver. He didn't want payment from her, but he knew that was the only way she could put faith in their agreement. Kyra lived in a world where people were motivated by money, so she'd believe in greed where nothing else would convince her.

Inside, he found her in the living room, staring out the window. Kyra didn't acknowledge him as he came in, didn't even look his way. Her posture said he was nothing to her, less than nothing. She'd know better than anyone how indifference could wound him deeper than anything else; he'd given her the blades with which to cut him. The silence weighed on him, so he passed through.

Bills lay scattered on the bed where they'd made love so many times. So this was how it would be. An endless ache seared him, nothing like he'd ever felt before. No more could he reach for her in the night, no more could he wrap his arms around her and bury his face in her hair. He didn't have any rights at all where she was concerned, and that seemed entirely wrong.

The easy course would be to leave the money and walk away. Just go. But no matter how much it hurt him to stay, he'd see this thing through for her. It was the least he could do. In his way, he always honored his commitments. She might not believe it, but he was a man of his word.

She'd tidied up as best she could. Reyes scrubbed the floor. He wanted no signs that VZ had caught up with him here. Monroe needed to think he was free and clear, right up until Reyes put a bullet in his brain. That would have to keep, however, until they completed Kyra's business. Then he'd be free to settle that personal score.

At last he took a shower, washing off all the dirt and dried blood, and then he dressed. It didn't take long to gather up his things. Part of him would like to burn this place down because it represented both the best days of his life, and the worst. Instead he walked with measured steps to the front room where she waited.

"Ready?"

"Sure. Let's go get Mia." She held out her hand for the keys, which were still in his jacket pocket.

I'm not worthy to drive the Marquis, I get it. Reyes turned them over without protest. "I'll have to direct you."

"That's not a problem. How long will it take us?"

"Two days," he guessed. "Driving eight to ten hours a day."

"Could we make it in one?"

He considered. "If we took turns driving and slept along the way."

"Two days it is," she said, dismissing his use as anything but a smoking gun. "They won't hurt her. She's bait. You should call him and tell him I'm on the way, just so they're sure I've taken the lure."

"You think that's a good idea? They'll know we're coming."

"No," she corrected. "They'll know *I'm* coming. If we play this right, they won't see you until it's too late."

Smart. She was so damn smart. No wonder she'd kept one step ahead of him for months. How many nights had he spent, studying her picture? Trying to understand the kind of woman who could live as she did. His imagination hadn't done her justice.

"All right. I'll make the call."

Reyes got out his phone and dialed Foster. To his surprise, he got voice mail. The man must have something major going on, because he'd never failed to pick up before. "I gave the girl your message, and she's heading your way. Good luck, man, you're going to need it."

"Very good," she said as he disconnected. "Casual. That should take care of Mia, assuming they haven't done anything to her before now." Her eyes lanced through him like a laser scalpel.

"I should have told you, but you would have insisted on leaving right then, and we needed to let the trail go cold. You can't help her if you get yourself arrested. Plus, your leg needed to heal some."

"I'm not interested in your rationalizations. Get your ass in the car. We have a long way to go—"

"And a short time to get there." He hummed a few bars of "Eastbound and Down" before he remembered she didn't want to be reminded of how much she'd shared with him. Lying in his arms, she'd talked about how much she loved watching old *Smokey and the Bandit* movies with her dad. They hadn't gotten cable most of the places they stayed, so late-night network movies had been their mainstay during her childhood.

Kyra went pale, and her fists clenched. "Shut it, you understand me? You don't know me, no matter what you think."

Reyes got in the Marquis. Since he understood why she was furious, he didn't argue. But he did know her, all the way down to the bone, and for a little while—the sweetest little while—she had been his.

CHAPTER 24

Whenever Kyra looked at him, she felt sick.

So she kept her eyes on the road, and her hands on the wheel, trying not to think how he'd duped her. Shame burned like acid. At any time, he could've killed her. How many nights had she lain in his arms? And how unspeakably sad—she'd wanted him almost from the moment she lay eyes on him. How was that for self-destructive?

She'd loved the hint of danger about him. Of course, she could never have imagined what he did for a living. What kind of person went around killing people? It was sick and insane, and she *hated* him for making a fool of her.

The scenery along the highway didn't vary much. First it was green, scattered with trees. Sometimes there were cows and horses standing near barbed-wire fences, watching the cars with dim disinterest. Sometimes the lanes were clogged with trucks, all trying to make a delivery before deadline. Numb, Kyra drove on.

It was a long day. She played the radio and tried to ignore him. He was smart enough to be quiet, not bothering her with rationalizations. Reyes knew she wasn't interested in hearing it. They stopped once for food, bathroom breaks, and gas, then she stopped once more for some replacement clothing. Then she drove another four hours.

By the time she stopped for the night, it was late. She chose a cheap motel off the interstate from a billboard with flickering lights that claimed rooms started at $29.95. The place had been painted at some point; maybe it was intended to be terracotta, but sun and wind had faded it to a pale peach with dirty streaks.

The man at the desk had to be a hundred if he was a day, and he was hard of hearing. She shouted her request for a room three times before finally getting through to him. After that, things went efficiently enough. She filled out her card with a flourish, signing the name Rachel Justice out of pure defiance. At this point she wanted to leave a trail back to Vegas. This would end now, one way or another. No more running, no more hiding.

Kyra took the key card, and let Reyes manage his own business. God, how humiliating. All this time, she'd been giving him a cut of their take, trying to show him the ropes, as if he needed it. Paid killers made top dollar; he hadn't been interested in the crumpled bills they collected at all. Everything he said—everything she *felt*—had been orchestrated to earn her trust, trick her into turning over the money. If she'd been a little less wary, she'd have a bullet in her head by now.

Kyra straightened her shoulders as she walked out of the dark, musty office. She limped, taking it slow. Her leg was sore, but nothing she couldn't handle. With Mia's life on the line, she wouldn't let it slow her down.

The cracked sidewalk had buckled, so she watched her step in heading for her room. This motel was shaped like a squared U with rooms on two levels. The upper balcony ran along the interior of the structure with the office in the middle. At the center of the U sat a neglected pool; in the guttering fluorescent lights, the water gleamed an oily black and littered with leaves. It didn't look as though anybody had used it in years.

The room was much as she'd expected, except smaller. There was only a double bed and a dresser, then beyond that, the tiny little bathroom. The beige carpeting was worn and stained, but what could you expect for thirty bucks? Kyra tossed her bag beside the bed and decided it was better she didn't have an ultraviolet light to find all the semen stains.

After wrapping a plastic bag around her calf, she took a long shower as if she could scrub away the memory of his touch. It didn't work, but she was more than clean when she stepped out onto the small, scratchy towel she'd spread on the floor. A second towel sufficed to dry off, though she could probably have used it as a loofah. Maybe she could use a vacation when this was all over; she'd go somewhere warm, where everything was clean and luxurious.

Kyra dressed in sweats and a T-shirt, left the light on, and curled up in the center of the bed. Silence made things worse, somehow. Tears prickled at the edges of her eyes, but she refused to cry just because she'd been stupid. It wasn't the first time, and it probably wouldn't be the last. She just had to tolerate him until they finished with Serrano. It was idiocy to imagine she could handle things alone. Sleep took a long time coming, and her dreams were full of an onyx-eyed man who carried a gleaming knife—and who kissed her with the sweetest longing, just before plunging the blade into her heart.

In the morning, someone tapped on her door. Kyra came awake, shivering and sweaty, but she couldn't remember anything. Caution made her tiptoe to the window to look out, despite the chain on the door. She found Reyes standing there in the early chill, his breath puffing out in smoky wisps. If she hadn't glimpsed the white bakery bag, she might've flipped him off through the glass and gone back to bed. With a mumbled curse, she let him in. He brought with him the scent of fresh coffee and fried dough.

Her stomach growled, but she fixed a hard stare on him, trying to seem cool when she wanted to go for him with her nails, hurt him a fraction as much as he had her. Unfortunately, her talent didn't work on him anymore, so he'd subdue her all too easily. Kyra regretted his immunity wholeheartedly.

"You can't buy me off with food. I despise you."

"I know," he said. "But you still need to eat." Reyes set her coffee cup on the chest along with a few sugar packets and two tiny cartons of nondairy creamer, then he put the pastry bag down as well. "Half a dozen mixed doughnuts. Enjoy."

"How do I know you didn't tamper with them?"

A flicker of something—anger, frustration?—rippled over his harsh face, the first visible emotional reaction since she'd found out the truth. Christ, she'd thought he was made of iron and obsidian. "Do you want me to taste the coffee? Take a bite out of each doughnut?" he asked, caustic. "But wouldn't that be worse than poison?" He paused. "A few days back, you were begging for my mouth."

She tried not to flinch. "I didn't know who you were, then. Now, for all I know, you intend to drug me and turn me over to Serrano. Maybe you're double-crossing *me*, not him, and this is the easiest way to get me and the car back to Vegas." As the hot, impulsive words poured out, she began to feel sick.

How could she be sure that wasn't the case? Maybe Mia wasn't even in Vegas, although how Reyes had found out about her was anybody's guess. She might be in Fargo, working, as she'd mentioned last time they talked. Kyra had her friend's cell number, but she never called. Those records could be subpoenaed, and she had warrants out. Mia didn't need law enforcement leaning on her. If she refused to cooperate—and she would—they could slap her with obstruction of justice, at the very least.

Should she risk calling from a pay phone? It might be worth the risk to check out Mia's situation for herself. A number of things could go wrong, but anything was better than not knowing.

Reyes regarded her, his dark face inscrutable. "You aren't going to believe anything I say. So just keep a close eye on me until actions establish what is true."

"I will." Kyra willed herself to stone and not remember how he could be fierce and gentle by turns, how for too brief a time, he'd given her everything she ever wanted. "Take a sip of the coffee and a bite from three random doughnuts for me, please."

He did as she asked. His stoicism gave the impression of masking a deep and brutal wound—and doubtless that was calculated as well. Sure, he was probably scarred for life over being found out. It must suck to find himself sleeping alone after so much pussy on tap. Kyra suppressed a bitter laugh over the idea she'd meant anything more than a job to him, more than convenient sex.

"I'll be in my room when you're ready to go," he said, letting himself out.

Her stomach rumbled. With a silent curse for the man who'd brought them, she devoured the doughnuts. Oddly, she couldn't make herself eat the part where he'd taken a bite. Instead she broke the pastry with her fingers and dropped it in the trash. Then she made the coffee pale and sweet as she liked it, guzzled it in a rush. When the sugar and caffeine hit her system, she felt almost equipped to face the day.

It didn't take Kyra long to get ready. She changed into jeans with holes in the knees and tugged a hoodie over her T-shirt. Snagging her backpack, she gave the room a final visual inspection to make sure she hadn't left anything behind, and then she slid out the door. Kyra crept past his room down to the office; there was a pay phone outside. She found Mia's number on a scrap of paper tucked in her wallet.

After scrounging up sufficient change, she dropped it into the machine and dialed. The phone rang four times and popped to voice mail. Mia's cheery voice said:

"I'm not available to take your call. Leave a message, please."

"Just wanted to let you know I'm on my way," she said quietly, and disconnected.

Reaching voice mail told her precisely nothing. If Serrano had Mia, it was unlikely he'd allow her to answer the phone. She might also be busy. It was pretty early. Calling Fargo information wouldn't help; Mia always stayed in furnished short-term housing, so she wouldn't show up on information.

But she could get the numbers of all the hotels that offered furnished corporate suites. Fargo wasn't enormous—how many could there be? It was better than being stupid and going blindly back to Vegas with a killer who had already deceived her once.

Kyra had to get change for the phone, and then she made the call and scribbled down all the numbers. Ten phone calls later, she'd discovered that nobody named Mia Sauter was currently staying—or had ever stayed—at any of the locations. That seemed pretty conclusive that Mia wasn't in Fargo. She turned, found Reyes leaning on the Marquis across the parking lot. No telling how long he'd been watching her. Kyra sauntered toward him, tucking her wallet back into her bag.

"Satisfied?" he asked. "Are we still heading to Vegas?"

God, how she hated to answer, "Yeah."

Reyes couldn't say he'd ever cared before what anyone thought of him, but he missed the light in her eyes when she looked at him. Now there was only suspicion and dislike. He couldn't complain. He'd earned it.

The damn stubborn woman wouldn't let him take his turn driving. He wasn't worthy to touch her sainted father's legacy or some such crap. He'd love to smash the shit out of her fantasy that Beckwith had been something special, but she didn't deserve that. Sometimes it was kinder to leave people their illusions.

By late afternoon they were in the Badlands, and the sun went down in a ball of fire, leaving streaks of red and orange to crack the sky. She didn't talk. Instead she sang along with the radio, ignoring him. It was ridiculous to be bothered by that, but he felt seven years old again, coming and going without acknowledgment. He could stand in a room with his dad for hours, and the old man would never say a word, lost in a smoky haze or simply plucking out bluesy notes for a song that would never be finished.

Her silence made him that helpless kid again, and he hated it. More than anything, he wanted to walk away. Forget his part in this. She'd laugh gleefully at the idea she could wound him, and he hoped she never figured out how much power she possessed.

They rolled into Vegas near midnight. The lights gave the city a festive, faintly decadent air. He'd always wondered what anthropologists would make of the place, once it lay in ruins a thousand years from now. They'd find a palace fit for a Roman emperor, an enormous Venetian villa, and a strange pyramid all in the same immediate area. No question, Vegas was a strange place, full of vice and urban magic.

For the right price, you could buy almost anything, which was why he kept an apartment here. The condo in Cali was the closest thing he had to a home, but he had four places total: Cali, New York, Vegas, and London. You never knew when things might get interesting, and you might want to slide out of the country for a while.

"I have a loft downtown." It was the first time he'd spoken in hours.

To his surprise she didn't argue. "Good for us. It will be better if we stay out of hotels. I don't want Serrano knowing we're in town until we've had a chance to scope out his movements, find out where he's keeping Mia and lay out a plan of attack."

Smart. He was struck again by her intelligent pragmatism. Kyra wouldn't focus on her hurt feelings until after they got the job done. A surge of admiration went through him like a spear.

"You'll want to turn left at the next light," he told her. "And then straight for three miles. I'll let you know as we get closer."

They reached the loft just before one, and Reyes directed her to his spot inside the parking garage. He had been a little worried that they might have trouble with bikers along the way, but apparently with Dwight dead, they'd lost interest in pursuing a vendetta. That qualified them as clever as hell in his book.

Kyra didn't seem pleased with the wrought-iron industrial cage lift that took them to the fifth floor. She kept peering down as if expecting something terrible to happen. Reyes didn't comment, merely led the way to the apartment, and let them both in. He had a different set of keys for each name, each life, but only the condo in Cali belonged to Porfirio Ten-Bears Reyes.

"It's a little Spartan," she said, as she surveyed the place.

That didn't seem to require an answer. He knew what she meant: one chair, no television, no pictures, no couch. A fine film of dust covered everything, and it felt close inside. Someone with time and imagination could probably do well with it; the hardwood floors were nice, and he quite liked the brick wall that accented the white plaster. A black spiral staircase led up to the bedroom, where he had an air mattress. It was a nice one, but anyone who came in would be able to tell nobody lived here long-term.

Kyra went to the balcony doors and opened them to let in some fresh air. Under other circumstances, he would have gone to the store and cooked for her again, but he didn't imagine she wanted to repeat the experience. She was the sort of woman who learned from her mistakes. His pain had shifted into quiet resignation. At this point he just hoped there would come a time when she could think about him without regret.

She tossed the greasy fast-food bags on the gray and black marble countertop. The galley kitchen was small, and he'd never bought food for the fridge. He couldn't remember spending more than a week here on any occasion. After this, he would have to sell it. He couldn't use the loft again without seeing her here, silhouetted by the city lights. A breeze blew in from outdoors, tinged with exhaust, and it spun through her curls like delicate fingers.

"Eat up," she invited.

But she didn't touch his food. Once she would've unfolded the foil and laid out his fries on top beside the burger, as if setting the table with expensive china. It was funny how such a number of small things added up to something important. This time, she left it in the bag, and he didn't want it. The smell of charred meat, grease soaking into soggy bread, did nothing for him.

"The bathroom is here." He pointed to the right of the door. "You can sleep upstairs. I'll camp out down here."

Kyra took a big bite out of her burger, chewed, swallowed, and then pointed a french fry at him. "You won't win points by being chivalrous. But I'm not arguing against taking the bed. You deserve to sleep on the floor like a dog."

He had another air mattress in the closet, which would make them equal in terms of comfort, but he decided not to point that out. As she finished her meal, he realized she'd thawed from silence to sniping, which had to be better. It *felt* better anyway, though perhaps that impression came as a result of upbringing. *Poor bastard,* he mocked himself. *All grown up and still tangled up with Daddy issues.*

She finished her food and muttered, “I’m gonna take a shower.”

Just a few days back, she would’ve dragged him in there with her and they would’ve made love beneath the steamy fall of water. He imagined her skin slick and wet, gleaming beneath his hands. Christ, these memories would drive him nuts.

Just when he thought he’d snap with the need to lash out, he realized something else. No matter what thoughts occupied her conscious mind, she didn’t fear him. Smart people just don’t mouth off to someone they think might put a bullet in them. Hope buoyed in his chest. Maybe if he showed her via action, as he’d said earlier, she might one day forgive him.

Reyes didn’t expect it. He never expected anything of anyone; it was easier that way. He didn’t get attached to people, places, or things. That way, he functioned as entirely self-sufficient and self-contained.

But he wasn’t. Not anymore. Not since he’d seen her bend over a pool table and sink a shot like she owned the place. As he listened to her belt out an awful, off-key rendition of “Brown-Eyed Girl” with him on the wrong side of the bathroom wall, his heart broke a little bit.

CHAPTER 25

Detective Sagorski was a fat fuck, Serrano thought—a waste of space. Doubtless he would milk the system for five more years, and then retire to drink beer on a hearty pension and the taxpayer's dollar. He'd been asking pointless questions for the last ten minutes, as if somebody like him could get Serrano to spill his guts.

His cheap brown polyester jacket strained at the seams, his shirt was badly wrinkled, and his tie sported a mustard stain. The asshole kept referring to his notebook, as if he couldn't remember what Serrano had said a few minutes before. He had bloodshot eyes and heavy hanging jowls that gave him the look of a tired basset hound.

Serrano tried to restrain his impatience. "Is there anything else I can do for you, detective?"

A spark of irritation showed in the other man's tired eyes. "I still have a few questions, if you don't mind." Though the words were polite, his tone wasn't.

"Go ahead." For the first time, a prickle of unease skated across his calm.

But Serrano hadn't gotten where he was by rattling easy. They'd have to do a lot more than send some toothless old dog on the verge of retirement to scare him.

"When was the last you saw Lou Pasternak and Joe Ricci?" The guy got to the point at last.

He pretended to think about it. "At a . . . gentleman's club. I can't remember exactly how long ago, though."

"Yes." Sagorski named the place. "I have the date. Witnesses say you exchanged heated words before you left."

That was a little too close for comfort. How the hell did they know to look at him for this? It didn't matter, he told himself. He was clean. He'd just done a little digging, made a few phone calls . . . and used the Russians as his triggermen. Nothing could be traced back to him. Even the Russians didn't know who had tipped them off.

"Nothing serious. They were just ribbing me a little bit."

"Over your recent romantic failure? It's too bad. We watched that video down at the precinct. One of our CIs gave us the heads-up."

Serrano's jaw clenched. "Probably. I can't remember."

"There's a lot you can't remember." In dogged persistence, Sagorski revealed he had the nature of a bulldog, not a basset, and once he sank his teeth into something, he wouldn't let go.

"Only criminals think they need to have an alibi ready," he said blandly. "I'm a businessman. Are you going to tell me what this is all about?"

As if he didn't know.

At that, the detective reached for his briefcase and withdrew a folder. "Sure. Pasternak and Ricci were found dead in their homes, three nights ago."

"That's too bad," he said. "This used to be such a nice town. Family friendly."

Sagorski ran his hands through thinning hair, leaving it standing on end like baby chick fluff. "Thing is, they were both shot twice in the back of the head."

He kept his expression neutral. "Strange coincidence."

Anybody with half a brain knew that was an execution-style shooting. You could pull some mope off the street and he'd tell you the same. That was the problem; everybody watching *CSI* thought they knew something.

The detective's mouth tightened. "We don't think it's a

coincidence, Mr. Serrano. They were business partners, so we think they got into something they shouldn't have."

Like laundering for the Armenians?

He raised his brows and leaned forward on his heavy mahogany desk. "How do you think I can help you with this, detective?"

"We're just beating the bushes." Sagorski tossed the folder on top of some paperwork Foster had brought him to sign the day before. "Hoping to find some leads. Go on, open it."

With growing trepidation, he did so. Glossy photos spilled out.

Jesus.

He'd understated the nature of their deaths. Serrano had seen some rough corpses in his time, but these sent a cold chill through even him. *Remind me never to get on the wrong side of Odessa.* Sagorksi had kindly provided both dorsal and ventral view. Whatever weapon they'd used had blown the back of their heads clean off. *It had to be high caliber. Overkill, really.*

But that wasn't the worst of it. Their hands had been hacked off at the wrists and stuffed into their mouths, and some crazy son of a bitch had carved Russian characters all over their bodies. Serrano didn't read Russian but he could guess what the letters said.

"Damn." There was no need to feign shock. Barayev was 100 percent crazier than he'd envisioned—and he had a good imagination.

"They did it while they were still alive," Sagorksi went on. "We're guessing they used a meat cleaver for the amputations. We think the knife work is meant as an object lesson. These men suffered a lot."

"I'm sorry to hear it." He was, actually. "They didn't deserve to go out like this."

Serrano would've been content with two shots to the back of the head, but he supposed the Red higher-ups felt there was some need to make an example of them. He could understand the reasoning; he worked in a similar fashion himself, though he'd never gone to such extremes. Quieter methods worked just as well for him since he didn't have a huge network to hide behind. That would entail trusting too many people with both his secrets and his money.

"So you don't know anything about this?"

They'd gotten a tip, he realized. There was no other reason they'd be looking so hard in his direction. Fury sparked through him. When Serrano found the son of a bitch who'd dimed him, he would make him so sorry. Then reason asserted itself. If their informant went missing after they talked to him, it would just persuade them he'd been telling the truth, even if they had no proof. He didn't need an army of law enforcement poking into every crevice.

"I wish I could be more help," he said. "Is there anything else, detective?"

"Actually, yes." Sagorski collected the pictures and tucked them back in his briefcase. "Do you know anything about Wayne Sweet? He was last seen in your company."

His polite smile froze. *Holy fuck.* Who had this bastard been talking to?

"He went to Switzerland with me," he answered readily enough. "To provide security. He met some ski bunny . . . they seemed to be having a good time, so I told him he could change his ticket and keep the suite for a week. Why? What's wrong?"

"He never made it home," Sagorski said. "His great-uncle . . ." He consulted his ubiquitous notebook once again. ". . . a Joseph Geller, reported him missing when he didn't show up to see him. Mr. Sweet visited once a month on Sunday, like clockwork."

Goddammit. Foster had checked his record and said he had no next of kin. Well, no fucking way. He wasn't going down for Wayne Sweet. They might suspect, but they didn't know.

"That's too bad. I'll send the old gent a fruit basket."

"Apparently Wayne was the only family poor Geller had left. He isn't going to shut up until we find him some answers." Though couched in innocuous terms, Serrano recognized that for a warning.

Sagorski may as well have said: *I'm onto you. I'll be digging in your trash, and I'm gonna keep coming until I find something.*

"I'd want to know, too," he said politely. "But if there's nothing else, I have work to do."

The cop rose, and with an effort, buttoned his suit jacket. "We'll be in touch. If you think of anything that could help, let us know."

"I'll do that."

Rage coiled through him, but Serrano waited a full five minutes before he picked up the lamp and hurled it at the door. His assistant came running, and she looked at the wreckage with wide eyes. "Everything all right, sir?"

"Fine," he gritted. "Get maintenance up here, will you? Damn thing had a short."

She scurried out as if she suspected he might launch something at her head next. Serrano swore over scaring her. He liked Sandy. The woman was a little timid, but she was efficient, and she didn't pester him with things she could handle herself. More important, she was reliable and loyal; she'd worked for him for fifteen years.

He called Foster and left a message when the asshole didn't answer his cell. "I want you up here as soon as you get in tonight. We need to talk."

If he hadn't been dumb enough to fall for Rachel Justice, Sweet wouldn't have posted that video. Pasternak and Ricci wouldn't have needed to go down for disrespecting him. They'd been his friends, once. Every rotten thing that had happened in the last six months could be traced directly to that bitch. And such irony—he'd wanted to go straight for her. Focus on his legitimate business interests, start a family. He hated how much he missed her, even now.

But she'd pay. And that would make everything else worthwhile.

Foster got the message marked urgent at four thirty that afternoon. He played it, deleted it, and ignored it. Whatever crisis Serrano was having, he could do it by himself. They were expecting him at Desert Winds to take care of Beulah and Lexie; he needed to sign the paperwork approving their transfer to an exclusive facility in Maryland. He was almost done here. It was time to start tying up loose ends in preparation for the greatest disappearing act of all time.

Even Houdini couldn't better it, he thought with a wry half smile.

He parked the Altima and strode up the walk toward the building. The head day nurse ushered him into the director's office, where everything was expensive and understated. He wouldn't be surprised if the plaque that read "Donald Moody" was embossed with real gold. Moody was a tall, thin man with a cavernous face. To Foster, he looked more like an undertaker, which didn't exactly recommend him as a manager for a long-term care facility.

Still, it didn't take long to sort things out. When money greased the wheels, everything was easier. The director produced the documents and Foster started signing them with a flourish that wasn't his own.

"We're sorry to see them go," Moody said.

You're sorry to lose my payments, you mean. Foster could count the times he'd spoken to this man on one hand, including patient intake. He offered a polite smile and continued writing the name that wasn't his own until he'd completed the stack.

Belatedly he realized the man was accustomed to acknowledgment when he spoke.

"I'm being transferred," he explained. "But the care they've received here has been stellar."

Moody smiled. "Glad to hear it. Obviously we take care of transport for you. You'll be able to see them in Maryland next week."

Foster calculated. Even if he hadn't completely wrapped up, it would be good to get them out of Vegas. Things would be coming to a head by then. It could get messy.

"That sounds excellent," he said, standing. "Is there anything else?"

"Not on our end." Moody handed him his copies of the paperwork. "You'll want to check with the facility in Maryland to make sure everything went smoothly."

"I will. Thanks."

They shook hands, and he left without seeing Lexie or Beulah. The old lady thrived on routine, so if he showed up on the wrong day, it would confuse her. He twinged with regret over needing to move her, as she'd gotten really used to this place, but it wouldn't be safe for her to stay once things heated up. Whatever else could be said of him, he looked after his dependents.

Foster made his way out, long strides eating up the distance back to his car. He hadn't spoken to Mia in days, but he knew she was here. After that near miss at the diner, she hadn't wanted to talk to him. He realized he'd injured her vanity, but explanations would only make it worse; it was better to retain this layer of constraint. She'd called him a few days back, though, to let him know Kyra was on the way.

How he'd smiled over that. Yes, matters were coming to a head, after a long roiling boil. Staying at his apartment, knowing somebody had been inside, took all of his control. But he went about his usual routine, knowing that any deviation would give away the game, and he'd come too far to fail now.

After he left Desert Winds, he grabbed a meal and then went to work at the usual time. Serrano would be furious by now. Foster passed through the Silver Lady, answering a few questions from security personnel along the way. Then, using his personal key, he took the executive express elevator up to the penthouse office. As usual, Sandy was already gone when he stepped off the lift and into the antechamber, so he let himself in.

"Where the fuck have you been?"

"Off work," he returned. "I'm not so much as half a second late, Mr. Serrano."

"We have a situation brewing here. Why the hell didn't you tell me Sweet had relatives, somebody to raise a fit when he went missing?"

Foster furrowed his brow, enjoying his part in the drama. "I checked his personnel file, sir. He listed 'no next of kin.' Would you like me to get it for you, so you can verify the documentation?"

The other man paced. "No, I don't want to see the damn file. Why didn't you dig deeper? I can't afford to work with someone who's sloppy."

"With all due respect, sir, my job is chief of security, not chief of your personal Gestapo." That subtle insubordination might be pushing it, but he needed to keep Serrano off balance or he might start looking too hard at various pieces of the puzzle.

Serrano narrowed his eyes dangerously. "For what I'm paying you, you're my bitch, and you do whatever I tell you to do. If I say bark, you make some noise. Get me?"

"Woof," Foster said.

"We could be in a world of shit over this."

What's this "we," white man? For obvious reasons he kept the joke to himself, merely listened with a grave, impenetrable patience as Serrano outlined the travails of his day. He'd already known most of it, or at least suspected, but it explained why Serrano was so worked up.

"You want me to look into this Sagorski?" he guessed. "See what I can find."

His boss nodded. "Yeah. There's no such thing as a clean cop, just one who hasn't been caught yet."

"I'm on it."

"That's all for tonight. Oh, and make sure we run clean games for the next month or so. Tell the dealers. I don't want to give them anything on me if they send undercover assholes sniffing around."

"Smart." Foster bit back a smile. "They got Capone on tax evasion, after all."

"Precisely. Now I'm going home. This place better be in one piece when I get back." Though Serrano's tone seemed jocular enough, Foster knew he was being warned.

I'm watching you. You made one mistake already. One more, and you're gone.

And Serrano didn't exactly offer a retirement plan to those who knew firsthand how he did business. That might just be the politest death threat he'd ever received.

Once the asshole left, Foster put the word out that they were going legit for the foreseeable future. No trick dealing, no fixes on roulette. The dealers groaned a little because they depended on their extra cut of the skewed winnings, but that couldn't be helped. He had to keep the man happy for a little while longer, however little he liked it.

Otherwise the night went smoothly enough, just the usual

snafus. He ejected a few drunks, caught a few people trying to work a new system, after buying some e-book online that had *foolproof* in the title. In the morning, he headed out, glad to put some miles between him and the Silver Lady.

Lately he'd found the place oppressive, and since he'd been forced to sever a satisfying sexual arrangement, he felt restless and prickly. Foster had no pressing business, so in the predawn coolness, he drove back to his apartment for a shower, food, and sleep, in that order.

Out of pure reflex, he surveyed the parking lot, checked all the paths. Foster didn't see anything out of place, no strange cars, no men lurking, and no sign of a tail. At that point, he left his vehicle and made for his building. Surprise sparked through him when he saw Mia sitting on the stairs, waiting for him.

Devoid of her usual high fashion, she wore black slacks and a matching pullover, almost as if she were dressed for a burglary. Doubtless that was her idea of what a woman wore for skulking around in the middle of the night. The dark colors should have made her skin look sallow. She should have looked frumpy. Instead she looked dangerous, and he wanted to touch her so badly he had to curl his hands into fists at his sides. He remembered she'd nearly kissed him, and for the first time in longer than he could recall, Foster could think of nothing to say.

She pushed to her feet. "You told me not to come to the casino again."

"Right," he agreed. "That would be a bad idea. Have you been here long?"

Stupid woman. Why couldn't she stay put? She shouldn't be roaming around at this hour.

Her being here was a bad idea, too, for several reasons. First off, he was tired and horny. He didn't know if he could trust himself to be alone with her. There came a point when he just didn't care what was right or fair; he could only think about what he wanted. Second, if someone was watching his place, they would've seen her by now, and he needed to keep her secret. She couldn't be allowed to fall into Serrano's hands. That would give him leverage.

"No, the cabbie dropped me off five minutes ago. I'm sorry

for dropping by like this, but I wasn't sure you'd take my call. Can I come up?" She actually seemed worried that she'd offended him with her unspeakable advances the other day.

Foster wanted to howl at the irony of it. What heterosexual male in his right mind refused to kiss a beautiful woman? Mentally he raised his hand and banged his head against a brick wall. No matter what she thought, it was for the best. The sooner she got out of his life, the better off they'd both be.

Regardless, they couldn't talk there. He'd left the bug in place, letting it report innocuous activity. He hoped he'd bored the crap out of whoever was listening to him. Maybe the sorry son of a bitch was asleep right now, but he'd review the logs later. That had to be Serrano's work, as the guy searched for some useful dirt. That was the way he worked. The Foundation would have moved on him long before now.

"That depends on what you want."

"Protection," she said baldly. "I think someone's after me, and I didn't know where else to go."

CHAPTER 26

Kyra tossed and turned on the air mattress.

It wasn't that the thing was particularly uncomfortable. She'd just gotten used to having a warm body in bed with her. And maybe she missed the sex, but it wasn't like she missed *him*. After all, to enjoy an encore, all she had to do was slip downstairs, tell him it didn't matter he was a lying bastard who'd been sent to kill her, and surrender her self-respect. The night was well advanced by the time she finally drifted off.

The sound of the shower woke her up. By the time she dressed and came down, she found him standing by the balcony doors in a pair of worn jeans, his hair sleek and dark against his head. The thin gray T-shirt molded to his shoulders and back, damp cotton revealing each shift. For a long, awful moment, she wanted nothing more than to lay her head between his shoulder blades, and she felt sick at the impulse.

"Is there a store within walking distance?"

"Several," he answered without asking why. "What do you need?"

"Ideally, a drug store, a thrift store, and an optician."

Reyes thought for a moment. "We're near downtown,

so you can find all three within a six-block radius."

That was good news. She got ready quickly, but Reyes insisted she wear a cap over her curls before he'd let her go out. Due to her leg, they walked slowly, and he showed no impatience when she needed to rest it. The bruises around his eyes had started to fade, but he looked like somebody had kicked the shit out of him. She should take pleasure in that. The cuts on his chest would scar.

They stopped first at the Walgreen's on the corner of Fourth and Fremont. They had a small grocery section, so he went to do a little shopping while she tried to decide on hair colors. She didn't want to keep it forever or have to re-dye later, so she needed something that washed out. Ordinarily she never messed with her hair; she liked the color. So he'd filled a basket with soups, juices, crackers, and junk food, and come back by the time she narrowed it down to two boxes of Clairol Natural Instincts.

"Which one?" she asked, not expecting him to care.

To her surprise, he set the basket down and took the boxes, considering the colors with all the care he'd give any weighty decision. She had to fight the ridiculous impression that he cared. "They're both nice," he said eventually, "but I think Navajo Bronze has too much red for your purposes. I'd go with Cinnamon Stick."

Astonished and off balance, she watched as he dropped the box in the red plastic basket and went to pay. By the time she caught up with him, he'd already checked out. Reyes took the bags and led the way out of the store.

"Where's the optician from here?"

"I think there's one on South Seventh . . . and there's a number of thrift stores on South Main. Up for a little walking?"

"You're the one carrying the bags." Kyra refused to give herself any quarter, despite the injured calf. "Did you get any perishables?"

"Nothing that won't keep. Let's take care of your errands."

Vegas during the day had a much different feel than at

night. Few cities had as much neon as you'd find here, but during the day everything looked deserted and quiet. People with hangovers no doubt hunkered down in their hotel rooms. You could almost figure people walking around downtown during the day lived and worked here.

At the optician she bought green contacts. They had no prescription and were disposable. The receptionist probably thought it was vanity, but she took care of the sale readily. Then they were on the way to the thrift store.

The first one they came to was run by a nonprofit organization called Opportunity Village. Kyra figured it was something like the Salvation Army. She went in and poked around through the used clothing, pulling out anything in her size that looked like a Sunday-school teacher might wear it. She wound up with a number of polyester print skirts and fussy button-up blouses. If she was going to snoop, trying to locate Mia, it made no sense to do it in a guise Serrano would immediately recognize.

She paid for her purchases, and Reyes took those bags as well. They didn't speak as they walked back to his loft. The day had already begun to heat up. Overhead the sun beat down even through her cap and found glimmering bits in the sidewalk. A few days back, he would've taken her hand, and it would have meant so much . . . because he could. He might've pushed her against the cool metal of that door, kissing her in the shadow of the building, before walking on. Now there was only silence, and she despised herself for being weak enough to mourn the dispelling of a lie.

Because it hurt to look at him, she dashed into the apartment as soon as he unlocked the door. "I'll be doing my hair."

"All right." She heard him go into the kitchen and start putting away the food.

Kyra leaned against the bathroom door for a moment. He'd bought cookies. Sweets. Frosted cupcakes. He didn't even eat that stuff. It had to be for her. For the love of God, *why*? *Never mind. Stay focused. You're the only thing standing between Mia and a permanent dirt nap.*

So she did her hair according to the directions and felt ridiculously sad when it was so dark when it dried. Next, she popped in the contacts—that quick, she became a green-eyed brunette. Once she put on the church-lady clothes, she hardly recognized herself. A pair of heavy, black wedge-heel sensible shoes completed the picture.

When she came out of the bathroom, he had two steaming bowls of soup waiting on the marble counter. She hesitated and then made her way over, hoisting herself onto the stool.

"Chicken noodle," he said. "You need something decent before you finish up with the sugar."

It wasn't worth arguing, although she didn't understand his obsession with what she ate. Kyra ate the damn soup and tried not to think about Mia, if she was safe, if she was scared. Her heart hurt for so many reasons. Once she'd finished, she gathered up her recently acquired pleather purse, and headed for the door.

Reyes blocked her path. "Don't go yet. You did a good job changing your appearance, but I have a few people I can talk to here first. Let me get the lay of the land before you hit the streets."

Kyra glared at him. "You make me sound like I'll be selling the goods."

"There's no point in you taking unnecessary risks. Serrano hired me through an intermediary, so he won't see me coming."

"It's *my* friend in Serrano's hands. Just who decides what's 'necessary' in this situation?" She stopped herself just before she yielded to the temptation to say, "You're not the boss of me." That was when she realized she was objecting to his plan on principle, not because there was anything tactically wrong with it.

"Give me three hours," he murmured. "If I can't turn up something useful, then we'll do it your way."

His low-key, unflappable demeanor was starting to get on her nerves. He acted like nothing touched him—nothing mattered. If you believed his face, Porfirio Ten-Bears Reyes was a crystal-clear pond, frozen all the way down to the rocky bottom. She hated how much she missed the illusion of warmth, the freedom to touch without taking, without worrying that the next touch would leave her head feeling like it had diamonds digging through her brain.

"All right." She paused, and then added grudgingly, "Do you need the keys to the Marquis?"

If he said yes, she was getting the money out of it before he took off. In fact, that might not be a bad idea anyway. Now that he knew where it was, she didn't feel good about letting him out of her sight.

He shook his head. "It draws attention. I'm better off leaving it in the garage."

Against her better judgment she sighed and sat down in the living room's only chair. "Three hours, not a minute more. If you're not back at . . ." Kyra checked her watch, "five forty-five, I'm going out to do my own legwork. Do you have anything to read?"

In answer, he ran upstairs, taking the steps two at a time. In motion Reyes was still the most beautiful man she'd ever seen, all dangerous, fluid grace, like knives spinning in the air above a juggler's head. When he returned, he handed her a book.

"*One Hundred Years of Solitude*," she read aloud. "Really?"

"I hope you like it." His onyx eyes said something else then, but she couldn't interpret the message. The moment passed, and he turned away, leaving her feeling as if she'd failed, somehow.

"Thanks." She thumbed the book and found it was a story of magical realism, whatever that meant. Maybe it would help her understand him.

To her surprise, Reyes leaned down and kissed her, a hard press of his lips that rang through her fierce and hot, echoing what she hadn't understood. Kyra gazed up in angry confusion, and took a swipe at him, but he'd already moved off toward the door.

"I'll be back," he promised. "Stay here. Stay safe."

Then he was gone, and Kyra began to read.

Reyes watched the parking garage for ten whole minutes after he left. He figured Kyra would give him at least that long before setting off on her own, if she'd lied to him. When the fifteen-minute mark came and went, he knew he had to get moving. She'd given him a time limit in which to ask around, and he damned well meant to be back on time, not give her an excuse to go out on her own.

Oh, he knew she was capable, more so than any woman he'd ever met. He'd never encountered anyone who could be a partner to him, not a liability, but Kyra qualified. But even she wasn't bulletproof. He didn't want to take chances with her. Even if she never forgave him, his world would be brighter for knowing she existed.

At last he took off, having no choice but to trust her promise. The irony didn't escape him. Reyes headed out on foot and made straight for the sweet cacophony of one of the downtown casinos. They all ran together here, lower budget than the ones on the Strip, less eye candy, more gambling specials. People who came down here were serious about winning and losing money, not necessarily looking for Cirque du Soleil, the Blue Man Group, or an aging lounge singer.

He picked one at random. Once inside, he bought a beer to blend in, popped the battery back in, and then made a call. "Apex?"

"What's up?" the guy said. "It's been awhile."

Reyes ignored the small talk, no time for it. "I need you to do a little checking on Gerard Serrano. His current financial situation, rumors around town."

"That won't come cheap. I'll have to rattle some cages, knock on some doors."

"Two large if you can get me something juicy in less than three hours."

"It's important—I hear you. I'll see what I can do."

"Bring the info to the bar at the Horseshoe. Don't call. I'm turning my cell off."

"Sounds like you're in some deep shit. Hope it don't splatter." His informant disconnected, leaving him to wait.

At the two-and-a-half-hour mark, Reyes was starting to get edgy. He'd put a lot of trust in Apex, a guy who'd worked for him off and on for several years. Just when he was about to head back to the loft, he saw the tall, skinny bastard weaving through the crowd toward him. Apex had added blue tips to the carmine streak in his dark hair, and he now sported five facial piercings instead of three. Otherwise he looked more or less the same.

"Let's get a table," he said in lieu of greeting.

Reyes followed him to a corner, where they could do business. It wouldn't do to draw attention by offering currency in the open. Somebody might take undue interest, thinking it was a drug deal instead of a simple money-for-info exchange. His ethnic heritage made that more likely; white people always seemed to think Latinos with cash were up to no good.

"What do you have for me?" Reyes asked.

"Pay me," Apex invited.

He slid a plain white envelope under the table, which the guy snagged and slid into his ripped jean jacket. The thing looked worse for the wear, hand painted with anarchy symbols and Chinese characters, held together with safety pins and affection. Reyes couldn't ever remember seeing Apex without it, no matter how hot it was. Beneath he wore one of his grubby T-shirts. This one read "Detroit Cobras."

"I hear three things. He's pissed because some bitch dumped him, one of his employees disappeared, and a cop named Sagorski is leaning on him. Thinks Serrano had something to do with taking out his competition. I hear it was a real professional hit, but messy, very messy. Sounds like it could be Serrano on a bad day. He ain't squeamish."

"Any evidence or they just like him for it?"

"Not sure. You didn't give me time to do a whole lot. If you want inside-the-precinct info, that's gonna take longer. And cost more."

Reyes waved that away. "I don't care who killed Serrano's competition, or what the five-oh think about it. Have you heard anything about a new woman? Has he been seen with anybody lately?"

"Nah, man. He seems to be off chicks. He spends all day at the casino, and then at night he might slide by one of his clubs, an upscale tittie bar or Farraday's, where he goes to hang with other rich fuckers." Bitterness salted Apex's voice, but Reyes didn't pursue it. Everybody had a pet hate.

So nobody had seen Mia coming or going. That meant Serrano had her locked down somewhere. This was where things would get interesting. It'd be hard as hell to figure out where he was keeping her, stage a rescue, and take the son of a bitch down quietly. They might need a little help.

"Can you swing by my place later? I have a special job for you."

A multipierced brow went up. "There's a reason we always meet in public places, dude. I don't jump like that."

"Ass," he muttered. "Bring a couple of your boys. I want you to do a little creeping for me."

"That'll cost you," Apex warned. "We ain't cheap."

"And you're not easy, either. I get it. Find out how many residences Serrano owns within reasonable driving distance for me, and then be there by eight." He scrawled the address on a cocktail napkin and slid it across the table.

Apex flashed a smile that rendered his features unexpectedly boyish. Not for the first time, Reyes wondered how old he was. The kid had been on his own for years, well before the age of majority, and he'd parlayed a nose for news into a lucrative business. He was also a fair hand at getting information he wasn't supposed to have, and not just about events in Vegas. He'd put Apex in his mid-twenties by now; they'd known each other awhile, but he couldn't be sure.

"Sounds like something fun is going down."

"Depends on your definition of fun."

"It's pretty loose." Apex stood and headed out without another word.

That was another thing about him; he didn't begin conversations with a hello or end them with a good-bye. He claimed life was too short to waste time on shit like that. Reyes watched him go, and then checked the time.

He swore. Only half an hour remained in the time limit Kyra had given him. She wasn't dumb, but she didn't like relying on him, either. She wanted to solve this problem on her own. Reyes tossed a twenty on the bar and quick-stepped toward the door. He didn't dare draw attention to himself by running.

Once outside, his strides lengthened. Reyes ran full out back toward the loft, convinced that he was going to be too late. What reason did she have to keep a promise to him? In her eyes, he was less than nothing, a murderer and a liar. He couldn't dispute either charge, didn't care to; it had never even bothered him until deceiving her.

His heart thundered in his ears. The apartment would be empty, just the lingering scent of coconut and the agony of not knowing what might be happening to her. She was a stubborn pain in the ass, and he didn't know why he cared. If she wanted to get herself killed, he shouldn't give a shit. God knew she couldn't wait to be shed of him.

By the time he got back to the building, his breath came in hard rasps, not from exertion but from fear. He could see it so clearly. Kyra would have slid out, trying to solve the problem on her own, after like half an hour. Some stooge who worked for Serrano would ID her, despite the new hair color, and they'd pick her up. They wouldn't know to be careful about touching her, and they'd manhandle her, leaving her with a terrible case of feedback. She wouldn't be able to use any of the abilities she'd stolen because of the pain. She'd be helpless in their hands.

Then he drew up short at finding the Marquis in the parking lot. It wasn't sure, he told himself. She might've gone out on foot, as he had. With his breath still shaky, he took the lift up and let himself in, fully prepared to find her gone, the apartment empty.

To his surprise, she was sitting in the chair where he'd left her, about a third of the way through the Marquez. She looked up with a bemused expression. "You're back."

"Yes." It seemed like he should say something else, but he had something squeezing at his heart, an emotion too profound to be relief.

"This is a weird book," she said, as if he hadn't run like hell to get back to her. "But compelling. I can't stop reading it. And I don't even understand what I like about it, you know?"

"Yeah," he said quietly. "I know all about that."

Then he began to fill her in on the emerging plan.

CHAPTER 27

Kyra had a serious case of confusion going on. She couldn't believe the crew Reyes had deputized. They'd started rolling in a little after eight, punkers and street thugs, all. They had an oddly alert air, though; none of them seemed to be junkies or 'heads, and they waited with good humor. Their leader, Apex, looked to her like a tropical fish, but he had a sharp mind, and he'd immediately gone to work on the laptop Reyes provided.

"You really think this will work?" she asked quietly.

Reyes studied her for a moment, somber, and his black eyes reminded her of a night without stars. "It has to. I'm out of ideas."

She wasn't overwhelmed with them, either. How hard they hit Serrano had to be tempered by her fear of what might happen to Mia caught in the crossfire. Kyra wished she'd never yielded to a weak impulse and confided in her friend. She'd never imagined Mia would come halfway around the world, trying to stop her, trying to *help* her. So much love and loyalty made her smile, even as worry gnawed a hole in her gut.

"I'm in," Apex said, after what seemed like forever, listening to him click the keys. "His phone records are right here."

Reyes took over the laptop then. "What's Mia's cell number?"

She thought it unlikely he'd have called her from his landline, but you never knew. She didn't spot it among the numbers called. Apex was skimming down the list over Reyes's shoulder. "Look, he's called this number twelve times in two days."

"You think he might be giving orders to guys guarding her?" Kyra asked.

"Can you find out who that number belongs to?" Reyes asked.

The hacker smiled. "Abso-fucking-lutely."

Reyes eased away from the laptop while Apex's boys milled around the loft. They'd complained about the lack of entertainment until their boss reminded them they were on a job, not here to have fun. Apex sat down again.

A few clicks and he said, "The number's unlisted, give me a minute." True to his word, he didn't take much longer before adding, "Bobby Rabinowitz. Serrano's been burning up the phone lines calling his money man."

"He's worried," Reyes guessed. "Checking out his options if he has to flee, how much money he can liquidate quickly."

"Because of the cop Apex said was leaning on him?" Kyra frowned. That didn't track with what she knew of Gerard Serrano. He was one tough son of a bitch, and he didn't scare easy. This wouldn't be the first time the police had looked his way.

"I don't think he's chatting with Rabinowitz because of Sagorski," Apex said.

She ran her hand through her hair, unnerved by the dark hue. "Then what?"

"If I knew that, I'd charge for the answer." Apex grinned, and for the first time, she noticed he had eyes that shone like slivers of jade.

"He calls this number a fair amount, too." She leaned forward, touching the screen as she counted. "Six times in the last few days."

"That's Foster's cell," Reyes said.

Kyra sighed. "So no help there."

"Here's another one." Apex pointed. "Four times. Either of you recognize it?"

"No." They spoke in unison.

"Then let's see who else he's been talking to." The hacker went to work, running the number through a series of programs. "Prepaid cell phone. Damn."

"That sounds like one of your colleagues," she said to Reyes. "You think?"

"Could be Van Zant," he admitted.

They'd never know because he'd buried the guy with his cell. Serrano might be calling a man who was six-feet deep, his phone vibrating away in his pants pocket. That image struck Kyra as more than a little macabre.

"Again, no help." She wanted to punch something.

The clock was ticking away. Every minute they spent trying to figure out where Mia was, her chance of survival went down. In many respects, this was like a kidnapping. They'd already lost valuable time.

"I don't think we're going to find anything out online," Apex said eventually. "It looks like this guy's too smart to leave a trail, point us the way."

"Agreed." Reyes spun to regard the rest of the crew who had been remarkably patient up until this point. "Time to move to phase two."

"Finally some action," one of them muttered.

"Keep your heads on straight," Apex warned. "No drinking, no gambling. I took the man's money in good faith, and I don't want any trouble in the casino that we haven't been paid for."

The plan was simple. Apex and crew would roll into the Silver Lady via the front doors. They'd start some low-level hassle: heckle dealers, mock the slot monkeys, maybe steal a few quarters. Eventually security would be dispatched to deal with them, at which point they'd do what they did best—run. Reyes had promised to bail out anybody who got caught. And while everybody was looking at the front doors, Kyra and Reyes would sneak in the back.

"Who's your best at security?" she asked.

Apex smiled. "I guess that would be me."

With a mental apology, she touched him lightly on the shoulder. "I should've guessed. Thanks for your help."

It had been long enough since she'd used the ability that she felt it flaring through her now, new neurons firing. She could tell Apex had noticed the theft, but he didn't know what to make of it. He frowned, glancing at where she'd touched him. Then he rubbed his shoulder, eyes narrowed.

Kyra jogged upstairs to get ready. Reyes made her wear one of her church-lady outfits, a pair of lime green double-knit polyester pants and a matching print blouse. For good measure, Kyra covered her freckles with foundation that make her skin look sun-damaged and orange. With her hair caught up in a barrette and a cheap pair of granny glasses, she hardly recognized herself.

"Damn." Apex offered up a wolf whistle, gently mocking.

Since she'd stolen from him, she let it go with a wry smile. Reyes paid her no attention, giving their crew a last-minute briefing. At last they were ready to go.

"You're crazy," Apex said. "It's gonna be hell getting up to the top floor, dude. But we'll do what we can to give you the opening. I'm just glad you paid up front."

Reyes laughed. "You wouldn't work for me any other way."

"Point. Let's roll out." He signaled to his boys and they took off.

"Just let me change."

Kyra almost said she liked him the way he was—and then she remembered that she didn't. Her heart hurt anew as she waited for him. She'd just gotten caught up in the excitement of planning their next move.

Within five minutes, he came downstairs wearing a sky blue leisure suit. He had on white shoes, a matching belt with enormous belt buckle, and he'd slicked his hair back with enough product to groom half of Manhattan. Somehow he'd managed to twist the leashed menace of his presence into a parody of itself; he'd become a joke.

"I'll never ask you to do anything I won't do myself."

Kyra couldn't help but laugh. "We look too goofy to be dangerous, is that it?"

"That's the idea. If they find us wandering where we shouldn't be, they won't immediately be on guard. That'll give us a few seconds to take care of business."

She knew what he meant. Sober now, she nodded. Maybe she didn't entirely like the idea of killing some unknown security guard, but she liked the idea of losing Mia even less. She'd do whatever it took to get her friend back.

Beyond this point, the plan was fluid. If they saw a chance, they'd take Serrano out, but they were hamstrung by not knowing where he'd stashed Mia. Reyes thought he had some failsafe in place—if the guards didn't hear from Serrano at a certain time, they'd kill her and clean up the scene.

Therefore, the primary objective was to get into security and make copies of the logs. They could review them elsewhere, and possibly figure out which of Serrano's men had taken her. At the least it might give them a direction to look, which was more than they had now.

"We need to make this fast. As of now, I can get us upstairs, but I don't know—"

"How long it'll last," he finished. "Let's go."

And so Kyra returned to the Silver Lady. In the one move Serrano would never anticipate, because assholes like him valued self above friendship, she walked right in the front door. She knew where the security cameras were, but she didn't look for them. Instead she feigned awe, gazing around at all the noise and flash. Serrano was like that, she thought, all sound and fury, signifying nothing. She couldn't remember where she'd heard that line, a movie maybe.

From her peripheral vision, she spotted Apex. Reyes gave him the signal as they passed through the casino. All the players were in place, so it was show time.

They couldn't be too direct in their approach to the doors at the back of the casino marked "private" but at the same time, they needed to be quick, or Kyra's stolen skill might go poof. Reyes knew a little about security, but he was no Apex, and he wouldn't want to bet their success on his rusty aptitude. It took all his self-control to lead them on a meandering path through the noisy casino.

He stopped twice to play the slots. Beside him, Kyra feigned an expression somewhere between disapproval and awe, as if she hadn't seen this place a hundred times before. He could almost believe she was a tourist from Minnesota.

Bells rang; lights flashed. The Silver Lady was perfectly garish. Too much time in a place like this could drive a man mad, and Reyes longed for somewhere quiet, but he'd see this damn thing through. He owed Kyra that much.

On cue, Apex's boys started some trouble. At first it was minor, and the security guys at the back of the room ignored it. Gradually, they escalated, and the guards had no choice but to move in. As soon as they did, Reyes took Kyra's hand, towing her toward the double doors that led into the private part of the casino.

That went without a hitch. Without the burly guys in suits, the door opened freely, as employees just had to flash a badge to get through. Security would get tougher as they went deeper. Kyra was silent beside him, completely focused on the mission. They followed the beige and bisque corridor down to a set of metal doors.

Their first challenge came in the form of a keypad. Reyes glanced at her in silent inquiry, and was surprised when she answered. Nobody had ever been able to read him like she did.

"I can do this," she said, already popping the panel to reroute the wires.

She worked for thirty seconds and then a spark lit up the display; the light flashed green. While he pushed the door open, she fit the cover back in place. It would withstand cursory scrutiny.

Inside the doors, he heard footfalls, more security. Fleetingly he wondered what the hell Apex was doing out there. But he'd paid well for a distraction, and his boys loved the chance to cause trouble for a guy like Serrano. Kyra was already looking for somewhere to hide. She found it in the form of a locked room.

"I have no tools. Shit. Credit card!" she demanded.

He gave her his AmEx, and she worked the door as the sound of running amplified. Any second now, they'd round the corner and find them. The lock snapped open and he shoved her through, not much caring what waited on the other side. He didn't want to fight this early in the game. If they started leaving bodies behind, it would get hard as hell to hide the fact they were coming. They'd find a small army waiting for them at the top. Plus, he objected on principle to killing guys who were just doing a job.

"Good work," he said softly, listening to the reinforcements run past.

When he turned, he saw they were in a room full of banquet supplies. Dining room chairs, replacement tables, linens, glasses . . . anything the restaurants on premises might need to replenish their stock. That gave him pause.

Maybe—

"They're gone. Should we roll out?"

Ignoring her, Reyes went over to some cardboard boxes, digging through. In the third one he checked, he hit pay dirt. He lifted a gray dress that looked about her size and tossed it at her. Finding something in his own size took more doing, but eventually he came up with a uniform that looked like it would work. Most likely some college athlete had worn it for a summer job. By the smell, these discards were none too clean, but they couldn't afford to be picky.

"Change," he said briefly.

She didn't argue, merely turned her back and skinned out of her clothes. His mouth went dry at seeing her sexy red underwear emerge from the green polyester nightmare he'd made her wear. Kyra scrambled into the maid outfit quicker than he got into the room-service uniform. He had the presence of mind to grab a tray and a silver dome from the shelving. If they could find her a cleaning cart, it would be even better. Nobody ever looked twice at janitorial staff. In fact, he'd used the ruse before, going where he wasn't supposed to be to kill some scumbag quietly.

When they slid out of the supply room, the corridor was empty. The fluorescent light seemed too bright after the shadows, but he set off with confidence. That was key. Look like you belong, and people are less likely to question you. As they went toward the service elevator, four more security guards blasted by them, but nobody said a word. They had their orders about dealing with the asshole punks on the floor.

Kyra gave him a look that asked, *It can't be this easy, can it?* Reyes shrugged, pushed the button for five, where she'd said security lay. Once, she'd had free run of this place, even a key to the executive express elevator. There was no point even thinking about that. Serrano was no fool; he would have had the controls changed as soon as he realized she'd played him.

The lift dinged, and the doors opened, revealing another hallway with more fluorescent lights and a few fake ficuses. They stepped out. Immediately to the left lay the security room with a full wall of constantly changing screens. On the right, there were a couple of small interview rooms, where they questioned people caught up to no good on Serrano's property. Foster also had an office on this level.

Reyes checked the time. It was almost ten. He hadn't thought to ask Kyra what hours Serrano worked, but maybe that would've changed after her defection. Was the son of a bitch up in his penthouse office even now, tormenting Mia? It would kill Kyra if anything happened to her friend, and whether he liked it or not, what hurt her, hurt him.

He didn't much like it.

"Ready?" she asked.

"Go for it."

She knocked.

One of the guards called through the door, "What?" He sounded bored and tired.

"I went in to clean the bathroom, and saw the toilet is overflowing into the hall. Should I call maintenance? I don't usually work this floor."

"Goddammit," the guard swore. "You had to have burritos, didn't you, Jackson?"

His partner made some unintelligible reply; Reyes heard the other guy laugh. Then the first man stepped out into the hall, and Reyes spun him headfirst into the wall. He didn't want to kill the poor bastard, but there was no surefire way to knock somebody out, unless you lived in the Star Trek universe or maybe a ninja movie.

The second guard heard something in the minor scuffle that alarmed him and by sound of chair legs scraping, pushed to his feet. "Mike?"

Kyra asked in a worried tone, "Wow, are you okay? Can you walk?"

Genius. That'd make Jackson think Mike had fallen somehow, maybe slipped in the imaginary water. He came out unsuspecting, looking to help, and Reyes met him with an uppercut followed by a right cross. From the point they acted against security, the clock was running.

First he made sure both guys were out, then he slung the first one over his shoulder and headed for the interview room. They had no windows for obvious reasons, just cameras to record the sessions. Reyes dumped Mike, and then went back for Jackson, who was already stirring. He hadn't been knocked out, merely dazed by the blow. With regret, Reyes hit him again before tossing him in with his buddy.

They needed to be quiet for a while. For good measure, he tied them with their own belts and gagged them with their own socks. *Poor bastards.* Jackson might remember to change his socks more often hereafter.

Kyra stood guard while he worked, bouncing with nervous energy. She had to know that every minute they remained increased their risk of discovery. The woman wasn't one to panic, though. She led the way into the security room and went immediately to work with the systems.

Luck had favored them so far. Her ability held while she found the last month's logs with a speed Apex might envy. Then again, it was *his* skill she was using, Reyes thought with a half smile. He marveled at the rarity of her while watching the hall, his turn to stand lookout.

"This is the whole month," she said a few seconds later. "If Mia came to the casino, we'll find out when, maybe who she talked to. I can burn it to a DVD and then we'll get the hell out of here. I can't see a way for us to get up to the penthouse tonight."

"How enterprising," a man said. "But you didn't need to come in person, you know. Reyes has my number. We could've done business over the phone."

Foster. Reyes would know that voice anywhere. But what the hell, he'd scanned that hall three seconds ago, and suddenly Foster was just . . . here. There was no cover. Nothing to hide behind. No shadows. Real people couldn't *do* that.

"We didn't want to insult you," Kyra told him. "Why don't you be a good lapdog and take us up to see your boss?" Reyes heard the bravado in her voice, the tremor she tried to hide.

"There's no point," Foster responded, cool as lemon gelato. "He isn't up there. You're welcome to the surveillance footage, but you'd be bored, I'm afraid. So why don't I save you the trouble? Mia came in. She talked to me. She *left* with me. Serrano trusts me to handle such things. But I'll give you an address. In fact, I've been ordered to provide it. Serrano really wants to see you, Kyra."

"What do *you* want?" Kyra wheeled from the station, hands curled into fists. Reyes wouldn't have been surprised if she'd gone for the bastard with her bare hands, but Apex was a thinker, not a fighter.

"Many things," Foster murmured. "And you, my dear, are going to make sure I get them."

CHAPTER 28

Ten minutes later, after Foster had them escorted from the building, Kyra studied the address in her hand. "It's a trap."

"Get an ax."

That surprised her into looking at him. They were standing on the sidewalk outside the Silver Lady, beneath the platinum neon bombshell curling her fingers in come-hither fashion. The light silvered his hair, raven wings frosted argent. "You've seen *Army of Darkness*?"

"Yeah. I love Bruce Campbell."

It made sense she supposed. What else would a guy like Reyes do for relaxation, other than watch monsters get dismembered? Oh, and read Marquez, apparently. To her mind, he didn't add up; the pieces didn't fit.

"My dad did, too," she said softly. "I always liked old movies better, but I watched my share of B movies with him." Then she remembered she didn't want to know anything else about him and made her tone businesslike. "It's too bad I had to tap Apex to get us in there, but done is done. I'll have to double dip and take the pain later."

"I don't want you doing that," Reyes said immediately.

She curled her lip. “I don’t give a shit. Use your head. If we go in like this, I’m the weakest link. I can defend myself in most situations, but this place will be crawling with Serrano’s goons. I expect a bloodbath in getting to him, don’t you?”

“And we’ll have to cut a path through them,” he agreed. “All right, then. I have a stop to make before we go in. What do *you* suggest?”

“We’ll take care of your business first.”

It made sense to get everything done before she found a target, so the least amount of time elapsed before they reached the address Foster had given them. First they went back to the apartment, taking a bus because cabs were easier to follow. They couldn’t afford to get hung up by thugs who might not have the latest game plan. Though it took a little longer, and their mission was time-critical, Kyra knew she had to make this count. They wouldn’t get another chance to save Mia.

At the loft, Kyra changed into a pair of tight black workout pants. They’d offer the best range of motion for fighting, even if they didn’t offer anything in the way of protection. But she was fresh out of flexible body armor, so this would have to do. A black T-shirt and sneakers completed the outfit. Boots would do more damage, but she wouldn’t be able to move as quickly.

With what she was planning, speed and reflex would come into play. While waiting for him—Reyes had gone to rummage around upstairs—she checked the phone book and then wrote down another address. They were almost ready. A few minutes later, he came back down apparently empty-handed.

“Got what you need?” she asked him.

He patted his jacket pocket. “Yeah, I’m good.”

They took the Marquis. From this point, there was no reason for subtlety. Serrano knew they were coming, and he *wanted* them to. Reyes gave her directions. The night was dark except for the neon everywhere. It gave everything a surreal painted air, as if they’d stepped into a modern art painting.

As it turned out, he needed to stop at a storage locker.

It was a small place downtown set between a daily parking lot and a building that looked as though it ought to be condemned. Reyes had a key to the gate that led around back to a warehouse, and then he used a second key to unlock the padlock on a back unit. She wasn't sure what she'd expected, but she found a bay full of junk: cardboard boxes, crates of dusty books, and even a dressmaker's mannequin. It looked like he'd cleaned out somebody's attic.

"What is all this stuff?" she asked.

"Camouflage."

He ignored the rest and went directly to a brass-bound trunk across which he'd tossed a colorful knit afghan. Inside the trunk lay a bunch of pulp paperbacks from the thirties and forties. Reyes got out a penknife and slid it down the side, popping out a false bottom. From inside, he lifted out a black duffel bag, then he replaced the wood back in place and rearranged the books before closing the trunk and covering it again.

"Your weapons cache," she guessed.

His smile came and went like a shadow. "I keep one in every town where I work. You never know when you'll find yourself needing firepower."

"We will. I can shoot," she added. "But if we're fighting inside, it may be dangerous to rely on weapons."

She took his silence for agreement. They went back to the Marquis, which they'd left in the alley outside the storage facility. The night air was cool for Vegas, a desert-scented wind sweeping the city. In the light from the dashboard, she read the address she'd scrawled. Mentally, she mapped it, and then started the car.

"Where are we going?"

Kyra didn't answer. She didn't want him here, didn't want his help. But she wasn't stupid enough to try this alone. Little as she liked it, she needed his expertise, so this would be the last thing they ever did together, and then she'd start forgetting he'd ever existed. She just wished it didn't hurt so fucking much.

They pulled up outside a martial arts studio. Kyra had checked the hours in the phone book ad, and they slid in just before the place closed. It was one of the few open this late. The last class had already gone, and the sensei was getting ready to lock up. Master Li was a small Japanese man in his late fifties, his salt-and-pepper hair worn clubbed back in a plain elastic band. According to the credentials on the wall, he was also an eighth-degree black belt.

"Can I help you?"

Kyra offered a sweet smile. "My husband was wondering if you had any positions open for instructors. He's studied Jendo, capoeira, and tarung derajat. Tell him, honey."

Seeming not to mind, Reyes recounted how he'd studied in Brazil, the Philippines, and Indonesia. Then he executed a few katas, showing his stuff. Despite everything, Kyra still felt a traitorous pleasure in watching him move. He possessed all the dangerous beauty of a honed knife.

Master Li asked Reyes a few questions and then said, regretful, "I don't have any openings at the moment, but your skills are most impressive. I wish I could help you."

She offered her hand. "Thanks anyway."

The sensei shook it, sending a spike of pain straight through her temples. Kyra swayed and Reyes supported her. "We need to get you something to eat. She has low blood sugar," he added, presumably for Master Li's benefit.

By the time he got her out to the car, she felt a little better. Apex's skill and the combat expertise she'd lifted didn't utilize the same part of the brain, so this would be tolerable. The aftermath would be brutal, given that she'd be making contact with a lot of people in the melee, but Kyra would worry about that after they saved Mia.

"Give me the keys."

For half a second, she considered arguing, but in truth, she needed the time to let things settle in her head. That would be easier with her eyes closed, doing relaxation and breathing exercises. So she tossed them to him, and he caught them in a jingle of metal.

Kyra slid into the car and leaned her throbbing head against the window. She breathed deeply, holding it for two beats, and then pushing the air out through her nose.

After five minutes or so, the pain had dulled enough to be manageable. She wouldn't win any spelling bees, but she could fight, and that was all that mattered.

"Better?"

"I'm fine," she growled. "Just get us there."

Before I crash.

When they pulled into the neighborhood, it wasn't what she expected. No lavish mansions, no gated communities. This was an average middle-class subdivision, each house more or less like its neighbor. She supposed he'd holed up at some unoccupied rental property; it wouldn't do for Serrano's own home to be spattered with blood. There were limits to what a cleanup crew could do.

"I'm parking here," he said quietly. "They know we're coming but there's no sense in making it easy for them. We'll go the rest of the way on foot."

Kyra nodded mutely. From Master Li, she had taken an unexpected lightness of movement. Her bones felt liquid, as if she could flow from place to place like the wind itself. She followed behind Reyes as he set off down the street.

At their turn, he stilled, and then pointed to the dark Ford Expedition parked near the curb. It was only one of two vehicles on the street. Everyone else had garaged their cars for the night. He tugged her arm and they slid sideways, which gave her a better vantage. She saw two men in silhouette from a driver passing in the other direction.

Lookouts.

Reyes motioned for her to get down, and she complied. By his gestures, he intended to take the driver, and he wanted her to get the guy on the passenger side. Kyra didn't need to be told this needed to be a permanent solution. The windows were rolled up, so that would make it tough hand to hand.

She tipped her head at the bag and he unzipped it silently. Within seconds, he'd fitted two guns with silencers. Reyes handed one to her, asking with his eyes whether she could use it. Kyra nodded. Then he gestured low. At first she didn't get it, but when he crawled under the SUV, she understood.

Once they were in position, directly beneath passenger and driver, she rolled over and removed the safety. In unison, they sent a spray of bullets up into the SUV. She imagined them striking their targets, blood and bone spattering everywhere. Better she couldn't see what she hit. Through the heavy reinforced metal, she couldn't even hear them cry out.

On his signal, she rolled outward and returned the weapon as she circled back around the SUV. Kyra didn't look, but Reyes checked their handiwork through the window, dispassionate.

"They're done," he said quietly. "Let's roll out."

From that point it was smooth sailing all the way up to the house. To her surprise, all the windows were dark. Shit. Maybe they'd been set up. Maybe nobody was here, and if they opened the door, wired to blow, the whole place would go up in flames. How far did they trust Foster?

By his expression, Reyes was wondering the same. "You think Mia's in there?"

"He said she was."

"It's your call," he said.

She wavered. "Yeah. Let's check it out. But we're not going in the front."

"One of the windows?" he suggested.

"Sounds good."

They circled around back and found a bedroom window. Kyra liked ranch houses; they were easy to enter. Reyes cut the screen and then produced a glass cutter. He etched a small circle and used a suction cup to pull it out silently. Her hand was small enough to reach the latch, so she unlocked it, and raised the frame. Reyes went in first and checked the room. When he indicated it was clear, she slid in after him.

Two guys sat lounging in the living room, watching TV in the dark. Rey slid up behind one, and broke his neck. Clean, quiet. Kyra struck with both hands across his throat, her hands like steel wedges. This one was a shooter; she felt the tingle run up her arm and into her fingertips. Suddenly, she wanted to use the gun in her pocket, but it was too much. Security, karate, marksmanship—it all twisted through her, making her realize she was on the verge of a full seizure. She hadn't had one of those since she was a kid.

Red laced her vision, and she wanted to puke.

"You're going to—to have to finish it," she choked out. "Please. I paid you well enough. Don't let anyone hurt her."

Reyes came over quietly, setting his hands on her shoulders. The warmth seemed to soak in through her skin, edging everything else out. Kyra concentrated on breathing, aware that she was wasting time.

"Stay with me," he breathed. "I never intended to take your money, but I knew you wouldn't trust me to stay the course unless you hired me. You're in this. You'll finish it. It won't be over in your head unless you do."

God, he knew her *so* well. She hated him for it. With his help she fought the seizure back. Who the hell knew what would happen later? She'd been so careful up until now. The important thing was, she could go on.

They just had to find Serrano. It was almost over. She should have been euphoric, but the suppressed pain made her feel nauseous instead. Kyra needed food and sleep . . . and Mia.

There were two more guards in the kitchen. Kyra shot one, knowing she couldn't take an extra theft tonight; she was saving the last one for Serrano. Reyes took his foe down in sweet silence, a flurry of kicks and punches so powerful the other guy hardly had a chance to respond, and then he caught the thug before he hit the ground.

Just hang on.

Serrano was in a back bedroom, talking to Mia in a low voice, trying to get her to tell him something about Kyra. So Foster hadn't lied. Mia sat tied to a chair, and her eyes were wide and dark with fear. She didn't appear to have any visible damage.

"I'll end her. I swear to God I will." Serrano put the gun to Mia's temple, and Kyra froze. She hoped Reyes had the sense not to do anything rash.

"Am I too late?" Foster asked, sauntering in. He held a Glock in one hand, which he trained on Reyes. "I hope I didn't miss the party."

"Foster." Relief colored Serrano's voice. "Thank God. How the hell did these two find me? I *distinctly* ordered you not to give them the go-ahead until morning when I had all my men in place."

"Let the girl go," he said. "Everything's under control now. Come on, Mia. It's almost over now." He held out a hand.

"Are you crazy?" she all but snarled. "You gave me to him, and now you just expect me to heel like a dog? I *trusted* you."

Foster was ice. "Your mistake. Come on now. Step away from him. Don't make me ask again."

"Oh, fuck it," Serrano said. "Take her. I lost my stomach for killing women years ago. Fix this for me, and there's a big bonus in it for you."

"That's good. Come on over here now." Mia did as Foster asked with reluctance, looking at him as if he were a snake charmer who could make her do things she didn't want to. Once Mia reached Foster's side, he turned the gun on Serrano. "Sorry about this," he added to her. "I hope you weren't scared, but he had guys on you, and I needed to buy a little more time. If I hadn't turned you over when I did, he'd have known."

Serrano looked pale and sick. "Known what?"

Foster smiled, and the gleam of his teeth sent a shiver through Kyra. She'd never seen anything like his look. "Mia, go on outside," he said. "We'll be there in a minute."

She looked at Kyra uncertainly. "Are you—"

"I'll be fine," Kyra said. "Go."

Mia went.

Reyes stirred, surprise mingling with conviction in his voice. "You hate him."

"More than you can possibly imagine," Foster agreed.

Serrano made a small sound over staring down the barrel of a gun held by a man he'd trusted. "We can talk about this. Whatever you think I did—"

Foster was implacable. "I know what you did. You won't be walking out of this room, one way or another."

"Why didn't you just shoot him long before I came along?" Kyra asked. "You had plenty of chances."

Hellfire lit the ice of his eyes from within, as if a

thousand lost souls lay trapped beneath their silvered surface. His tone was savage. "Because that was too simple. You see, Kyra, I wanted him to suffer. I had to find something worse for him. I could only cause him physical pain, but you . . . *you* broke his heart."

That was too much for Serrano, who apparently couldn't stand being ignored. "The bitch did nothing of the kind."

"No?" Foster laughed. "These poems prove otherwise." He lofted a silver USB drive. Kyra started with shock, and he glanced her way. "Didn't know that, did you? He planned to give them to you on your wedding night. After you left, they took a sad turn." Foster quoted aloud, "Darkness, unlit by stars/Now that you have gone, neither bread nor meat holds any savor./Sorrow pure unhallowed blue/I am desolate with loss of you."

Reyes seemed to come to some realization, and his expression held something like pity as he gazed at Serrano. "That's why you were so set on wiping her out. Not because she lied or even because she dented your pride. Because she *left* you."

"Fuck," Serrano said in disgust. "Kill me now, Foster. Spare me the psychoanalysis from a bastard who's more screwed up than I am."

"I don't work for you anymore," he said quietly. "I've accepted another offer. Kyra, he's yours now. Do with him as you will." As he passed by, Foster tossed her the USB drive. "I'd have them published posthumously if I were you. Imagine how he'll writhe, humiliated in hell."

Then Foster glanced at Reyes. "Don't worry about your failure to complete the job. You did exactly as I expected, and the stain on your record dies with him." He paused at the door. "By the way, if you have the stomach for it, I suggest chopping off his hands and etching him with some Russian characters. There's a cop named Sagorski who'd love to hear about it."

That took all the defiance out of Serrano, who gazed wildly between Kyra and Reyes. "Don't. Jesus, no. Can't we come to some kind of agreement? Keep the money. I can give you more if you want."

"I have the stomach for it," Reyes said, smiling. "If the client pays for it, I'm happy to make the hit look like it came down from a certain criminal contingent. I'm good at emulating M.O."

A surge of pure fury went through Kyra. "No, he's mine."

Foster slid out whistling a tune she couldn't place. She tucked the poems into her pocket, and stared at Serrano. He looked older than his late forties now, frail somehow. It roused no pity in her.

"At least tell me why," Serrano begged. "What the hell did I ever do to you?"

She lashed out with a spin kick, knocking him to the ground. "You took away the only person who ever gave a shit about me," she snarled. "You had an old man beaten up, and he died in an alley like a dog. He didn't even *cheat* you, asshole. He won nothing! His system didn't work, but you never show mercy, do you?" Hate spread like wildfire through her. "And neither will I."

That was what he was best at, after all. No mercy.

She hit him again and again. Rage took her. When she came to herself long minutes later, she heard Serrano moaning in pain, and his face was damn near unrecognizable. Reyes silently handed her the gun, and she finished what she'd started so many months before with two shots to the back of the head.

Serrano died with tears in his eyes.

Kyra stood for a moment studying her handiwork. "That's for you, Dad."

"It's over, then. He's dead, and you've still got the money."

She swung her gaze his way, armored with violence. It made it easier to strike, hoping it would hurt him, even a little. God, she'd told him she was falling in *love* with him. Between the stink of Serrano's voided bowels and the crash she was fighting back by the skin of her teeth, it was all she could do to stay on her feet now.

"Yeah. And we're done, too. It's been . . . interesting,

Reyes. Don't follow. Don't try to find me. I don't want to see you again."

Kyra stumbled out to look for Mia, leaving him alone in the house of the dead.

CHAPTER 29

Reyes researched his next job a hell of a lot better.

As Foster had promised, nobody seemed to know that his last contract had gone wrong. The offers poured in as they always had, and he continued to pick and choose. He reviewed Interpol files for Nicolao Vadas and he didn't like what he saw, including the names of his movies and the pictures of his victims. After due investigation, he chose the job in Budapest for several reasons, though it wasn't even close to the highest bid.

One: it was across an ocean from Kyra Marie Beckwith. Two: the scumbag deserved to die. The e-mail came in through layers of encryption from a bereaved father in Hungary; his daughter had been lured into the life with promises of a film career, and she was dead by fifteen of a drug overdose. The man was a grocer, but he'd scraped up fifteen grand. Reyes would've done the job for $5.95. Odd as it might sound to a normal, he needed a righteous killing to feel clean.

A lesser factor . . . he'd discovered that Monroe was hiding there. After giving him up to Van Zant, he had reason to fear. He'd considered the man a friend, but he should know better than anyone, friendship could be bought and sold like anything else. Monroe had to know Reyes would come for him.

So he booked himself on an overnight flight. He couldn't outrun the memories, but maybe it would help to be a world away. Rising costs kept people from traveling, so he had an empty seat next to him in first class. The pretty blond flight attendant showed signs of interest, but he kept his expression impassive and turned his face toward the window. Thereafter, she kept her attention professional.

He took out *One Hundred Years of Solitude* and brushed his fingers over the cover. In his mind's eye, he could see Kyra curled up in his loft, reading it. Reyes placed his fingers where she'd held it. For a long, aching moment, he let himself remember.

Then he opened the book.

The flight was long, but uneventful. They landed at JFK with a minimum of fuss, and then he had a connection in two hours. He didn't try to sleep. His eyes felt achingly dry, full of grit and weariness. He bought a coffee to combat the feeling. Reyes couldn't remember the last time he'd slept well.

Liar. It was at the little house in the woods, the last time you held her.

Along with the other passengers, he boarded the flight to Amsterdam just before midnight. He accepted a pillow and blanket to make his flight more pleasant, but in truth, he just wanted an excuse to shut everyone out. After refusing dinner service, he dozed in fits and starts, and dreamed of a woman's freckled face.

Eight hours later, the Boeing put down in Amsterdam, where he went through immigration, baggage claim, and customs. Most countries were like that these days, even if you were only passing through. Reyes rechecked his luggage and barely made his connection to Budapest.

This was the last leg of the journey. It felt like he'd been traveling forever, though it had only been a little over a day. He never traveled directly to a hit, so there would be other stops to cloud the waters. Time-consuming, but it had helped more than once in throwing people off his trail. He paused at a currency exchange for some forints.

As it was late morning, Reyes went directly to an apartment building near the opera house where he had rented a studio apartment before. It was white stone with ornate cornices and small balconies beneath each window. Some residents would plant flowers in the springtime. The owners kept small furnished rentals for travelers, offering more privacy and self-sufficiency than a hotel. Budapest was a gorgeous city, and if he hadn't been so damn tired, he would've appreciated it more.

Reyes knocked on the manager's door, Istvan Laszlofi, as he recalled. The man came to the door eventually, clad in tan slacks and a white undershirt. His thinning hair was mussed, and by his expression, he'd interrupted a meal. The manager raised bushy brows, coal black in contrast to his silver hair.

"Nekem bérelnem kell egy szobát." He wasn't fluent, but he had enough conversational Hungarian to ask to rent a room.

"Milyen hosszú?"

A week ought to do it. If his business didn't take that long, he'd let the guy keep the extra cash. *"Hét nap."*

The manager named a sum; he paid out the bills and received a key in return. As if he knew Reyes wasn't fluent, the man spoke slowly in telling him that he had a room upstairs, first door on the right. Reyes nodded in thanks and jogged up the stairs.

He didn't have much stuff to stow, but he needed to get some sleep. The studio was small, even by European standards. Technically he supposed one could call it a loft, but there were no stairs, just an actual ladder leading up to a deep ledge where they'd stashed a mattress.

The downstairs held a small fridge with a white microwave sitting atop it. There was also a black futon, hardwood floors, and a TV. Just one window. The balcony would make it hard to get in. He peered out at the street, which was narrow, lined with trees in clay pots.

The small bathroom, done in plain white ceramic tile, held a shower stall, an economy toilet, and a pedestal sink. The kitchen was nothing but two burners, four cupboards, and a sink. Most important, it would be impossible to get in here without him noticing. He'd bed down upstairs for better security; there was no way he'd sleep through anyone coming up that ladder. Nobody should know he was here—he hadn't even confirmed with the client yet—but he hadn't survived all these years in this line of work by being less than cautious.

A long nap left him feeling better mentally. Reyes took a quick shower and headed out. As he typically did, he bought a prepaid cell phone to use with this particular client. Once the job was done, he would discard it. He visited an Internet café and sent an e-mail with the number, nothing more. Reyes was sitting in a restaurant eating a hearty bowl of soup when his cell went off.

"Mack," he answered.

"You take job?" The heavily accented voice belonged to the bereaved father.

Reyes remembered a picture of a young girl, facedown in her own vomit. He'd done the research, no margin for error. "Yes. I'm sending you some numbers. Wire the funds, and I'll take care of the problem by tomorrow."

"Promise to God?" Maybe he didn't speak the language fluently, but he'd understood yes at least.

The call completed, Reyes went to a different Internet café. He added instructions in Hungarian to complete the transfers. Two e-mails later, he had an address. His client was smart; he didn't put anything incriminating in his messages, just the bare details. The grocer knew where to find the skin peddler. He just didn't have the skills to take him out.

Not tomorrow. Today. Now. He needed this. Needed to feel clean again by doing something worthwhile, make the world a better place by taking a scumbag out of it. And maybe the expiation would take away some of the pain that throbbed through him as if his whole body had become a rotten tooth.

Reyes stopped by a pawnshop and bought a knife. They were easier to lay hands on in Europe. He could kill with his bare hands, but it was likely he was walking into heavy artillery. He wasn't suicidal; he wanted to walk out again. However much he hurt, he wasn't ready to call it quits. Time would heal this over. He'd get used to being alone. He just needed to immerse himself in routine again. Remember his life without her.

The club was down by the river, a shoddy building made of crumbling red bricks. Reyes strode through the alley, circling around behind. It was littered with empty cans, broken bottles, and discarded needles. This was how he lived, cleaning out the gutters.

Two men were unloading a shipment of liquor as he passed by. They didn't question him, as he strode through the back door as if he owned the place. He passed through a filthy kitchen, where an elderly woman was making soup. The dance floor looked strange and deserted, swimming with shadows. Toward the back, a stage stood empty. Later, some naked woman would wrap herself around the pole. Upstairs, there was a red velvet room, where men pushed little girls to the floor and made them weep, and someone else recorded it.

This was his world. It had never seemed so strange, so alien, before.

Only one table was occupied. Four men were playing cards. He recognized Nicolao Vadas from his mug shot: tall and thin with a scar on his left cheek, a beak of a nose, and full lips that he constantly wet with his tongue. He'd been arrested many times, but his lawyers always got him out. Like a cockroach, he'd keep coming back until someone stepped on him hard enough to break him.

"What are you doing here?" Vadas demanded in Hungarian.

In answer, Reyes spiked a knife up through his jaw and into his brain.

His three men scrambled for their weapons. The pistols lay among scattered cards and poker chips. He felt disconnected, as if they could shoot him, and he wouldn't even feel it. Lightning fast, Reyes grabbed the closest guy's hand and slammed it to the table. In the same motion, he used the bastard as his personal shield. He took his HK away and leveled it on the thug across the table with his fingers edging toward his gun.

"I was only paid to kill him," he said in badly accented Hungarian. "Do you three want to walk away?"

Whatever they saw in his eyes, they decided not to fight. The other two backed out of the club slowly, showing their hands. They'd just find some other asshole to work for, but until someone else judged them bad enough to put down, he wouldn't touch them. If he went around killing everyone *he* thought deserved to die, he'd skip far beyond the thin line that kept him sane. He pocketed the HK.

Reyes let go of the third guy, who ran, slipping and sliding in his haste, toward the exit. He stared down at Nicolao Vadas, who would never hurt another kid. His dead eyes gazed at nothing. Was there expiation in that filmy look? Drawing a cloth from his jacket, he cleaned the handle, but he left the blade in place. He hadn't touched it.

Maybe this would make up for what he'd almost done, the woman he might've killed. Maybe in time, the ache would go away.

He took out his throwaway cell phone and snapped a picture. He'd send this by courier to the grocer as proof of a job well done. Reyes met no opposition as he left the club. If he'd been a different sort of man, he might've burned it down.

Instead he wiped down the phone, and went out into the street, where a light rain had begun to fall. Passing cars splashed him, and a kid in a Citroen flipped him off as he crossed. He walked, head down, one of the few without an umbrella.

At a small office supply store, he bought a brown envelope, and then went to a third Internet café. He used the web to request a pickup from Kenguru Boy courier service. Choosing immediate and express got him service right away. He'd only been there half an hour when the young man showed up on a motorcycle. Cash changed hands.

The courier spoke lightly accented English. "Thank you, sir. We will make sure your parcel arrives within two hours. This address is not far." His eyes said it would've been easy for Reyes to deliver it himself.

Yeah, he knew that, but clients never saw his face.

Except Serrano at the end, and he took it to his grave.

Ruthlessly, Reyes pushed the memory down. He didn't want to remember that job or how it ended. He preferred to forget what he'd done to tie up loose ends and the anonymous call he'd made to Sagorski, who was doubtless rubbing his hands together in glee over such a juicy case.

Now he had only one more task left in Budapest.

In truth he had no heart for it, but if he didn't make an example of Monroe, people would think they could get away with crossing him. According to Intel for which he'd paid a premium, Monroe was hiding out in a squat down near the Danube. Unless he'd scrambled since then, this would be quick.

Reyes rented a motorbike so he could travel fast, weaving in and out of city traffic. Down by the river, it smelled of damp wood and rotten fish. There was a web of warehouses and abandoned buildings in this section, but the one he sought had some unmistakable graffiti on it: a blond woman wearing a red shirt and a mournful look, naked from the waist down.

He found it on his second circuit. After parking the bike, he pulled the HK out of his pocket and disengaged the safety. He hadn't come to talk. The gray building had many broken windows. A gate across the doorway was supposed to discourage trespassers, but it was possible to edge it outward enough to slip past.

Inside it stank of urine. He searched three floors methodically, ignoring the presence of other squatters, who peered at him with starving eyes, their faces withered with hunger and drink. Deep down he'd never doubted he would find Monroe on the top floor, having claimed the best digs even in a place like this.

Monroe had an ego and a taste for comfort that didn't echo in his work ethic. Reyes had always found his laissez faire attitude toward life refreshing. Not anymore. It was weakness, pure and simple.

It became obvious where he was hiding by the shiny new locks. Reyes kicked the door with all his strength; new locks could only do so much good when the door was flimsy and half rotten. When Reyes burst in, Monroe was using his laptop to steal signal from some business nearby. Likely he was working for somebody, stealing info he wasn't supposed to have, as he'd done so many times for Reyes.

Monroe had turned an abandoned office into a decent apartment. He had a mattress and some furniture, tables and chairs with hardware set up. At any given time he could be cloning credit cards from stolen receipts, pirating DVDs, or something even less reputable, such as creating incriminating blackmail videos out of personal photos uploaded to private Flickr accounts.

Reyes had always known the guy wasn't exactly humanitarian-of-the-year material, but he'd never thought Monroe would roll, not after he'd saved his life in Prague. He'd thought they were friends, or as close as guys like them got. He looked younger than he was, a boyish thirty, with fair hair and blue eyes. If he had to shave once a week, it was a miracle.

"Shit," Monroe said, freezing.

"Weren't you expecting me?"

His throat worked, and he clutched his laptop as if it could shield him from what was coming. "Not this fast."

"No? See, word got out. That you worked for me, and then you turned. People were eager to give you up. In my line of work, we can't afford to trust people who turn out to be unreliable."

"He threatened to kill me, man. He rousted me in Phoenix. I had him in my house, ice pick in my eye. You know Van Zant; he's a crazy son of a bitch." Then he seemed to stop and think. "Was, I guess. *Was* a crazy son of a bitch. Anyway, I knew you could take him. I'm sorry, but I'm not dying for you, dude. It wasn't just the money."

"But you took it, didn't you?"

And Kyra might've died because you're a spineless prick. Because I trusted you. An icy rage took hold of him. This much he could do for her. Would do. He'd make things right, even if she never knew.

Monroe hunched his shoulders defensively. "Yeah. I needed the cash. It's getting harder to make a living like this, and security online gets better every day."

"Lucky, you don't have to worry about that anymore." The numbness threatened again, washing in like fog on a rocky beach. It eclipsed the cold fury. Maybe on some level, it should have bothered him to snip this last loose end. He'd felt something for this guy once. Now he didn't seem to feel anything at all, as if he were in a boat washing farther and farther from shore.

His expression became bewildered. "What, online security?"

"No." Reyes smiled. "Living." He picked up a pillow from the mattress, covered the barrel of the HK, and shot Monroe in the head.

In the future, he'd have to find another hacker, someone else to access classified information. Maybe Apex could step up. Reyes would make sure there were no personal connections, going forward. And he wouldn't turn to that person when he was in trouble. At least he'd learned a valuable lesson over the past months: you could only ever rely on yourself. He wouldn't make that mistake again.

He wiped the gun and left it on Monroe's body. It was never smart to carry a murder weapon with you. Reyes retraced his steps through the squat.

"There's a bunch of good stuff upstairs," he said to the homeless in Hungarian.

Soon Monroe's stuff would be stolen, including IDs. If he knew anything about such places, all the evidence would be compromised long before the cops were alerted.

By some miracle, the bike was still where he'd left it. He fired it up and spun away from the last connection to the mess he'd made. There was nothing left to do.

He stopped at a petrol station just before returning the bike. Gassing up didn't cost much; the tank was small. Afterward, he went into the restroom and washed his hands, scrubbing diligently. Prolonged immersion with simple soap and water would defeat a gunshot residue test. He knew these things because he was careful and precise. He knew what he needed to do to survive. Now he just had to get back to it.

It was over. Everything. Over. He'd never see her again. Never go looking. Because that was what she wanted, and the best thing he could do for her was leave. He'd always known it would end that way, no matter how sweet it seemed. Reyes wouldn't grieve for something that had never belonged to him.

It was time to get back to work, back to his life. Time to do what he did best. Time to forget there had ever been a woman who held him because she wanted to.

He had nothing *but* time, spread out before him like a wasteland.

CHAPTER 30

It had been a week since they left Las Vegas.

And she'd crashed hard once she got them to safety. Mia told her they'd spent a whole day hiding in a hotel off the strip, but she couldn't remember it. Since then, Mia had been moody and uncommunicative, totally unlike herself. Focusing on her friend's problems distracted Kyra from thinking about her own, but she didn't want to push. After leaving the rental house, she'd found Mia shivering outside despite the relative warmness of the air.

Kyra had taken her hand, despite the pain, and led her to the Marquis. She didn't want to stick around in case one of the neighbors called the police. The other woman roused only long enough to request they pick up her things, and then she closed her eyes. Kyra had no choice but to hang tough, despite the pain spiking through her brain. She'd overloaded her circuits, and there was no help for it but medication and rest.

That set the tone for the next several days. They drove in near silence, both nursing private grief.

In Colorado, she had the Marquis painted white on the off chance anyone was still looking for her. The switched plates should do some good as well, as long as she drove within the speed limits and didn't attract police attention. Mia huddled against the door, head against the window. Kyra had never seen her like this: so small and scared.

Just what the hell had happened? But any attempt to find out met with a wall of silence. Her friend wasn't ready to talk, and Kyra had to respect that.

A rest stop where they used the bathroom had a small visitor's center, and Kyra picked up a brochure for a gorgeous hotel called Chateau on the Lake. It promised soothing tranquility set amid pastoral beauty, lush gardens, in-house spa, massage therapy, tennis courts—pure luxury. Somewhere to rest sounded wonderful.

As they walked back to the Marquis, she asked, "What do you think?" and passed the flyer to her friend.

Mia read it over as she climbed into the passenger seat. "I could use it."

They didn't need a vacation as much as a place to lick their wounds. While Kyra didn't know exactly what had happened between Mia and Foster, she recognized the wreckage in her eyes. God, she felt more or less the same, as if she'd been hit by a car, the scars too deep for anyone else to see.

She drove. The Marquis responded like a familiar friend, comfortable beneath her hands. Kyra focused on breathing, and tried to tell herself she didn't hurt. She'd give anything if that wasn't true of Mia.

By the end of the seventh day, they reached Branson, Missouri. Mia used her cell to call the hotel on the flyer to find out if they had a room. They did, and she reserved it.

Chateau on the Lake lay some four miles from the theaters and eight miles from downtown, but Kyra didn't imagine they'd want to explore the homey attractions. At least she didn't. She intended to hole up, order room service, and try to forget.

The place was every bit as beautiful as the pictures claimed. Nestled amid trees and gardens, the yellow building gleamed in the last rays of the sun, gilding it. She hoped that meant they'd find some respite there. While Mia got her stuff, Kyra pulled the money case out of the floor of the car and tucked it into her duffel bag.

She didn't think Reyes would come looking for her, but she didn't mean to leave the money unattended until then. Her father had died, and she'd suffered for it, so she didn't mean to let anyone take it.

Inside, it was positively lavish. Mia took care of check-in because a place like this didn't work on a cash-only basis. She'd dip into her stash to cover her part of the stay. A bellman took their luggage—paltry as it was—up to their rooms, and Kyra tipped him.

The room was every bit as nice as the lobby led her to believe: two full-sized beds with adjustable mattresses, rich mahogany furnishings, echoed in the window treatment. The walls were painted rich ochre, lending a warm air that was echoed in the colorful swirls of the bedspreads. Sateen-covered cushions sat at artful angles on the bed, and there were mints on the pillows.

Kyra tossed her bag beside the bed closest to the door. If someone came in on them, she was best suited to dealing with the problem. Mia wasn't used to this shit; for all their friendship, they'd lived very different lives, and she was sorry she'd whispered even a hint of her intentions. It had been a rare phone conversation where, in a moment of weakness, she felt so totally alone that she just wanted someone to know where she was and what she was up against. She hadn't reckoned on Mia's sweet, fierce loyalty.

"Here's the deal," she said, dropping onto the bed. "Tonight we take hot baths. Order room service, including ice cream, and we get something girlie on pay-per-view. I'm not going to ask you any questions. But tomorrow we talk."

Mia raised her brows. "I will if you will."

Did she think I didn't want to? Kyra considered. *Possible.* She didn't know what kind of cues she'd been giving. It had been everything she could do to go through the motions without a full collapse.

"I'm just . . . raw," she answered at last. "But I want to talk to you about it. You're all I have left."

Mia's dark eyes glinted. "You, too. I don't see my mom anymore, you know."

"I'm sorry." She hugged Mia, knowing it wouldn't be bad or unpleasant.

Her friend was good with numbers, which was a particularly low-key talent. Mia wouldn't need to tally any figures tonight anyway. Thereafter, they followed through with her plan—with one amendment. They used the spa before wading into personal matters, and it turned into a whole day of steaming, massage, yoga, hair, manicures, and pedicures, though Kyra requested the same person handle all of her treatments. They considered it a harmless eccentricity and granted the request. By the time they got back to the room, she almost didn't hurt anymore. Maybe she could talk with equanimity now.

TV off, they sat on the beds cross-legged, facing each other. Mia smiled, but it was tinged with melancholy. "It's been a long time since we did this."

"Yeah." Her throat clogged, as if physical comfort cleared the way for emotional baggage to break open, like luggage tossed too hard on a conveyer at the airport.

"So this Serrano had something to do with your dad dying . . . and then he sent someone after you. . . . What happened between you two? Though I wasn't in the room very long, I saw how he looked at you."

Shock went through her. "You didn't see anything. You were scared to death."

"That doesn't make me blind or stupid," Mia snapped. "I thought we were opening up? Stop stalling. I don't show you mine, if you don't show me yours."

She clenched her teeth and spoke through them. "We had . . . chemistry. I thought I might be falling for him until I found out he was hired to kill me."

"No shit," Mia said. "You know, some of us take our thrills in smaller doses. I just date married guys for instance."

"It wasn't on purpose, ass." But she smiled nonetheless.

The pressure in her chest eased a little, enough that she no longer felt like each breath sent a knife through her chest. God, she hated being stupid, and she'd been a class-A fool where he was concerned. Maybe she'd live through this after all.

"Tell me the sex was worth it, at least."

Kyra thought about that, and a little shiver rolled through her. "Yeah. It was."

"That's something at least."

"What about you and Foster?"

"No sex."

With a scowl, Kyra folded her arms. "You know what I'm asking."

"You want to know what happened. How I ended up tied to a chair." Mia drooped a little, studying her lap. "I came looking for you . . . and ran into him. He said he'd help me. At first he seemed to. He kept me in the loop whenever he talked to your hit man."

"Reyes. And he's not mine."

"Whatever. He kept me away from the casino. Didn't want his boss seeing me, he said. But he must've been followed to one of our meetings because the next time I went out, I noticed I had somebody following me. I couldn't think what else to do, so I went to him for help."

"And he turned you over to Serrano." Kyra's hands curled into fists. "No wonder you were terrified. I'm so sorry."

"Not your fault," Mia said automatically. "Well, actually it is, but not . . . directly. It's not like you told me to trust him. It's just . . . worse because I . . . liked him." She squeezed her eyes shut. "At one point I tried to kiss him and he jerked away like I had screaming fourth grade cooties."

"He's a weird one," Kyra said. "But don't take it personally. He had some vendetta against Serrano. He was using both of us."

"He whispered to me not to be scared—that Serrano wouldn't do anything to me before you got there—but how the hell was I supposed to believe that, after he lied about taking me someplace safe?" Mia's wounded eyes demanded an answer.

Kyra didn't have one. "We sure can pick 'em. But we'll be okay, right? It'll just take time."

The other woman shrugged. "I guess."

She felt oddly diffident about asking this. "Speaking of time . . . I wondered if you could take some off. I'd really like to just . . . I dunno. Hang out with you. Take a long break and start figuring out what to do next."

Mia nodded slowly. "I'd like that. I wouldn't mind going somewhere warm. We can lay in the sun for a while and bask away our sorrows."

"Sounds fantastic." If it couldn't take away the pain, at least they'd have sunshine. She hesitated, and then added: "I got away with a huge amount of money, and I need to get it out of the country. I was hoping you could help me with that."

A frown knit her friend's dark brows together. "You know I specialize in catching people who try to do that, right?"

"Does that mean you can't help me?"

A fulminating silence. Kyra opened her eyes wide, trying to appear cute and imploring. It wasn't her best look.

"You know I can," Mia muttered. "Let's take that vacation and then we'll talk more. I'll think about it as we go."

"Okay." She knew the other woman well enough to realize that pushing at this point would just make Mia dig her heels in. A maybe was almost as good as a yes.

They stayed almost a week in Missouri. From there they meandered south, heading toward Florida. Mia wanted to go to Disney for some reason, and because it tickled Kyra's sense of the absurd, she went along with it.

You just killed a bunch of guys, took revenge on your father's murderer, got your heart broken, and stole three million dollars. What are you going to do now?

I'm going to Disney World.

And they did.

Mia rented a condo for a few weeks in Davenport, a two bedroom place with a long balcony and tropical décor. The plants were fake, and the floors were tiled in cool faux-marble. It had no soul, just like Reyes's loft.

After the first week, which passed in a flurry of tourist attractions, they spent the time lounging in the sun and catching up. She bought a bikini and high-SPF sunscreen. Mia bronzed like a goddess, but Kyra just gained another layer of freckles.

Time went in spurts, alternating fast and slow. Sometimes a patch of days sped by when she hardly thought of him at all. And sometimes she woke in a tangle of sweat-hot sheets, her body straining for someone who wasn't there.

She didn't want to remember lying in his arms in the backseat of the Marquis, didn't want to listen to his raw, whispered confessions that made her feel as though she was the only one he'd ever trusted enough to talk to. And she didn't want to remember that, in the end, she'd just been a job to him.

Not when he'd been so much more.

Kyra could no longer deny that was true. Though she had no personal experience to draw on, it seemed her tentative assessment of "I think I'm falling for you" hadn't encompassed the whole. In truth, she'd fallen like a brick, and she still hadn't hit bottom.

If there were a pill that could make her forget, she'd take it.

But there wasn't, so she had to soldier on.

They'd been living in the condo for a month when Mia came in from the pool, looking brighter and more resolute than she had in weeks. It seemed she was finally starting to heal. That was good for her, bad for Kyra because she knew what was coming. Mia must be tired of the holding pattern and wanted to get back to her life.

That made total sense; she understood. Even so, she braced herself.

"I have a job offer," Mia said without preamble.

"And you want to take it."

"It's lucrative."

"It's fine," Kyra told her. "Go. I'm all in one piece. We've had our bonding time. I'll stay out of trouble."

Mia sank down slowly on the white and wicker sofa. "I don't want to leave you. You're . . . not okay."

"Sure I am."

Mia touched her arm. Evidently she didn't mean to start work today. She'd known about Kyra's ability for a long time, but it had never altered the way she treated her. Kyra loved her fiercely for that.

"You're *not*. I hear you crying in your sleep sometimes."

She cringed. That was beyond what she could tolerate, weakness displayed when she let her guard down. How utterly pathetic.

"I just miss my dad." Which was true. It wasn't all of it, but it was true.

"Yes. But you're still thinking about someone else, too."

"I . . . no. It's not like that." Kyra spun to her feet and paced. "It *shouldn't* be. I just . . . I can't get him out of my head. And instead of getting better, it just hurts more. I . . . ache." She rubbed her chest against the tightness that thoughts of him always created. "I miss being touched. I miss *him*."

Kyra knew she could never lie to Mia. She might be able to indulge in an impressive self-delusion, but Mia was too canny to be fooled. She found herself thinking how he'd helped her, how he hadn't hurt her, no matter his orders. It would be crazy to go looking for round two with a guy like that, no matter how great the sex. Besides, she didn't even know where to start. It wasn't like they'd exchanged e-mail addresses.

Two days ago, she'd discovered that he had been telling the truth. At some point he'd put the money back. In the end he'd stayed with her because he *wanted* to, until she told him to go.

"Oh, honey," Mia said softly. "I didn't know. But you really—"

"Yeah." Kyra wiped her eyes. "Most women pick a douche bag for their first relationship, but I take the cake. You've broken up with guys before, right? Does it eventually stop hurting?" She hated how sad she sounded.

"Eventually. Sometimes it takes years, depending on how much you felt, how deep it ran. There was this guy in college—God, I was crazy about him, and he left me for someone else. Sometimes . . . I still talk to him in my head. I miss him. There's a little love left for him, even now."

"So it doesn't go away altogether if it's real." Kyra sighed and walked over to the window to gaze out; she could see the pool from here. She wondered where he was, if he'd forgotten about her by now.

Mia shook her head. "You just push it down and function until the day you meet someone who sparks something stronger than what's left."

"That's the saddest thing I ever heard."

"Welcome to the real world, babe. It's not all skin games and winning bets."

She turned. "You think my dad did me a disservice by raising me like he did."

"It doesn't matter, not anymore. It only matters what you

do now." Mia came over and hugged her, head on her shoulder. "How bad is he, really?"

"Reyes?" Kyra returned the hug and stepped back. "I know he's done time. I know he kills people. He claims just the ones who have it coming. Bad enough, right? I should forget him."

"You were never very good at doing what you should," Mia noted. "And you're not a bastion of moral fiber, either."

"Speaking of which . . . I hate to ask, but—"

"What have I decided about helping with your cash situation?"

"Yeah." A smiled flickered across Kyra's mouth. "You know me too well."

"I want to take care of you before I go," Mia answered. "That means making sure you have something to live on while you heal, and it's not safe for you to be carrying around this much money."

Kyra shook her head. "You know I can't open an account here—a wanted felon with that much money? No thanks."

"I've been thinking about that. I caught a number of guys who were moving capital around in the islands, stealing from corporate accounts, and trying to bury it. All I had to do was follow the money."

Her mouth twisted. "You're talking about guys who got caught."

"Yes, but that's because they weren't happy once they got it out of the country. And they used wires from existing bank accounts. We're not going to do that."

"What's your plan then?" Kyra found herself reluctantly interested.

"We charter a sailboat to Barbados. They don't look too hard at tourists coming in and out of the islands. Once there, you can open an offshore account for a million cash. Your warrants aren't the kind to get you flagged in international databases."

"That's . . . genius."

"Do you have a passport?"

Kyra nodded. "Dad insisted. He said you never knew when you might have to make a run for the border. I keep it in my purse, just in case."

"Depending on where you disembark in Barbados, your passport may or may not be scanned. It would be to your advantage to stay out of the system," Mia added, unnecessarily. "But again, even if they do, your warrants won't qualify for extradition. You're what we call a low-priority criminal."

She smiled reluctantly. "It sounds doable. Do you know anyone who could help me? If not," she hastened to add, "I can take care of it. You've given me the idea. That's more than enough. Take your job. I'll be fine. I just . . . need to get away."

The islands sounded wonderful, even better than Florida. No clocks, nowhere to be. Maybe she'd even buy a house and invite Mia to come visit. Kyra wasn't sure she was ready to settle down for good, but it might be nice to have a home base for a change. She'd tasted that in the form of a person, and now she found herself hungry for it. Maybe a place could offer some facsimile of belonging.

Mia leveled a long look on her with an inscrutable half smile before saying, "I might. Let me make some calls."

CHAPTER 31

The arrangements took another week.

Mia shopped and made a few adjustments to her professional wardrobe. With her deep tan, she looked fabulous in white and ivory, so she loaded up on pale suits that made her look like a million bucks. Kyra envied the way she could so easily look put together, no matter how quickly she got ready.

And then it was time for good-byes at the ungodly hour of half past dawn. Despite the hour, Mia fussed like a mama hen with her last chick. "You'll meet your ride this afternoon in Miami, right? Dock twelve. Don't forget."

"I got it," Kyra said, waving the address. "Good luck."

They hugged. Downstairs, the cabbie leaned on the horn. Mia let herself out of the condo with a final wave. She was taking a taxi to the airport because she didn't like public farewells. They promised to call, all the usual stuff. Work had her heading to New Zealand, and Kyra thought the contract sounded like a fantastic opportunity.

Now she just had to get her stuff together, not that she had much. Afterward, she took a bath in preparation for an early start. At least the brown rinse had come out of her hair, finally, and the sun had lightened it further, streaking it almost white in places. There was no point in dressing up for a boat ride, plus it would look suspicious, so she dragged on a bikini and pulled a pair of cutoffs over the bottoms.

Kyra added a pair of sandals, sunglasses, and sunscreen. This stuff smelled like coconut, and the scent brought to mind the way Reyes had buried his face in her hair, breathing her in. An ache curled through her. Kyra rubbed her chest, trying to make it go away. The need to see him, touch him, almost hurt, but she didn't have a way to get in touch with him, even if she wanted to.

"Jesus," she muttered. "Stop already."

With a final glance at the condo, she picked up her bags and headed out the door. It had brightened into a sunny morning—as if there were any other kind outside of hurricane season. In no particular hurry, Kyra made sure she drove the speed limit, and she made the drive in less than four hours. She stopped at a seafood place for lunch, and then took the long way to the marina, enjoying the sight of sails on the horizon. Soon she'd take her place among them.

People walked along the beach wearing very little, showing off tight bodies and dark tans. Kyra felt like she should be driving a convertible to fit the setting, but she wasn't lighthearted enough for that anyway. She'd put up a good front for Mia, knowing her friend wouldn't take the job any other way, but she wasn't looking forward to this trip. So many things could go wrong . . . she was sure Mia had lined up reliable help, but still. She was a little light on trust these days.

At ten minutes before the appointed hour, she reached the dock. Kyra paid for parking, figuring she'd talk to the guy first. If she didn't like what she saw, she wasn't going out on the ocean with him; that was damn sure, no matter how highly recommended he came. Her gut seldom steered her wrong.

With one very notable exception: not *thinking about him.*

If she thought he seemed trustworthy, she'd make arrangements to store her car while she was gone. Kyra didn't know how long she planned to stay in Barbados. She was back to taking things as they came.

Dock 12 held a thirty-some-odd-foot sailboat, a Hunter Legend. It wasn't new, but it was well kept. That seemed to be a good sign. She wasn't going to be any help out on the water, but she could follow directions. If her "tour guide" had patience, she'd learn.

Suddenly nervous about making a good impression, she called out as she came up the gangplank. "Hey, I'm a little early. I hope you don't mind."

No answer.

Tentative, Kyra stepped on to the boat, which rocked gently with the water, butting up against the pier. She called out again and walked the length of the craft. On her second pass, she glimpsed the shadow of someone coming from belowdecks. Then a male silhouette swung into view.

Before she ever saw his face, she knew by the way he moved. All the breath ran out of her in a little *oof*, as if he'd punched her in the chest. Reyes looked a little thinner, but still tall, still imposing. His knife-blade cheekbones seemed sharper, his eyes blacker than sin, and lacking all softness. He gazed at her for a long moment in silence.

"You," she said.

"Me."

"How did you find me?"

When I told you not to. She wasn't sure if that was what she still wanted. It had been nearly two months. Seeing him roused a painful ache. It twisted through her like a cyclone, leaving wreckage in its wake.

"Technically," he murmured, "you found me."

God, he was so remote, so distant. Even the sunlight didn't seem to warm him; it merely glazed his raven hair with blue. He wore nothing but a pair of white swim trunks, slung low. They revealed the taut slope of his abdomen, the hollow of his hip. She felt like she could eat him with her eyes and tried not to show it.

"Semantics. Answer the question."

"I was surprised to hear from Foster. He had a message for me—"

"Mia," she guessed.

Reyes nodded. "I called her. We . . . talked."

Kyra winced. She could only imagine what her friend

might've said. *Please don't let him know I've been crying in my sleep.*

"And? What did she say?"

"That she had reservations about putting you back in touch with someone like me, and that if I ever hurt you again, she'd hunt me down and kill me." His expression said he took Mia seriously—as well he should.

"Oh," Kyra said in a small voice. "Anything else?"

"She asked if I knew anyone who could help you take a little money to Barbados, and she said she thought we had unfinished business. We came to an agreement."

"You? Mia hired *you*? Knowing that you once tried to kill me." She'd smack her friend the next time she saw her. Jesus. Talk about not needing enemies.

"Not exactly," he said in a voice so soft and low she almost lost the words amid the slosh of the waves. "I do pro bono work sometimes, but this is more a labor of love. And let's be clear, Kyra. I never tried to hurt you. I was hired to, but almost from the moment I saw you, it was something else. Foster was counting on that."

She closed her eyes, shutting out the bleak intensity of his eyes. Though he hadn't moved—he was eerie in his stillness—the angle of his hands gave her the impression he was fighting in silence not to reach out.

"How can I ever trust you?" Kyra gave a shuddery sigh. "I wish—I wish we could turn back the clock. I wish you hadn't lied. I wish you were just that drifter I picked up, who made me feel like the most important person in the world."

"You are," he said quietly. "I came from Thailand for you, because Mia said she could probably get you here. I'd have come from Zimbabwe, Outer Mongolia, or a prison in Central America. In truth, I came through hell getting here . . . because for me that's anywhere you're not."

"Oh, Rey," she whispered, and put out her hands.

His fingers twined with hers and he drew her to him with exquisite tenderness, as if she were a dove that could die of fright in his hands. But that wasn't what she wanted. She stretched up and fisted her hands in his hair, pulling his mouth to hers.

He tasted of French vanilla coffee, rich and sweet. This

powerful man trembled against her. He smelled of sea and sunshine, layered with a kiss of citrus. Kyra had never wanted anything more than his bare skin against hers.

She broke away, breathless. "Is there a cabin?"

Kyra knew he wasn't Prince Charming. If anything, he was the prince of darkness. He had a record and a history of violence, but he'd never hurt her on purpose. She knew that now. And if it hadn't been for Foster's machinations, she would never have met him.

"Yes. We'll be several days on the ocean . . . if you're going with me." His dark eyes said she had a choice—that he'd walk away and let her go, even if it killed him.

Like hell.

"Not if." She punctuated the words with a feathery kiss. "When. But I want you first. I need you. I haven't been touched in nearly two months, and I miss you. I miss being part of you."

"Kyra," he said, touching his brow to hers. "You never stopped."

A little moan escaped her because her whole body streamed with warmth. It was almost too much. She tugged at his hand because she *could.* She was just a woman with him. His woman.

In answer, he swung her into his arms and navigated the ramp that led down into the cabin. They passed through a tiny galley, an equally small dining area with the table folded down, and into the berth. Reyes tossed her onto the blue-patterned bedspread.

"I don't think I'll have much patience," he warned with a tight smile.

She moved her shoulders in a shrug. "Then it'll be like the first time."

"Better. Because I know you now."

His hands moved on her, shaping the lines over her body. With his lips he found each new freckle, licking a path that drove her wild and left her writhing on the bed. Her bikini top disappeared with a twist of his clever fingers and he bent his head to her breast, his mouth full of heat and homage. With each touch, each brush of his lips, he said:

You are the only woman in the world. The sun rises and falls with you.

She shivered in reaction as he worked the denim down her hips. The spandex of her suit was damp already; he had her twisting with need. Quickly she skinned the bottoms off and tugged at his trunks, but he slid down, his jaw scraping tender skin.

"What happened to not having much patience?" she demanded, as he rubbed his open mouth against her belly.

He gave an eloquent shrug, touching his lips to hers, petal soft. Then his tongue slid and delved. She cried out, pleasure spreading like fireworks along her nerves. Kyra cupped his head in her hands, and urged him on. With a fierce and devastating hunger, he devoured her, nuzzling her through one orgasm, and then two. Her hips bucked, and she arched against his mouth, open to him, and wanting more.

When she felt boneless and spent, he slid upward, their skin sweat-slick. His weight pressed her down into the mattress. Dizzy and blissful, she heard him rummaging. A crinkle of foil, then he came into her, inch by delicious inch. Hard and hot, filling her up. Kyra felt the throb of his blood pulsing through him.

Nothing had ever been like this. Ever.

Instead of going wild inside her, he lay down, precious in his stillness, as if he wanted to imprint the feel of her body beneath him in case the memory had to last. Only after she, too tantalized for further patience, began to work her hips, did he move.

He stroked her hair compulsively as he thrust, brushing it back from her face. Reyes gazed down at her upturned face, his lips near to hers so he could claim her next exhaled breath. Kyra wrapped her arms around his shoulders, her legs around his hips, and held on tight.

Her whole body worked with his, push-slide, as need spiraled. Tingles skated through her nervous system, and her heart went wild. His strokes became quick and shallow, the muscles of his butt bunching against her ankles.

"Kyra . . ." He turned his face into her neck, licking up her sweat.

When he came, she came, a hot and seamless slide into pleasure so profound she couldn't see for the tears stinging her eyes. For long moments, she held him in trembling lethargy, welcoming his weight. His fingers stirred in her hair, stroking.

"It was never quite like that," she whispered.

"No. Now I know the value of what I hold."

Inexplicably, she wanted to weep in earnest, just sob against his chest. Compulsively she shaped letters on his chest, writing her name in some primitive need to claim. But that made no sense at all.

"Would you have come looking for me?"

His hair slid against her cheek as he shook his head. "No. You told me not to."

She huffed softly. "Like you always do as you're told."

"I want you to be happy." He sealed a kiss into her palm. "Even if that means staying a world away from you."

"You know . . ." She rolled to face him. "I am. But let's be clear—that's because you're right here with me. Should we get up?"

"Soon."

Four hours later, they did. It was early evening when they surfaced. She rinsed off in the tiny shower; there wasn't room for two. Then she went on deck to watch him fiddling with various ropes and gizmos on the boat.

"You sure you know what you're doing?"

"I'll get us there. Trust me."

To her surprise, she did. But looking out toward the parking lot, she realized she'd left one thing undone, if she truly meant to sail away with him. "I'll be right back."

Reyes froze. "Will you?"

She touched a hand to his waist. "Of course. Do you think I came all this way to fuck and leave you?"

His somber look all but broke her heart. "I hope not."

"Then trust *me*."

He gave a nod and continued with his work. At this point, he'd still let her walk away and take some petty revenge. That, more than anything else, reassured her. This was right;

she was sure of it. Bag in hand, Kyra ran down the gangplank. She returned within five minutes, and he seemed surprised to see her.

"Are we almost ready to take off?"

The sky blazed sapphire on the horizon, lit with scarlet and umber. Soon, they would go that way, and spend their first night on the water. Reyes followed her gaze; perhaps her train of thought as well.

A smile kindled in his eyes, stars on black velvet, and then found outlet on a mouth both beautiful and cruel. "Yes. We're fully stocked, and ready to get underway."

"That includes the galley, right?" She hesitated, suddenly shy. "Will you . . . cook for me again?"

"Yes." No hesitation, no adornment. Kyra had the feeling she could have asked for a kidney or his right hand, and he would've said the same.

This was harder, so hard, a ridiculous question from someone who never wanted ties, never wanted the same man for more than one night. But she did, desperately.

Him. Only him.

"Will you stay with me?"

"Always."

The intensity of the moment sent her scrambling back, seeking something light to dispel the ache that demanded his hands on her. "Are you going to quit killing people?"

He raised his brows then. There was a limit to how much he would grant; he was what he was. "Are you going to quit conning them?"

She grinned. "It's not the same. But . . . we'll discuss our options."

They stood on the deck together for a few moments more. His dark gaze traced the path toward the parking lot, where she'd left the last link to her father, the last link to her old life. He knew, of course.

"We can't take it with us." Melancholy laced his tone.

"That's okay," she said. "I'm ready to let Myrna go. I left the keys in the ignition, free to anyone who wants to claim her. I like the idea of letting fate decide."

He searched her face. "Are you sure?"

"I found something more important than the car."

"Oh, yeah?" Lines of tension bracketed his mouth, as if he were afraid to hope for too much even now. She saw how his fist furled at his side, a quiet defense.

Kyra closed her eyes and leaped. "You. I love *you*. It scares the hell out of me, but . . . I'm willing to give this a try if you are. Wherever it takes us."

"You're my beating heart," he said simply. "Where you go, I do."

And that was everything. They raised the sails and slid away from the dock out onto the vast blue sea.

Turn the page for a special preview of
Ava Gray's next novel

SKIN TIGHT

Coming Summer 2010
from Berkley Sensation!

CHAPTER 1

PRESENT DAY, VIRGINIA

"I understand your father was Iranian," the interviewer said delicately. "And you still have relatives there, including your grandfather and numerous cousins."

He was a silver-haired man, clad in a navy blue suit. His pale blue shirt and gray tie said he was conservative, somewhat lacking in imagination. Mia had learned to read people, based on the clothing they chose.

The hotel conference room was nearly as nondescript as her interviewer. Painted beige with a faux-wood theme, she could have been in any hotel in any part of the country. There were no windows to distract her from the inappropriate question.

She had impeccable references. At first she didn't doubt Micor Technologies would select her, even from a large pool of qualified candidates. Her track record for ferreting out the truth made her the ideal choice. And indeed, everything had been going well until the management ran across her ethnic background.

Mia raised a brow. "How is that relevant?" Oh, he didn't come right out and say it. But she knew what he was trying to imply. "May I remind you that discrimination is still illegal in the United States?"

Collins was a smart man; he could read between the lines and he knew that after asking about her father's country of origin, she had a case, should she pursue the matter. If he didn't want to hire her, he shouldn't have asked.

His mouth was tight when he offered the contract, standard terms. She had ninety days to unearth evidence of who was misappropriating company funds. They thought it was someone in accounting, but couldn't be sure because the culprit was clever.

"I'll come in under the pretext of updating the company software." Fortunately, she knew enough about computers to make that fiction convincing.

"I'm afraid that won't do," Collins said, shaking his head.

She paused, pen hovering above the pristine white contract. "What won't?"

"We can't have word getting out that we've hired a consultant. No, Miss Sauter, we need you on the payroll as an official employee. Otherwise, it will raise eyebrows. Our work is so sensitive that we never bring in contractors. Fortunately, we have an IT opening at the moment. Since a monkey could do it, I am sure you will have no trouble balancing that workload against your investigation."

Gazing into his eyes, she had the uncanny sensation he wanted her to fail. That offended her on so many levels that she couldn't begin to tabulate them. And considering her math aptitude, that was saying something.

"No problem at all," she said coolly and scrawled her signature on the contract.

This particular job required an extensive background check and the signing of a nondisclosure agreement. Collins showed his displeasure every step of the way. He was one who thought dark hair and eyes meant secret ties to the Al Qaeda.

They concluded their business with a faux-civility that left her angry. Mia went from the conference room to her hotel room, changed into workout clothes, and then spent an hour pummeling a target at the gym. She didn't often lose her temper, but few things set her off as much as bigotry.

Then she wrapped up negotiations with the old couple, sealing the deal on their arrangement. Their condo would do nicely, it seemed.

It was under less than ideal circumstances she got ready for work on Monday. Last night, the nightmares had come before she enjoyed more than a couple hours sleep. Mia loathed herself for being so weak, but she couldn't seem to shake the trauma of how helpless she'd felt, tied to a chair with a dirty rag in her mouth. It seemed as if she should be over it, as she'd come to no physical harm.

To offset that sense of vulnerability, she dressed in a black suit with a blue, lace-trimmed camisole beneath it: strength, underscored with softness. Mia knew what men saw when they looked at her; she planned that reaction from her coral-frosted mouth to the matching lacquer on her nails. She had long since learned to make the exterior camouflage the computer within. Men were never impressed that she could add a column of twelve four-digit numbers in her head in less than ten seconds.

Mia took a last look around the place she would call home for the next three months. Unlike most of her contracts, this job wasn't situated in a city large enough to offer corporate housing, but she'd gotten lucky with a snowbird couple heading to Arizona for the winter. Mia didn't think Virginia winters were terrible, but the old folks did.

They'd given her a great deal on the place—almost no rent at all—saying she was doing them a favor, and they could rest easy knowing someone would water their plants and look after their fat, lazy cat. Mia wasn't a pet person, but she figured she could handle food and water for three months. The ginger tabby glared at her from its hiding spot beneath the coffee table.

"I'll be back by six, Peaches."

That cat looked remarkably indifferent.

Mia stepped out into the brisk morning air and turned her face up to the sky. It promised to be a glorious day, clear, cool, and lovely. Too bad she would spend it trying to figure out who was the biggest liar.

With a mental shrug, Mia made her way to the rental car. She'd long since sold her own vehicle because she worked overseas too often to make it practical. Now she included use of a vehicle as part of her contract fee, and it was surprising how few companies balked. If they needed someone to sort their financial embarrassment quickly and quietly, they had bigger issues than whether to pay for the long-term rental of a Ford Focus.

This car was blue and nondescript in every way. That was good. She didn't want to draw attention with flash. In her line of work, it would be best if nobody noticed her at all.

The drive didn't take long, not that Mia was surprised. Before she'd come to an agreement on the condo, she'd timed the commute. If traffic was good and road conditions favorable, she could cover the distance in fourteen minutes.

Micor Technologies sat outside the city limits, surrounded by acres of woods instead of an industrial park. That struck Mia as more than a little odd, but maybe they did testing here that wouldn't be safe in a high population center. She had no idea what the company did; that information had no bearing on her task.

She pulled up to the gate, where an armed guard sat inside a glass booth. "Badge," he said, extending a hand.

"This is my first day. I'm to report to HR to have one made."

"I'll need your driver's license. I'm sure you understand I have to call this in."

Interesting. She'd interviewed off-site at a local hotel. Though she'd driven the commute, she'd never come to the gate before. At other facilities where she'd worked, the guards were less attentive. That suggested a curious level of security.

"No problem." Mia handed her ID over, and the man got on the phone. It took about five minutes for him to confirm her claim.

"You're to go straight in and park in the west lot. Go directly through those doors, and the corridor will take you to human resources. If you don't comply with these instructions exactly, you may have difficulties." His face broke into a half-smile, softening the sternness of his warning.

"And you don't want to be late on your first day, right?"

"Absolutely not. Thank you."

Mia pulled forward and followed the drive to the west lot, as instructed. She told herself the warning flags raised by procedure here was none of her business. Like any other job, she'd find the guilty party, deliver the evidence, and move on. She hadn't taken a vacation since she spent a few weeks in Florida with her friend Kyra last year, so maybe she'd relax a bit before accepting the next job.

No point in getting ahead of herself, though.

She parked and climbed out of the Focus, studying the complex for a moment. It was a sprawling series of interconnected buildings, all gleaming white metal. The structure looked even more out of place, surrounded by an electrified fence and miles of trees. Again, not her concern, even if insistent warning bells had started going off.

Her heels clicked as she crossed the parking lot. The door wasn't secured, but there were cameras at this entrance, tracking her every movement. If she veered right or left, she had no doubt someone would come to collect her. Mia followed instructions and continued down the corridor until she came to a suite of offices.

There, a well-coiffed woman in middle years sat behind the reception desk. The room was elegantly appointed in maroon and gray. Abstract art adorned the walls, but Mia didn't care for it. To her, it resembled nothing so much as blood spatters.

"May I help you?" the receptionist asked.

"Mia Sauter. I need to have my security badge made up."

"Oh, that's right. I'm Glenna Waters. Thomas Strong is the director, but he won't be able to meet with you today. But no worries, I can handle this."

"Thanks."

Mia smiled her appreciation and followed the other woman behind the beige partition, where she stood before a black curtain and had her picture taken. Glenna worked with several different machines, and it took fifteen minutes for her to present a freshly magnetized, freshly laminated card.

"There you are. You'll want to wear this at all times." She flicked her own security tag. "I can give you a lanyard or a clip. Which do you prefer?"

"The clip, please."

Glenna finished the badge and handed it over. "You're assigned to IT, which is down the hall from accounting. I'll give you a map of the facility to help you find your way. This place can be tricky, but as long as you stay in the admin area you'll be fine."

"There are labs on premises?" Mia couldn't believe she'd asked that. It was none of her business, nothing to do with the job. Hopefully Glenna would take it as casual interest.

The other woman nodded. "Yes, ma'am. The labs are past the security doors in the east wing."

"Will off-limits areas be clearly marked?" She tried a smile. "I don't want to wander wrong looking for the lounge."

"Your mag strip won't let you wander into restricted areas, don't worry."

"Good to know. I've never worked anywhere like this before."

Glenna nodded. "Most of us hadn't. You'll find it's a good place, though. They take care of their employees. Great benefits and retirement plan. I'll set you up an appointment with Mr. Strong to talk about rollover of your 401K."

That would be natural if she worked here for real. But Mia didn't have a 401K plan to transfer. Her money was invested in a varied portfolio.

"That won't be necessary," she said. "I had to cash out recently. Family illness."

Glenna's face softened in sympathy. "I'm sorry to hear that."

She offered a wave in acknowledgment as she left HR, badge clipped to the lapel of her jacket. Following the map proved no hard task and soon she presented herself in IT, ready to begin. She loved this part of her job: the hunt for clues, following the trail, analyzing patterns of data. And she was good at it for reasons nobody had ever discerned.

After all, it took a thief to catch a thief.

Over the years, he had been known by so many names, he had almost forgotten his own. For the last three months, he had been Thomas Strong. Once the man known as Addison Foster left Vegas, he'd sloughed his old identity like a snake outgrowing its skin. Though he'd always known this last task would require patience, lately, he found himself suffering from its lack. Despite his near perfect disguise, he was no closer to accessing the secure part of the facility than he had been a year ago, right after he orchestrated the death of Gerard Serrano.

As director of human resources, he had his fingers on everyone who hired in and out of the facility. In theory, it sounded good. He thought he'd have access to all employees, even the lab workers. But their nondisclosure agreements prevented them from talking to him about their research, once they commenced in the restricted areas. That meant he'd been reduced to a glorified paper pusher with no promise of ever getting closer than he was.

That was unacceptable.

He just needed to find the right angle. Maybe one of the geeky techs would be amenable to seduction. At this point, it was the only approach he hadn't tried. There were no other weaknesses in security; he'd already tested it extensively. If nothing else, that alone confirmed he'd come to the right place. That part of the complex wouldn't be locked down if they didn't have impressive secrets to keep.

He had a feeling he knew exactly what they were hiding.

The intercom buzzed. "Mr. Strong, your two o'clock is here."

His jaw clenched. Glenna meant well, but she was both managing and proprietary, so she wanted to know where he was at all times in case someone called looking for him. Strong wasn't used to accounting for his movements; working for prior employers, he'd grown used to a certain amount of freedom, as they had cared more about results than schedules.

He tapped the button to answer. "Great. Send him in."

This joker wanted to talk about possible career advancement. He worked in accounting, but he wanted lab management. He'd seen an interior job posting and sought to apply for it, even though his resume was years too light and his education somewhat inadequate. Jenkins was convinced he had what it took, however, and spent forty-five minutes telling Strong what he thought he wanted to hear.

"I'm a people person," Jenkins was saying. "I can get results, too. They like me. I'm wasted in accounting. Any dork can crunch numbers. But give me five minutes with a guy, and I can tell you exactly what makes him tick."

This should be good.

Strong raised a brow. "Oh, really?"

"Yep." Confident he was on the right track, Jenkins leaned forward. "Want me to analyze you?"

He smiled. "Absolutely."

"You live alone," Jenkins began. "You're career-driven, so you put work ahead of relationships. You're self-contained and professional, but you enjoy the outdoors. I can tell that by the calluses on your hands." He paused, as if to assess the effect of his recitation.

"Very good, Mr. Jenkins." He was careful to keep his expression noncommittal.

But frankly, that wasn't half-bad. He was inclined to favor the guy's application to get him out of accounting. Best to send Jenkins back to his desk before he noticed anything else, however.

His days had become a miserable wasteland of such appointments. Glenna was too efficient to permit gaps in his calendar that allowed him to roam around the facility. Sometimes he manufactured events to cover his absence, but if that happened too often, she started asking questions. Unfortunately, she was clever, honest, and hardworking.

He would like very much to fire her. There was no cause, however, and he had a soft spot for her, as much as she annoyed him. He did his best to live up to the image she cherished of him because her wildest dreams were oddly sweet, innocent in a way that moved him. At this point, all Glenna wanted from life was a fair boss who appreciated her work and respected her efforts. He couldn't punish her for that.

By the time he got rid of Jenkins, it was nearly three, but he had two disciplinary cases and a directors meeting thereafter, which took him well past five. And so he'd wasted another day. He wasn't used to such a crushing lack of progress. It was unthinkable he could get this close to finishing what he'd started and come up against an impassable wall.

Tomorrow would be different. It had to be.

He stepped into the hallway. It was quiet in the complex this late. Most admin staff went home promptly at five, trusting their work could keep until the morning. The meeting had run long, however, with a couple of blowhards squabbling about God only knew what. Strong had learned months back to appear attentive while in fact he heard nothing.

As he strode toward the exit, he heard the delicate clicking of feminine heels. Someone had worked nearly as late as him tonight. He hastened his step, half-hoping to encounter one of the lab techs, even though he knew it was unlikely by the sound of her shoes. Lab techs wore sneakers or comfortable crepe soles.

When he came around the corner, he stopped walking. Shock ricocheted through him. He recognized this woman, even from the back. Last year, he'd spent enough time staring at the swell of her ass to know it in his sleep. If that wasn't enough, she was dressed in one of her familiar, sharply tailored suits and she had her raven hair bound in a complicated twist at the nape of her neck. The black pumps made the most of her legs, giving her calves a tremendously sexy curve.

His heart gave an unsteady, excited thump at seeing her after all these months. He calmed himself with some effort. Her reasons for being here had nothing to do with him. Thinking back, he recalled she worked as a consultant, specializing in corporate embezzlement. Intriguing to find her here. That meant there was trouble on the premises, something they needed an expert to resolve.

Did that mean someone high up the food chain had gotten cold feet? Started withdrawing his share of the profits to make a run for it? He might be able to leverage that once he discovered the identity of that individual.

Having Mia Sauter around would complicate his life, no question. He'd fought the attraction in Vegas, knowing it wasn't fair. He couldn't let her get close to him; he couldn't bear her pain when she realized he was everything she wanted... and no one in particular. Since Lexie's accident, few things retained the capacity to touch him, but Mia's expression when she realized he'd betrayed her to Serrano still put razors to his skin.

It would be painful to see her every day, but if their paths crossed, he just had to treat her with polite indifference. She'd never know him. Nobody ever did.

For no reason he could fathom, she paused with one hand on the metal handle of the door. He froze. She appeared to be staring at his image in the glass, and then she whirled. Anger sparked from her in near visible waves as she stalked back toward him. By her look, she recognized him.

He stood frozen. This was unprecedented. He was clad in the armor of expectation. She should have no reason to expect to find him here. Ergo, he should be someone else in her eyes, someone she'd never seen.

And yet, she jabbed her finger into his sternum, contempt tightening her mouth. "What are you doing here? I told you, I only contacted you for Kyra. Nothing else could have impelled me to get in touch with you."

His breath went out in a rush. There was no mistaking her recognition now, but he tried to play it off. Perhaps he could convince her she was mistaken. "I'm sorry, miss. Do I know you?"

Another jab with her index finger. "Do you think this is *funny*, Foster?" Then her gaze narrowed on his badge. "Or should I say Strong? What are you up to? Maybe you're the one who's—"

"Shhh." He tried to glare her into silence, but she was having none of it. Luckily the cameras here didn't pick up sound, or he might have some explaining to do. "I'm sure you have questions, but we can't talk here."

"Oh, no," she bit out. "The last time I fell for your cloak and dagger bullshit, I wound up tied to a chair. You tell me what's going on, *right now*, or I march back to my desk and call Collins. I'm supposed to report any irregularity around here, so I'm sure he'd be interested in what I know about you."

Beneath her anger, he could see the wound. She'd trusted him. So few people did; Lexie had been one of them, and look what it cost her.

"Mia, please." He felt strange and off-kilter.

Nobody *ever* saw him. He couldn't stem the irrational hope that she was different. He had no right to wish for it, nor did he deserve it, but even if she hated him, it meant more than she could ever realize to be certain she looked at him and saw only the reflection in his mirror.

"You're a bastard," she said quietly. "Give me one reason I shouldn't turn you in."

ABOUT THE AUTHOR

Ava Gray is the pen name for a national bestselling author with three ongoing series. She has a degree in English Literature, but before she began writing full-time, she was a clown, a clerk, a voice actress, and a savior of stray kittens, not necessarily in that order. She lives in sunny Mexico with her husband, two children, two cats, and one very lazy dog. You can find out about her work at www.avagray.com.